ACCLAIM FROM THE U.K. FOR

The Vintage Book of War Fiction

"A substantial—and compelling—read. . . . There is little glorification of war and much thoughtful, intense writing."
—*The Times*

"The range is international, the impeccable standards of writing never dip; this is some of the finest writing about war this [past] century."
—*The Independent on Sunday*

"The collection is taken to a higher plane with the many pleasant surprises."
—*The Irish Times*

"Whatever strategies the writer finds to deal with war, the sheer physical impact of conflict seldom fails to shock."
—*The Guardian*

The Vintage Book of War Fiction

SEBASTIAN FAULKS worked as a journalist for fourteen years before taking up writing books full time in 1991. He is the author of *The Girl at the Lion d'Or, A Fool's Alphabet, The Fatal Englishman, Charlotte Gray, On Green Dolphin Street,* and the internationally bestselling *Birdsong*. He lives with his family in London.

JÖRG HENSGEN was born in Germany and studied at the universities of Wuppertal, Göttingen, and Hamburg. He now lives in London and works as an editor.

The Vintage Book of
War Fiction

EDITED BY SEBASTIAN FAULKS
AND JÖRG HENSGEN

Vintage Books
A Division of Random House, Inc.
New York

A VINTAGE BOOKS ORIGINAL, SEPTEMBER 2002

The Cataloging-in-Publication Data is on file at the Library of Congress.

Vintage ISBN: 1-4000-3040-4

www.vintagebooks.com

Printed in the United States of America
10 9 8 7 6 5 4 3 2 1

CONTENTS

INTRODUCTION

THIS IS A book of extracts from works of fiction set in the wars of the twentieth century, and, when you come to think about it, the strangest thing about such books is that there are not more of them. Once the young literary form of the novel had decided, 250 years or so ago, that it would do more than tell stories, that it was uniquely suited by its access to inward psychological development and boundless narrative to explore 'human nature' and that that would be, for many writers and readers, its highest aim, then you would have thought that most ambitious novelists would have looked to see what conditions of existence offered them the most extreme and therefore, presumably, most rewarding circumstances for their study. War, surely, would have been the answer. If the writing of fiction had been undertaken not by writers but by scientists, they would certainly have seized on the dramatic potential of armed conflict for their experiments. These, they would have argued, are the ideal laboratory conditions for this examination of humanity; only under these intense pressures, both on the battlefield and behind it, both in the generations that fought and in their children, would the transcendent or outer qualities of humankind become visible.

Artists, however, aren't like that. Writers write what they can; they write books about the stories or people that have moved them, without analysing, necessarily, the effects their work will have on their readers. They certainly don't view it as scientific enterprise in which the rewards are bestowed on those who work at the frontiers of knowledge. Perhaps they should, but they don't; and the other deterrent fact about war as a subject or background for fiction is that it is so disgusting. Which writer would willingly immerse himself for two or three years in this drab world of units and numbers, of industrial metal and meaningless death, without women or children or costume or domestic drama or even interesting food and drink? Laboratory of souls maybe, they would reply, but what a repellent and austere one.

Well, there are ways round that problem; in fact there are more ways of disarming a reader's natural disinclination to read about such things than of overcoming the writer's reluctance to write about them. I remember the reactions of friends and colleagues who asked me what I was writing in the early 1990s when I told them it was a novel set in the First World War. They thought I was insane. No one (or no one they could think of) had written a novel in England about this war since . . . well, since Robert Graves—or perhaps that wasn't a novel. Anyway, it would be impossible to improve on the great books of the 1920s; war was a subject for decrepit old men in Aldershot bungalows; and, outside the British Legion library, it would have no sale at all. Oddly enough when the novel, *Birdsong,* came out in 1993 and met with some success, many of the same people assured me it was because I had 'jumped on a First World War bandwagon'.

It does seem that war has to some extent come back into play as a background or setting for serious fiction, though writers today are unlikely to follow the direct course to the Front of Erich Maria Remarque or even the twisting paths of Evelyn Waugh, whose *Sword of Honour* trilogy fully digested a personal experience of combat before setting it in a social context. They will look for different angles. The fall-out, the repercussions, the social eddies that begin from the hideous collisions of metal and flesh; the historical, post-Freudian, even the comic or ironic dimensions: these are likely to be of interest to modern writers, at the end of an old century and the start of a new millennium. How did we get here? Has ever there been such a century for killing as the one we have just endured? What did it mean? Have we really thought it through?

Pat Barker, Sebastien Japrisot, William Boyd, Louis de

Bernières and others have recently used war for their own fictional ends; it serves a purpose in a wider artistic scheme. But one of the first things that will strike readers of this anthology is the high proportion of novelists who are drawing on their own experiences, recycled or recrafted to varying degrees, and the low proportion who have gone in with the pure, disinterested eye of fiction. Many writers have used the form of the novel as little more than a convenience for what is at heart a documentary account of what happened to them. We have tried, on the whole, to favour full-blown fiction over lightly fictionalised autobiography, though there were instances of fact-based fiction where the writing itself was so compelling (Sassoon, Tim O'Brien), so successfully transformed (Hemingway, Norman Mailer) or else dealt with an experience or a conflict that would otherwise have been unrepresented (Malraux) that we were glad not to be inflexible.

There seems little doubt that the main impulse of a writer such as A.D. Gristwood was a documentary one. He wanted to get down on paper what the Great War was like, and if that meant inventing a perfunctory story and changing a few names, so be it. Later generations have been thankful for what he did, and such purpose can give real power to the writing, as it did to the overtly political novel *Under Fire,* which its author, Henri Barusse, hoped would help to stop the fighting. Witnessing what no human being had ever seen before, however—slaughter of ten million men for no apparent reason—proved an experience difficult to transmute into fiction, and there are not many outstanding novels to emerge from 1914–18. Exceptions include books by Henry Williamson, Frederic Manning, R.H. Mottram and Richard Aldington; unfortunately, Ford Madox Ford's Tietjens tetralogy, the most highly esteemed of all, defeated our attempts to find an extract that was both representative and self-contained.

In compiling this anthology we were aware of the attraction of good writing for its own sake but also of the need to be to some extent representative—to vary the contents by nationality of author, by conflict, by type of combat (by air and sea as well as by land), but above it all by tone. There is no shortage of novels that describe bullet wounds and bombardments; there are not so many that talk about what was going on elsewhere. For this reason we were particularly pleased to include extracts from Elizabeth Bowen, Jean-Louis Curtis and John Horne Burns. Where it seemed possible, we looked to include humorous writing (Louis de Bernières, Laurie Lee, Christopher John Farley), or incidents that illuminated peripheral or contingent aspects of war—Wolfgang Koeppen's Nazi on the loose in Rome, for instance, Stratis Myrivilis's unashamed description of the beauty of firepower or Kurt Vonnegut's wry account of literary profiteering.

With Vonnegut and Joseph Heller, we have cheated. We wanted to include them both out of admiration for their writing and because the theatres of war they wrote about (Dresden and the US airforce in the Mediterranean, respectively) were intriguing. However, we feared to bore readers with writing that would be too familiar to them, so in these two instances (only) we have taken extracts from the writers' accounts of their novels rather than from the novels themselves.

Traditionally, the art of the anthologist is one of compromise, of steering a course between the Scylla of overfamiliarity and the Charybdis of too many unknowns. It is something like that of the music promoter who will use his star attractions to 'break' new acts and who will also make sure that while the main act plays songs from their new album they also include their greatest hits. Our rule of thumb was that if the Rolling Stones were going to play, they should give it all they've got; and if your curiosity does not flare up at the sight of Hemingway's name, I hope at least you won't deny yourself the intense pleasure of re-reading the extract in question.

The novelists' techniques evolved as the wars themselves become different, and to some extent the literary style was affected by the military circumstances. Many English novelists of the Great War were acting as auxiliary reporters: 'Look,' they were saying, 'no one really told you before what it was like'—and their ambitions were essentially journalistic. Those who went artistically further found what they could do constrained by the static nature of trench warfare. It is not surprising that, not only surveying an unprecedented human holocaust but watching it from a hole in the ground for months on end, these men produced such introspective books.

The Second World War brought, superficially, a completely different set of problems and responses. The combatants were unillusioned from the start. They knew how gruesome war would be, they knew that they had been dropped into it by inept politicians, but in place of the innocent patroitism of their fathers they had a proper moral cause to fight for; or at the very least, they were defending their homes. This was an inter-continental war fought in the jungle, the desert, by sea and by air. There was much less problem here about getting word home of what was going on; the difficulty was more that there was so much happening on so many different fronts that many voices and their stories were in danger of going unheard. To novelists, however, this multiplicity was an advantage, and made this the easiest war to write about. In the 1950s Alistair MacLean chose the Atlantic Convoys, in the 1960s John Fowles the German occupation of a Greek island; as late as 1995 Robert Harris found secret dramas at Bletchley. The growth of air war, of radar and the improvement of communications made this, frankly, more exciting than the trenches; and all novelists from Allied countries could approach the subject with a certain moral ease denied to Heinrich Böll or Shusaku Endo.

Writing from Vietnam became different again. Like the First World War, this proved a difficult experience to digest, and it was some time before American film-makers, in particular, were able to approach the subject. The amount of information had increased and so had access to it, particularly by television camera; but the combat was contained, peculiar and morally doubtful: drafted young civilians fighting a guerrilla war from helicopter gunships with napalm in a country they had never heard of . . . this was not Normandy or Iwo Jima. American writers eventually seemed to agree on a strategy to deal with it, and it seems to have been by recourse to what you might call a rock'n'roll style. When you read American accounts of Vietnam, it is very hard not to hear in them the tones of Haight Ashbury, of Jerry Rubin and the Yippies and the entire fusion of high and popular culture that was taking place in America at the time. The results are both shocking and poignant. It was as though Wyoming and Georgia, so reluctantly transplanted to the undergrowth of Vietnam, decided on its return that from now on it would speak its own demotic; that if Washington had sent them there, from now now on Washington would hear about it in their way, in their language. The literary craft of Larry Heinemann and Philip Caputo is far subtler than that, of course; but there is something insistently democratic in the way these people wrote which is analogous to the low-key yet haunting inscriptions of the Vietnam Memorial itself.

Whereas in Europe, the idiom of the commanders (even of an SAS officer such as Sir Peter de la Billiere) has retained a wistful air, a tacit acknowledgement that war is a dreadful last resort, American military leaders from MacArthur onward have shown a much franker relish in the way they speak of their business. When General Norman Schwarzkopf declared of the Iraqi army in 1991 that he was going to 'cut it off, then kill it', he may have been making a reference to Hannibal's action at Cannae, but his private soldiers ignorantly used the language of the video game, while the Nato commanders in the Kosovo conflict seemed to believe that war could actually be waged as at a games console, safe from harm, with only the enemy targets open to damage. It is possible to envisage on the ground in bombed Belgrade or mutilated Kosovo the dramatically complex circumstances that might give rise to fiction in due course, but you feel it would be certain to come from those countries and not from the ranks of the arm's-length Nato air forces. Perhaps that is unfair. The story of a troubled pilot who has inadvertently bombed the refugees he is meant to help, attacked the liberation army who are his allies or destroyed the embassy of a non-engaged enemy country is not without potential.

As for the West's most recent war, on what President Bush has called 'the axis of terror,' it seems likely that film-makers will be the first to respond. Most observers of the terrorist attacks of September 11, 2001, were at once queasily struck by the way the television pictures evoked so many mindless Hollywood bang-fests, and it was easy to conjecture the morbid contribution made by such exploitative films to the minds of the terrorists, already confused by material envy, sexual frustration and shame at the institutional failure of their religion. Yet Hollywood is nothing if not thick-skinned, and that awful day will doubtless provide a backdrop for many movies over the next few years. As for the air and ground war in Afghanistan itself, it seems too remote and too specialized— not just professional soldiers, but specialized units within those forces—to have a wider human resonance. The SAS memoir is already an established and fast-selling genre in Britian, but it relies for its effect on a documentary thrill that follows the breaking of professional confidences. Does this mean that war novels are finished?

As serious fiction has moved further from plot and incident, the reader's hunger for books that impose an artistic and comforting pattern on the random events of life is less often satisfied. War can still deal with big events, while violent accidents or sudden reversals are considered melodramatic in ordinary fiction. Only in a war novel can you respectably kill off your main character with a stray sniper's bullet, yet such deaths are in some way emblematic, in extreme form, of the inexplicable randomness of life events as we experience them from day to day in peace. A parent who has lost a child in a car accident may find greater affinity with the narrative emergencies of people in a wartime novel than in one that deals with a married woman's failed love affair or a sensitive young man's sexual awakening.

It still seems to me strange, when I came to think of it, that there are not more war books.

The bulk of the hard work that has gone into this anthology has been done by my co-editor Jörg Hensgen; his reading, researching, editing and organising have been prodigious. While I am happy to accept the blame for any shortcomings, the credit for any strengths this book may have is more likely to be his. I confess that occasionally during our collaboration I salved my guilt at the inequity of our contributions by reflecting that I was the first male member of my family for more than 100 years who, when confronted by a German of the same generation, had at least not tried to kill him.

Sebastian Faulks

The Vintage Book of War Fiction

Bruce Chatwin

Volunteers

When the First World War broke out in August 1914, both the volunteers who marched through the streets of Paris, London and Berlin, and the crowds who cheered them believed that the war would be over by Christmas. The 'Spirit of 1914' was still powerful four months later when the war reached the small Welsh village of Rhulen, as described here by Bruce Chatwin in his novel On the Black Hill *(1982).*

THEN THE WAR came.

For years, the tradesmen in Rhulen had said there was going to be war with Germany, though nobody knew what war would mean. There had been no real war since Waterloo, and everyone agreed that with railways and modern guns this war would either be very terrible, or over very quickly.

On the 7th of August 1914, Amos Jones and his sons were scything thistles when a man called over the hedge that the Germans had marched into Belgium, and rejected England's ultimatum. A recruiting office, he said, had opened in the Town Hall. About twenty local lads had joined.

'More fool them,' Amos shrugged, and glared downhill into Herefordshire.

All three went on with their scything, but the boys looked very jittery when they came in for supper.

Mary had been pickling beetroot, and her apron was streaked with purple stains.

'Don't worry,' she said. 'You're far too young to fight. Besides, it'll probably be over by Christmas.'

Winter came, and there was no end to the war. Mr Gomer Davies started preaching patriotic sermons and, one Friday, sent word to The Vision, bidding them to a lantern lecture, at five o'clock, in the Congregation Hall.

The sky was deepening from crimson to gunmetal. Two limousines were parked in the lane; and a crowd of farm boys, all in their Sunday best, were chatting to the chauffeurs or peering through the windows at the fur rugs and leather upholstery. The boys had never seen such automobiles at close quarters. In a nearby shed, an electric generator was purring.

Mr Gomer Davies stood in the vestibule, welcoming all comers with a handshake and muddy smile. The war, he said, was a Crusade for Christ.

Inside the Hall, a coke stove was burning and the windows had misted up. A line of electric bulbs spread a film of yellow light over the planked and varnished walls. There were plenty of Union Jacks strung up, and a picture of Lord Kitchener.

The magic lantern stood in the middle of the aisle. A white sheet had been tacked up to serve as a screen; and a khaki-clad Major, one arm in a sling, was confiding his box of glass slides to the lady projectionist.

Veiled in cigar smoke, the principal speaker, Colonel Bickerton, had already taken his seat on the stage and was having a jaw with a Boer War veteran. He extended his game leg to the audience. A silk hat sat on the green baize tablecloth, beside a water-carafe and a tumbler.

Various ministers of God – all of whom had sunk their differences in a blaze of patriotism – went up to pay their respects to the squire, and show concern for his comfort.

'No, I'm quite comfortable, thank you.' The Colonel enunciated every syllable to perfection. 'Thank you for looking after me so well. Pretty good turn-out, I see. Most encouraging, what?'

The hall was full. Lads with fresh, weatherbeaten faces crammed the benches or elbowed forward to get a better look at the Bickertons' daughter, Miss Isobel – a brunette with moist red lips and moist hazel eyes, who sat below the platform, composed and smiling, in a silver fox-fur cape. From her dainty hat there spurted a grey-pink glycerined ostrich plume. At her elbow crouched a young man with carroty hair and mouth agape.

It was Jim the Rock.

The Joneses took their seats on a bench at the back. Mary could feel her husband, tense and angry beside her. She was afraid he was going to make a scene.

The vicar of Rhulen opened the session by proposing a vote of thanks to Mr Gomer Davies for the use of the Hall, and electricity.

Rumbles of 'Hear! Hear!' sounded round the room. He went on to sketch the origins of the war.

Few of the hill-farmers understood why the murder of an Archduke in the Balkans should have triggered off the invasion of Belgium; but when the vicar spoke of the 'peril to our beloved Empire' people began to sit up.

'There can be no rest,' he raised his voice, 'until this cancer has been ripped out of European society. The Germans will squeal like every bully when cornered. But there must be no compromise, no shaking hands with the devil. It is useless to moralize with an alligator. Kill it!'

The audience clapped and the clergyman sat down.

Next in turn was the Major, who had been wounded, he said, at Mons. He began with a joke about 'making the Rhine whine' – whereupon the Colonel perked up and said, 'Never cared for Rhine wines myself. Too fruity, what?'

The Major then lifted his swagger stick.

'Lights!' he called, and the lights went off.

One by one, a sequence of blurred images flashed across the screen – of Tommies in camp, Tommies on parade, Tommies on the cross-Channel ferry; Tommies in a French café; Tommies in trenches; Tommies fixing bayonets, and Tommies 'going over the top'. Some of the slides were so fuzzy it was hard to tell which was the shadow of Miss Isobel's plume, and which were shell-bursts.

The last slide showed an absurd goggle-eyed visage with crows' wings on its upper lip and a whole golden eagle on its helmet.

'That,' said the Major, 'is your enemy – Kaiser Wilhelm II of Germany.'

There were shouts of 'String 'im up' and 'Shoot 'im to bloody bits!' – and the Major, also, sat down.

Colonel Bickerton then eased himself to his feet and apologized for the indisposition of his wife.

His own son, he said, was fighting in Flanders. And after the stirring scenes they'd just witnessed, he hoped there'd be few shirkers in the district.

'When this war is over,' he said, 'there will be two classes of persons in this country. There will be those who were qualified to join the Armed Forces and refrained from doing so . . .'

'Shame!' shrilled a woman in a blue hat.

'I'm the Number One!' a young man shouted and stuck up his hand.

But the Colonel raised his cufflinks to the crowd, and the crowd fell silent:

'. . . and there will be those who were so qualified and came forward to do their duty to their King, their country . . . and their womenfolk . . .'

'Yes! Yes!' Again the hands arose with fluid grace and, again, the crowd fell silent:

'The last-mentioned class, I need not add, will be the aristocracy of this country – indeed, the only true aristocracy of this country – who, in the evening of their days, will have the consolation of knowing that they have done what England expects of every man: namely, to do his duty . . .'

'What about Wales?' A sing-song voice sounded to the right of Miss Bickerton; but Jim was drowned in the general hullabaloo.

Volunteers rushed forward to press their names on the Major. There were shouts of 'Hip! Hip! Hurrah!' Other voices broke into song, 'For they are jolly good fellows . . .' The woman in the blue hat slapped her son over the face, shrieking, 'Oh, yes, you will!' – and a look of childlike serenity had descended on the Colonel.

He continued, in thrilling tones: 'Now when Lord Kitchener says he needs you, he means YOU. For each one of you brave young fellows is unique and indispensable. A few moments ago, I heard a voice on my left calling, "What about Wales?"'

Suddenly, you could hear a pin drop.

'Believe you me, that cry, "What about Wales?" is a cry that goes straight to my heart. For in my veins Welsh blood and English blood course in equal quantities. And that . . . that is why my daughter and I have brought two automobiles here with us this evening. Those of you who wish to enlist in our beloved Herefordshire Regiment may drive with me . . . But those of you, loyal Welshmen, who would prefer to join that other, most gallant regiment, the South Wales Borderers, may go with my daughter and Major Llewellyn-Smythe to Brecon . . .'

This was how Jim the Rock went to war – for the sake of leaving home, and for a lady with moist red lips and moist hazel-coloured eyes.

Louis-Ferdinand Céline

COULD I BE THE LAST COWARD ON EARTH?

The narrator of Céline's novel Journey to the End of the Night *(1932) too has volunteered to join the army after seeing soldiers and military bands parading through the streets of Paris. But his feelings of patriotism soon give way to the realization that he has made a big mistake: 'The music had stopped . . . I was about to clear out. Too late! They'd quietly shut the gate behind us civilians. We were caught like rats.'*

WHEN YOU'RE IN, you're in. They put us on horseback, and after we'd been on horseback for two months, they put us back on our feet. Maybe because of the expense. Anyway, one morning the colonel was looking for his horse, his orderly had made off with it, nobody knew where to, probably some quiet spot that bullets couldn't get to as easily as the middle of the road. Because that was exactly where the colonel and I had finally stationed ourselves, with me holding his orderly book while he wrote out his orders.

Down the road, away in the distance, as far as we could see, there were two black dots, plunk in the middle like us, but they were two Germans and they'd been busy shooting for the last fifteen or twenty minutes.

Maybe our colonel knew why they were shooting, maybe the Germans knew, but I, so help me, hadn't the vaguest idea. As far back as I could search my memory, I hadn't done a thing to the Germans, I'd always been polite and friendly with them. I knew the Germans pretty well, I'd even gone to school in their country when I was little, near Hanover. I'd spoken their language. A bunch of loud-mouthed little halfwits, that's what they were, with pale, furtive eyes like wolves; we'd go out to the woods together after school to feel the girls up, or we'd fire pop-guns or pistols you could buy for four marks. And we drank sugary beer together. But from that to shooting at us right in the middle of the road, without so much as a word of introduction, was a long way, a very long way. If you asked me, they were going too far.

This war, in fact, made no sense at all. It couldn't go on.

Had something weird got into these people? Something I didn't feel at all? I suppose I hadn't noticed it . . .

Anyway, my feelings toward them hadn't changed. In spite of everything. I'd have liked to understand their brutality, but what I wanted still more, enormously, with all my heart, was to get out of there, because suddenly the whole business looked to me like a great big mistake.

'In a mess like this,' I said to myself, 'there's nothing to be done, all you can do is clear out . . .'

Over our heads, two millimetres, maybe one millimetre from our temples, those long searching lines of steel, that bullets make when they're out to kill you, were whistling through the hot summer air.

I'd never felt so useless as I did amidst all those bullets in the sunlight. A vast and universal mockery.

I was only twenty at the time. Deserted farms in the distance, empty wide-open churches, as if the peasants had gone out for the day to attend a fair at the other end of the district, leaving everything they owned with us for safe-keeping, their countryside, their carts with the shafts in the air, their fields, their barn yards, the roads, the trees, even the cows, a chained dog, the works. Leaving us free to do as we pleased while they were gone. Nice of them, in a way. 'Still,' I said to myself, 'if they hadn't gone somewhere else, if there were still somebody here, I'm sure we wouldn't be behaving so badly! So disgustingly! We wouldn't dare in front of them!' But there wasn't a soul to watch us! Nobody but us, like newlyweds that get down to the dirty business when all the people have gone home.

And another thought I had (behind a tree) was that I wished Déroulède* – the one I'd heard so much about – had been there to describe his reactions when a bullet tore open his guts.

Those Germans squatting on the road, shooting so obstinately, were rotten shots, but they seemed to have ammunition to burn, whole warehouses full or so it seemed to me. Nobody could say this war was over! I have to hand it to the colonel, his bravery was remarkable. He roamed around in the middle of the road, up and down and back and forth in the midst of the bullets as calmly as if he'd been waiting for a friend on a station platform, except just a tiny bit impatient.

One thing I'd better tell you right away, I'd never been able to stomach the country, I'd always found it dreary, those endless fields of mud, those houses where nobody's ever home, those roads that don't go anywhere. And if to all that you add a war, it's completely unbearable. A sudden wind had come up on both sides of the road, the clattering leaves of the poplars mingled with the little dry crackle aimed at us from down the road. Those unknown soldiers missed us every time, but they spun a thousand deaths around us, so close they seemed to clothe us. I was afraid to move.

That colonel, I could see, was a monster. Now I knew it for sure, he was worse than a dog, he couldn't conceive of his own death. At the same time I realized that there must be plenty of brave men like him in our army, and just as many no doubt in the army facing us. How many, I wondered. One or two million, say several millions in all? The thought turned my fear to panic. With such people this infernal lunacy could go on for ever . . . Why would they stop? Never had the world seemed so implacably doomed.

Could I, I thought, be the last coward on earth? How terrifying! . . . All alone with two million stark raving heroic madmen, armed to the eyeballs? With and without helmets,

* Paul Déroulède (1847–1914). Writer and politician. Extreme nationalist, supporter of General Boulanger and founder of the League of Patriots.

without horses, on motorcycles, bellowing, in cars, screeching, shooting, plotting, flying, kneeling, digging, taking cover, bounding over trails, bombarding, shut up on earth as if it were a loony bin, ready to demolish everything on it, Germany, France, whole continents, everything that breathes, destroy, destroy, madder than mad dogs, worshipping their madness (which dogs don't), a hundred, a thousand times madder than a thousand dogs, and a lot more vicious! A pretty mess we were in! No doubt about it, this crusade I'd let myself in for was the apocalypse!

You can be a virgin in horror the same as in sex. How, when I left the Place Clichy, could I have imagined such horror? Who could have suspected, before getting really into the war, all the ingredients that go to make up the rotten, heroic, good-for-nothing soul of man? And there I was, caught up in a mass flight into collective murder, into the fiery furnace . . . Something had come up from the depths, and it was happening now.

The colonel was still as cool as a cucumber, I watched him as he stood on the embankment, taking little messages sent by the general, reading them without haste as the bullets flew all around him, and tearing them into little pieces. Did none of those messages include an order to put an immediate stop to this abomination? Did no top brass tell him there had been a misunderstanding? A horrible mistake? A misdeal? That somebody's got it all wrong, that the plan had been for manœuvres, a sham battle, not a massacre! Not at all! 'Keep it up, colonel! You're doing fine!' That's what General des Entrayes,* the head of our division and commander over us all, must have written in those notes that were being brought every five minutes by a courier, who looked greener and more shitless each time. I could have palled up with that boy, we'd have been scared together. But we had no time to fraternize.

So there was no mistake? So there was no law against people shooting at people they couldn't even see! It was one of the things you could do without anybody reading you the

---

* Entrayes derives from *entrailles*, entrails ('blood and guts').

riot act. In fact, it was recognized and probably encouraged by upstanding citizens, like the draft, or marriage, or hunting! . . . No two ways about it. I was suddenly on the most intimate terms with war. I'd lost my virginity. You've got to be pretty much alone with her as I was then to get a good look at her, the slut, full face and profile. A war had been switched on between us and the other side, and now it was burning! Like the current between the two carbons of an arc lamp! And this lamp was in no hurry to go out! It would get us all, the colonel and everyone else, he looked pretty spiffy now, but he wouldn't roast up any bigger than me when the current from the other side got him between the shoulders.

There are different ways of being condemned to death. Oh! What wouldn't I have given to be in prison instead of here! What a fool I'd been! If only I had had a little foresight and stolen something or other when it would have been so easy and there was still time. I never think of anything. You come out of prison alive, you don't out of a war! The rest is blarney.

If only I'd had time, but I didn't. There was nothing left to steal. How pleasant it would be in a cosy little cell, I said to myself, where the bullets couldn't get in. Where they never got in! I knew of one that was ready and waiting, all sunny and warm! I saw it in my dreams, the prison of Saint-Germain to be exact, right near the forest. I knew it well, I'd often passed that way. How a man changes! I was a child in those days, and that prison frightened me. Because I didn't know what men are like. Never again will I believe what they say or what they think. Men are the thing to be afraid of, always, men and nothing else.

How much longer would this madness have to go on before these monsters dropped with exhaustion? How long could a convulsion like this last? Months? Years? How many? Maybe till the whole world's dead, and all these madmen? Every last one of them? And seeing that events were taking such a desperate turn, I decided to stake everything on one throw, to make one last try, to see if I couldn't stop the war, just me, all by myself! At least in this one spot where I happened to be.

The colonel was only two steps away from me, pacing. I'd

talk to him. Something I'd never done. This was a time for daring. The way things stood, there was practically nothing to lose. 'What is it?' he'd ask me, startled, I imagined, at my bold interruption. Then I'd explain the situation as I saw it, and we'd see what he thought. The essential is to talk things over. Two heads are better than one.

I was about to take the decisive step when, at that very moment, who should arrive at the double but a dismounted cavalryman (as we said in those days), exhausted, shaky in the joints, holding his helmet upside-down in one hand like Belisarius,* trembling, all covered with mud, his face even greener than the courier I mentioned before. He stammered and gulped. You'd have thought he was struggling to climb out of a tomb, and it had made him sick to his stomach. Could it be that this spook didn't like bullets any more than I did? That he saw them coming like me?

'What is it?' Disturbed, brutally, the colonel stopped him short; flinging at him a glance that might have been steel.

It made our colonel very angry to see that wretched cavalryman so incorrectly clad and shitting in his pants with fright. The colonel had no use for fear, that was a sure thing. And especially that helmet held in the hand like a bowler was really too much in a combat regiment like ours that was just getting into the war. It was as if this dismounted cavalryman had seen the war and taken his hat off in greeting.

Under the colonel's withering look the wobbly messenger snapped to attention, pressing his little finger to the seam of his trousers as the occasion demanded. And so he stood on the embankment, stiff as a board, swaying, the sweat running down his chin strap; his jaws were trembling so hard that little abortive cries kept coming out of him, like a little dog dreaming. You couldn't make out whether he wanted to speak to us or whether he was crying.

Our Germans squatting at the end of the road had just

---

* Byzantine general (500–565) who, according to legend, was blinded by order of Emperor Justinian. Numerous paintings show him as a beggar, holding out his reversed helmet for alms.

changed weaponry. Now they were having their fun with a machine gun, sputtering like handfuls of matches, and all around us flew swarms of angry bullets, as hostile as wasps.

The man finally managed to articulate a few words:

'Colonel, sir, Sergeant Barousse has been killed.'

'So what?'

'He was on his way to meet the bread wagon on the Etrapes road, sir.'

'So what?'

'He was blown up by a shell!'

'So what, dammit!'

'That's what, colonel, sir.'

'Is that all?'

'Yes, sir, that's all, colonel sir.'

'What about the bread?' the colonel asked.

That was the end of the dialogue, because, I remember distinctly, he barely had time to say 'What about the bread?' That was all. After that there was nothing but flame and noise. But the kinds of noise you wouldn't have thought possible. Our eyes, ears, nose and mouth were so full of that noise that I thought it was all over and I'd turned into noise and flame myself.

After a while the flame went away, the noise stayed in my head, and my arms and legs trembled as if somebody were shaking me from behind. My limbs seemed to be leaving me, but then in the end they stayed on. The smoke stung my eyes for a long time, and the prickly smell of powder and sulphur hung on, strong enough to kill all the fleas and bedbugs in the whole world.

I thought of Sergeant Barousse, who had just gone up in smoke as the man had told us. That was good news. Great, I thought to myself. That makes one less stinker in the regiment! He wanted to have me court-martialled for a tin of meat. 'It's an ill wind,' I said to myself. In that respect, you can't deny it, the war seemed to serve a purpose now and then! I knew of three or four more in the regiment, real scum, that I'd have gladly helped to make the acquaintance of a shell, like Barousse.

As for the colonel, I didn't wish him any harm. But he was dead too. At first I didn't see him. The blast had carried him up an embankment and laid him down on his side, right in the arms of the dismounted cavalryman, the courier, who was finished too. They were embracing each other for the moment and for all eternity, but the cavalryman's head was gone, all he had was an opening at the top of the neck, with blood in it bubbling and glugging like jam in a pan. The colonel's belly was wide open and he was making a nasty face about it. It must have hurt when it happened. So much the worse for him! If he'd got out when the shooting started, it wouldn't have happened.

All that tangled meat was bleeding profusely.

Shells were still bursting to the right and left of the scene.

I'd had enough, I was glad to have such a good pretext for clearing out. I even hummed a tune, and reeled like when you've been rowing a long way and your legs are wobbly. 'Just one shell!' I said to myself. 'Amazing how quick just one shell can clean things up. Could you believe it?' I kept saying to myself. 'Could you believe it!'

There was nobody left at the end of the road. The Germans were gone. But that little episode had taught me a quick lesson, to keep to the cover of the trees. I was in a hurry to get back to our command post, to see if anyone else in our regiment had been killed on reconnaissance. There must be some good dodges, I said to myself, for getting taken prisoner . . . Here and there in the fields a few puffs of smoke still clung to the ground. 'Maybe they're all dead,' I thought. 'Seeing they refuse to understand anything whatsoever, the best solution would be for them all to get killed instantly . . . The war would be over, and we'd go home . . . Maybe we'd march across the Place Clichy in triumph . . . Just one or two survivors . . . In my dream . . . Strapping good fellows marching behind the general, all the rest would be dead like the colonel . . . Like Barousse . . . like Vanaille (another bastard) . . . etc. They'd shower us with decorations and flowers, we'd march through the Arc de Triomphe. We'd go to a restaurant, they'd serve us free of charge, we'd never pay for anything any more, never as long as we lived! We're heroes! we'd say when they brought the bill . . . defenders of the *Patrie*! That would do it! . . . We'd pay with little French flags! . . . The lady at the cash desk would refuse to take money from heroes, she'd even give us some, with kisses thrown in, as we filed out. Life would be worth living.'

As I was running, I noticed my arm was bleeding, just a little though, a far from satisfactory wound, a scratch. I'd have to start all over.

It was raining again, the fields of Flanders oozed with dirty water. For a long time I didn't meet a soul, only the wind and a little later the sun. From time to time, I couldn't tell from where, a bullet would come flying merrily through the air and sunshine, looking for me, intent on killing me, there in the wilderness. Why? Never again, not if I lived another hundred years, would I go walking in the country. A solemn oath.

Walking along, I remembered the ceremony of the day before. It had taken place in a meadow, at the foot of a hill; the colonel had harangued the regiment in his booming voice: 'Keep your courage up!' he had cried. 'Keep your courage up! and *Vive la France*!' When you have no imagination, dying is small beer; when you do have imagination, dying is too much. That's my opinion. My understanding had never taken in so many things at once.

The colonel had never had any imagination. That was the source of all his trouble, especially ours. Was I the only man in that regiment with an imagination about death? I preferred my own kind of death, the kind that comes late . . . in twenty years . . . thirty . . . maybe more . . . to this death they were trying to deal me right away . . . eating Flanders mud, my whole mouth full of it, fuller than full, split to the ears by a shell fragment. A man's entitled to an opinion about his own death. But which way, if that was the case, should I go? Straight ahead? My back to the enemy. If the MPs were to catch me roaming around I knew my goose was cooked. They'd give me a slapdash trial that same afternoon in some deserted classroom . . . There were lots of empty classrooms wherever we went. They'd play court martial with me the way

14

kids play when the teacher isn't there. The noncoms seated on the platform, me standing in handcuffs in front of the little desks. In the morning they'd shoot me: twelve bullets plus one. So what was the answer?

And I thought of the colonel again, such a brave man with his breastplate and his helmet and his moustaches, if they had exhibited him in a music hall, walking as I saw him under the bullets and shellfire, he'd have filled the Alhambra, he'd have outshone Fragson,* and he was a big star at the time I'm telling you about. Keep your courage down! That's what I was thinking.

After hours and hours of cautious, furtive walking, I finally caught sight of our men near a clump of farmhouses. That was one of our advance posts. It belonged to a squadron that was billeted nearby. Nobody killed, they told me. Every last one of them alive! I was the one with the big news: 'The colonel's dead,' I shouted, as soon as I was near enough. 'Plenty more colonels where he came from.' That was the snappy comeback of Corporal Pistil, who was on duty just then, what's more, he was organizing details.

'All right, you jerk, until they find a replacement for the colonel, you can be picking up meat with Empouille and Kerdoncuff here, take two sacks each. The distribution point is behind the church . . . the one you see over there . . . Don't let them give you a lot of bones like yesterday, and try and get back before nightfall, you lugs!'

So I hit the road again with the other two.

That pissed me off. 'I'll never tell them anything after this,' I said to myself. I could see it was no use talking to those slobs, a tragedy like I'd just seen was wasted on such swine! It had happened too long ago to capture their interest. And to think that a week earlier they'd have given me four columns and my picture in the papers for the death of a colonel the way I'd seen it. A bunch of halfwits.

The meat for the whole regiment was being distributed in a summery field, shaded by cherry trees and parched by the

---

* Popular cabaret singer early in the century.

August sun. On sacks and tent cloths spread out on the grass there were pounds and pounds of guts, chunks of white and yellow fat, disembowelled sheep with their organs scattered every which way, oozing intricate little rivulets into the grass round about, a whole ox, split down the middle, hanging on a tree, and the four regimental butchers all hacking away at it, cursing and swearing and pulling off choice morsels. The squadrons were fighting tooth and nail over the innards, especially the kidneys, and all around them swarms of flies the like of which one sees only on such occasions, as self-important and musical as little birds.

Blood and more blood, everywhere, all over the grass, in sluggish confluent puddles, looking for a congenial slope. A few steps further on, the last pig was being killed. Four men and a butcher were already fighting over some of the prospective cuts.

'You crook, you! You're the one that made off with the tenderloin yesterday!'

Leaning against a tree, I had barely time enough to honour that alimentary dispute with two or three glances, before being overcome by an enormous urge to vomit, which I did so hard that I passed out.

They carried me back to the outfit on a stretcher. Naturally they swiped my two oilcloth sacks, the chance was too good to miss.

I woke to one of the corporal's harangues. The war wasn't over.

David Malouf

INVISIBLE ENEMIES

When Jim Saddler, the protagonist of David Malouf's novel
Fly Away Peter (1982), leaves rural Australia for the trenches
of France, he is at first proud to have become part of history
and fascinated by 'vast numbers of men engaged in an
endeavour that was clearly equal in scale to anything the
Pharaohs had imagined'. But he soon learns that he has
instead become part of the bizarre machine of trench warfare
where death can come at any moment and the enemy can't
even be seen.

OFTEN, AS JIM later discovered, you entered the war
through an ordinary looking gap in a hedge. One minute you
were in a ploughed field, with snowy troughs between ridges
that marked old furrows and peasants off at the edge of it
digging turnips or winter greens, and the next you were
through the hedge and on duckboards, and although you
could look back and still see farmers at work, or sullenly
watching as the soldiers passed over their land and went
slowly below ground, there was all the difference in the world
between your state and theirs. They were in a field and very
nearly at home. You were in the trench system that led to the
war.

But at Armentières, on that first occasion, you came to the
war from the centre of town. Crossing Half-past Eleven
Square (it was called that because the Town Hall clock had

17

stopped at that hour during an early bombardment; every-thing here had been renamed and then named again, as places and streets, a copse, a farmhouse, yielded up their old history and entered the new) you turned left and went on across Barbed-wire Square till you came to a big red building called the Gum-boot Store. There, after being fitted out with rubber boots that went all the way to mid-thigh, and tramping about for a few minutes to get used to the things, you were led away into the grounds of another, larger building, this time of brick, that was an Asylum; and from there, via Lunatic Lane, into the lines. Lunatic Lane began as a cobbled street, then became dirt, and before you quite knew it you were on planks. From this point the duckboards, for all their twisting and turning, led straight to the war.

They began to move up just at dusk, and by the time night fell and the first flares became visible, throwing their yellow glare on the underside of clouds and falling at times in a shower of brilliant stars, they were in the support line, stumbling in the dark through a maze of communication trenches, round firebays and traverses, jostling water-bottles, messtins, entrenching tools, grunting with the effort of trying to keep up, and quite blind except for the warning passed back from man to man of a hole up ahead in the greasy duckboards – *But where? How far? Am I almost on it?* – or a wire obstacle overhead.

The deeper they went the worse it got. In places where seepage was bad the duckboards were a foot under water. Once a whole earthwall had fallen and the passage was so narrow they could barely squeeze through: the place had been hit by a 'minnie'. They met two stretcher bearers moving in the opposite direction with a man who screamed, and some of the moisture, Jim thought, as they brushed in passing, must be blood. They hurried to keep up with the man in front and were soon breathless and sweating, partly because of the cracking pace that was being set – the men up front must actually have been running – but also because they were so keyed-up and eager to get there at last and see what it was. Everything here was so new, and they didn't know what might happen next, and when it did happen, how they would meet it. There was no stopping. If a man paused to adjust his pack or got his rifle caught in an overhead entanglement the whole troop might take a wrong turning and be lost in the dark.

The smell too got worse as they pushed further towards it. It was the smell of damp earthwalls and rotting planks, of mud impregnated with gas, of decaying corpses that had fallen in earlier battles and been incorporated now into the system itself, occasionally pushing out a hand or a booted foot, all ragged and black, not quite ingested; of rat-droppings, and piss, and the unwashed bodies of the men they were relieving, who also smelled like corpses, and were, in their heavy-eyed weariness as they came out, quite unrecognizable, though many of them were known to Jim by sight and some of them even by name; the war seemed immediately to have transformed them. They had occupied these trenches for eleven days. 'It's not so bad,' some of them mumbled, and others, with more bravado, claimed it was a cake-walk. But they looked beaten just the same.

They stayed eleven days themselves, and though the smell did not lessen, they ceased to notice it; it was their own. They were no longer the 'Eggs a-cook' of the easy taunt: 'Verra nice, verra sweet, verra clean. Two for one.' They were soldiers like the rest. They were men.

For eleven days they dug in and maintained the position. That is, they bailed out foul water, relaid duckboards, filled and carried sandbags to repair the parapet, stood to for a few minutes just before dawn with their rifles at the ready, crouched on the firestep, waiting – the day's one recognition of the reality of battle – then stood down again and had breakfast. Some days it rained and they simply sat in the rain and slept afterwards in mud. Other days it was fine. Men dozed on the firestep, read, played pontoon, or hunted for lice in their shirts. They were always cold and they never got enough sleep. They saw planes passing over in twos and threes, and occasionally caught the edge of a dogfight. Big black cannisters appeared in the sky overhead, rolling over and over, very slowly, then taking a downward path; the earth shook. You got used to that, and to the din.

Jim never saw a German, though they were there alright. Snipers. One fellow, too cocky, had looked over the parapet twice, being dared, and had his head shot off. His name was Stan Mackay, and it worried Jim that he couldn't fit a face to the name even when Clancy described the man. He felt he ought to be able to do that at least. A fellow he had talked to more than once oughtn't to just go out like that without a face.

Snipers. Also machine-gunners.

One of them, who must have had a sense of humour, could produce all sorts of jazz rhythms and odd syncopations as he 'played' the parapet. They got to know his touch. Parapet Joe he was called. He had managed, that fellow, to break through and establish himself as something more than the enemy. He had become an individual, who had then of course to have a name. Did he know he was called Parapet Joe? Jim wondered about this, and wondered, because of the name, what the fellow looked like. But it would have been fatal to try and find out.

One night, for several hours, there was a bombardment that had them all huddled together with their arms around their heads, not just trying to stop the noise but pretending, as children might, to be invisible.

But the real enemy, the one that challenged them day and night and kept them permanently weary, was the stinking water that seeped endlessly out of the walls and rose up round their boots as if the whole trench system in this part of the country were slowly going under. Occasionally it created cave-ins, bringing old horrors back into the light. The dead seemed close then; they had to stop their noses. Once, in heavy rain, a hand reached out and touched Jim on the back of the neck. 'Cut it out, Clancy,' he had protested, hunching closer to the wall; and was touched again. It was the earth behind him, quietly moving. Suddenly it collapsed, and a whole corpse lurched out of the wall and hurled itself upon him. He had to disguise his tendency to shake then, though the other fellows made a joke of it; and two or three times afterwards, when he dozed off, even in sunlight, he felt the same hand brush his neck with its long curling nail, and his scalp bristled. Once again the dead man turned in his sleep.

Water was the real enemy, endlessly sweating from the walls and gleaming between the duckboard-slats, or falling steadily as rain. It rotted and dislodged A-frames, it made the trench a muddy trough. They fought the water that made their feet rot, and the earth that refused to keep its shape or stay still, each day destroying what they had just repaired; they fought sleeplessness and the dull despair that came from that, and from their being, for the first time, grimily unwashed, and having body lice that bred in the seams of their clothes, and bit and itched and infected when you scratched; and rats in the same field-grey as the invisible enemy, that were as big as cats and utterly fearless, skittering over your face in the dark, leaping out of knapsacks, darting in to take the very crusts from under your nose. The rats were fat because they fed on corpses, burrowing right into a man's guts or tumbling about in dozens in the bellies of horses. They fed. Then they skittered over your face in the dark. The guns, Jim felt, he would get used to; and the snipers' bullets that buried themselves regularly in the mud of the parapet walls. They meant you were opposed to other men, much like yourself, and suffering the same hardships. But the rats were another species. And for him they were familiars of death, creatures of the underworld, as birds were of life and the air. To come to terms with the rats, and his deep disgust for them, he would have had to turn his whole world upside down.

All that first time up the line was like some crazy camping trip under nightmare conditions, not like a war. There was no fight. They weren't called upon in any way to have a go.

But even an invisible enemy could kill.

It happened out of the lines, when they went back into support. Their section of D company had spent a long afternoon unloading ammunition-boxes and carrying them up. They had removed their tunics, despite the cold, and scattered about in groups in the thin sunlight, relaxed in their shirtsleeves, were preparing for tea. Jim sat astride a blasted trunk and was buttering slabs of bread, dreamily spreading them thick with golden-green melon and lemon jam. His favourite. He was waiting for Clancy to come up with water, and had just glanced up and seen Clancy, with the billy in one hand and a couple of mugs hooked from the other, dancing along in his bow-legged way about ten yards off. Jim dipped his knife in the tin and dreamily spread jam, enjoying the way it went over the butter, almost transparent, and the promise of thick, golden-green sweetness.

Suddenly the breath was knocked out of him. He was lifted bodily into the air, as if the stump he was astride had bucked like an angry steer, and flung hard upon the earth. Wet clods and buttered bread rained all about him. He had seen and heard nothing. When he managed at last to sit up, drawing new breath into his lungs, his skin burned and the effect in his ear-drums was intolerable. He might have been halfway down a giant pipe that some fellow, some maniac, was belting over and over with a sledge hammer. *Thung. Thung. Thung.*

The ringing died away in time and he heard, from far off, but from very far off, a sound of screaming, and was surprised to see Eric Sawney, who had been nowhere in sight the moment before, not three yards away. His mouth was open and both his legs were off, one just above the knee, the other not far above the boot, which was lying on its own a little to the left. A pale fellow at any time, Eric was now the colour of butcher's paper, and the screams Jim could hear were coming from the hole of his mouth.

He became aware then of blood. He was lying in a pool of it. It must, he thought, be Eric's. It was very red, and when he put his hands down to raise himself from his half-sitting position, very sticky and warm.

Screams continued to come out of Eric, and when Jim got to his feet at last, unsteady but whole (his first thought was to stop Eric making that noise; only a second later did it occur to him that he should go to the boy's aid) he found that he was entirely covered with blood – his uniform, his face, his hair – he was drenched in it, it couldn't all be Eric's; and if it was his own he must be dead, and this standing up whole an illusion or the beginning of another life. The body's wholeness, he saw, was an image a man carried in his head. It might persist after the fact. He couldn't, in his stunned condition, puzzle this out. If it was the next life why could he hear Eric screaming out of the last one? And where was Clancy?

The truth hit him then with a force that was greater even than the breath from the 'minnie'. He tried to cry out but no sound came. It was hammered right back into his lungs and he thought he might choke on it.

Clancy had been blasted out of existence. It was Clancy's blood that covered him, and the strange slime that was all over him had nothing to do with being born into another life but was what had been scattered when Clancy was turned inside out.

He fell to his knees in the dirt and his screams came up without sound as a rush of vomit, and through it all he kept trying to cry out, till at last, after a few bubbly failures, his voice returned. He was still screaming when the others ran up.

He was ashamed then to have it revealed that he was quite unharmed, while Eric, who was merely dead white now and whimpering, had lost both his legs.

That was how the war first touched him. It was a month after they came over, a Saturday in February. He could never speak of it. And the hosing off never, in his own mind, left him clean. He woke from nightmares drenched in a wetness that dried and stuck and was more than his own sweat.

A few days later he went to sit with Eric at the hospital. He had never thought of Eric as anything but a nuisance, and remembered, a little regretfully now, how he and Clancy had tried to shake him off and how persistent he had been. But Clancy, behind a show of tolerant exasperation, had been fond of the boy, and Jim decided he ought, for Clancy's sake, to pay him a visit. He took a bar of chocolate. Eric accepted it meekly but without enthusiasm and hid it away under his pillow.

They talked about Clancy – there was nothing else – and he tried not to look at the place under the blanket where Eric's feet should have been, or at his pinched face. Eric looked scared, as if he were afraid of what might be done to him. *Isn't it done already?* Jim asked himself. *What more?*

'One thing I'm sorry about,' Eric said plaintively. 'I never learned to ride a bike.' He lay still with the pale sweat gathering on his upper lip. Then said abruptly: 'Listen, Jim, who's gunna look after me?'

'What?'

'When I get outa here. At home 'n all. I got no one. Just the fellers in the company, and none of 'em 'ave come to see me except you. I got nobody, not even an auntie. I'm an orfing. Who's gonna look after me, *back there?*'

The question was monstrous. Its largeness in the cramped space behind the screen, the way it lowered and made Eric sweat, the smallness of the boy's voice, as if even daring to ask might call down the wrath of unseen powers, put Jim into a panic. He didn't know the answer any more than Eric did and the question scared him. Faced with his losses, Eric had hit upon something fundamental. It was a question about the structure of the world they lived in and where they belonged in it, about who had power over them and what responsibility those agencies could be expected to assume. For all his childish petulance Eric had never been as helpless as he looked. His whining had been a weapon, and he had known how to make use of it. It was true that nobody paid any attention to him unless he wheedled and insisted and made a nuisance of himself, but the orphan had learned how to get what he needed: if not affection then at least a measure of tolerant regard. What scared him now was that people might simply walk off and forget him altogether. His view of things had been limited to those who stood in immediate relation to him, the matron at the orphanage, the sergeant and sergeant major, the sisters who ran the ward according to their own or the army's rules. Now he wanted to know what lay beyond.

'Who?' he insisted. The tip of his tongue appeared and passed very quickly over the dry lips.

Jim made a gesture. It was vague. 'Oh, they'll look after you alright Eric. They're bound to.'

But Eric was not convinced and Jim knew that his own hot panic had invaded the room. He wished Clancy was here. It was the sort of question Clancy might have been able to tackle; he had knocked about in the world and would have been bold enough to ask, and Jim saw that it was this capacity in Clancy that had constituted for Eric, as it had for him, the man's chief attraction: he knew his rights, he knew the ropes.

'I can't even stand up to take a piss,' Eric was telling him. The problem in Eric's mind was the number of years that might lie before him – sixty even. All those mornings when he would have to be helped into a chair.

'No,' Jim asserted, speaking now for the charity of their people, 'they'll look after you alright.' He stood, preparing to leave.

'Y' reckon?'

'Of course they will.'

Eric shook his head. 'I don't know.'

'Wilya come again, Jim?' A fine line of sweat drops on the boy's upper lip gave him a phantom moustache. 'Wilya, Jim?' His voice sounded thin and far away.

Jim promised he would and meant it, but knew guiltily that he would not. It was Eric's questions he would be unable to face.

As he walked away the voice continued to call after him, aggrieved, insistent, 'Wilya, Jim?' It was at first the voice of a child, and then, with hardly a change of tone, it was the voice of a querulous old man, who had asked for little and been given less and spent his whole life demanding his due.

Outside, for the first time since he was a kid, Jim cried, pushing his fists hard into his eye-sockets and trying to control his breath, and being startled – it was as if he had been taken over by some impersonal force that was weeping through him – by the harshness of his own sobs.

Erich Maria Remarque

HOW LONG IT TAKES FOR A MAN TO DIE!

Published in 1929, All Quiet on the Western Front *is arguably the most famous war novel of the century. Its impact is mainly due to the fact that it crossed the national boundaries of friend and foe and described the universal human tragedy of war. Through the eyes of the nineteen-year-old German soldier Paul Bäumer, Erich Maria Remarque portrays a 'generation that was destroyed by the war – even those of it who survived the shelling'. In the following extract, Bäumer is sent on reconnaissance patrol into no man's land where, for the first time, he encounters the enemy at close quarters.*

I SLIP WARILY over the edge, and snake forwards. I creep along on all fours; things are going well, I fix the direction, look about me and take note of the pattern of artillery fire so that I can find my way back. Then I try to make contact with the others.

I am still afraid, but now it is a rational fear, which is just an extraordinarily enhanced cautiousness. It is a windy night, and the shadows move back and forth in the sudden flashes from the gunfire. By this light you can see too much and too little. Often I freeze suddenly, but there is never anything there. In this way I get quite a long distance forward, and then turn back in a curve. I haven't made contact. Every few feet closer to our trench makes me more confident, but I still move as fast as I can. It wouldn't be too good to stop one just at this moment.

And then I get another shock. I'm no longer able to make out the exact direction. Silently I crouch in a shell hole and try and get my bearings. It has happened more than once that a man has jumped cheerfully into a trench, and only then found out that it was the wrong side.

After a while I listen again. I still haven't sorted out where I am. The wilderness of shell holes seems so confusing that in my agitated state I no longer have any idea which way to go. Maybe I am crawling parallel with the trenches, and I could go on for ever doing that. So I make another turn.

These damned Verey lights! It feels as if they last for an hour, and you can't make a move, or things soon start whistling round you.

It's no use, I've got to get out. By fits and starts I work my way along. I crawl crabwise across the ground and tear my hands to pieces on ragged bits of shrapnel as sharp as razorblades. Often I get the impression that the sky is becoming lighter on the horizon, but that could just be my imagination. Gradually I realize that I am crawling for my life.

A shell hits. Then straight away two more. And then it really starts. A barrage. Machine-guns chatter. Now there is nothing in the world that I can do except lie low. It seems to be an offensive. Light-rockets go up everywhere. Incessantly.

I'm lying bent double in a big shell hole in water up to my waist. When the offensive starts I'll drop into the water as far as I can without drowning and put my face in the mud. I'll have to play dead.

Suddenly I hear their shellfire give way. Straight away I slip down into the water at the bottom of the shell hole, my helmet right on the back of my neck and my mouth only sufficiently above water to let me breathe.

Then I remain motionless – because somewhere there is a clinking noise, something is coming closer, moving along and stamping; every nerve in my body tenses up and freezes. The clinking noise moves on over me, the first wave of soldiers is past. All that I had in my head was the one explosive thought: what will you do if someone jumps into your shell hole? Now

I quickly pull out my small dagger, grip it tight and hide it by keeping my hand downwards in the mud. The idea keeps pounding in my brain that if anyone jumps in I'll stab him immediately, stick the knife into his throat at once, so that he can't shout out, there's no other way, he'll be as frightened as I am, and we'll attack each other purely out of fear, so I have to get there first.

Now our gun batteries are firing. There is an impact near me. That makes me furiously angry, that's all I need, to be hit by our own gunfire; I curse into the mud and grind my teeth, it's an outburst of rage, and in the end all I can do is groan and plead.

The crash of shells pounds against my ears. If our men launch a counter-offensive, I'm free. I press my head against the earth and I can hear the dull thunder like distant explosions in a mine – then I lift my head to listen to the noises above me.

The machine-guns are rattling away. I know that our barbed-wire entanglements are firm and pretty well undamaged; sections of them are electrified. The gunfire increases. They aren't getting through. They'll have to turn back.

I collapse into the shell hole again, tense almost to breaking point. Clattering, crawling, clinking – it all becomes audible, a single scream ringing out in the midst of it all. They're coming under fire, the attack has been held off.

It's got a little bit lighter. Footsteps hurry by me. The first few. Past me. Then some more. The rattle of the machine-guns becomes continuous. I am just about to turn round a bit when suddenly there is a noise and a body falls on to me in the shell hole, heavily and with a splash, then slips and lands on top of me –

I don't think at all, I make no decision – I just stab wildly and feel only how the body jerks, then goes limp and collapses. When I come to myself again, my hand is sticky and wet.

The other man makes a gurgling noise. To me it sounds as

if he is roaring, every breath is like a scream, like thunder – but it is only the blood in my own veins that is pounding so hard. I'd like to stop his mouth, to stuff earth into it, to stab again – he has to be quiet or he'll give me away; but I am so much myself again and suddenly feel so weak that I can't raise my hand against him any more.

So I crawl away into the furthest corner and stay there, my eyes fixed on him, gripping my knife, ready to go for him again if he moves – but he won't do anything again. I can hear that just from his gurgling.

I can only see him indistinctly. I have the one single desire – to get away. If I don't do so quickly it will be too light; it's already difficult. But the moment I try to raise my head I become aware that it is impossible. The machine-gun fire is so dense that I would be full of holes before I had gone a step.

I have another go, lifting up my helmet and pushing it forwards to gauge the height of fire. A moment later a bullet knocks it out of my hand. The gunfire is sweeping the ground at a very low level. I am not far enough away from the enemy trenches to escape being hit by one of the snipers the moment I tried to make a break for it.

It gets lighter and lighter. I wait desperately for an attack by our men. My knuckles are white because I am tensing my hands, praying for the firing to die down and for my mates to come.

The minutes trickle past one by one. I daren't look at the dark figure in the shell hole any more. With great effort I look past him, and wait, just wait. The bullets hiss, they are a mesh of steel, it won't stop, it won't stop.

Then I see my bloodied hand and suddenly I feel sick. I take some earth and rub it on to the skin, now at least my hand is dirty and you can't see the blood any more.

The gunfire still doesn't die down. It's just as strong now from both sides. Our lot have probably long since given me up for lost.

It is a light, grey, early morning. The gurgling still continues. I block my ears, but I quickly have to take my hands away from them because otherwise I won't be able to hear anything else.

The figure opposite me moves. That startles me, and I look across at him, although I don't want to. Now my eyes are riveted on him. A man with a little moustache is lying there, his head hanging lopsidedly, one arm half-crooked and the head against it. The other hand is clasped to his chest. It has blood on it.

He's dead, I tell myself, he must be dead, he can't feel anything any more; that gurgling, it can only be the body. But the head tries to lift itself and for a moment the groaning gets louder, the forehead sinks back on to the arm. The man is not dead. He is dying, but he is not dead. I push myself forward, pause, prop myself on my hands, slip a bit further along, wait – further, a terrible journey of three yards, a long and fearsome journey. At last I am by his side.

Then he opens his eyes. He must have been able to hear me and he looks at me with an expression of absolute terror. His body doesn't move, but in his eyes there is such an incredible desire to get away that I can imagine for a moment that they might summon up enough strength to drag his body with them, carrying him hundreds of miles away, far, far away, at a single leap. The body is still, completely quiet, there is not a single sound, and even the gurgling has stopped, but the eyes are screaming, roaring, all his life has gathered in them and formed itself into an incredible urge to escape, into a terrible fear of death, a fear of me.

My legs give way and I fall down on to my elbows. 'No, no,' I whisper.

The eyes follow me. I am quite incapable of making any movement as long as they are watching me.

Then his hand falls slowly away from his chest, just a little way, dropping only an inch or two. But that movement breaks the spell of the eyes. I lean forward, shake my head and whisper, 'No, no, no' and lift up my hand – I have to show him that I want to help him, and I wipe his forehead.

The eyes flinched when my hand came close, but now they lose their fixed gaze, the eyelids sink deeper, the tension eases.

I open his collar for him and prop his head a bit more comfortably.

His mouth is half open and he makes an attempt to form some words. His lips are dry. I haven't got my water bottle, I didn't bring it with me. But there is water in the mud at the bottom of the shell hole. I scramble down, take out my handkerchief, spread it out, press it down, then cup my hand and scoop up the yellow water that seeps through it.

He swallows it. I fetch more. Then I unbutton his tunic so that I can bandage his wounds, if I can. I have to do that anyway, so that if I get caught the other lot can see that I tried to help him, and won't shoot me outright. He tries to push me away, but his hand is too weak. The shirt is stuck fast and I can't move it aside, and since it is buttoned at the back there is nothing for it but to slit it open.

I look for my knife and find it again. But as soon as I start to cut the shirt open his eyes open wide again and that scream is in them once more, and the look of panic, so that I have to close them, press them shut and whisper, 'I'm trying to help you, comrade, *camarade, camarade, camarade –*' and I stress the word so that he understands me.

There are three stab wounds. My pack of field dressings covers them but the blood flows out underneath, so I press them down more firmly, and he groans.

It's all I can do. Now we must just wait, wait.

Hours. The gurgling starts up again – how long it takes for a man to die! What I do know is that he is beyond saving. To be sure, I have tried to convince myself otherwise, but by midday this self-delusion has melted away, has been shot to pieces by his groans. If I hadn't lost my revolver when I was crawling along I would shoot him. I can't stab him.

By midday I am in that twilight area where reason evaporates. I am ravenously hungry, almost weeping for want of food, but I can't help it. I fetch water several times for the dying man and I drink some of it myself.

This is the first man I have ever killed with my own hands, the first one I've seen at close quarters whose death I've

31

caused. Kat and Kropp and Müller have all seen people they have hit as well, it happens often, it's quite common in hand-to-hand fighting –

But every gasp strips my heart bare. The dying man is the master of these hours, he has an invisible dagger to stab me with: the dagger of time and my own thoughts.

I would give a lot for him to live. It is hard to lie here and have to watch and listen to him.

By three in the afternoon he is dead.

I breathe again. But only for a short time. Soon the silence seems harder for me to bear than the groans. I would even like to hear the gurgling again; in fits and starts, hoarse, sometimes a soft whistling noise and then hoarse and loud again.

What I am doing is crazy. But I have to have something to do. So I move the dead man again so that he is lying more comfortably, even though he can't feel anything any more. I close his eyes. They are brown. His hair is black and slightly curly at the sides. His mouth is full and soft underneath his moustache; his nose is a little angular and his skin is tanned – it doesn't seem as pale as before, when he was still alive. For a moment his face even manages to look almost healthy, and then it gives way quickly to become the face of a dead stranger, one of the many I have seen, and every one of them looks alike.

His wife is bound to be thinking of him just now: she doesn't know what has happened. He looks as if he used to write to her a lot; she will go on getting his letters, too – tomorrow, next week – maybe a stray one in a month's time. She'll read it, and he'll be speaking to her in it.

My state of mind is getting worse all the time, and I can't control my thoughts. What does his wife look like? Like the slim dark girl in the house by the canal? Doesn't she belong to me? Perhaps she belongs to me now because of all this! If only Kantorek were sitting here by me! What if my mother saw me in this state – The dead man would surely have been able to live for another thirty years if I'd taken more care about how I was going to get back. If only he had been running a couple of yards further to the left he'd be back in his trench over there writing another letter to his wife.

But this will get me nowhere, it's the fate we all share. If Kemmerich's leg had been a few inches further to the right, if Haie had leaned an inch or two further forward –

The silence spreads. I talk, I have to talk. So I talk to him and tell him directly, 'I didn't mean to kill you, mate. If you were to jump in here again, I wouldn't do it, not so long as you were sensible too. But earlier on you were just an idea to me, a concept in my mind that called up an automatic response – it was a concept that I stabbed. It is only now that I can see that you are a human being like me. I just thought about your hand-grenades, your bayonet and your weapons – now I can see your wife, and your face, and what we have in common. Forgive me, *camarade*! We always realize too late. Why don't they keep on reminding us that you are all miserable wretches just like us, that your mothers worry themselves just as much as ours and that we're all just as scared of death, and that we die the same way and feel the same pain. Forgive me, *camarade*, how could you be my enemy? If we threw these uniforms and weapons away you could be just as much my brother as Kat and Albert. Take twenty years from my life, *camarade*, and get up again – take more, because I don't know what I am going to do with the years I've got.'

He is silent, the front is quiet apart from the chatter of machine-guns. The bullets are close together and this is not just random firing – there is careful aiming from both sides. I can't get out.

'I'll write to your wife,' I tell the dead man breathlessly, 'I'll write to her, she ought to hear about it from me, I'll tell her everything that I'm telling you. I don't want her to suffer, I want to help her, and your parents too and your child –'

His uniform is still half open. It is easy to find his wallet. But I am reluctant to open it. Inside it will be his paybook with his name. As long as I don't know his name it's still possible that I might forget him, that time will wipe out the image of all this. But his name is a nail that will be hammered into me and that can never be drawn out again. It will always have the power to bring everything back, it will return constantly and will rise up in front of me.

I hold the wallet, unable to make up my mind. It slips out of my hand and falls open. A few pictures and letters drop out. I collect them up and go to put them back in, but the pressure that I am under, the complete uncertainty of it all, the hunger, the danger, the hours spent with the dead man, these things have all made me desperate, and I want to find out as quickly as possible, to intensify the pain so as to end it, just as you might smash an unbearably painful hand against a tree, regardless of the result.

There are photographs of a woman and of a little girl, small amateur snapshots, taken in front of an ivy-covered wall. There are letters with them. I take them out and try to read them. I can't understand most of them, since they are difficult to decipher and I don't know much French. But every word I translate hits me like a bullet in the chest – or like a dagger in the chest –

My head is nearly bursting, but I am still able to grasp the fact that I can never write to these people, as I thought I would earlier on. Impossible. I look at the photos again; these are not rich people. I could send them money anonymously, if I start earning later. I cling to this idea, it is at least a straw to grasp at. This dead man is bound up with my life, and therefore I have to do everything for him and promise him everything so that I can be rescued. I swear wildly that I will devote my whole existence to him and to his family. I assure him of this with wet lips, and deep within me, while I am doing so, there is the hope that I can buy my own salvation that way, and maybe get out of this alive – it's a little trick of the mind, because what you promise are always things that you could only see to *afterwards*. And so I open the paybook and read slowly: Gerard Duval, compositor.

I write down the address on an envelope with the dead man's pencil, and then in a great hurry I shove everything back into his tunic again.

I have killed Gerard Duval, the printer. I think wildly that

34

I shall have to become a printer, become a printer, a printer –

By the afternoon I am calmer. All my fears were groundless. The name no longer bothers me. The attack has passed. 'Well, pal,' I call across to the dead man, but now I say it calmly, 'Your turn today, mine tomorrow. But if I get out of all this, pal, I'll fight against the things that wrecked it for both of us: your life, and my –? Yes, my life too. I promise you, pal. It must never happen again.'

The sun's rays are slanting. I am numb with exhaustion and hunger. Yesterday seems nebulous to me. I no longer have any hopes of getting out of here. So I doze fitfully, and don't even realize that it is evening again. Twilight. It seems to come quickly now. Another hour. If it were summer, another three hours. Another hour.

Now I suddenly start to tremble in case anything goes wrong. I am not thinking about the dead man any more, he's of no importance to me. All at once my desire for life comes back and everything that I promised before gives way in face of that desire. But just so as not to attract bad luck at this stage I babble mechanically, 'I'll do everything, everything that I promised you' – but I know already that I won't.

It suddenly occurs to me that my own mates might shoot at me if I crawl their way: they don't know it's me. I'll shout out at the first possible point where they might understand me. Then I'll wait there, I'll lie in front of the trench until they answer.

The first star. The front is still quiet. I breathe out and talk to myself in my excitement: 'Don't do anything stupid now, Paul – keep calm, Paul, calm – then you'll be OK, Paul.' It's a good move for me to say my own name, because it sounds as if someone else were doing it, and is that much more effective.

The darkness deepens. My agitation subsides and to be on the safe side I wait until the first light-rockets go up. Then I crawl out of the shell hole. I have forgotten the dead man. In front of me is the young night and the battlefield bathed in pale light. I pick out a shell hole; the moment the light dies away I rush across, feel my way onwards, get to the next one, take cover, hurry on.

I get nearer. Then by the light of one of the rockets I see something in the barbed-wire that moves for a moment before it stops, so I lie still. The next time, I spot it again, it must be men from our trench. But I'm still cautious until I recognize our helmets. Then I shout.

My own name echoes back to me straight away as an answer: 'Paul – Paul.'

I shout again. It is Kat and Albert, who have come out with a tarpaulin to look for me.

'Are you wounded?'

'No, no –'

We tumble into the trench. I ask for something to eat and gobble it down. Müller gives me a cigarette. I give a brief account of what happened. After all, it is nothing new; that sort of thing has happened plenty of times. The only difference in the whole thing was the night attack. But once in Russia Kat had to lie up for two days behind the Russian lines before he could break through.

I don't say anything about the dead printer.

It's not until the following morning that I find I can't hold out any longer. I have to tell Kat and Albert. They both calm me down. 'You can't do anything about it. What else could you do? That's why you're out here.'

I listen to them, comforted, feeling better because of their presence. What sort of rubbish did I dream up in that shell hole?

'Have a look at that,' says Kat, and points.

There are some snipers standing on the parapet. Their rifles have telescopic sights and they are keeping an eye on the sector facing our trench. Every so often a shot rings out.

Then we hear shouts – 'That was a hit!' 'Did you see how high he jumped?' Sergeant Oellrich turns around proudly and notes his score. He is in the lead in today's shooting list with three direct hits confirmed as certain.

'What do you think of that?' asks Kat.

I nod.

'If he goes on that way he'll have another sharpshooter's badge by this evening,' reckons Kropp.

'Or he'll soon be promoted to staff sergeant,' adds Kat.

We look at each other.

'I wouldn't do it,' I say.

'All the same,' says Kat, 'it's a good idea for you to watch him just now.'

Sergeant Oellrich goes back to the fire-step. The end of his rifle moves this way and that.

'You don't need to waste another thought on that business of yours,' nods Albert.

I can't even understand it myself any more.

'It was just because I had to stay there with him for such a long time,' I say. 'After all, war is war.'

There is a short, dry crack from Oellrich's rifle.

A.D. Gristwood

THE WASTELAND

'Before the world grew mad, the Somme was a placid stream of Picardy, flowing gently through a broad and winding valley northwards to the English Channel. It watered the country of simple rural beauty.' These are the opening words of The Somme, *published in 1927 and praised by H.G. Wells as 'a book that every boy with a taste for soldiering should be asked to read and ponder.'* A.D. Gristwood's novel has survived the change of literary climate better than those of most of his British contemporaries.

IT WAS A gloriously hot and sunny day in September. The Loamshires were in newly won trenches outside Combles. The town, or the battered husk that represented it, had fallen that morning, but the battalion was far from feeling any flush of victory. Even the unheard-of event of the French advancing past Combles in clearly visible columns of fours failed to rouse them. Every one was languid and weary and dispirited.

The trenches had been abandoned by the Germans only yesterday, and everywhere lay scattered their arms and clothing. And not only arms! Sprawling over the parapets were things in rags of grey and khaki that had once been men. As far as the clothing went nothing extraordinary was visible, but the dead men's faces were black with a multitude of flies. These indeed were the worst horror. Everywhere they found carrion and ordure, and, disturbed by the traffic of the trench, the buzzing cloud revealed raw festering flesh where once had been a happy human countenance. Fresh from such a feast, they settled on living men and shared their rations: sluggish, bloated creatures, blue and green and iridescent. Well was Beelzebub named the Prince of Flies!

Sometimes the Germans had buried their dead in the floor of the trench, where, baking in the sun, the earth had cracked into star-shaped fissures. A foot treading unwarily here sunk suddenly downwards, disturbing hundreds of white and wriggling maggots. In one place a hand with blue and swollen fingers projected helplessly from the ground. 'O death, where is thy sting? O grave, where is thy victory?'

An order had been given that, in consolidating the trench, as soon as pick or shovel should disturb the dead, the hole should be filled in again and the earth beaten down. Often fragments of blanket or clothing gave warning, and sometimes the sudden gush of escaping gases. Not a hundred yards to the left lay Leuze Wood, captured by the battalion a fortnight ago. Little progress had been made since then, and, in so exposed a position, the dead could not always be buried. Moreover, fatigue and the indifference of desperation made their presence of little account, and thus there lay in the billows of tumbled earth a company of dead men half-buried, flung there like puppets thrown down by a child. Close to the trench a man of the Loamshires stood nearly upright, buried to the waist, his arms fast bound to his side, his glassy eyes wide open to the sky, his face stained livid yellow from the fumes of an explosion. Who he was no one knew: doubtless his dear ones were writing to him in hope and trust for his welfare: doubtless they had prayed that night for his safety. And all the time he stood there, glaring upwards as though mutely appealing from Earth to Heaven.

The carrion reek of putrefaction filled the wind. For twenty-four hours drum-fire had deafened all the world, and sleep had been a matter of dozes between hours of horror. Hostile shelling, occasional casualties, the dead weight of fatigue, the grim barrenness of what was called a 'victory', the vista of months ahead – fear ever lying in wait to grow to panic – small wonder if these things had damped men's spirits! There had indeed been current that morning rumours of relief, promptly discountenanced by experienced cynics. (And every one who had been in France for a month was a cynic.) There were even tales of a Divisional Rest for a month, laughed to scorn even more readily.

Hence the glittering wonder of the event. To a party of men carrying petrol-tins on a water-fatigue appeared an immaculate being in red tabs. He seemed strangely out of place in that Golgotha – and yet not so out of place. 'Who are you men?' 'Tenth Loamshires, sir.' 'What are you doing?' 'Water party, sir.' 'You don't want any water. You're relieved tonight. Go down to the "Cookers" and wait orders there. Don't take those things back – the less movement we have the better.' Thus the beneficent decree of the Dynast. Soulless plodding changed to eager haste; tongues were unloosed. A sergeant was heard to say: 'That ends the bloody Somme for us,' and in less than a minute every one was repeating the words like a hope of salvation.

The 'Cookers' lay in a deep hollow a mile to the rear of the line. The place was known as 'Death Valley', by no means without reason. There were the foremost batteries, and the fatigue party waited until dusk in a whirlpool of hurry. The 'Big Push', to use the euphemistic cant of the day, was in full cry. Always new guns were arriving, and ammunition-limbers, ration-wagons, water-carts, field-kitchens, mules, stores of the Royal Engineers, camouflage materials, corrugated iron, timber, barbed wire, sandbags in thousands. No lorries or ambulances could reach Death Valley, however, which lay far from paved roads among the uplands of the Somme. The hill-side tracks had been utterly obliterated by the weeks of shell-fire since the bloodstained 1st July, and all the countryside was a wilderness. To write 'a wilderness' is easy, but to realize the appearance of the landscape you must have seen it. Thereabouts the country is open downland, after the manner of Sussex, largely grass-covered, and sprinkled capriciously with rare patches of woodland. From the crests of the ridges mile upon mile of country was visible, and everywhere the land lay utterly waste and desolate. Not a green thing survived the harrowing of the shells. Constant barrages had churned the land into a vast desert of shell-craters, one intersecting another like the foul pock-markings of disease. To look over these miles of blasted country, thus scarified to utter nakedness, was to see a lunar landscape, lifeless, arid and accursed.

At night this sense of other-wordliness was stronger than ever. In the dense darkness, where to show a light was probably suicide, the dismal sea of craters was lit only by the flash of guns and the noiseless ghastly glare of Verey lights. In the white radiance of the magnesium flares all things seemed to await judgment, and the ensuing utter darkness came with the suddenness of doom. From dusk to dawn they traced in the sky their graceful parabolas, hanging long in the air as though unwilling to cease their brooding over it. Always they seemed cold, revealing, pitiless, illuminating with passionless completeness this foul chaos of man's making, unutterably sad and desolate beneath the stars. From far behind the line you could trace the course of the trenches by their waxing and waning, and the veriest child at home knew the danger of their all-revealing splendour.

By day the hills were deserted, and only in the valleys and hollows was movement visible. In daylight those open ridges might only be crossed in safety by small parties of perhaps twenty men – lost in the vastness of the landscape. Larger parties drew gun-fire, and road traffic could by no means face the wilderness. It was in such small parties that the Loamshires had first found their way to Combles from the flesh-pot of Amiens: their first sight of the Somme battlefield was gained from the Crucifix above Death Valley. This ancient iron cross, rusty, bent, and ominous, yet remained as a notorious landmark on the hill-side, and from the shattered trenches near by they looked forward across the valley to a hideous welter of dust and smoke and intolerable noise. A heavy bombardment was in progress, and great spouts of flying earth sprang skywards unceasingly. Not a yard of the tortured earth appeared immune from these volcanoes, and it seemed impossible that a man could live five minutes within the zone of their tumult. And yet they knew that men were facing their utmost shock and horror not a mile from where they were standing, and it was all too obvious that their turn awaited them. Tiny dust-coloured figures could be seen moving amid the welter, surviving by a miracle. The continuous hullabaloo of guns smote their ears with a vicious perseverance of shock. There, across the valley, lay the reeking core of this desolation, smoking, flaming, forcing itself with hideous toil and confusion towards an unknown decision. For miles to north and south stretched this artificial Hell, and the reek of it darkened the autumn sky.

Within the region of desolation the rare woods were matchwood only, shattered stumps of trees, bristles of timber splintered and torn to fantastic shreds and patches. Each wood was a maze of ruined trenches, obstructed by the fallen riven trunks of trees, dotted with half-obliterated dugouts, littered with torn fragments of barbed wire. This, indeed, was largely twisted and broken by shell-fire, but in rusted malignancy it yet remained fiercely hindering. Immediately after their final capture (for commonly they changed hands half a dozen times in a week) these woodlands of the Somme represented the apotheosis of Mars. There lay the miscellaneous debris of war – men living, dying and dead, friend and foe broken and shattered beyond imagination, rifles, clothing, cartridges, fragments of men, photographs of Amy and Gretchen, letters, rations, and the last parcel from home. Shells hurling more trees upon the general ruin, the dazing concussion of their explosion, the sickly sweet smell of 'gas', the acrid fumes of 'H.E.', hot sunshine mingling with spouts of flying earth and smoke, the grim portent of bodies buried a week ago and now suffering untimely resurrection, the chatter of machine-guns, and the shouts and groans of men – such were the woods of the Somme, where once primroses bloomed and wild rabbits scampered through the bushes.

Rarely are there many men visible, and the few are hot, grimy and exhausted beneath their ludicrous shrapnel helmets shaped like pie-dishes. They move slowly because they can by no means move otherwise. The mud from recent rains has caked on the skirts of their great-coats, and their boots and puttees are coated white and yellow with soil. Probably they last shaved a week ago, and have since washed in shell-holes. They are irritable, quarrelsome, restless even in their fatigue, with dark shadows beneath their eyes and drawn, set faces. That little group carrying a stretcher, plodding slowly, with eyes fixed on the ground and faces of a strange dead, yellowish hue, is leaving the front line. For perhaps forty-eight hours the men have been lying in holes and ditches, 'being shelled to hell'. They passed the time as best they might – smoking, dozing, eating, quarrelling, drinking, cleaning rifles that were instantly fouled again by the drifting dust. They dared not leave their holes even to relieve the demands of nature. Vermin maddened them and only ceased their ravages in the cool of the night. Occasionally a shell struck home and they saw their friends mangled to red tatters. Sometimes men were numbed to idiocy by concussion; sometimes they were buried alive in the earthquake of a collapsing trench; sometimes a lucky man secured an arm wound and 'packed up' for hospital before their envying eyes. Perhaps an exposed position involved digging. Chalk is tough to handle, and the spur of shell-fire, if it goads to exertion, does little to invigorate. And this is why they seem dazed, with the haggard beaten air of suffering children. But at least their faces are set towards the old familiar world of trees and fields and farm-yards; of women and children; of red-roofed estaminets where *vin rouge* restores the hearts of men, of straw barns where lives oblivion.

It will be said that here is no trace of the 'jovial Tommy' of legend, gay, careless, facetious, facing all his troubles with a grin and daunting the enemy by his light-heartedness. We all know the typical Tommy of the war correspondents – those ineffable exponents of cheap optimism and bad jokes. ''Alf a mo', Kaiser', is the type in a nutshell. A favourite gambit is the tale of the wounded man who was smoking a Woodbine. Invariably he professes regret at 'missing the fun', and seeks to convey the impression that bayonet fighting is much like a football match, and even more gloriously exciting. It was such trash that drugged men's minds to the reality of war. Every one actively concerned in it hated it, and the actual business of fighting can never be made anything but devilish. It is even divested of the old hypocritical glories of music and gay colours (and so far, indeed, the change is for the better). The patriots at home urged that 'it was necessary to keep up the nation's spirit; nothing would have been gained by unnecessary gloom,' but a people that must be doped to perseverance with lies is in an evil case, and the event of these Bairnsfather romances was a gigantic scheme of falsehood. How bitterly it was resented the nation never knew.

From Death Valley the Loamshires marched over the hills to Meaulte. At the tail-end of the march they were dog-weary, but twelve hours' sleep on straw went far to restore them. For twenty-four hours the joy of release was undimmed. With clean, vermin-free underclothing, and after a long night's rest and a hot shower-bath, once more it was possible to think sanely; the lowering cloud of urgent danger was lifted for a season. Perhaps it was a cynical enjoyment, but the bands that played in the square, the cosy, crazy little shops where wrinkled old women sold delicious coffee, the roaring tide of khaki, drunk and sober, in the streets, made them forget altogether those thousands suffering and dying in the furnace not half a dozen miles away. Meaulte lies on the edge of the 'old front line' and, to normal eyes, was hideous enough. The houses had been shelled to greater or less dilapidation, and dust lay thick on every road and yard. The shops, even when intact, were blighted with a hopeless dirt and squalor. Hardly a house remained in occupation, and the few inhabitants, lost in the crowd of troops, sold coffee, *vin rouge*, biscuits, chocolate, tinned fruits and cigarettes as the last resource against ruin. Every garden had run wild, and the autumn flowers were dusty and stunted among the weeds. It was a foul-mouthed, jostling throng that filled the streets, their pockets temporarily full and hearts light by reason of a week's respite. Small wonder drunkenness and debauchery ran riot in the place. They were the only means of forgetting.

From this grey pandemonium the men of the Loamshires hoped to march westwards again to the real France beyond the battle zone. Divisional Rest was due, and already that month the brigade had lost more than half its strength at Leuze Wood. New drafts had restored their numbers, but some weeks of work together would be required to restore the battalions to efficiency. But, quenching the sergeant's pious hope, came on the second morning the order to 'parade for pay and stand by ready to move off in an hour's time'. The news came like a blow, and the delayed pay an hour before departure seemed a refinement of exasperation. Of what use was money if the creditors were to be moved away from all chance of spending it? During pay-parade the company commanders, haranguing their men, told them that they were to return to the 'forward area' (blessed euphemism) for ten days, and that the battalion's sole duty lay in the construction of a forward-trench as close as might be to the German lines. They were assured, with a particularity that seemed almost suspicious, that during this 'tour in the line' they were to be used only as pioneers. Certainly they had done Yeomen's service on the Somme, both on the 1st July at Gommecourt and on the 9th September at Leuze Wood, and undoubtedly the new drafts were inexperienced and unassimilated. But already the rumoured Divisional Rest had been cut down from a month to a day, and dark suspicions grew like the rank weeds of Meaulte.

Trones Wood of ill memory was their destination, and the march there filled the greater part of two days. After a night in old German dugouts, the official Reserve positions were found to be nothing more than a series of shelter trenches midway between Trones Wood and Guillemont. These were the merest slots in the ground, none more than five feet deep. Wrapping themselves in blankets and ground-sheets, and covering the tops of the trenches with pilfered timber and sheets of corrugated iron, they made themselves as comfortable as might be. These narrow ditches resembled the drainage-trenches of a London suburb in the heyday of its development towards villadom, but the grimly humorous found a resemblance to graves. By good management it was just possible to curl up head to head in the slots, and the impedimenta of equipment were jammed haphazard into holes and corners. After dark no lights were allowed above ground, but, by shutting in a section of trench with ground-sheets, the feeble illumination of candles was available to those who had the good fortune to possess any. Crawling along these narrow alley-ways at night, dodging beneath ingenious erections of blankets, stumbling over a long litter of men and equipment, you would imagine yourself in an overcrowded coal-mine, where fools performed the simplest tasks with incredible toil. To turn, you must stand up, and to venture out of the trench was to invite the immediate disaster of falling headlong into a shell-hole. Once you had lost your bivouac it might take you half an hour to recover it.

Fortunately, the rain held off until the evening of the Loamshires' departure. Even two hours had sufficed to transform the trenches into slimy morasses, with equipment and personal belongings fast sinking into the mud. Utterly forlorn these 'homes' seemed in their inundation, and, with nowhere to sit in comfort, men were the less sorry to leave them. Two days and nights saw them back again, so exhausted after their march that it was easy enough to fall asleep in the rain, often with nothing but a wet ground-sheet between the sleeper and a puddle. This time they occupied other trenches behind the wood, wider and less exasperatingly crowded. Here it was necessary to carve shelters in the sides of the trenches, using rubber sheets and blankets as the outer trenchward wall. Coiled up in these lairs, you could at least avoid the rain, and by sharing your bivouac it was even possible to lie warm. (To neutralize this luxury, the lice were the more active in snugger quarters.)

For several days their time was passed chiefly in salvage-fatigues. These involved the tiresome quartering of long acres of ground, and the collection and sorting into a variegated dump of all the litter of the battlefield. Not far from Trones Wood a blown-in trench held thousands of Mills bombs. These ingenious weapons are rendered harmless by a steel safety-pin, which rusts with damp. So long as they are undisturbed they are innocuous, but they have been known to lie forgotten and unheeded for weeks only to explode with fatal results at an inadvertent kick. Thus it was delicate work disinterring them from the earth and debris in which they were nearly buried; but by a fluke of good fortune none had rusted sufficiently to fracture the pins, and there were no casualties.

In fine weather they were almost happy, and, dog-tired always, sound sleep came as a gift in the most cramped quarters. In the freshness of the morning the breakfasts of fragrant bacon were glorious indeed. The hot strong tea, and white bread far better than they were getting at home, were wolfed with eager appetite, and always there was a rush to the sooty dixie for the sake of the bacon-fat and greasy crackling that afford so tasty a dish when bread is used to sop them. Often porridge was added, so thick that it was possible to invert the dixie and no harm done. Unaffectedly living to eat, meals and mails were the only landmarks in monotonous days. For dinner came potatoes boiled in their skins and nondescript watery stew. On gala days roast beef appeared, and sometimes duff took the place of nauseous rice.

Apart from fatigues, drill consisted only in the inspection of rifles, but excuse for a full-dress parade was found in a message from the Brigadier. To hear his sacred words the battalion was drawn up in mass behind the wood, where a prying aeroplane might have stirred the enemy's artillery to serious activity. (But obviously risks must be run to hear a General's voice.) It seemed that that great man loved his men like a father, and that his children were to be praised for their prowess. They had done splendidly, and the high standard attained was never to be lowered. To the old hands the General expressed his thanks; to the new he said approximately 'Go thou and do likewise'. All and sundry were bidden 'never to forget the traditions of their battalion and brigade', and it was obvious that storms were to be expected. The proceedings terminated with the distribution of 'Divisional Cards', for all the world like prizes at a Sunday-school Treat, and the shame of the recipients was only equalled by the ribaldry of the audience. For these cards certified that the holder had distinguished himself in action at such a time and such a place, and even bore the signature of Olympus. The theory was that by this means a spirit of emulation was aroused, and it was reckoned that three of these cards meant a military medal in the rations. 'The Tommies are such children!' Such was life in Reserve.

Stratis Myrivilis

THE BEAUTY OF THE BATTLEFIELD

In his novel Life in the Tomb *(1924), the Greek writer Stratis Myrivilis gives a harshly realistic yet reflective account of the trench warfare at the Macedonian front in 1917–18, where the Greek army fought Bulgarian and German forces. While observing an artillery duel, the narrator becomes fascinated by the visual beauty of the lights and the magnificent spectacle of the falling bombs. He recognizes that the bombardment is not just cruel and inhuman but also 'divinely majestic': 'Man becomes Titan who makes Earth howl beneath his blows.'*

ONE GETS USED to anything sooner or later. I have noticed that human beings possess an inexhaustible inner reserve of adaptive capability which rescues them from great misfortunes and especially from madness. Here, for example, our way of life has already become a stable condition. Sometimes it occurs to me that if the stories about eternal torments in hell were accurate, each of the damned would have all the time in the world to grow used to his tortures through and through, and consequently could puff his cigarette to his heart's content inside the cauldron of brimstone, lighting it from the very flames that were harrowing him.

We either sleep during the day, lying on our backs in the darkness, or talk and play cards, our candles burning. The latter we do less and less frequently, however, because no one has the slightest appetite for idle prating. When we open our mouths it is only to pronounce the barest minimum of words necessary for our duties, or to indulge in smut, or to hurl curses at each other. Soon enough, in any case, we are overcome by sleep as though by some disease, a sleep full of exhaustion, nightmares, and wet dreams. The men awake soaked in sweat and semen.

But as soon as darkness falls, this whole world comes to life and emerges from its caverns in order to fight: to wage war. Under the cover of darkness, hordes of implement-laden soldiers peek over the rim of the trench and leap across the top in successive ranks, then proceed slouchingly, and with sluggish movements, towards no man's land. Deprived of cigarettes, with an absolute minimum of noise, they advance in this robot-like manner in order to dig, or set up entanglements, or keep their ears cocked at a listening post, or lie in ambush. Sometimes they return depleted, in which case the Order of the Day strikes certain names off the company rolls and Balafaras obtains certain home addresses so that he may dispatch his 'lovely letters', neatly typewritten.

The pyramidal ridge of Peristeri – the 'Dove' – looms blacker and fiercer than ever in the darkness. It is swaddled in mystery, and its tip touches the sky. The oppressive silence which this fortified mountain exudes is more frightening than a thousand-mouthed cannonade.

Suddenly a slender red line burgeons from one of the flanks and ascends. The men fall flat on their faces then, no matter where they happen to be, because the top of this luminous, fading stem will blossom before long into a brilliant flower of light, a miniature sun. A flare like this ignites high above us in the atmosphere and hovers there, swaying in balance, as it shines down upon us with unbearable brilliance. Then it flounders in mid-air and sails off attentively into the void. It is the Dove's lightly sleeping eye, an eye whose lid lifts suspiciously in the night so that this powerful lantern may search gruffly to see where we are and what we are doing. An area of many square kilometres is illuminated as though in daylight. The lantern advances with such slow-moving deliberation that you would think some invisible giant were holding it in his enormous hand as he strolled from place to place, urgently looking for something on the ground. Eventually it descends ever so slowly and goes out, or else disappears behind some hill. No one budges during this interval; no one breathes. Soon another flare ignites, and then another and another; they follow each other in close succession, coming from both sides now. If a person ignorant of the war observed all this outpouring of light as it bathed the mountains, he would mistake it for a celebration of joy and kindness. The other evening an illuminating rocket like this fell on Magarevo, a deserted hamlet which sits between the Bulgarians and us. It landed on a rooftop and started a conflagration which destroyed three houses, after which the fire subsided of its own accord. (No one went to extinguish it!) The empty village was illuminated funereally all the while, its casements swinging open, the house-interiors filled with darkness. Ignited flares have also fallen into patches of dry grass or amidst the wheat which ripened in vain for the absent reapers who will never again come with their scythes and merry songs. The fields burn and burn, until they grow tired of burning. Occasionally an attack, reconnoitring mission, or *coup de main* occurs in a nearby sector. At such times the spectacle is unimaginably grand. Igniting beside the white flares are chromatic ones – green, red, yellow, maroon – which promenade across the sky like multicoloured caterpillars or drag their bodies laboriously between the stars as though they were fiery but wounded dragons all coiled in upon themselves. A cherry-dark stalk germinates with a whistle and explodes at its tip, whereupon varicoloured stars gush upward in a veritable geyser above our heads, then drip down in clusters, fading as they descend. All this is an agreed-upon signal for artillery barrages and other types of fire.

The cannonade begins close on the rockets' heels. It comes from the Dove, or from us, or sometimes from both at once. The batteries seek mutual annihilation. This is known as an 'artillery duel'. What happens at such times is terrible but also beautiful. Alas, I cannot escape calling it 'beautiful' since it is the most majestic spectacle a man can ever hope to experience. When the action falls outside our sector I creep into the trench, glue my chin to the soil of the parapet, and become nothing but two eyes and a pair of ears diffused into this strange universe, a being who throbs with pride as well as wretchedness.

Diamond necklaces string themselves along the base of the mountains; the gems sparkle each in turn in the darkness, then fade. These are the salvos, discharged in regular succession. Next, the valleys start to roar. They weep, reverberate with imploring moans, shriek, howl protractedly, and bellow. Absolute silence metamorphoses instantaneously into pandemonium. The atmosphere smacks its lips; it whistles fervidly with its fingers inserted into a thousand mouths. Whole masses of air shift position with violent movements; the sky rips from end to end like muslin. Invisible arrows pass across the void. Angry vipers lunge this way and that. On all sides are lashes incising the air and pitilessly thrashing the weeping hills, which huddle and curl into balls as though wishing to be swallowed into the bowels of the earth, in order to escape. The caves moan and sob in woeful groans. A thousand titans yawp in consternation, chew their fingers with obstinate despair, and holler. The atmosphere vibrates then like a bow-string and men's hearts quake like aspen leaves in a storm.

The passing shells cannot be seen; you sense them, however, with your entire body – their location at every instant, how fast they are travelling, where they will land. Some of them remind you of an object breaking the surface of a lake; they make a refreshing noise, a kind of lapping, as though they were speeding along on peaceful waters. Others create a fearful racket. Imagine colossal iron bridges erected in the darkness between the Dove and us, and rickety wagons passing over them with full loads of clattering metal tools. That is how they sound. Still others whistle almost gleefully at a standard pitch. These have been christened 'nightingales' by the men, and in truth they actually do resemble birds that have flown the coop and soared unrestrainedly into the empyrean, whistling the song of freedom.

Audible amid all these frenzied night-cries, amid this entire chaos of sound, are the amazing wails of exploding shells. A shell, when it bursts, howls with vengeful wrath. It is a blind monster, all snout and nothing else, which charges the earth and rips it to shreds with its iron fangs. Millions of men have packed their hatreds into the ample belly of this mechanized brute, have stamped their enmity tightly in, and sent the beast out to bite. When a shell explodes, all of these hatreds lurking there by the thousands, all of these satanic embryos imprisoned in the steel womb, are released like a pack of rabid dogs which then race to the attack yelping their own disparate cries that are so mournful and strange.

When I find myself near a bursting shell I invariably have this feeling that human voices are inside it, voices which shriek with unappeasable passion. Inside a shell, I insist, are howling people foaming at the mouth and grinding their jaws together. You can hear the hysterical screech of the murderer as he nails his dagger into warm flesh; you can recognize the victory-cry of the man who drives his weapon into the breast of a hated foe, then, clutching the hilt in his palm, twists the knife in the wound, voluptuously bellowing his satiated passion and drinking down in a daze the agony of the other, who writhes beneath his powerful knee and thrashes about on the ground, spewing his life out through his throat, along with the blood.

Whenever the shells begin to rake our own trench along with the others, we worm into our dugouts and await orders. No one remains in the trench itself except the sentries, and they are relieved more frequently at such times.

A bombardment is the most supremely powerful sensation that a man can experience. You lie flat on your face at the bottom of the trench or in an underground shelter. Your mouth tastes like plaster of Paris; your soul is held in thrall by profound grief and pulsating terror, by a preoccupation which shrinks you, makes you roll up into yourself and take refuge in the kernel of your existence – a kernel which you desire to be tiny as a cherry-pit and hard and impenetrable as a diamond. Your soul is on its knees. Filled with wonder and sacred awe, it prays fervidly of its own accord. You neither understand nor recognize the words it uses (this is the first time in your life you have heard them), and it directs its supplications to a God whose existence you had never even suspected. Your soul is a tiny lamp-flame, a sickly wavering flicker which totters this way and that in an effort to separate from its wick and be sucked gently upward by the famished void.

A bombardment is extraordinarily cruel and inhuman. It is horrible, but also divinely majestic. Man becomes a Titan who makes Earth howl beneath his blows. He becomes Enceladus and Typhon, raises up mountains, juggles lightning bolts playfully in his hands, and causes indomitable natural forces to mewl like whipped cats.

Is it not man 'who looketh on the earth, and it trembleth; who toucheth the mountains, and they smoke'?

Ernest Hemingway

GOING BACK

In A Farewell to Arms *(1929) Ernest Hemingway tells the story of an American volunteer in the ambulance service at the Italian front. Recovering from his wounds in hospital, the narrator falls in love with Catherine, an English nurse. In this extract Hemingway brings a characteristically clear-eyed quality to a familiar moment in a young soldier's life.*

THE NIGHT I was to return to the front I sent the porter down to hold a seat for me on the train when it came from Turin. The train was to leave at midnight. It was made up at Turin and reached Milan about half-past ten at night and lay in the station until time to leave. You had to be there when it came in, to get a seat. The porter took a friend with him, a machine-gunner on leave who worked in a tailor shop, and was sure that between them they could hold a place. I gave them money for platform tickets and had them take my baggage. There was a big rucksack and two musettes.

I said good-by at the hospital at about five o'clock and went out. The porter had my baggage in his lodge and I told him I would be at the station a little before midnight. His wife called me 'Signorino' and cried. She wiped her eyes and shook hands and then cried again. I patted her on the back and she cried once more. She had done my mending and was a very short dumpy, happy-faced woman with white hair. When she cried her whole face went to pieces. I went down to the corner where there was a wine shop and waited inside looking out the window. It was dark outside and cold and misty. I paid for my coffee and grappa and I watched the people going by in the light from the window. I saw Catherine and knocked on the window. She looked, saw me and smiled, and I went out to meet her. She was wearing a dark blue cape and a soft felt hat. We walked along together, along the sidewalk past the wine shops, then across the market square and up the street and through the archway to the cathedral square. There were streetcar tracks and beyond them was the cathedral. It was white and wet in the mist. We crossed the tram tracks. On our left were the shops, their windows lighted, and the entrance to the galleria. There was a fog in the square and when we came close to the front of the cathedral it was very big and the stone was wet.

'Would you like to go in?'

'No,' Catherine said. We walked along. There was a soldier standing with his girl in the shadow of one of the stone buttresses ahead of us and we passed them. They were standing tight up against the stone and he had put his cape around her.

'They're like us,' I said.

'Nobody is like us,' Catherine said. She did not mean it happily.

'I wish they had some place to go.'

'It mightn't do them any good.'

'I don't know. Everybody ought to have some place to go.'

'They have the cathedral,' Catherine said. We were past it now. We crossed the far end of the square and looked back at the cathedral. It was fine in the mist. We were standing in front of the leather goods shop. There were riding boots, a rucksack and ski boots in the window. Each article was set apart as an exhibit; the rucksack in the centre, the riding boots on one side and the ski boots on the other. The leather was dark and oiled smooth as a used saddle. The electric light made high lights on the dull oiled leather.

'We'll ski some time.'

'In two months there will be skiing at Mürren,' Catherine said.

'Let's go there.'

'All right,' she said. We went on past other windows and turned down a side street.

'I've never been this way.'

'This is the way I go to the hospital,' I said. It was a narrow street and we kept on the right-hand side. There were many people passing in the fog. There were shops and all the windows were lighted. We looked in a window at a pile of cheeses. I stopped in front of an armorer's shop.

'Come in a minute. I have to buy a gun.'

'What sort of gun?'

'A pistol.' We went in and I unbuttoned my belt and laid it with the empty holster on the counter. Two women were behind the counter. The women brought out several pistols.

'It must fit this,' I said, opening the holster. It was a grey leather holster and I had bought it second-hand to wear in the town.

'Have they good pistols?' Catherine asked.

'They're all about the same. Can I try this one?' I asked the woman.

'I have no place to shoot,' she said. 'But it is very good. You will not make a mistake with it.'

I snapped it and pulled back the action. The spring was rather strong but it worked smoothly. I sighted it and snapped it again.

'It is used,' the woman said. 'It belonged to an officer who was an excellent shot.'

'Did you sell it to him?'

'Yes.'

'How did you get it back?'

'From his orderly.'

'Maybe you have mine,' I said. 'How much is this?'

'Fifty lire. It is very cheap.'

'All right. I want two extra clips and a box of cartridges.'

She brought them from under the counter.

'Have you any need for a sword?' she asked. 'I have some used swords very cheap.'

'I'm going to the front,' I said.

'Oh yes, then you won't need a sword,' she said.

I paid for the cartridges and the pistol, filled the magazine and put it in place, put the pistol in my empty holster, filled the extra clips with cartridges and put them in the leather slots on the holster and then buckled on my belt. The pistol felt heavy on the belt. Still, I thought it was better to have a regulation pistol. You could always get shells.

'Now we're fully armed,' I said. 'That was the one thing I had to remember to do. Someone got my other one going to the hospital.'

'I hope it's a good pistol,' Catherine said.

'Was there anything else?' the woman asked.

'I don't believe so.'

'The pistol has a lanyard,' she said.

'So I noticed.' The woman wanted to sell something else.

'You don't need a whistle?'

'I don't believe so.'

The woman said good-by and we went out on to the sidewalk. Catherine looked in the window. The woman looked out and bowed to us.

'What are those little mirrors set in wood for?'

'They're for attracting birds. They twirl them out in the field and larks see them and come out and the Italians shoot them.'

'They are an ingenious people,' Catherine said. 'You don't shoot larks do you, darling, in America?'

'Not especially.'

We crossed the streets and started to walk up the other side.

'I feel better now,' Catherine said. 'I felt terrible when we started.'

'We always feel good when we're together.'

'We always will be together.'

'Yes, except that I'm going away at midnight.'

'Don't think about it, darling.'

We walked on up the street. The fog made the lights yellow.

'Aren't you tired?' Catherine asked.

'How about you?'

'I'm all right. It's fun to walk.'

'But let's not do it too long.'

'No.'

We turned down a side street where there were no lights and walked in the street. I stopped and kissed Catherine. While I kissed her I felt her hand on my shoulder. She had pulled my cape around her so it covered both of us. We were standing in the street against a high wall.

'Let's go some place,' I said.

'Good,' said Catherine. We walked on along the street until it came out on to a wider street that was beside a canal. On the other side was a brick wall and buildings. Ahead, down the street, I saw a streetcar cross a bridge.

'We can get a cab up at the bridge,' I said. We stood on the bridge in the fog waiting for a carriage. Several streetcars passed, full of people going home. Then a carriage came along but there was someone in it. The fog was turning to rain.

'We could walk or take a tram,' Catherine said.

'One will be along,' I said. 'They go by here.'

'Here one comes,' she said.

The driver stopped his horse and lowered the metal sign on his meter. The top of the carriage was up and there were drops of water on the driver's coat. His varnished hat was shining in the wet. We sat back in the seat together and the top of the carriage made it dark.

'Where did you tell him to go?'

'To the station. There's a hotel across from the station where we can go.'

'We can go the way we are? Without luggage?'

'Yes,' I said.

It was a long ride to the station up side streets in the rain.

'Won't we have dinner?' Catherine asked. 'I'm afraid I'll be hungry.'

'We'll have it in our room.'

'I haven't anything to wear. I haven't even a night-gown.'

'We'll get one,' I said and called to the driver.

'Go to the Via Manzoni and up that.' He nodded and turned off to the left at the next corner. On the big street Catherine watched for a shop.

'Here's a place,' she said. I stopped the driver and Catherine got out, walked across the sidewalk and went inside. I sat back in the carriage and waited for her. It was raining and I could smell the wet street and the horse steaming in the rain. She came back with a package and got in and we drove on.

'I was very extravagant, darling,' she said, 'but it's a fine nightgown.'

At the hotel I asked Catherine to wait in the carriage while I went in and spoke to the manager. There were plenty of rooms. Then I went out to the carriage, paid the driver, and Catherine and I walked in together. The small boy in buttons carried the package. The manager bowed us toward the elevator. There was much red plush and brass. The manager went up in the elevator with us.

'Monsieur and Madame wish dinner in their rooms?'

'Yes. Will you have the menu brought up?' I said.

'You wish something special for dinner. Some game or a soufflé?'

The elevator passed three floors with a click each time, then clicked and stopped.

'What have you as game?'

'I could get a pheasant, or woodcock.'

'A woodcock,' I said. We walked down the corridor. The carpet was worn. There were many doors. The manager stopped and unlocked a door and opened it.

'Here you are. A lovely room.'

The small boy in buttons put the package on the table in the centre of the room. The manager opened the curtains.

'It is foggy outside,' he said. The room was furnished in red plush. There were many mirrors, two chairs and a large bed with a satin coverlet. A door led to the bathroom.

'I will send up the menu,' the manager said. He bowed and went out.

I went to the window and looked out, then pulled a cord that shut the thick plush curtains. Catherine was sitting on the bed, looking at the cut glass chandelier. She had taken her hat off and her hair shone under the light. She saw herself in one of the mirrors and put her hands to her hair. I saw her in three other mirrors. She did not look happy. She let her cape fall on the bed.

'What's the matter, darling?'

'I never felt like a whore before,' she said. I went over to the window and pulled the curtain aside and looked out. I had not thought it would be like this.

'You're not a whore.'

'I know it, darling. But it isn't nice to feel like one.' Her voice was dry and flat.

'This was the best hotel we could get in,' I said. I looked out the window. Across the square were the lights of the station. There were carriages going by on the street and I saw the trees in the park. The lights from the hotel shone on the wet pavement. Oh, hell, I thought, do we have to argue now?

'Come over here please,' Catherine said. The flatness was all gone out of her voice. 'Come over, please. I'm a good girl again.' I looked over at the bed. She was smiling.

I went over and sat on the bed beside her and kissed her.

'You're my good girl.'

'I'm certainly yours,' she said.

After we had eaten we felt fine, and then after, we felt very happy and in a little time the room felt like our own home. My room at the hospital had been our own home and this room was our home too in the same way.

Catherine wore my tunic over her shoulders while we ate. We were very hungry and the meal was good and we drank a bottle of Capri and a bottle of St Estephe. I drank most of it but Catherine drank some and it made her feel splendid. For dinner we had a woodcock with some soufflé potatoes and purée de marron, a salad, and zabaione for dessert.

'It's a fine room,' Catherine said. 'It's a lovely room. We should have stayed here all the time we've been in Milan.'

'It's a funny room. But it's nice.'

'Vice is a wonderful thing,' Catherine said. 'The people who go in for it seem to have good taste about it. The red plush is really fine. It's just the thing. And the mirrors are very attractive.'

'You're a lovely girl.'

'I don't know how a room like this would be for waking up in the morning. But it's really a splendid room.' I poured another glass of St Estephe.

'I wish we could do something really sinful,' Catherine said. 'Everything we do seems so innocent and simple. I can't believe we do anything wrong.'

'You're a grand girl.'

'I only feel hungry. I get terribly hungry.'

'You're a fine simple girl,' I said.

'I am a simple girl. No one ever understood it except you.'

'Once when I first met you I spent an afternoon thinking how we would go to the Hotel Cavour together and how it would be.'

'That was awfully cheeky of you. This isn't the Cavour is it?'

'No. They wouldn't have taken us in there.'

'They'll take us in some time. But that's how we differ, darling. I never thought about anything.'

'Didn't you ever at all?'

'A little,' she said.

'Oh you're a lovely girl.'

I poured another glass of wine.

'I'm a very simple girl,' Catherine said.

'I didn't think so at first. I thought you were a crazy girl.'

'I was a little crazy. But I wasn't crazy in any complicated manner. I didn't confuse you did I, darling?'

'Wine is a grand thing,' I said. 'It makes you forget all the bad.'

'It's lovely,' said Catherine. 'But it's given my father gout very badly.'

'Have you a father?'

'Yes,' said Catherine. 'He has gout. You won't ever have to meet him. Haven't you a father?'

'No,' I said. 'A step-father.'

'Will I like him?'

'You won't have to meet him.'

'We have such a fine time,' Catherine said. 'I don't take any interest in anything else any more. I'm so very happy married to you.'

The waiter came and took away the things. After a while we were very still and we could hear the rain. Down below on the street a motor car honked.

> '"But at my back I always hear
> Time's winged chariot hurrying near,"'

I said.

'I know that poem,' Catherine said. 'It's by Marvell. But it's about a girl who wouldn't live with a man.'

My head felt very clear and cold and I wanted to talk facts.

'Where will you have the baby?'

'I don't know. The best place I can find.'

'How will you arrange it?'

'The best way I can. Don't worry, darling. We may have several babies before the war is over.'

'It's nearly time to go.'

'I know. You can make it time if you want.'

'No.'

'Then don't worry, darling. You were fine until now and now you're worrying.'

'I won't. How often will you write?'

'Every day. Do they read your letters?'

'They can't read English enough to hurt any.'

'I'll make them very confusing,' Catherine said.

'But not too confusing.'

'I'll just make them a little confusing.'

'I'm afraid we have to start to go.'

'All right, darling.'

'I hate to leave our fine house.'

'So do I.'

'But we have to.'

'All right. But we're never settled in our home very long.'

'We will be.'

'I'll have a fine home for you when you come back.'

'Maybe I'll be back right away.'

'Perhaps you'll be hurt just a little in the foot.'

'Or the lobe of the ear.'

63

'No I want your ears the way they are.'

'And not my feet?'

'Your feet have been hit already.'

'We have to go, darling. Really.'

'All right. You go first.'

We walked down the stairs instead of taking the elevator. The carpet on the stairs was worn. I had paid for the dinner when it came up and the waiter, who had brought it, was sitting on a chair near the door. He jumped up and bowed and I went with him into the side room and paid the bill for the room. The manager had remembered me as a friend and refused payment in advance but when he retired he had remembered to have the waiter stationed at the door so that I should not get out without paying. I suppose that had happened; even with his friends. One had so many friends in a war.

I asked the waiter to get us a carriage and he took Catherine's package that I was carrying and went out with an umbrella. Outside through the window we saw him crossing the street in the rain. We stood in the side room and looked out the window.

'How do you feel, Cat?'

'Sleepy.'

'I feel hollow and hungry.'

'Have you anything to eat?'

'Yes, in my musette.'

I saw the carriage coming. It stopped, the horse's head hanging in the rain, and the waiter stepped out, opened his umbrella, and came toward the hotel. We met him at the door and walked out under the umbrella down the wet walk to the carriage at the curb. Water was running in the gutter.

'There is your package on the seat,' the waiter said. He stood with the umbrella until we were in and I had tipped him.

'Many thanks. Pleasant journey,' he said. The coachman lifted the reins and the horse started. The waiter turned away under the umbrella and went toward the hotel. We drove down the street and turned to the left, then came around to the right in front of the station. There were two *carabinieri* standing under the light just out of the rain. The light shone on their hats. The rain was clear and transparent against the light from the station. A porter came out from under the shelter of the station, his shoulders up against the rain.

'No,' I said. 'Thanks. I don't need thee.'

He went back under the shelter of the archway. I turned to Catherine. Her face was in the shadow from the hood of the carriage.

'We might as well say good-by.'

'I can't go in?'

'No.'

'Good-by, Cat.'

'Will you tell him the hospital?'

'Yes.'

I told the driver the address to drive to. He nodded.

'Good-by,' I said. 'Take good care of yourself and young Catherine.'

'Good-by, darling.'

'Good-by,' I said. I stepped out into the rain and the carriage started. Catherine leaned out and I saw her face in the light. She smiled and waved. The carriage went up the street, Catherine pointed in toward the archway. I looked, there were only the two *carabinieri* and the archway. I realized she meant for me to get in out of the rain. I went in and stood and watched the carriage turn the corner. Then I started through the station and down the runway to the train.

The porter was on the platform looking for me. I followed him into the train, crowding past people and along the aisle and in through a door to where the machine-gunner sat in the corner of a full compartment. My rucksack and musettes were above his head on the luggage rack. There were many men standing in the corridor and the men in the compartment all looked at us when we came in. There were not enough places in the train and everyone was hostile. The machine-gunner stood up for me to sit down. It was a very tall gaunt captain of artillery with a red scar along his jaw. He had looked through the glass on the corridor and then come in.

'What do you say?' I asked. I had turned and faced him. He was taller than I and his face was very thin under the shadow of his cap-visor and the scar was new and shiny. Every one in the compartment was looking at me.

'You can't do that,' he said. 'You can't have a soldier save you a place.'

'I have done it.'

He swallowed and I saw his Adam's apple go up and then down. The machine-gunner stood in front of the place. Other men looked in through the glass. No one in the compartment said anything.

'You have no right to do that. I was here two hours before you came.'

'What do you want?'

'The seat?'

'So do I.'

I watched his face and could feel the whole compartment against me. I did not blame them. He was in the right. But I wanted the seat. Still no one said anything.

Oh, hell, I thought.

'Sit down, Signor Capitano,' I said. The machine-gunner moved out of the way and the tall captain sat down. He looked at me. His face seemed hurt. But he had the seat. 'Get my things,' I said to the machine-gunner. We went out in the corridor. The train was full and I knew there was no chance of a place. I gave the porter and the machine-gunner ten lire apiece. They went down the corridor and outside on the platform looking in the windows but there were no places.

'Maybe some will get off at Brescia,' the porter said.

'More will get on at Brescia,' said the machine-gunner. I said good-bye to them and we shook hands and they left. They both felt badly. Inside the train we were all standing in the corridor when the rain started. I watched the lights of the station and the yards as we went out. It was still raining and soon the windows were wet and you could not see out. Later I slept on the floor of the corridor; first putting my pocket-book with my money and papers in it inside my shirt and trousers so that it was inside the leg of my breeches. I slept all

66

GOING BACK

night, waking at Brescia and Verona when more men got on the train, but going back to sleep at once. I had my head on one of the musettes and my arms around the other and I could feel the pack and they could all walk over me if they wouldn't step on me. Men were sleeping on the floor all down the corridor. Others stood holding on to the window rods or leaning against the doors. That train was always crowded.

William Boyd

NARROW ESCAPES

In June 1917, the war had been waged for almost three years, and more and more new recruits were brought into the trenches of the Western Front. They too had to experience what thousands of others had gone through before, as described here in William Boyd's novel The New Confessions *(1987).*

WE MISSED THE Battle of Messines Ridge by a few days. The huge mines were exploded beneath it on the 7th June, and thus was initiated the Third Battle of Ypres, which lasted, in fits and starts, until mid-November. In fact everything stopped shortly after Messines for a couple of months until the offensive was renewed again at the end of July. Meanwhile the 13th (public school) service battalion of the Duke of Clarence's own South Oxfordshire Light Infantry moved into the Ypres Salient.

We had hoped, indeed, Colonel O'Dell had assured us, that we were to be reunited with the regiment, but this was not to be. On June 17th we found ourselves posted to corps reserve behind Bailleul some dozen miles from Ypres. We were billeted in a farm across the road from a battalion of Australian pioneers. The bombing section of D company pitched its tent and thus began the familiar round of equipment cleaning, fatigue parties and sports. My God, I was sick of sports by then! Football, badminton, rugby, cricket, everything – even battalion sized games of British Bulldog.

We could hear the guns on the front clearly. Somehow they sounded different from the long-range boom of the siege artillery at Nieuport – like the small thunder of a skittle ball, more sinister and dangerous, knocking things down. One week we laid a corduroy road of raw sappy elm planks for the use of a battery of heavy howitzers – squat, musclebound guns with fist-sized rivets – that fired a fat shell a foot in diameter. These guns were towed into place – hence the road – by traction engines. Standing back fifty yards, fingers in our ears, we watched their first salvo. The earth shivered, the guns disappeared in smoke. It took five minutes to load them; the shells were trundled up on light railways and then, with some difficulty, winched into the breech with primitive-looking block and tackle rigged beneath wooden tripods.

Boredom set in again, but it was of a slightly different order: beneath it lay a seam of excitement. An offensive was on; fairly soon, surely, it would be our turn for a 'stunt'. There was real enthusiasm in our tent, shared by everyone with the exception of Pawsey and myself. Even Noel Kite said he was keen to 'have a go at the Teutons'. Ralph the dog, whom we had brought from Nieuport, became the bombing section mascot. I have a photograph of us all, taken with Somerville-Start's box camera. There they sit – Kite, Bookbinder, Somerville-Start (Ralph panting between his knees), Druce, Teague, Pawsey and the others whose names I cannot recall – grinning, fags in mouths, caps pushed back, shirtsleeved, collars open, Teague clutching a Mills bomb in each hand. We look like a typically close bunch of 'mates', cheery and convivial. It is an entirely illusory impression. The months at Nieuport had forged few bonds. If truth be told we all rather grated on each other's nerves. We were like schoolboys at the end of term, needing some respite from the close proximity.

At the end of June we marched from Bailleul through Locre and Dickebusch to Ypres. The countryside had a look of certain parts of England. Gentle hills, red-tiled cottages and farms, scattered woods, and along the lanesides, a profusion of lilac, may and laburnum bushes. We skirted the shattered town and went into reserve trenches on the left bank of the Ypres canal. This was the first time the battalion came under fire from a few stray shells. We all thought we were blasé about shelling after the artillery duels at Nieuport but this was our first experience of real explosions. I remember seeing the puffs of dirt erupt and collapse in the fields across the canal and thought they possessed a fragile transient beauty – '*earth trees that live a split-second*' – I wrote in my diary. A few landed in the reserve lines, knocking down a couple of poplars, but I registered no alarm. There seemed nothing inherently dangerous in them – as threatening as the puffs of smoke that drifted harmlessly in the sunlit air after the clods of earth had thumped to the ground.

A and B companies went into the front line to relieve a battalion of the Royal Sussex Regiment. Two days later I went up myself as part of a ration party, carrying four gallons of tea in a couple of petrol cans.

What can I tell you about the Ypres front in early July 1917? Later, I used to explain it to people like this:

Take an idealized image of the English countryside – I always think of the Cotswolds in this connection (in fact, to be precise, I always think of Oxfordshire around Charlbury, for obvious reasons). Imagine you are walking along a country road. You come to the crest of a gentle rise and there before you is a modest valley. You know exactly the sort of view it provides. A road, some hedgerowed lanes, a patchwork of fields, a couple of small villages – cottages, a post-office, a pub, a church – there a dovecot, there a farm and an old mill; here an embankment and a railway line; a wood to the left, copses and spinneys scattered randomly about. The eye sweeps over these benign and neutral features unquestioningly.

Now, place two armies on either side of this valley. Have them dig in and construct a trench system. Everything in between is suddenly invested with new sinister potential: that neat farm, the obliging drainage ditch, the village at the crossroads become key factors in strategy and survival. Imagine running across those intervening fields in an attempt to capture positions on that gentle slope opposite so that you may advance one step into the valley beyond. Which way will you go? What cover will you seek? How swiftly will your legs carry you up that sudden gradient? Will that culvert provide shelter from enfilading fire? Is there an observation post in that barn? Try it the next time you are on a country stroll and see how the most tranquil scene can become instinct with violence. It only requires a change in point of view.

Of course as the weeks go by the valley is slowly changed: the features disappear with the topsoil; buildings retreat to their foundations; trees become stumps. The colours fade beneath the battering until all you have is a homogeneous brown dip in the land between two ridges.

But I thought only of my idyllic prospect as I peered out through a thin embrasure in the sandbags as our tea was issued in the trenches. Admittedly the landscape in that part of Belgium is flatter and there are no real hedgerows, but as I looked out through our wire across a grassy meadow which ascended a gentle slope to the ridge opposite I thought I might as well be in a valley in Oxfordshire. There were hawthorn bushes and scrubby hedges marking the intersections of field boundaries. I saw an unpaved road, small clumps of trees (somewhat knocked about), a group of farm buildings (ditto), but essentially it was no more than a section of run-of-the-mill countryside. If it had not been for the enemy wire and the dark outline of the earthworks of their trench system, I might not have been able to stifle a yawn. The evening sun was pleasantly warm and I could see wisps of smoke rising from their lines. No man's land. It was unimpressive.

We spent a week on the canal bank during which we had two days and two nights in the line. There, I was gratified to discover – despite the occasional barrages – that I was not panic-stricken. It was still close enough to my experience of the trenches at Nieuport not to be too unnerving.

The most irritating consequence of our first visit to the trenches at the Salient was that we became lousy. I tried all the usual remedies: powder; hours of diligent nit-picking, like an ape; a candle-flame run up and down the seams, but nothing worked. Eventually I used to turn my shirt inside out, wear it that way for a couple of days, then turn it back again, and so on. It seemed to regulate the itching at least. I was always scratching but it no longer rose to peaks of intolerability.

After our time at the front we duly marched back to Bailleul and routine re-established itself. Cleaning, drilling, sports, working parties and occasional visits to cafés in the town. I gained a real impression, too, of the vast organism that is an army: all those separate units that allow the whole to function – ordnance, transport, clothing, feeding, animals, signals, engineering, road-building, policing, communications, health and sanitation . . . There was an invisible city camped in the fields around Ypres and it required its civil servants, pay-masters, administrators, labour force and undertakers to make it function. The part the 13th battalion played in its organization was to dig cable ditches for the signallers, muck out open-air stables in the brigade transport lines, help lay tracks for light railways, stand guard over vast supply dumps, dig graves and latrines at a field hospital. We were no more than ants in an ant heap. But at the same time in those weeks of waiting I played atrociously in goal for the D company football team (we lost 11–2 against the Australian pioneers); came down with a dose of influenza; wrote a letter to my father and three to Hamish; almost had a fist fight with Teague when he accused me of stealing; felt bored, sexually frustrated, tired and occasionally miserable and one night dreamt vividly of my death – eviscerated by a German with an entrenching tool. I oscillated between the roles of soulless functionary and uniquely precious individual human being; from the disposable to the *sine qua non*.

It all came to an end on July 16th when the guns started up again in earnest. Then the one week barrage preliminary to the attack was extended to two as the renewed offensive was continually delayed. For the first few nights the firework display on the horizon was tremendous but as it continued night after night it became only another source of grumbles. The 13th was not even in reserve for the big push of July 31st. The day the battle proper began we were marched to a sugar-beet factory near Locre for delousing.

We marched back to our billets that evening in heavy rain. It rained constantly for the next four days and nights. Suddenly the dark damp countryside seemed to ooze foreboding. Rumour abounded about the attack – all of it baleful. A company of the Australians – out rewiring one night – took heavy casualties ('heavy casualties' – a bland, soft phrase). I asked one man what it had been like. 'Fuckin' shambles,' he said.

On August 7th we were moved back up to brigade reserve on the canal bank. Before we occupied the trenches we were paraded in a field where Colonel O'Dell addressed us. The battalion, he said, had been ordered to provide reinforcements for other units in the brigade. I do not remember the details; two companies were going to the Royal Welch, I think. D company was to be attached to a battalion of the Grampian Highlanders.

I already thought of us as the 'unlucky' 13th and this latest move seemed to me yet another turn for the worse. Teague and Somerville-Start, however, rejoiced. There was much excited talk about the 'Jocks' and their fighting spirit, and ill-informed speculation about this venerable regiment's battle honours.

The next night we set off, having left most of our kit at the battalion dump. Ralph was entrusted to the quartermaster. The 'bombers' made a great fuss of their farewells, you would have thought they were saying goodbye to their grandmothers. I had nothing to do with it – I was glad to be rid of the animal at last.

It took hours to join our new unit. There was immense toing and froing behind the front. We followed duckboard and fascine paths across black fields and were often redirected back down them. Once we eventually gained the trench system we were continually halted to allow a passage of ration and ordnance parties, engineers and signallers. Eventually we found the right communication trench. We toiled up this. Ahead I heard Louise reporting to an officer in the Grampians. Soon we were deployed in the support lines.

It was immediately clear that these trenches were not what we were used to: no dugouts, not even ledges cut for sleeping. I put my waterproof cape on the ground and sat down, my back against the rear wall. Druce passed among us checking all was well. I tipped my helmet forward and tried to sleep. My nostrils were full of the smell of wet earth and from the right came Bookbinder's body odour – truly appalling, a vile hogo. On my left Pawsey was having a shit in his helmet – he was too scared to go to the latrine sap.

From my diary:

August 9th 1917. Our first morning with the Grampians. Woken by random shelling. Stand to. Misty dawn. Up ahead, beyond our wire, a low ridge and two obliterated farms. Over to our right, according to Druce, the Frezenburg–Zonnebeck road. I can see no sign of it.

It is not very evocative, I admit. The biggest shock for me was not the shelling but the transformation in the landscape. All the ground as far up as the ridge looked as though it had been badly ploughed. Almost all the long grass and shrubs that I had seen five weeks earlier had disappeared. I could not see behind me, nor much to either side, but the countryside we occupied was a more or less uniform dark brown. It was hard to believe we were in high summer. I was also – curiously, for I am not particularly fastidious – somewhat offended at the mess everywhere. The trench was full of litter – empty tins, discarded equipment, boxes and fragments of boxes – and through slits in the parapet of sandbags no man's land seemed to be scattered with heaps of burst mattresses. I swear it was five minutes before I realized they were dead bodies.

Druce sent me, Kite and Somerville-Start into the Grampians' trenches to draw our water ration for the section. We passed along the support line through our company looking for the lead-off trench to the battalion ration store. We turned the corners of a fire-bay.

'Where are the Grampians?' Kite asked.

'Another ten yards.'

We came out of the fire-bay. Five very small men – very small men indeed – sat around a tommy-cooker brewing tea. They looked at us with candid hostility. They wore kilts covered with canvas aprons. Their faces were black with mud, grime and a five-day growth of beard. Two of them stood up. The tops of their heads came up to my chest. Neither of them could have been more than five feet tall. Bantams . . . These were the 17th/3 Grampians, a Bantam battalion, every man under the army's minimum height of five foot three inches. Kite and Somerville-Start were both taller than six feet.

'What the fuck are youse cunts looking at?' one of the men said in a powerful Scottish accent.

'*What?*' Kite said, unable to conceal his astonishment.

'Rations,' I said. At least I could understand. He told me where to go.

We made our way diffidently along the support trench until we found the supplies' sap. There, a dozen Bantams were collecting rations. We waited our turn uneasily, like lanky anthropologists amongst a pygmy tribe. We stood head and shoulders above these tiny dirty men. They seemed more like goblins or trolls than members of the same race as ourselves. The Bantams appeared indifferent to our presence, but we were all ill at ease, full of bogus smiles, as if we suspected some elaborate practical joke were being played on us and had not quite divined its ultimate purpose. We gladly picked up our petrol cans of water and headed back.

The Bantams did not like us. It cannot just have been because of our height, though it has to be said that as ex-public schoolboys we were on average taller than the other ranks in most regiments. I suspect it was a combination of our stature, our voices, our bearing and our Englishness that let us down. It did not help when on our way back that first day Kite said loudly 'I think they're rather sweet little chaps. Is it true they've been specially bred?' In any event, there swiftly grew up an invisible barrier between our company flanks and the Bantams on either side. It was so uncomfortable that we demanded our own ration parties which, somehow, Louise managed to arrange for us. The company's first deaths in action were sustained in this way. The pipe band were carrying up dixies of hot stew when they 'got a shell all to themselves', as the saying had it. Four were killed and three were wounded. It shocked us all profoundly: the pipe band had seemed indestructible. Louise, I recall, took it particularly badly.

Trench routine continued as normal for the next few days. My diary records the daily round:

Sentry duty 4 a.m.–6 a.m. Stand to. B'fast – tea, pickled mackerel, biscuit. Repaired trenches. Ration carrying. Lunch: beef stew, biscuits. Slept. Sentry duty 6 p.m.–8 p.m.

It rained from time to time and I grew steadily dirtier. I watched my uniform take on that particular look common to heavily soiled clothes – one sees it on tramps and refugees, for example. The fibres of the material seem to become bulked out with dirt so that jacket and trousers look as if they have been cut from a thick coarse felt. Creases at armpits, elbows and backs of knees develop a permanent concertina-ed effect – rigid and fixed. Your hair dulls, then becomes oily, and then transforms into a matt, clotted rope-end. Finger nails are rimmed with earth; your hands hard and calloused as a peasant's. Your beard grows. Your head itches, itches all day long.

We knew our 'stunt' was approaching as the ridge in front of us steadily took more shelling. Tension increased, and the routine wariness that had characterized our waking moment was replaced by neurotic edgy alarm. We kept expecting to be pulled out of the line for a period of rest before the attack but we appeared to have been forgotten. Even Teague and Somerville-Start were subdued. As for myself, I had evolved a new approach. I decided to be logical. I was going, as far as possible, to *think* my way to survival, even if it meant disobeying orders.

We stood to at half past four, an hour before dawn. Our

objectives were the two ruined farms. D company was going for the right-hand one, along with the Bantams on our right flank. We were to capture the farm, secure it and repel any counterattack until the second wave passed us. All night the ridge had been pounded by our guns. As we lined up in the fire trench the bombardment was still going on. Louise passed among us, white-faced and muttering what I suppose were words of encouragement. I could not hear him above the noise of the shells. Beside me stood Pawsey. On the other side was Somerville-Start. He held a ladder, so did I. I was as ready as I would ever be.

But I had forgotten about the rum. The quartermaster-sergeant passed among us pouring out the tots from the big ceramic bottle. The rum looked black, evil, thick as molasses. I drank my allocation – half a wine glass, I suppose – in two gulps, and I was seriously drunk within a minute. I saw Pawsey vomit his issue and lean gagging against the trench wall. Somerville-Start's face wore a kind of fixed, zealous grimace – he was breathing fiercely through his nose, both hands on his ladder.

Then everyone urinated. I suppose an order must have been given. The trench filled with vinegary urine-steam. I was giddy. I felt the trench had acquired a steep, dipping gradient to the left, down which I might at any moment slide. I held on to my ladder, and adjusted the weight of my sack of bombs. I never heard the whistle go but suddenly I saw people begin to climb their ladders. Somerville-Start and I set off simultaneously.

I do not remember my first unprotected view of no man's land – that initial astonishing second – because Somerville-Start got shot in the mouth. The moment his face cleared the parapet I saw his teeth shatter as they were hit by the bullet and a plume of blood, like a pony tail, issued from the nape of his neck. Several teeth, or teeth fragments, hit me in the face, stinging me like thrown gravel, and one piece cut me badly above my right eye. My eye filled with warm blood and I blundered over the sandbags blindly, wiping my eye with my sleeve. I sensed Pawsey going by me. My vision cleared and I saw him running off in the direction of the ridge. There was no sign of the ridge itself – the creeping barrage some fifty yards in front of us obscured everything.

'Think!' I said out loud. I crouched down and scampered forward, almost on all fours, like a baboon.

'*Stand up, that man!*' somebody bellowed.

I ignored him.

We were now, I realized, being shelled in our turn and I suppose there must have been machine-gun fire from somewhere because I saw some Bantams on my right gently falling over. I scrabbled after the creeping barrage, dragging my rifle on the ground. As far as I was concerned the world was still canted over towards the left and I kept falling over heavily on my left side, bruising my left knee. I moved like some demented cripple.

Then a shell exploded near me and the blast of air snatched my rifle from my grasp and whipped my helmet from my head. Warm earth hit my face and I felt the weal of the chin strap hot on my throat. I was stunned immobile for some seconds. Then, crab-like, I scuttled into the fuming crater.

Kite was already there, on his back, wounded. He held up the stump of his right arm, fringed like a brush, not bleeding but clotted with earth.

'Somebody's gone and shot my bloody arm off!' he shouted.

I blinked. I screwed up my eyes to adjust focus.

'Damn nuisance,' Kite said. He seemed wholly unperturbed.

I wondered if I should help him.

'D'you want a hand?' I yelled, in all innocence.

'Very funny, Todd,' he said petulantly. 'Hardly the time or place.' He began to move. 'I can make it on my own.' He crawled back towards our lines.

I looked around. I could not see a soul. The din was so general it seemed quite normal, like the factory floor of an iron foundry . . . I still had my sack of bombs. I wondered where I should throw them. I slithered forward, past some small dead Bantams. I saw what looked like a horrifically mangled side of beef, flayed by a maniac butcher with an axe. At the top there was an ear, some hair and part of a cheek. At the bottom, a bare knee with a smudge of dirt on it.

I crawled on until I reached some tangled wire. The German line? I glanced back. I could make out nothing. I turned: was that the farmhouse up ahead? It should have been easy for me to determine – we were meant to run uphill after all – but my dipping, left-biased world had made me immune to gradients. I had the disarming impression, all at once, that I was in fact moving parallel to our front line. So I turned, with some difficulty, right, leaning into the slope and felt I was falling. I immediately ran across Pawsey and Louise. Pawsey was shot through the chest. He had dry cherry foam on his lips. He was trying to speak but only pink bubbles formed and popped in his mouth. Louise, I guessed, had gone to help him and – so it seemed – had been caught by a concentrated burst of machine-gun fire in the throat, which was badly torn. He was quite dead. One bullet had taken off his nose with the neatness of a razor.

I looked up. The barrage had lifted. I could not hear the dreary clatter of machine-gun fire. I saw Bantams running back to our lines. More bubbles popped between Pawsey's lips. I grabbed him under the arms and began to drag him back to safety. I had not gone ten yards when he died. There is an unmistakable limpness about a dead person that no living being can imitate. Instinct tells you when it has arrived. But I needed no instinct, remember: I had dragged dead men from the surf at Croxyde Bains. Poor Pawsey felt the same.

I laid him down. There was no point in dragging back a dead man. Heavy firing was coming from further up the line, and a few shells were now bursting on the ridge, more an acknowledgement of the attack's failure than an attempt to silence the German guns. My section of no man's land was now strangely quiet. All the same I zig-zagged back to the lines moving carefully from shell hole to shell hole. In one particularly large hole I saw a couple of Bantams searching corpses for loot. I passed by on the other side.

I was helped into the trench by men I did not recognize.

This must be the second wave of the attack, I guessed, whose presence had not been required. I was passed down the line into the support trenches. Eventually I found my bits and pieces and sat down. I felt terrible. My brain was tender and bruised. I was nauseous. My mouth was dry and rank. My legs were visibly shaking and my joints ached. So this is battle fatigue, I thought. I know now I was suffering from a massive hangover. My first.

After a while I managed to light a cigarette. I put my trench cap on and waited for the others. Then I began to remember, piecemeal. Kite, with no hand. Louise and Pawsey dead . . .

A corporal from another platoon came over. He looked very tired.

'Any sign of Lieutenant McNeice?'

I told him about Louise. And Kite and Pawsey. I wondered if the others were all right.

'I don't know,' he said. 'I can't find a soul from my platoon.'

'You haven't seen any of my lot, have you?'

'I saw someone . . . well, *explode*. Must have been a bomber. Whole sacks of bombs went up. Took about five chaps with him.'

'Good God!'

'Are you all right?' he said. 'You've got blood all over your face.'

'Just a scratch,' I said reflexively, followed by a warm spurt of pride at my nonchalance. I put my hand up to my forehead. I felt a curious lump embedded above my eyebrow. It moved. I plucked it out with a wince. It was a tooth. One of Somerville-Start's incisors. I still have the scar.

The delayed shock arrived about an hour later. It was not so much what I had witnessed that overwhelmed me as the retrospective sense of awful peril I had been in. I saw myself running foolishly here and there about the battlefield, some-how avoiding the multitudinous trajectories of thousands of pieces of whizzing hot metal. I was not grateful for my luck. I was horrified, if you like, that I had used up so much. We all have narrow escapes in life, of some of which we are entirely unaware. What upset me was the hundreds of thousands of narrow escapes I must have had during my few hectic minutes in no man's land. I was convinced I had overdrawn my balance of good fortune; that whatever haphazard benevolence the impassive universe might hold towards me was all but gone.

Siegfried Sassoon
My Own Little Show

The poet Siegfried Sassoon describes his war experiences in his autobiographical novel Memoirs of an Infantry Officer *(1930). In 1917 he has lost all faith in the war and becomes increasingly hostile towards the official line and 'the people at home who couldn't understand'. He decides that the only way out of this senseless situation is to embark on 'death or glory' and to 'make a little drama out of my own experience'. This opportunity arises when he has to lead a bombing party into the enemy trenches.*

Part of the interest of the passage lies in the question of what level of irony Sassoon is dealing in; a question thrown into a harsher light by the extract from Pat Barker's Regeneration *that follows.*

ON SATURDAY AFTERNOON we came to Saulty, which was only ten miles from Arras and contained copious indications of the offensive, in the form of ammunition and food dumps and the tents of a Casualty Clearing Station. A large YMCA canteen gladdened the rank and file, and I sent my servant there to buy a pack full of Woodbines for an emergency which was a certainty. Canteens and *estaminets* would be remote fantasies when we were in the devastated area. Twelve dozen packets of Woodbines in a pale green cardboard box were all that I could store up for the future consolation of B Company; but they were better than nothing, and the box was no weight for my servant to carry.

Having seen the men settled into their chilly barns and sheds, I stuffed myself with coffee and eggs and betook myself to a tree stump in the peaceful park of a white château close to the village. Next day we were moving to our concentration area, so I was in a meditative mood and disposed to ask myself a few introspective questions. The sun was just above the tree-tops; a few small deer were grazing; a rook flapped overhead; and some thrushes and blackbirds were singing in the brown undergrowth. Nothing was near to remind me of the war; only the enormous thudding on the horizon and an aeroplane humming across the clear sky. For some obscure reason I felt confident and serene. My thoughts assured me that I wouldn't go back to England tomorrow if I were offered an improbable choice between that and the battle. Why should I feel elated at the prospect of the battle, I wondered. It couldn't be only the coffee and eggs which had caused me to feel so acquiescent. Last year, before the Somme, I hadn't known what I was in for. I knew now; and the idea was giving me emotional satisfaction! I had often read those farewell letters from second-lieutenants to their relatives which the newspapers were so fond of printing. 'Never has life brought me such an abundance of noble feelings,' and so on. I had always found it difficult to believe that these young men had really felt happy with death staring them in the face, and I resented any sentimentalizing of infantry attacks. But here I was, working myself up into a similar mental condition, as though going over the top were a species of religious experience. Was it some suicidal self-deceiving escape from the limitless malevolence of the front line? . . . Well, whatever it was, it was some compensation for the loss of last year's daydreams about England (which I could no longer indulge in, owing to an indefinite hostility to 'people at home who couldn't understand'). I was beginning to feel rather arrogant toward 'people at home'. But my mind was in a muddle; the war was too big an event for one man to stand alone in. All I knew was that I'd lost my faith in it and there was nothing left to believe in except 'the Battalion Spirit'. The Battalion Spirit meant living oneself into comfortable companionship with the officers and NCOs around one; it meant winning the respect, or even the affection, of platoon and company. But while exploring my way into the war I had discovered the impermanence of its humanities. One evening we could be all together in a cosy room in Corbie, with Wilmot playing the piano and Dunning telling me about the eccentric old ladies who lived in his mother's boarding house in Bloomsbury. A single machine-gun or a few shells might wipe out the whole picture within a week. Last summer the First Battalion had been part of my life; by the middle of September it had been almost obliterated. I knew that a soldier signed away his independence; we were at the front to fight, not to think. But it became a bit awkward when one couldn't look even a week ahead. And now there was a steel curtain down between April and May. On the other side of the curtain, if I was lucky, I should meet the survivors, and we should begin to build up our little humanities all over again.

That was the bleak truth, and there was only one method of evading it; to make a little drama out of my own experience – that was the way out. I must play at being a hero in shining armour, as I'd done last year; if I didn't, I might crumple up altogether. (Self-inflicted wounds weren't uncommon on the Western Front, and brave men had put bullets through their own heads before now, especially when winter made trench warfare unendurable.) Having thus decided on death or glory, I knocked my pipe out and got up from the tree stump with a sense of having solved my problems. The deer were still grazing peacefully in the park; but the sun was a glint of scarlet beyond the strip of woodland and the air was turning chilly. Along the edge of the world that infernal banging was going on for all it was worth. Three Army Corps were to attack on Easter Monday.

'*Secret*. The Bombing Parties of 25 men will rendezvous at 2.30 a.m. tomorrow morning, 16th inst. in shafts near C Coy. HQ. The greatest care will be taken that each separate

Company Party keeps to one side of the Shaft and that the Dump of Bombs be in the trench at the head of these shafts, suitably split. The necessity of keeping absolute silence must be impressed on all men. These parties (under 2nd Lt. Sherston) will come under the orders of O.C. Cameronians at ZERO minus 10. Lt. Dunning and 2 orderlies will act liaison and report to O.C. Cameronians at ZERO minus 5. While the parties are in the shaft they must keep a free passage way clear for runners, etc.'

Such was the document which (had I been less fortunate) would have been my passport to the Stygian shore. In the mean time, with another two hours to sit through, we carried on with our world without end conversation. We were, I think, on the subject of Canterbury Cricket Week when my watch warned me that I must be moving on. As I got up from the table on which we'd been leaning our elbows, a blurred version of my face looked at me from the foggy mirror with an effect of clairvoyance. Hoping that this was an omen of survival, I went along to the rendezvous-shaft and satisfied myself that the bombing parties were sitting on the stairs in a bone-chilling draught, with my two subordinate officers in attendance.

Zero hour was 3 a.m. and the prefatory uproar was already rumbling overhead. Having tightened my mud-caked puttees and put my tie straight (there was no rule against wearing a tie in an attack) diffidently I entered the Cameronian HQ dug-out, which was up against the foot of the stairs. I was among strangers, and Zero minus 10 wasn't a time for conversational amenities, so I sat self-consciously while the drumming din upstairs was doing its utmost to achieve a reassuring climax. Three o'clock arrived. The tick-tacking telephone-orderly in a corner received a message that the attack had started. They were over the barrier now, and bombing up the trench. The Cameronian Colonel and his Adjutant conversed in the constrained undertones of men who expect disagreeable news. The Colonel was a fine-looking man, but his well-disciplined face was haggard with anxiety. Dunning sat in another corner, serious and respectful, with his natural jollity ready to come to the surface whenever it was called for.

At the end of twenty minutes' tension the Colonel exclaimed abruptly, 'Good God, I wish I knew how they're doing!' . . . And then, as if regretting his manifestation of feeling, 'No harm in having a bit of cake, anyhow.' There was a large home-made cake on the table. I was offered a slice, which I munched with embarrassment. I felt that I had no business to be there at all, let alone helping to make a hole in the Colonel's cake, which was a jolly good one. I couldn't believe that these competent officers were counting on me to be of any use to them if I were required to take an active part in the proceedings upstairs. Then the telephone-orderly announced that communication with Captain Macnair's headquarters had broken down; after that the suspense continued monotonously. I had been sitting there about two and a half hours when it became evident that somebody was descending the steps in a hurry. HQ must have kept its cooking utensils on the stairs, for the visitor arrived outside the doorway in a clattering cascade of pots and pans. He was a breathless and dishevelled sergeant, who blurted out an incoherent statement about their having been driven back after advancing a short distance. While the Colonel questioned him in a quiet and controlled voice I rose stiffly to my feet. I don't remember saying anything or receiving any orders, but I felt that the Cameronian officers were sensitive to the delicacy of my situation. There was no question of another slice of home-made cake. Their unuttered comment was, 'Well, old chap, I suppose you're for it now.'

Leaving them to get what satisfaction they could from the sergeant's story, I grinned stupidly at Dunning, popped my helmet on my head, and made for the stairway. It must have been a relief to be doing something definite at last, for without pausing to think I started off with the section of twenty-five who were at the top of the stairs. Sergeant Baldock got them on the move at once, although they were chilled and drowsy after sitting there for over three hours. None of them would have been any the worse for a mouthful of rum at that particular moment. In contrast to the wearisome candlelight of the lower regions, the outdoor world was bright and breezy; animated also by enough noise to remind me that some sort of battle was going on. As we bustled along, the flustered little contingent at my heels revived from its numbness. I had no idea what I was going to do; our destination was in the brain of the stooping Cameronian guide who trotted ahead of me. On the way we picked up a derelict Lewis gun, which I thought might come in handy though there was no ammunition with it. At the risk of being accused of 'taking the wrong half of the conversation' (a favourite phrase of Aunt Evelyn's) I must say that I felt quite confident. (Looking back on that emergency from my arm-chair, I find some difficulty in believing that I was there at all.) For about ten minutes we dodged and stumbled up a narrow winding trench. The sun was shining; large neutral clouds voyaged willingly with the wind; I felt intensely alive and rather out of breath. Suddenly we came into the main trench, and where it was widest we met the Cameronians. I must have picked up a bomb on the way, for I had one in my hand when I started my conversation with young Captain Macnair. Our encounter was more absurd than impressive. Macnair and his exhausted men were obviously going in the wrong direction, and I was an incautious newcomer. Consequently I had the advantage of him while he told me that the Germans were all round them and they'd run out of bombs. Feeling myself to be, for the moment, an epitome of Flintshire infallibility, I assumed an air of jaunty unconcern; tossing my bomb carelessly from left hand to right and back again, I inquired, 'But where *are* the Germans?' – adding 'I can't see any of them.' This effrontery had its effect (though for some reason I find it difficult to describe this scene without disliking my own behaviour). The Cameronian officers looked around them and recovered their composure. Resolved to show them what intrepid reinforcements we were, I assured Macnair that he needn't worry any more and we'd soon put things straight. I then led my party past his, halted them, and went up the trench with Sergeant Baldock – an admirably impassive little man who never ceased to behave like a perfectly trained and confidential man-servant. After climbing over some sort of barricade, we went about fifty yards without meeting anyone. Observing a good many Mills bombs lying about in little heaps, I sent Baldock back to have them collected and carried further up the trench. Then, with an accelerated heart beat, I went round the corner by myself. Unexpectedly, a small man was there, standing with his back to me, stock still and watchful, a haversack of bombs slung over his left shoulder. I saw that he was a Cameronian corporal; we did not speak. I also carried a bag of bombs; we went round the next bay. There my advent-urous ardour experienced a sobering shock. A fair-haired Scotch private was lying at the side of the trench in a pool of his own blood. His face was grey and serene, and his eyes stared emptily at the sky. A few yards further on the body of a German officer lay crumpled up and still. The wounded Cameronian made me feel angry, and I slung a couple of bombs at our invisible enemies, receiving in reply an egg-bomb, which exploded harmlessly behind me. After that I went bombing busily along, while the corporal (more artful and efficient than I was) dodged in and out of the saps – a precaution which I should have forgotten. Between us we created quite a demonstration of offensiveness, and in this manner arrived at our objective without getting more than a few glimpses of retreating field-grey figures. I had no idea where our objective was, but the corporal informed me that we had reached it, and he seemed to know his business. This, curiously enough, was the first time either of us had spoken since we met.

The whole affair had been so easy that I felt like pushing forward until we bumped into something more definite. But the corporal had a cooler head and he advised discretion. I told him to remain where he was and started to explore a narrow sap on the left side of the trench. (Not that it matters whether it was on the left side or the right, but it appears to be the only detail I can remember; and when all is said and done, the war was mainly a matter of holes and ditches.) What I expected to find along that sap, I can't say. Finding nothing, I stopped to listen. There seemed to be a lull in the noise of the attack along the line. A few machine-guns tapped, spiteful and spasmodic. High up in the fresh blue sky an aeroplane droned and glinted. I thought what a queer state of things it all was, and then decided to take a peep at the surrounding country. This was a mistake which ought to have put an end to my terrestrial adventures, for no sooner had I popped my silly head out of the sap than I felt a stupendous blow in the back between my shoulders. My first notion was that a bomb had hit me from behind, but what had really happened was that I had been sniped from in front. Anyhow my foolhardy attitude toward the Second Battle of the Scarpe had been instantaneously altered for the worse. I leant against the side of the sap and shut my eyes . . . When I reopened them Sergeant Baldock was beside me, discreet and sympathetic, and to my surprise I discovered that I wasn't dead. He helped me back to the trench, gently investigated my wound, put a field-dressing on it, and left me sitting there while he went to bring up some men.

After a short spell of being deflated and sorry for myself, I began to feel rapidly heroical again, but in a slightly different style, since I was now a wounded hero, with my arm in a superfluous sling. All my seventy-five men were now on the scene (minus a few who had been knocked out by our own shells, which were dropping short). I can remember myself talking volubly to a laconic Stokes-gun officer, who had appeared from nowhere with his weapon and a couple of assistants. I felt that I must make one more onslaught before I turned my back on the war and my only idea was to collect all available ammunition and then renew the attack while the Stokes-gun officer put up an enthusiastic barrage. It did not occur to me that anything else was happening on Allenby's Army Front except my own little show. My overstrained nerves had wrought me up to such a pitch of excitement that I was ready for any suicidal exploit. This convulsive energy might have been of some immediate value had there been any objective for it. But there was none; and before I had time to inaugurate anything rash and irrelevant Dunning arrived to relieve me. His air of competent unconcern sobered me down, but I was still inflamed with the offensive spirit and my impetuosity was only snuffed out by a written order from the Cameronian Colonel, who forbade any further advance owing to the attack having failed elsewhere. My ferocity fizzled out then, and I realized that I had a raging thirst. As I was starting my return journey (I must have known then that nothing could stop me till I got to England) the MO came sauntering up the trench with the detached demeanour of a gentle botanist. 'Trust him to be up there having a look round,' I thought. Within four hours of leaving it I was back in the Tunnel.

Back at Battalion Headquarters in the Tunnel I received from our Colonel and Adjutant generous congratulations on my supposedly dashing display. In the emergency candlelight of that draughty cellar recess I bade them good-bye with voluble assurances that I should be back in a few weeks; but I was so overstrained and excited that my assurances were noises rather than notions. Probably I should have been equally elated without my wound; but if unwounded, I'd have been still up at the Block with the bombing parties. In the meantime, nothing that happened to me could relieve Battalion HQ of its burdens. The Adjutant would go on till he dropped, for he had an inexhaustible sense of duty. I never saw him again; he was killed in the autumn up at Ypres . . . I would like to be able to remember that I smiled grimly and departed reticently. But the 'bombing show' had increased my self-importance, and my exodus from the front line was a garrulous one. A German bullet had passed through me leaving a neat hole near my right shoulder-blade and this patriotic perforation had made a different man of me. I now looked at the war, which had been a monstrous tyrant, with liberated eyes. For the time being I had regained my right to call myself a private individual.

Pat Barker

FINISHED WITH THE WAR

While on convalescence in England, Siegfried Sassoon decided not to go back to France and publicized his reasons in a declaration which was printed in The Times *in July 1917. Sassoon expected to be court-martialled; instead he was found to be in need of psychiatric treatment and sent to Craiglockart War Hospital, a hospital for shell-shocked officers. These events lie at the centre of Pat Barker's novel* Regeneration *(1991), the first in a trilogy about the distinguished psychologist W.H.R. Rivers.*

Finished with the War
A Soldier's Declaration

I AM MAKING this statement as an act of wilful defiance of military authority, because I believe the war is being deliberately prolonged by those who have the power to end it.

I am a soldier, convinced that I am acting on behalf of soldiers. I believe that this war, upon which I entered as a war of defence and liberation, has now become a war of aggression and conquest. I believe that the purposes for which I and my fellow soldiers entered upon this war should have been so clearly stated as to have made it impossible to change them, and that, had this been done, the objects which actuated us would now be attainable by negotiation.

I have seen and endured the suffering of the troops, and I can no longer be a party to prolong these sufferings for ends which I believe to be evil and unjust.

I am not protesting against the conduct of the war, but against the political errors and insincerities for which the fighting men are being sacrificed.

On behalf of those who are suffering now I make this protest against the deception which is being practised on them; also I believe that I may help to destroy the callous complacence with which the majority of those at home regard the continuance of agonies which they do not share, and which they have not sufficient imagination to realize.

S. Sassoon
July 1917

BRYCE WAITED FOR Rivers to finish reading before he spoke again. 'The "S" stands for "Siegfried". Apparently, he thought that was better left out.'

'And I'm sure he was right.' Rivers folded the paper and ran his fingertips along the edge. 'So they're sending him here?'

Bryce smiled. 'Oh, I think it's rather more specific than that. They're sending him to *you*.'

Rivers got up and walked across to the window. It was a fine day, and many of the patients were in the hospital grounds, watching a game of tennis. He heard the *pok-pok* of rackets, and a cry of frustration as a ball smashed into the net. 'I suppose he is – "shell-shocked"?'

'According to the Board, yes.'

'It just occurs to me that a diagnosis of neurasthenia might not be inconvenient confronted with this.' He held up the Declaration.

'Colonel Langdon chaired the Board. *He* certainly seems to think he is.'

'Langdon doesn't believe in shell-shock.'

Bryce shrugged. 'Perhaps Sassoon was gibbering all over the floor.'

'"Funk, old boy." I know Langdon.' Rivers came back to his chair and sat down. 'He doesn't *sound* as if he's gibbering, does he?'

Bryce said carefully, 'Does it matter what his mental state is? Surely it's better for him to be here than in prison?'

'Better for *him*, perhaps. What about the hospital? Can you imagine what our dear Director of Medical Services is going to say, when he finds out we're sheltering "conchies" as well as cowards, shirkers, scrimshankers and degenerates? We'll just have to hope there's no publicity.'

'There's going to be, I'm afraid. The Declaration's going to be read out in the House of Commons next week.'

'By?'

'Lees-Smith.'

Rivers made a dismissive gesture.

'Yes, well, I know. But it still means the press.'

'And the minister will say that no disciplinary action has been taken, because Mr Sassoon is suffering from a severe mental breakdown, and therefore not responsible for his actions. I'm not sure *I*'d prefer that to prison.'

'I don't suppose he was offered the choice. Will you take him?'

'You mean I *am* being offered a choice?'

'In view of your case load, yes.'

Rivers took off his glasses and swept his hand down across his eyes. 'I suppose they *have* remembered to send the file?'

Light from the window behind Rivers's desk fell directly on to Sassoon's face. Pale skin, purple shadows under the eyes. Apart from that, no obvious signs of nervous disorder. No twitches, jerks, blinks, no repeated ducking to avoid a long-exploded shell. His hands, doing complicated things with cup, saucer, plate, sandwiches, cake, sugar tongs and spoon, were perfectly steady. Rivers raised his own cup to his lips and smiled. One of the nice things about serving afternoon tea to newly arrived patients was that it made so many neurological tests redundant.

So far he hadn't looked at Rivers. He sat with his head slightly averted, a posture that could easily have been taken for arrogance, though Rivers was more inclined to suspect shyness. The voice was slightly slurred, the flow of words sometimes hesitant, sometimes rushed. A disguised stammer, perhaps, but a life-long stammer, Rivers thought, not the recent, self-conscious stammer of the neurasthenic.

'While I remember, Captain Graves rang to say he'll be along some time after dinner. He sent his apologies for missing the train.'

'He *is* still coming?'

'Yes.'

Sassoon looked relieved. 'Do you know, I don't think Graves's caught a train in his life? Unless somebody was there to *put* him on it.'

'We were rather concerned about you.'

'In case the lunatic went missing?'

'I wouldn't put it quite like that.'

'I was all right. I wasn't even surprised, I thought he'd slept in. He's been doing a . . . a lot of rushing round on my behalf recently. You've no idea how much work goes into *rigging* a Medical Board.'

Rivers pushed his spectacles up on to his forehead and massaged the inner corners of his eyes. 'No, I don't suppose I have. You know this may sound naïve but . . . to *me* . . . the accusation that a Medical Board has been rigged is quite a serious one.'

'I've no complaints. I was dealt with in a perfectly fair and reasonable way. Probably better than I deserved.'

'What kind of questions did they ask?'

Sassoon smiled. 'Don't you know?'

'I've read the report, if that's what you mean. I'd still like to hear your version.'

'Oh: "Did I object to fighting on religious grounds?" I said I didn't. It was rather amusing, actually. For a moment I thought they were asking me whether I objected to going on a crusade. "Did I think I was qualified to decide when the war should end?" I said I hadn't thought about my qualifications.'

He glanced at Rivers. '*Not true*. And then . . . then Colonel Langdon asked *said* "Your friend tells us you're very good at bombing. Don't you still dislike the Germans?"'

A long silence. The net curtain behind Rivers's head billowed out in a glimmering arc, and a gust of cool air passed over their faces.

'And what did you say to that?'

'I don't remember.' He sounded impatient now. 'It didn't matter what I said.'

'It matters now.'

'All right.' A faint smile. '*Yes*, I am quite good at bombing. *No*, I do not still dislike the Germans.'

'Does that mean you once did?'

Sassoon looked surprised. For the first time something had been said that contradicted his assumptions. 'Briefly. April and May of last year, to be precise.'

A pause. Rivers waited. After a while Sassoon went on, almost reluctantly. 'A friend of mine had been killed. For a while I used to go out on patrol every night, looking for Germans to kill. Or rather I told myself that's what I was doing. In the end I didn't know whether I was trying to kill them, or just giving them plenty of opportunities to kill me.'

'"Mad Jack."'

Sassoon looked taken aback. 'Graves really *has* talked, hasn't he?'

'It's the kind of thing the Medical Board would need to know.' Rivers hesitated. 'Taking *unnecessary* risks is one of the first signs of a war neurosis.'

'Is it?' Sassoon looked down at his hands. 'I didn't know that.'

'Nightmares and hallucinations come later.'

'What's an "unnecessary risk" anyway? The maddest thing *I* ever did was done under orders.' He looked up, to see if he should continue. 'We were told to go and get the regimental badges off a German corpse. They reckoned he'd been dead two days, so obviously if we got the badges they'd know which battalion was opposite. Full moon, not a cloud in sight, *absolutely mad*, but off we went. Well, we got there –

95

eventually – and what do we find? He's been dead a helluva lot longer than two days, and he's French anyway.'

'So what did you do?'

'Pulled one of his boots off and sent it back to battalion HQ. With quite a bit of his leg left inside.'

Rivers allowed another silence to open up. 'I gather we're not going to talk about nightmares?'

'You're in charge.'

'Ye-es. But then one of the paradoxes of being an army psychiatrist is that you don't actually get very far by *ordering* your patients to be frank.'

'I'll be as frank as you like. I did have nightmares when I first got back from France. I don't have them now.'

'And the hallucinations?'

He found this more difficult. 'It was just that when I woke up, the nightmares didn't always stop. So I used to see . . .' A deep breath. 'Corpses. Men with half their faces shot off, crawling across the floor.'

'And you were awake when this happened?'

'I don't know. I must've been, because I could see the sister.'

'And was this always at night?'

'No. It happened once during the day. I'd been to my club for lunch, and when I came out I sat on a bench, and . . . I suppose I must've nodded off.' He was forcing himself to go on. 'When I woke up, the pavement was covered in corpses. Old ones, new ones, black, green.' His mouth twisted. 'People were treading on their faces.'

Rivers took a deep breath. 'You say you'd just woken up?'

'Yes. I used to sleep quite a bit during the day, because I was afraid to go to sleep at night.'

'When did all this stop?'

'As soon as I left the hospital. The atmosphere in that place was really terrible. There was one man who used to boast about killing German prisoners. You can imagine what living with *him* was like.'

'And the nightmares haven't recurred?'

'No. I do dream, of course, but not about the war. Sometimes a dream seems to go on after I've woken up, so there's a kind of in-between stage.' He hesitated. 'I don't know whether that's abnormal.'

'I hope not. It happens to me all the time.' Rivers sat back in his chair. 'When you look back now on your time in the hospital, do *you* think you were "shell-shocked"?'

'I don't know. Somebody who came to see me told my uncle he thought I was. As against that, I wrote one or two good poems while I was in there. We-ell . . .' He smiled. '*I* was pleased with them.'

'You don't think it's possible to write a good poem in a state of shock?'

'No, I don't.'

Rivers nodded. 'You may be right. Would it be possible for me to see them?'

'Yes, of course. I'll copy them out.'

Rivers said, 'I'd like to move on now to the . . . thinking behind the Declaration. You say your motives aren't religious?'

'No, not at all.'

'Would you describe yourself as a pacifist?'

'I don't think so. I can't possibly say "*No* war is ever justified", because I haven't thought about it enough. Perhaps some wars are. Perhaps this one was when it started. I just don't think our war aims – *whatever they may be* – and we don't know – justify this level of slaughter.'

'And you say you *have* thought about your qualifications for saying that?'

'*Yes*. I'm only too well aware of how it sounds. A *second-lieutenant*, no less, saying "The war must stop". On the other hand, I have *been* there. I'm at least as well qualified as some of the old men you see sitting around in clubs, cackling on about "attrition" and "wastage of manpower" and . . .' His voice became a vicious parody of an old man's voice. '"*Lost heavily in that last scrap*." You don't talk like that if you've watched them die.'

'No intelligent or sensitive person would talk like that anyway.'

A slightly awkward pause. 'I'm not saying there are no

exceptions.'

Rivers laughed. 'The point is you hate civilians, don't you? The "callous", the "complacent", the "unimaginative". Or is "hate" too strong a word?'

'No.'

'So. What you felt for the Germans, rather briefly, in the spring of last year, you now feel for the overwhelming majority of your fellow-countrymen?'

'Yes.'

'You know, I think you were quite right not to say too much to the Board.'

'That wasn't my idea, it was Graves's. He was afraid I'd sound too sane.'

'When you say the Board was "rigged", what did you mean?'

'I meant the decision to send me here, or somewhere similar, had been taken before I went in.'

'And this had all been fixed by Captain Graves?'

'Yes.' Sassoon leant forward. 'The point is they weren't going to court-martial me. They were just going to lock me up somewhere . . .' He looked round the room. '*Worse* than this.'

Rivers smiled. 'There *are* worse places, believe me.'

'I'm sure there are,' Sassoon said politely.

'They were going to certify you, in fact?'

'I suppose so.'

'Did anybody on the Board say anything to you about this?'

'No, because it was –'

'All fixed beforehand. Yes, I see.'

Sassoon said, 'May I ask you a question?'

'Go ahead.'

'Do *you* think I'm mad?'

'No, of course you're not mad. Did you think you were going mad?'

'It crossed my mind. You know when you're brought face to face with the fact that, yes, you did see corpses on the pavement . . .'

'Hallucinations in the half-waking state are surprisingly common, you know. They're not the same thing as psychotic hallucinations. Children have them quite frequently.'

Sassoon had started pulling at a loose thread on the breast of his tunic. Rivers watched him for a while. 'You must've been in agony when you did that.'

Sassoon lowered his hand. 'No-o. *Agony's* lying in a shell-hole with your legs shot off. I was *upset*.' For a moment he looked almost hostile, then he relaxed. 'It was a futile gesture. I'm not particularly proud of it.'

'You threw it in the Mersey, didn't you?'

'Yes. It wasn't heavy enough to sink, so it just' – a glint of amusement – '*bobbed* around. There was a ship sailing past, quite a long way out, in the estuary, and I looked at this little scrap of ribbon floating and I looked at the ship, and I thought that me trying to stop the war was a bit like trying to stop the ship would have been. You know, all they'd've seen from the deck was this little figure jumping up and down, waving its arms, and they wouldn't've known what on earth it was getting so excited about.'

'So you realized *then* that it was futile?'

Sassoon lifted his head. 'It still had to be done. You can't just acquiesce.'

Rivers hesitated. 'Look, I think we've . . . we've got about as far as we can get today. You must be very tired.' He stood up. 'I'll see you tomorrow morning at ten. Oh, and could you ask Captain Graves to see me as soon as he arrives?'

Sassoon stood up. 'You said a bit back you didn't think I was mad.'

'I'm quite sure you're not. As a matter of fact I don't even think you've got a war neurosis.'

Sassoon digested this. 'What have I got, then?'

'You seem to have a very powerful *anti*-war neurosis.'

They looked at each other and laughed. Rivers said, 'You realize, don't you, that it's my duty to . . . to try to change that? I can't pretend to be neutral.'

Sassoon's glance took in both their uniforms. 'No, of course not.'

Sebastien Japrisot

THE WOMAN ON LOAN

Some soldiers were prepared to do anything to get out of the war. Desertion was the obvious but also the most dangerous expedient. In his novel A Very Long Engagement *(1991), Sebastien Japrisot tells the story of a woman who, after the war, tries to find out what happened to her fiancé, who had been court-martialled for self-mutilation. During her investigations she learns of another soldier's desperate – and rather unusual – attempt to obtain the ticket home.*

ELODIE GORDES
43, Rue Montgallet
Paris
Wednesday, July 7

Mademoiselle,

I thought it easier for me to write you and here I have started this letter over a good three times now. I do not understand how what hurts me so much in the telling will be of use to you, or what it has to do with the death of your fiancé, but you say it is vital and I felt such sorrow in you, the other day, I would be ashamed to make you suffer even more by remaining silent. Only I beg of you, do not speak to anyone of what I will tell you, as until today I have not revealed these things to another soul.

In that photo of those bound soldiers I was much distressed

to see Kléber Bouquet, but when I said I did not know him it was only half a lie. Before the war, for more than three years my husband spoke often of him, as they shared the money they earned every Saturday at the open-air market where they hawked their furniture, but I never saw him. I did not even know his name, for my husband called him the Eskimo.

Now, so that you will understand me, I must speak of certain matters, and these above all I beg you to keep secret because the happiness of the children is at stake.

AS I WRITE this the children have been long abed, today is Friday, making it two nights ago that I began this letter. I feel worry and trepidation as I come to what you desired to know all in an instant, that day of the thunderstorm, like a bolt from on high. No doubt I cannot help putting off the telling, but there is something else too, I am trying to make you understand that ours was a folly like many another which would never have come to pass without the war. The war destroyed everything, even Benjamin Gordes, and finally the Eskimo, and simple good sense, and me.

In August of 1914, grief-stricken as I was knowing he might never return, I was relieved to learn from his first letter that my husband had met up in his regiment with his friend from the furniture market. He had always spoken of the Eskimo with a fondness I felt in him for no other. He admired him for his steadiness, his cheerfulness, his air of adventure, and most likely he felt admired in return for his skill as a cabinet-maker. One proof of how deep this friendship went was that when mobilization came, Benjamin, as the father of five children, should have been assigned to the territorial army and remained back at the home front to repair roads or train tracks, but no, he insisted on going off with the rest of his regiment. He told me: 'I would rather be with the Eskimo than with some lot of old men who'll get bombarded anyway. As long as we can be together, I'll not feel so afraid.' Perhaps it gnawed at his conscience, I admit, to be excused for children that were his in name only. That was him all over, more's the pity.

101

I will not dwell on what those terrible years were for me, you have certainly lived through the same heartache. Apart from the children, my days were given over to waiting. Waiting for a letter, waiting for the official daily bulletin, waiting for the next day to come so that I might spend it waiting. Benjamin had never much taken to writing, for he stupidly feared to make a fool of himself, still he did not ever let me go long without news, though of course we were at the mercy of the post office. I already told you he did not speak of the war to me, which is true, but the longer the war lasted, the more sadness and discouragement I could feel in his letters. His spirits lifted only when he mentioned the Eskimo, and that is how I learned his name. 'Yesterday I went with Kléber to see a show, some entertainment for the troops, we laughed heartily.' 'I must go, duty calls, Kléber and I take on two unwary grenadiers in a game of manille.' 'Remember, in your next package, to send some shag for Kléber, always puffing away on that pipe of his.' 'Kléber has it on good authority, we will soon be going on leave.'

Leave. This word came up again and again. In fact, Benjamin's first leave was after the fighting in Artois, at the end of July 1915. That made it almost one year to the day he had been gone. To say he was a changed man does not come close, for he was not the same man at all. Doting on the children one moment, shouting at them the next for making too much of a racket. And then he would sit silent at the table after meals for a long time, finishing up his bottle. He hardly ever touched wine before the war and now he had to have his bottle at noon and suppertime. One day during that week at home he went over to his workshop and returned after nightfall unsteady on his feet and smelling of drink. I had put the children to bed. That was the evening I first saw him cry. He could not stomach any more of the war, he was afraid, he had a terrible sense that if he did not do something, he would never come home again.

The next day, sober once more, he held me in his arms, he told me: 'Don't be angry with me, I've taken to drink like some others because out there it's the only way I can keep going. I never thought to see the day I would do such a thing.'

He left. His letters grew sadder still. I found out later that his regiment was in Champagne during the autumn and winter, and outside Verdun in March of 1916. He came home on leave on April 15, I remember it was a Saturday. He was more thin and pale than ever, with something dead, yes, something already dead in his eyes. He had stopped drinking. He saw the children growing up without him, he tried to take an interest in them but they quickly wore him out. He told me, in our bed where he no longer felt desire for me, lying in the dark: 'This war will never end, the Boches are being massacred and so are we. You don't know what courage is until you see the English fight, but their courage is not enough, nor is ours, nor is the enemy's. We are drowning in mud. It will never end.' Another night, when I lay huddled close to him, he said: 'Either I desert and they catch me or I need another child. When you have six children, they send you home for good.' After a long silence, in a changed voice, he said: 'You understand?'

Do you understand? I feel sure you understand what he meant. I am certain you are already laughing and making fun of me as you read this.

Please excuse me. That was a foolish thing to say. You are not laughing at me. You would like your fiancé to come home, too.

That night, I told Benjamin he had gone mad. He fell asleep. Me, I could not. He came back to it the next day and the others as well, whenever the children could not hear us. He would say: 'You will not be deceiving me, because I am the one asking you to do it. And what difference can it make since the other five are not mine in any case? Would I want such a thing if my blood were strong enough to give you the sixth child? Would I want this if I were free of all ties and a fatalist like Kléber?'

He had said the name: Kléber.

One afternoon we were outdoors, we had left the children for an hour with the downstairs neighbours, the two of us were walking along the Quai de Bercy, and he told me: 'You must promise me before I go. With Kléber, it doesn't bother me. All I can see is that then I would be out of it and we would be happy, as though the war had never been.'

The day he left, I went with him to the station. At the Gare du Nord he kissed me through the bars of the gate, he looked at me, I had the terrible feeling I did not know him any more. He said: 'I understand, you feel you no longer know who I am. Yet it really is me, Benjamin. But I cannot survive any longer, save me! Promise you'll do it. Promise.'

I nodded to say yes, I was weeping. I watched him trudge away in his uniform, a dirty blue colour it was, carrying his helmet and haversacks.

I am telling you about my husband, and about myself, not about Kléber Bouquet. And yet it was Kléber who told me, later on, what I would come to believe: you take what comes, when it comes, you do not struggle against the war, or against life, or against death, you pretend, and the only master of this world is time.

Time only made Benjamin's obsession worse. What he could no longer bear was how the war went on and on. All he spoke of in his letters was the month when Kléber would be on leave. All he wanted to know from me was what my best days would be to conceive a child.

I wrote him: 'Even if it takes, there would still be eight or nine months to wait, the war will be over by then.' He wrote back: 'What I need is hope. If I could find reason to hope again for eight or nine months, that would already be something.' And Kléber told me: 'When we were in Artois, Benjamin lost heart to see all those dead bodies, the horrible wounds, and the butchery of Notre-Dame-de-Lorette and Vimy, across from Lens. Poor Frenchmen, poor Moroccans, poor Boches. They tossed them into carts, one after another, as though they had never been anything at all. And one time there was a fat fellow up in a cart packing in the corpses, arranging them so they would take the least amount of space, and he walked all over them. So Benjamin yelled at him, calling him every name in the book, and this man jumped on him and they fought rolling around on the ground like dogs.

Maybe Benjamin had no heart left for war, but he had courage enough to tangle with a big lout trampling on the bodies of fallen soldiers.'

Mademoiselle, I do not know if I am making clear to you what I mean, that nothing is ever black or white, because time turns everything to grey. Today, Sunday, July 11, having written this letter by fits and starts, I am no longer the same person I was last Wednesday when I was so afraid to speak to you of these matters. Now I tell myself that if my memories can help you, the pain they cost me is a small price to pay. To be frank, there is something for me in this as well, I am no longer ashamed, it is all as one to me.

Kléber Bouquet arrived on leave in June of 1916. On June 7, a Monday, he left a note in my mailbox saying he would come by the following afternoon and if I did not want to see him, he would understand, I had only to hang a coloured cloth in a window facing the street. The next morning I took the children to their Aunt Odile in Joinville-le-Pont, telling her merely that I had some things to attend to and might be busy for a few days.

At around three o'clock in the afternoon, watching from the window of my bedroom, I saw a man stop on the pavement across the street and look up at my building. He was in light-coloured summer clothing, wearing a boater. We looked at each other for a few moments, stock-still, both of us, and I could not bring myself to give him the slightest sign. Finally he crossed the street.

I did not open the door until I heard his footsteps reach our landing, then I went to the dining room. He came in, taking off his straw hat, almost as ill at ease as myself, saying simply: 'Hello, Elodie.' I replied hello. He closed the door, came into the room. He was as Benjamin had described him to me: a robust man with a placid face, a frank look in his eyes, with brown hair and moustache, and the large hands of a carpenter. The only thing missing from the portrait was his smile, but this was quite beyond him, while as for me, I leave you to imagine. We surely seemed like two foolish actors at a loss for their lines. I have no idea how, after a few seconds when I no longer dared look him in the face, I was able to say: 'Do sit down, I've made some coffee.'

In the kitchen my heart was pounding, my hands were shaking. I brought out the coffee. He was sitting at the table, he had placed his boater on the sofa where my sister-in-law Odile sleeps when she stays with us. It was a hot day but I did not dare open the window for fear we might be seen from the building next door. I said: 'You may take off your jacket if you'd like.' He thanked me, he hung his jacket on the back of his chair.

We drank our coffee sitting across from each other at the table. I could not bring myself to look at him. Like me he did not want to speak of Benjamin or the front, which would naturally remind us of him. To relieve our embarrassment he recounted his younger days in America with his brother Charles, who had stayed behind there, and also his friendship with Little Louis, who had been a boxer and now owned a bar where he staged Seltzer-bottle fights with his customers. I looked up just then and saw his smile, it was childlike and comforting, this smile truly did change him wonderfully.

Next he asked me if he could smoke a cigarette. I went to fetch him a saucer for an ashtray. He smoked a Gauloise bleue. He was silent now. We could hear children playing outside. After only a few puffs he put out his cigarette in the saucer. Then he stood up and said in a gentle voice: 'It was a ridiculous idea. But we can lie to him, you know, pretend we did. Maybe it will give him some peace of mind out in the trenches.'

I did not answer. Still I could not look him in the face. He took up his boater from the sofa. He said: 'Leave a message for me with Little Louis, Rue Amelot, if you wish to speak with me before I go back.' He went towards the door. I stood up as well, I was there before him to keep him from leaving. After a moment, when I looked him finally straight in the eye, he pressed me against his shoulder, his hand was in my hair, we stood like that without a word. And then I pulled away from him, I went back into the dining room. Before he had arrived I had tried to prepare the bedroom, by this I mean to remove whatever might remind us of Benjamin, but I had given up this idea and did not wish to go with him into that room or the children's bedroom.

Without turning around, I took off my dress by the sofa and everything else as well. As I did this he kissed the back of my neck.

That evening he took me to a restaurant on Place de la Nation. He smiled at me across the table and I felt that nothing was quite real, that I was not truly myself. He told me of a prank he had played with Little Louis on a stingy customer, I was not listening carefully to what he said, too busy looking at him, but I laughed to see him laughing. He told me: 'You should laugh more often, Elodie. The Inuit, the people we call Eskimos, they say when a woman laughs a man should count the teeth she shows, for he will take the same number of seals on his next hunt.' I laughed again, but not for long enough for him to count on more than five or six in the bag. He told me: 'No matter, we'll order something else, I never did like seal.'

Walking me home in the darkness of the Rue de Sergent-Bauchat, he slipped an arm around my shoulders. Our steps echoed in an empty world. No suffering anywhere, no tears, no mourning, no one anywhere or any thought for tomorrow. On the front step of my building his large hands were holding mine, his boater was tipped back on his head, he told me: 'If you asked me to come up it would make me happy.'

He came up.

The following afternoon I went to his place, on the Rue Daval, a room beneath the eaves. His workshop was down in the courtyard.

The day after that, Thursday, he came back to my flat for lunch. He brought red roses, a cherry tart, his trusting smile. We ate our meal naked, after making love. And we made love all afternoon. He was taking the train in the morning. He had told the truth to the woman he had lived with before the war, and she had left him, taking all her belongings I pretended not to see the day before. He said: 'These things always work out in the end.' Time . . . I do not know if I loved him, if he loved me, outside of the laughable interlude I have described to you. Today I remember the last time I saw Kléber. He was on the landing just about to go downstairs. I stood at my door. He tipped his boater, he smiled, his voice was so low it was almost a murmur, he said: 'When you think of me, show him many seals. You'll bring me luck.'

I believe you understand what followed, at least what Benjamin made of those three days, since you asked me in the car, in the pouring rain, if I was the reason they quarrelled. They quarrelled because we are people, not things, and no one, not even the war, can change that.

I did not get pregnant. Flying in the face of everything, Benjamin was stubbornly jealous, or he became that way. He must have pushed Kléber to the limit and so heard truths that were unbearable. And once again, time did its work. Benjamin's questions in his letters, after he learned he had gained nothing in lending me to his friend, were like a hail of bullets: how and where I had undressed, had it upset me to be possessed by another, how many times during those three days, in what position, and above all, aching, throbbing, that obsession with finding out if I'd shared his pleasure. Yes, I had shared it, from the first time to the last. I can certainly tell you: that had never happened to me before. My mason? I had naïvely imagined I felt the woman's share of it, less than what one finds stroking oneself in bed. Benjamin? To please him, I would pretend.

The hour is late, the gentleman who was with you will come for this letter. I think I have told you everything. I never saw Benjamin again, I never saw Kléber again, and in 1917 I found out by chance, which makes such a bad job of things, that he was not ever going to come home either. Now I work, I raise my children as best I can. The two oldest, Frédéric and Martine, help me as much as they are able. I am twenty-eight years old, I wish only to forget. I trust in what he said, the man of my interlude: the only master of us all is time.

Adieu, mademoiselle.
Elodie Gordes.

Isaac Babel

TREASON

Arguably the most important result of the First World War was the Russian Revolution of October 1917. One of the most vivid descriptions of the events that followed the Revolution can be found in Isaac Babel's collection of short stories, Red Cavalry (1926). *A bespectacled Jewish intellectual, the author participated as a war correspondent in the Red Army campaign in Poland in 1920 where he joined a regiment of Cossacks – former Tsarist troops and the feared enemy of the Eastern European Jews, but now part of the Red Army.*

Although he is passionately on the side of the Revolution, Babel gives a devastating account of the barbarism of war. 'Treason', however, is one of his lighter stories, and although originally written as a propaganda piece on Red Army morale, today it reads more like a parody.

COMRADE INVESTIGATOR BURDENKO. To your question I reply that my Party number is 2400, issued to Nikita Balmashov by the Krasnodar Party Committee. My life before 1914 I explain as domestic: I did arable farming with my parents and transferred from arable farming into the ranks of the Imperialists to defend Citizen Poincaré* and the butcher

---

* President of the French Republic.

of the German Revolution, Ebert-Noske* – they, one must suppose, were asleep and as they slept dreamed of a way to lend assistance to my native settlement of St Ivan in the Kuban district. And so the rope uncoiled until the time when Comrade Lenin together with Comrade Trotsky redirected my brutal bayonet and pointed it towards a given set of intestines and a new piece of belly fat that suited it better. Ever since that day, I bear the number 2400 on the butt of my sharp-eyed bayonet, and it is rather embarrassing and all too ridiculous for me to hear now from you, Comrade Investigator Burdenko, this unseemly cock and bull story about the unknown N— Hospital. I don't give a shit about that hospital, and almost never fired at it or attacked it – it could not have happened. Being wounded, we all three of us, namely the soldier Golovitsyn, the soldier Kustov and I, had a fever in our bones, and did not attack, but only wept, standing in hospital dressing-gowns in the square amidst the free population, Jews by nationality. And regarding the three panes of glass which we damaged with an officer's revolver, I tell you on my honour that the panes were not serving their appointed purpose, being in the storeroom where they were not needed. Even Dr Yaveyn, seeing this bitter shooting of ours, merely made mockery with various smiles, standing at the window of his hospital, which can also be confirmed by the above-mentioned free Jews of the town of Kozin. Concerning Dr Yaveyn I can also, Comrade Investigator, submit the material evidence that he made fun of us when the three of us wounded men, namely the soldier Golovitsyn, the soldier Kustov and I, originally presented ourselves for treatment, and with his very first words he announced to us, all too coarsely: 'You fighting men will each of you go and take a bath in the bathroom and drop your weapons and your clothes this minute; I'm afraid there'll be an infection from them, they're going straight into my storeroom . . .' Where-upon, beholding in front of him a beast, and not a man,

---

* Ebert was the President of the German Weimar Republic and Noske his Minister of Defence. Balmashov conflates them into one person.

soldier Kustov stuck out his broken leg and questioned how there could be any infection in a sharp Kuban sabre, except for the enemies of our revolution, and was also interested to find out more about the storeroom, whether there was really a Party soldier there in charge of the stuff or, on the contrary, one of the non-Party masses. Then Dr Yaveyn evidently realized that we were perfectly able to understand treason. He turned his back and, without another word, sent us off to the ward, and again with various smiles, where we went hobbling on various legs, waving our crippled arms and holding on to one another, as the three of us are countrymen from the St Ivan settlement, namely Comrade Golovitsyn, Comrade Kustov and I, we are countrymen with the same fate and whoever's got a broken leg holds his comrade by the arm, and whoever doesn't have an arm leans on his comrade's shoulder. In accordance with the order that had been issued, we went into the ward, where we expected to see cultural-education work and devotion to the cause, but what did we see as we entered the ward? We saw Red Army men, all of them infantry, sitting on the made beds playing draughts, and with them tall nurses, completely smooth, standing by the windows and doling out sympathy. At the sight of this, we stopped as though we had been struck by thunder.

'Your war's over, lads,' I exclaim to the wounded men.

'That's right, it is,' the wounded men reply, moving their draughts that are made of bread.

'It's a bit soon,' I says to the wounded men, 'it's a bit soon for you soldiers to have finished with the war when the enemy is moving about softly-softly fifteen versts from the town and when one reads in the *Red Trooper* newspaper that our international position is just horrible and the horizon is filled with clouds.' But my words bounced off the heroic soldiers like sheep droppings off a regimental drum, and instead of a proper conversation what happened was that the sisters of mercy led us over to our beds and again began to go on and on about giving up our arms, as though we'd already been beaten! They caused Kustov no end of agitation on that account, and he began picking at his wound, which was

111

situated on his left shoulder, above the valiant heart of a fighting man and proletarian. Seeing this, the nurses quietened down a bit, but they quietened down only for a very short time, and then started once more to engage in the jeering that is common to the non-Party masses and began to send those who were willing to haul the clothes off us as we slept or made us play theatrical roles for cultural-educational work dressed in women's clothes, which is not seemly.

Unmerciful sisters. Several times they tried using sleeping powder to get our clothes, so we began to take turns at sleeping, keeping one eye open, and even went to the toilet on lesser business in full uniform with revolvers. And when we had suffered like this for a week and a day we began to ramble in our speech, had visions and, finally, waking up on the accursed morning of 4 August, saw that we were lying in numbered overalls like penal convicts, without our weapons and without the clothes that had been woven by our mothers, those weak old women in the Kuban . . . And the sun, we saw, was shining gloriously, and the trench soldiers, among whom we three Red cavalrymen had suffered so much, were making fools of us, and with them the unmerciful sisters, having slipped us sleeping powder the night before, were now shaking their young breasts at us and bringing us cocoa in dishes, and milk in the cocoa enough to drown in! At the sight of this merry carousal the soldiers thumped their crutches horribly loud and pinched our sides as though we were prostitutes, saying that Budyonny's First Cavalry Army had finished its war, too. But no, curly-headed comrades who feed your very marvellous bellies so that at night you sound like machine-guns, it has not finished its war, and all it was was that, having asked to leave the room like it was for necessary business, the three of us went outside into the yard and from the yard we rushed all in a fever and with black gaping wounds to Citizen Boyderman, the chairman of the district revolutionary committee, without whom, Comrade Investigator Burdenko, this misunderstanding about the shooting most possibly would never have existed, i.e. without that chairman who made us completely lose our wits. And although we can give no firm material evidence against Citizen Boyderman, the thing is that when we looked in on the chairman we directed our attention upon a citizen of elderly years in a sheepskin coat, a Jew by nationality, who was sitting at a table, a table so piled with papers that it is not a pretty sight to see . . . He casts his eyes now this way, now that, and it's plain to see that he can't make head nor tail of those papers, those papers are a misery to him, all the more so when I tell you that unknown but honoured soldiers go in threateningly to see Citizen Boyderman and ask him for rations, and if it's not them it's local Party workers reporting on counter-revolution in the surrounding villages, and then immediately rank and file workers from the Centre appear, wanting to get married in the district revolutionary committee in the very shortest time and without delay . . . So we too with raised voices explained the incident of treason at the hospital, but Citizen Boyderman only stared at us, and cast his eyes now this way, now that, and stroked our shoulders, which is not authority and is unworthy of authority, issued no resolution of any kind, but merely announced: 'Comrade soldiers, if you love Soviet authority, then leave these premises,' to which we were unable to agree, i.e. to leave the premises, but demanded to see his identity card, on the non-production of which we lost consciousness. And, being without consciousness, we came out on to the square in front of the hospital, where we disarmed the militia in the person of one cavalry-man and with tears in our eyes violated three poor-quality panes of glass in the above-mentioned storeroom. In the face of this inadmissible fact, Dr Yaveyn made faces and mocking grimaces, and this at the moment when Comrade Kustov was about to die of his illness within four days!

In his short Red life Comrade Kustov was agitated about treason beyond all bounds, that treason that is winking at us from the window, there it goes, mocking at the coarse proletariat, but the proletariat, comrades, knows itself that it's coarse, this causes us pain, it burns our souls and tears with fire the prisons of our bodies and the gaols of our hateful ribs . . .

Treason, I tell you, Comrade Investigator Burdenko, is laughing at us from the window, treason is up and about in our house with its boots off, treason has thrown its boots over its shoulder so as not to make the floorboards creak in the house it is burgling . . .

Laurie Lee

THANK GOD FOR THE WAR

The Spanish Civil War (1936–9) was the politically most significant conflict between the two world wars, second in importance only to the Russian Revolution. It drew volunteers from all over the world who joined the Republican army to defend democracy against the Fascist troops of General Franco.

It is strange, however, that so little fiction has come out of the Spanish Civil War. With the notable exception of Ernest Hemingway's For Whom the Bell Tolls, *the best-known works on the war are memoirs, such as George Orwell's* Homage to Catalonia *or, from a Spanish perspective, Arturo Barea's trilogy,* The Forging of a Rebel.

Laurie Lee too published his reminiscences in the form of a memoir, A Moment of War *(1991), although in recent years attention has been brought to the fictional character of his writing. The following extract recounts what life was like in the International Brigade – and how the war had some rather unexpected liberating effects.*

ON A BLEAK naked hill above the town, Figueras Castle stood like a white acropolis – a picturesque assemblage of towers and turrets, walled in by great slabs of stone. The approach road was suitably stark and forbidding, but once I'd passed inside the huge nail-studded doors, I got an impression of almost monastic calm. Indeed the Castle, clamped down on these rocks many centuries ago as a show of force commanding Spain's northern frontiers, appeared now as something a touch over-theatrical, and rather lacking any original ferocity.

But this was the 'Barracks', the place to which I had been delivered, the collecting point for volunteers entering Spain from the north. My escort, warmer and more cheerful now after several more stops on the road for anis and coñac, seemed in a natural hurry to get rid of me, and pushed me inside a glass-fronted box-office just inside the gate.

'We brought you another one!' he shouted to anyone who might be listening. 'He's English, I think – or Dutch.' With that, he threw my bags across the floor, slapped me on the back, gave me a heavy-lidded wink and left.

An official, bowed at his tiny desk, looked at me with a kind of puff-eyed indifference. Then he sniffed, asked me my name and my next of kin, and wrote down my answers in a child's exercise book. As he wrote he followed the motions of the pen with his tongue, breathing hard and sniffing rhythmically as he did so. Finally, he asked for my passport and threw it into a drawer, in which I saw a number of others of different colours.

'We'll take care of that for you,' he said. 'Would you like some prophylactics?'

Not knowing what these were, I nevertheless said yes, and he handed me a bagful which I stowed away in my pocket. Next he gave me a new hundred peseta note, a forage-cap with a tassel, and said, 'You are now in the Republican Army.' He considered me dimly for a moment, then suddenly shot to his feet, raised his fist and saluted.

'Welcome, comrade!' he cried. 'You won't be here long. As soon as we collect a convoy together we pass you away. In the meantime you have training, political education, fraternal discussion, much to do. Study victory. See a doctor. Dismiss!'

He spoke with a curious accent. It could have been Catalan or French. He kicked my bags back towards me and turned away. I picked them up and went out into the courtyard.

It was now about noon, with the sun at its low winter strength, and across the northern horizon the mountains caught it like broken glass, each peak flashing with blue and white light. Away to the south the land sank in frozen waves, while to the east lay the violet sea. After my two weeks underground the light burned my eyes, and it took some while to get used to the view, focus on its range and open distances, which were immense and exhilarating. The Castle and its courtyard seemed lifted in pure blue air and pressed close to a cold clear sky. I ceased to wonder how I had got here at last. It was simply a moment of magical arrival.

The Castle courtyard was bounded by a bare white-washed wall along the top of which stood pots of crumpled geraniums. Some thirty or forty men lounged round the base of the wall, talking and smoking or eating lumps of bread. A ragged lot, dressed in an odd medley of clothes – some in civvies (as I was), others in long capes like Berbers, or in flashy jackets like white African hunters, while some had their heads thrust through jagged holes cut from the middle of military blankets.

I sat down on the edge of a little group, and was addressed in English by a chap who called himself Danny. Danny was a bone-thin Londoner, all nose and chin, with a small bent body and red wrinkled hands. He was twenty-two, an unemployed docker from Bermondsey, undernourished and frail; when he moved, his limbs seemed to flap and flutter like wallpaper on an abandoned house.

''Ere we are then, eh?' he kept saying with a kind of sneezing giggle. Over and over again. Peering at me, then at the great mountain landscape, and clasping his bony knees with his hands. 'Said I'd never make it – the lads. The old woman too. What they call this then? I got 'ere, didn't I?'

He'd clench up his tiny hands and look round him with a trembling squint. A shaking hiss came out of his thin sad mouth. 'We're 'ere then, ain't we? . . . Eh, Doug? Eh?' He turned to a man squatting beside him. 'An' 'ere's another one, eh?' he said, pointing a finger at me. 'They're coming over in bleedin' droves.'

The Scot looked at me bleakly, as though he doubted I'd be much of a reinforcement. They'd been at the Barracks a week, they said, and both showed a mixture of bravado and bewilderment, though the Scot also seemed to have a profane contempt for most of the others around him.

'Look at this bugga',' he said, jerking a finger at Danny. ''E dunno a gun fra' a stick a' rock. If we canna' do better'n tha', Guid 'elp us.'

Danny stiffened and gave him a shrivelled look.

'But we're 'ere then, ennit?' he said.

It was true – and we were. Danny pointed out the others gathered in the courtyard, sitting and standing in their little groups, some playing cards, or just whistling, or staring into the distance, some fast asleep with the daylight exhaustion of waiting. Everybody was here, said Danny: Dutch, Germans and Poles. Exiles from Paris, a sprinkling of thugs on the run from Marseilles, a few Welshmen from the valleys, some Durham miners, Catalans, Canadians, Americans, Czechs, and half a dozen pale and speechless Russians.

The Welsh, in their huddles, were talking Welsh. The Durham miners were protesting about the food. The Scot, who seemed to have found some brandy from somewhere, was rising on the peak of spluttering Olympian disdain.

'We gotta anni-hi-late the lot of 'em,' he growled. 'Teach 'em political authority. Or wipe 'em all out. Thas what we gotta do.'

''E's so drunk,' said Danny, ''e don't know which side 'e's on yet – do ya, you 'eathen bastard?'

Two young men, in dark suits, were playing chess on the ground, using stones in scratched squares in the sand. They were solemn, concerned, and cast disapproving glances at Doug. They talked together formally, in the accents of clerks.

This, again, was not quite what I'd expected. In this special army I'd imagined a shoulder-to-shoulder brotherhood, a brave camaraderie joined in one purpose, not this fragmentation of national groups scattered around the courtyard talking wanly only to each other. Indeed, they seemed to share a mutual air of unease and watchfulness, of distrust and even dislike.

I left Danny and Doug and wandered casually around,

pretending I'd been here for weeks. But the pattern of that first morning was to be repeated during the whole length of my stay. The French crooks crouched in corners, shrugging and scowling; the Poles sat in princely silence sunning their beautiful cheekbones. The Czechs scribbled pamphlets and passed them to each other for correction; while the Russians seemed to come and go mysteriously as by tricks of the light. The British played cards and swore.

But we were a young and unclassifiable bunch on the whole, with mixed motives and humours, waiting to test our nerves in new fields of belief. The Castle and its courtyard was our starting-point – a square of pale sunlight surrounded by snow.

How had we all got here? Some by boat, some by illegal train-shuttles from France, but most smuggled from Perpignan by lorry. I hadn't known, in my solitary ignorance, that there was this well-organized traffic for volunteers running from London through Paris into Spain. Which was why I'd done the daft thing and come on my own, and even chosen winter to do it. Nevertheless, I heard later that my progress had not gone altogether unnoticed. I must have been watched through France, and all the way from Perpignan. Of that I was never entirely certain, but if it was true it probably saved my life.

Figueras had once been a fine hill town, with ordered streets and pretty houses, and open spaces for walking in the evening. War had shrivelled and emptied it, covered it with a sort of grey hapless grime so that even the windows seemed to have no reflections. The gathering twilight also seemed to bring an unnatural silence, as if all life had gone into hiding.

Down near the station, however, were a couple of low-roofed taverns, bare and cold, with streaming wet floors. Doug and Ulli led me first into one, and then into the other, where they were clearly already well known and where the stooping old women behind the bar threw up their hands at the sight of them.

They were not the taverns I remembered – those with great sweating wine-casks and glistening bottles labelled with posturing bullfighters. Indeed, I could see no drink at all, so in the second bar I asked for some coffee, and was given a glass of hot brown silt tasting of leather and rust.

'Leave all tha',' said Doug, 'an' come along wi' us.' We went down some steps into a dim-lit cellar whose walls were covered with anarchist posters – vivid stark images of fists and faces, mouths crying defiance, shouting blasts for freedom, guns and flags held high, banners billowing with slogans, all in bright, hard, primary colours.

A thin old man in a corner quickly turned his back on us as we entered, bent low, and tried to hide something under his cloak. There was a brief flapping and squawking from between his legs as he furtively pushed a chicken into a sack.

'All right, Josepe,' said Ulli, poking round the littered cellar. 'Where is it? Out with it, man.'

'Ay – ay,' wheezed the ancient. 'Again the Frenchman, by God! Why don't you go away to your country?'

Ulli, in Spanish, and Doug, with black Scots oaths, began to bully and tease the old man till he folded and scrabbled across the room. Mumbling of foreign evils and the curses of war, he searched through some sacking and turned up a stained goatskin flask.

We sat on the floor and passed it round between us. It was a country *coñac*, vitriolic and burning.

Josepe kept the struggling chicken huddled under his cloak and watched us peevishly while we drank. The black hairy flask smelt richly of goat and resin, the *coñac* of bitter oils. But it stung, and warmed us deep inside, just right for three men sitting on a cellar floor.

'Bless this place,' Doug grunted, wiping his mouth. 'I never wanna leave it – never.'

Danny came suddenly down the steps on his little web-like feet, noiseless, nose-poking, apologetic.

'Well, 'oo'd a' believed it?' he giggled. ''Ere we are again then, eh? Got a drop left for me? No offence, a' course.'

Doug looked at him with distaste, but passed him the

coñac. Danny nodded jerkily to each of us, and drank.

Only a few days in Spain, ripe for Freedom and the Cause, and here we were, squatting in the cellar of a northern tavern, bullying a crazed old man and getting drunk.

When we'd emptied a third leather flask, Josepe begged plaintively for payment, and Doug gave him a new hundred peseta note.

'No, no!' whimpered Josepe, waving it away.

'Guid Goverrment money,' said Doug, screwing it into his hand. 'Take it mon – it's a soldier's wages.'

The old man bunched up his knees and hissed and grizzled, pushing at Doug with his tiny fists.

'No, no!' he wailed. 'It is not to be borne! Carmelita! Eulalia! Come!'

A slim gliding figure, as light as a greyhound, moved softly down the cellar steps. The man reached out a shaking hand and gripped the girl by the shoulder while the chicken broke from his cloak and flew into the wall.

'Where've you been, whore?' he growled, pinching the girl viciously. 'Why did you leave me again to the Frenchmen?'

She turned her head towards us.

'Give him something,' she whispered. 'Belt, scarf, cigarettes – anything. But quickly; he's going mad.'

The girl wore the tight black dress of the villages, and had long Spanish-Indian eyes. She pushed the old man up the stairs and told him to go to bed. Doug, Ulli and Danny followed behind him, singing brokenly and urging him on.

A winter sunset glow shone through a high grille in the wall, and I was aware, behind the sharp smell of coñac, of something softer and muskier. The young girl, crouching low in the shadows, had loosened her dress and was pouring brandy over her bare bruised shoulder.

She rubbed the liquor into her flesh with long brown fingers and watched me warily as she did so. Her eyes were like slivers of painted glass, glinting in the setting sun. I heard the boys upstairs stamping and singing to the breathy music of an old accordion. But I couldn't join them. I was trapped down here, in this place, this cellar, to the smell of *coñac* and this sleek animal girl.

She was stroking, almost licking, her upper arms, like a cat, her neck arched, her dark head bowed. She raised her eyes again, and we just stared at each other before I sat down beside her. Without a word, she handed me the flask of *coñac*, turned her bare shoulder towards me, and waited. Her skin was mottled by small purple bruises that ran backwards under her dress. I poured some drops of *coñac* into the palm of my hand and began to rub it awkwardly over her damp hot flesh. The girl sighed and stiffened, then swayed against me, leading me into a rhythm of her own.

The frayed black dress was now loose at the edges and gave way jerkily to my clumsy fingers. The girl's eyes were fixed on mine with a kind of rapt impatience. With a slight swerve of her shoulders she offered more flesh for healing. I rubbed more coñac into the palms of my hands. Slowly, as my touch followed her, she lay back on the sacking. The boys upstairs were singing 'Home on the Range'.

Apart from the quick stopping and starting of her breath, the girl was silent. The red blanket of sunset moved over her. Her thin dancer's body was now almost bare to the waist and revealed all the wispy fineness of a Persian print. It seemed that in some perverse way she wished to show both her beauty and its blemishes. Or perhaps she didn't care. She held my hands still for a moment.

'Frenchman,' she said thickly.

'English,' I said woodenly.

She shrugged, and whispered a light bubbling profanity – not Catalan but pure Andaluz. Her finger and thumb closed on my wrist like a manacle. Her body met mine with the quick twist of a snake.

When the square of sunset had at last moved away and died, we lay panting gently, and desert dry. I took a swig from the goatskin and offered it to her. She shook her head, but lay close as though to keep me warm. A short while ago she had been a thing of panicky gasps and whimpers. Now she looked into my eyes like a mother.

'My little blond man,' she said tenderly. 'Young, so young.'

'How old are you, then?' I asked.

'Fifteen . . . sixteen – who knows?' She sat up suddenly, still only half-dressed, her delicate bruised shoulders arched proudly.

'I kill him.'

'Who?'

'The old one. The grandfather. He maltreats . . . Thank God for the war.'

The chicken, huddled fluffily against the wall in the corner, seemed now to be asleep. The girl turned and tidied me briskly, then tidied herself, settling her clothes around her sweet small limbs. Then she lifted her long loose hair and fastened it into a shining bun. The stamping and singing upstairs had stopped.

I was astonished that this hour had been so simple yet secret, the opening and closing of velvet doors. Eulalia was not the sort of Spanish girl I'd known in the past – the noisy steel-edged virgins flirting from the safety of upstairs windows, or loud arm-in-arm with other girls in the *paseo*, sensual, cheeky, confident of their powers, but scared to be alone with a man.

Eulalia, with her beautiful neck and shoulders, also had a quiet dignity and grace. A wantonness, too, so sudden and unexpected, I felt it was a wantonness given against her will. Or at least, if not given willingly, it was now part of her nature, the result of imposed habit and tutoring.

As she pulled on her tattered slippers, she told me she would not stay long in Figueras. She'd come from the south, she said – she didn't know where – and had been working here as a house-drudge since she was ten. Once she would have stayed on till body and mind were used up; the sexually abused slattern of some aged employer, sleeping under the stairs between calls to his room. Not any more, she was now free to do as she wished. Spain had changed, and the new country had braver uses for girls such as she. She need stay no longer with this brutal pig of an innkeeper. She would go to Madrid and be a soldier.

It had grown dark and cold in the cellar. Suddenly she turned and embraced me, wrapping me urgently in her hot thin arms.

'Frenchman!' she whispered. 'At last I have found my brother.'

'Englishman,' I said, as she slipped away.

The next day, in the evening, a child brought me a message, and as soon as I was free I slipped down to the town. This time I went alone, but not immediately to Josepe's, but first to an old wine bar up near the Plaza. The first man I saw was the giraffe-necked Frenchman from the Pyrenees who had guided me over the last peak of the mountains. He'd been taciturn, gruff: 'Don't do this for everyone,' he'd said. 'Don't think we run conducted tours.' Which was exactly what he was doing, as I could see now. Beret and leather jacket, long neck still lagged with a scarf, he stood in the centre of the bar talking to a group of hatless young men, each looking slightly bewildered and carrying little packages. Smoking with rapid puffs, eyes shifting and watchful, marshalling his charges with special care, he handed each one a French cigarette, then pushed them towards the door. His coat was new, and his shoes well polished, and clearly he had walked no mountain paths lately. Perhaps he'd brought this little group across the frontier by truck. As he left the room, he brushed against me, caught my eye for a moment and winked . . .

I went down the street in the freezing rain and found Felipe's bar closed and dark. Through a crack in the shutters I could see a glimmer of candles and some old women sitting by a black wooden box. Bunches of crape hung over the mirror behind the bar which was littered with broken bottles. I was wondering why, and from whom, the message had been sent up to the Barracks. It had certainly been laconic enough. The boy had simply sidled in and asked me if I was 'Lorenzo the Frenchman', and then muttered, 'You've got to go down to Felipe's.'

I knocked on the door and presently one of the old women

let me in. She asked who I was and I told her. 'Where's Don Felipe?' I said, and she showed her gums briefly, then said, 'Bang! He's gone to the angels.' She stabbed a finger at the open box, and there he was, his face black and shining like a piece of coal. 'Bang!' said the old woman again, with a titter, then crossed herself. 'God forgive him.'

Where was Eulalia? I asked. 'She went in a camion,' she said. 'An hour ago. Away over there . . .' I could get no more from her, except that the old man had been shot and that, in her opinion, he was without shame and deserved it.

Looking into the crone's bright death-excited eyes, and smelling the hot pork-fat of the candles, I knew that this was not a wake, or even a mourning, but a celebration of something cleared from their lives. I also knew that Eulalia, my murderous little dancer, had called me to show me what she'd done, but called me too late, and had gone.

André Malraux

CRASH

First published in 1937, André Malraux's Days of Hope *gives an optimistic account of the first months of the Spanish Civil War when with initial victories over the Fascists, everything seemed to be going well. Malraux, who had helped to organize an international air squadron to fight for the Republican cause, cast his experiences as a novel and here describes the tragic outcome of an unsuccessful air raid.*

ATTIGNIES WAS SEMBRANO'S bomber. The crews of the two planes had been mixed up: in his machine were Pol, the mechanic, and Attignies. Sembrano had brought his second pilot with him, a Basque named Reyes. At their southernmost aerodrome they had found some bombs that they had had to change, and a degree of confusion worthy of Toledo; nearing Malaga, the refugees one hundred and fifty thousand strong, streaming along the coast road; then, beyond, the Fascist cruisers trailing their smoke-clouds through the brilliant morning light as they made for Almeria; finally, the first of the combined Italian and Spanish motorized columns. Seen from the planes, it looked as if it must catch up the exodus within a few hours. Attignies and Sembrano had exchanged glances and come down as low as possible. Nothing more could be seen of the column.

To speed his return, Sembrano opened out his engine and turned out to sea.

When Attignies looked round, the mechanic was rubbing his hands, which were covered with oil from the bomb-releasing controls. Attignies looked at the sky in front again, full of round clusters of cumulus-cloud reminding him of the animated cartoons; eighteen enemy pursuit planes – overdue – were approaching in two groups. And still more behind, probably.

Their bullets began whizzing through the front gun-turret.

Sembrano felt a ferocious cudgel-blow on his right arm, which went limp. He turned to the second pilot: 'Catch hold of the stick!' Reyes was holding not the joystick but his stomach, with both hands. But for the belt which held him up, he would have fallen on top of Attignies, who lay prone behind his seat, with one foot a mass of blood. Now that the enemy fighter was behind their plane, it would probably fire on them from above; there was no possible protection; faced with that number of enemies, the five Republican fighters had to cover the escape of the other heavy bomber, which was in a better position to put up a fight. The holes in the fuselage were like shell-holes: the Italians were using big quick-firers. Was the tail gunner wounded?

As Sembrano turned to look, the starboard engine caught his eye; it was alight. Sembrano cut it out; all his machine-gunners had stopped firing now. The plane was losing height every second. Attignies was bending over Reyes, who was down off his seat and calling repeatedly for something to drink. 'A stomach-wound,' thought Sembrano. A new enemy onslaught swept over the plane, only hitting the right wing. Sembrano was piloting with his feet and his left arm. Blood was trickling gently down his cheek; he had probably been hit in the head, too, but he felt no pain. The plane sank lower and lower. Behind, Malaga; beneath, the sea. Just the other side of a strip of sand ten yards wide, a reef of rocks.

Parachutes were out of the question. The enemy fighter was following, and their machine was already too low. To climb was impossible; the elevator, probably torn by the explosive bullets, scarcely answered the controls. The water was so near now that the lower gunner drew in his projecting turret and lay flat in the cockpit; his legs, too, were covered with blood. Reyes had closed his eyes and was talking Basque. The wounded men were no longer watching the enemy fighter, from which only a few final bullets were reaching them now; they were watching the sea. Several of them could not swim – if swimming were possible with an explosive bullet in one's foot, arm, or stomach. They were more than half a mile from the shore, and a hundred feet above the sea; beneath them, twelve or fourteen feet of water. The enemy fighter returned, opening fire with every gun again; the bullets wove a pattern of red streaks like a spider's web around their plane. Beneath Sembrano the clear calm morning waves threw back the sunlight placidly; the best thing was to shut one's eyes and let the plane drop slowly down, until . . . Suddenly he noticed Pol's face, alarmed, blood-stained, but still to all appearances jubilant. Spurts of red flame flashed round the blood-soaked cockpit, in which Attignies was now bending over Reyes, who was down off his seat and seemed to be *in extremis*. Pol's face, the only one of which Sembrano could get a full view, was also streaming wet; but in the smooth cheeks of the fat, vivacious Jew burned such a desire for life that the pilot made a last effort to use his right arm. The arm had disappeared. With all the strength of his legs and left arm he pulled the plane's nose up.

Pol, who had lowered the wheels, now began to take them in again. The body of the plane glided along the surface of the water like a flying-boat; for a moment it slowed up, then plunged deeper into the waves and capsized. They struggled against the water which came flooding into the plane, like so many drowned cats. It stopped short of what was now the roof of the body. Pol threw himself against the door, tried to open it in the normal way, downwards; failed, realized that now that they were upside down he ought to look for the handle at the top, but the door had been jammed by an explosive bullet. Sembrano, having righted himself in the overturned plane after seeing the pilot's cabin tilt over in front of him, was groping for his arm in the water like a dog chasing its tail; the blood from his wound was leaving bright red stains in the water, already pink, that filled the cockpit, but his arm was where it should be. The lower gunner had forced a way through one of the main panels of his turret, which had come open during the somersault. Sembrano, Attignies, Pol, and he succeeded in getting out and at last found themselves facing the endless stream of fugitives, with the upper halves of their bodies in the open air and their legs in the water.

Attignies was shouting as he propped himself against the mechanic. But the waves drowned his voice. Maybe the peasants saw him beckoning to them as they fled, but that was all. And Attignies knew that each member of a crowd believes that an appeal for help is meant for his neighbour. A peasant was walking along the beach. Attignies crawled as far as the sand: 'Come and help them!' he shouted as soon as he was within earshot. 'Can't swim,' the other answered. 'It's not deep.' The peasant stood there. When he saw Attignies close beside him, out of the water, he said at last: 'I've got a family.' And moved away. It may have been true, and what help was to be expected from a man who would leave that headlong flight to wait patiently for the Fascists? Perhaps he was suspicious; Attignies's fair and strongly moulded head looked too much like the Malaga peasant's conception of a German pilot. In the east, the Republican planes were just disappearing over the tops of the mountains. 'Let's hope that they'll send a car for us,' Attignies muttered.

Pol and Sembrano had got all the wounded out, and had carried them to the beach.

A group of *milicianos* broke off from the surging mass of fugitives. Poised on the roadside embankment, and as a result much taller than the crowd, they seemed more in keeping with the rocks and heavy banks of cloud than with living things; as though nothing which did not join in the stampede could be alive. Their eyes fixed on the plane, which was burning itself out and sending short flames out of the waves that hid the colour of the wing-bands, they dominated the rush of jutting shoulders and upraised hands like keepers of some legendary vigil. Between their legs, wide splayed to resist the sea-wind, the heads seemed fluttering past like dead leaves. At last they began moving down towards Attignies. 'Help the wounded!' They waded out to the plane, step by step, impeded by the water. The last man stopped and took Attignies's arm on his shoulder.

'D'you know where there's a telephone?' Attignies asked him.

'Yes.'

The *miliciano* belonged to the village trainband; without artillery and without machine-guns, they were going to attempt to defend their homes of rubble against the Italian mechanized columns. On the road, in tacit sympathy with them, one hundred and fifty thousand unarmed citizens out of the two hundred thousand inhabitants of Malaga were flying till their last breath from 'the liberator of Spain'.

They stopped half-way up the bank. 'People who say bullet-wounds don't hurt can have this one!' thought Attignies; and the sea-water did not improve matters. Above the embankment, the bent figures were still retreating eastwards; some walking, some running. In front of many mouths a fist held up an ill-defined object, as if all were playing on some silent bugle; they were eating. Some short, thick, vegetable; celery, perhaps.

'There's a field of them,' said the *miliciano*. An old woman trotted down the bank, shrieking; went up to Attignies and held out a bottle. 'The poor things poor little lads!' She saw the others below, withdrew her bottle before Attignies had taken it, and hurried down as quickly as she could, shouting the same words again and again.

Attignies trudged up the slope, leaning on the *miliciano*. Women went running past, stopped, started to scream when they saw the wounded airmen and still smouldering plane, and ran on.

'The Sunday promenade,' reflected Attignies bitterly, as he reached the road. Against the background of the noises of the flight, punctuated by the pulsing of the sea, another sound, and one which Attignies recognized, was growing more insistent every second: an enemy pursuit plane. The crowd scattered; they had already been bombed and machine-gunned.

It was making straight for the big bomber, where the last flames were dying into the sea. The *milicianos* were already carrying the wounded away; they would reach the road before the enemy plane arrived. They did their best to make the crowd lie down but nobody heard them. On Sembrano's instructions the *milicianos* laid the wounded at the foot of the little wall. The plane came down very low, circling over the multi-seater, which with its undercarriage sticking into the air and the glowing sparks coursing over it looked like a chicken on a spit. A photograph was no doubt taken, and the plane flew away again. 'Don't forget your lorries' feet are sticking in the air as well!' Attignies grinned.

A cart was passing. Attignies stopped it, and took his arm off the *miliciano*'s shoulder. A peasant girl gave up her place for him, and went and squatted between an old woman's legs. The cart started off again. There were five peasants in it. Nobody had asked any questions, and Attignies had not said a word; the whole world, just then, was moving in the same direction.

Heinrich Böll

THE POSTCARD

When Heinrich Schnitzler, the protagonist of Böll's post-humously published novel, The Silent Angel *(1992), returns to the ruins of his hometown at the end of the Second World War, he recalls the deceptively undramatic way the war had first entered his life.*

THE POSTCARD ARRIVED one morning while he was still sleeping, on the first day of his vacation and his mother had thought, It's nothing important. The postman had handed her a whole packet: the newspaper, a few catalogues, a letter, a statement of account for her pension, and she'd signed a receipt for something or other. Anyhow it was hard to see in the semi-darkness of the vestibule, and it was dark in the hall as well; only indirect light entered through the large greenish glazing above the hallway door. His mother had leafed through the pile quickly and tossed the postcard on the table in the hall before she went into the kitchen, an ordinary printed postcard that she considered totally unimportant.

He slept late that day. It was the first day of his life, if you could call it a life. Up till then everything had been school – school, poverty, apprenticeship, hardship – and the day before he'd finally passed his apprentice's exam and gone on vacation . . .

*

When she returned he was still sleeping, and the small, white postcard was still lying there. She put her shopping bag on the table and picked up the small, typed card, and now, in spite of the darkness, she suddenly saw the strange red marks on it, a white card with a red rectangle, and inside the red rectangle, spiderlike, a thick black *R*. A vague feeling of uneasiness swept over her. She let the card fall to the table; there was something strange about it. She didn't know you could register postcards, too; a registered postcard seemed suspicious, it frightened her. She picked up her bag quickly and went into the kitchen. Maybe it's a certificate from the chamber of commerce, she thought, or some professional group like that, saying that he's passed his exam, something important that had to be registered. She felt no curiosity, just uneasiness. She set the bowl down on the table and pushed open the shutter because it had suddenly turned dark outside, and saw the first drops already beginning to fall in the courtyard, plump, round drops, falling slowly and heavily, fat ink blots on the asphalt. The carpenters stood in their blue aprons in the courtyard in front of their shop, quickly draping a canvas over a large window frame. The drops fell faster and more thickly, rattling now. She heard the men laugh before they disappeared behind the dusty panes of their basement workshop . . .

She removed the cloth from the table, took the kitchen knife from the drawer, pushed the bowl into place and began to prepare the cauliflower with trembling hands. The large, bold-faced *R* inside the red rectangle produced a fear in her that was gradually turning to nausea; her head started to spin, she had to pull herself together.

Then she started to pray. Whenever she was frightened, she prayed. As she did, a fitful series of random images floated through her mind – her husband, who had been dead for six years, standing at the window, grimacing as the first major deployment passed by below.

She thought too of the birth of her son during the Great War, that tiny, gaunt little boy, who never did get very strong . . .

Then she heard him go into the bathroom. The helpless stirring in her breast remained, a clump of pain and agitation, fear and suspicion, and a longing to cry that she had to choke back.

When he emerged from the bathroom his mother was already setting the table in the living room. The room was tidy and clean, flowers stood on the table, along with butter, cheese, sausage, and the brown coffeepot, the yellow cosy, and a can of milk, and on his plate he saw a large, tin box with cigarettes. He gave his mother a kiss and felt her trembling; he looked at her in shocked surprise as she suddenly burst out crying. Perhaps she was crying for joy. She held his hand tight and said softly, still crying, 'You mustn't be angry. I wanted to make it so nice.' She pointed at the table, crying harder, then broke out in violent sobs, and he saw her broad, handsome face swimming in tears. He didn't know what to do. He stammered, 'My God, Mother, it's nice, it really is.'

'It is,' he said again. She looked at him, searching his face, and tried to smile.

'Really,' he said, before going into the bathroom. He quickly donned a fresh shirt, put on a red tie and hurried back out. His mother was already sitting there; she'd taken off her apron, brought her cup from the kitchen and was smiling at him.

He sat down and said, 'I slept wonderfully.'

She thought he really did look better. She took the cosy off the coffeepot and poured him a cup, followed by a thick stream of canned milk. 'Didn't you read a little too long?'

'No, not at all,' he said with a smile. 'I was tired yesterday, too tired.' He opened the tin box, lit a cigarette, began to stir his coffee slowly and looked into his mother's eyes. 'Everything's so nice,' he said.

Without changing her expression she said, 'There's some post.' He saw the corners of her mouth tremble. She bit her lip; she couldn't speak, and a dry, deep sob arose. Suddenly he knew that something had happened, or was about to happen. He knew it. The post had caused it, it had something to do with the post. He looked down, stirred his cup, inhaled more deeply on his cigarette, and took a sip from time to time. He had to give her time. She didn't want to cry, but she had something to say and she had to have time to recover fully from her long, dry sob before she could speak again. It was something to do with the post. He would never forget that sob for the rest of his life, a sob that contained everything, all the horror not one of them could have known about then. It was a sob that cut like a knife. His mother sobbed, she sobbed just once, a long, drawn-out, deep sob, and still he looked downward, staring at the surface of his coffee cup in which the canned milk had now dispersed to a smooth and even light brown. He saw the tip of his cigarette, saw the ash tremble, grey and silver, and at last he sensed that he could look up.

'Yes,' she said softly, 'Uncle Eddy wrote. He's an assistant schoolmaster now, but he's been transferred, too. He says the whole thing makes him sick.'

'Yes, of course,' he said. 'It would make any normal person sick.'

She nodded. 'And my pension statement,' she said. 'There's less again.' He laid his hand on hers, which seemed small, broad and worn atop the blossom white tablecloth. His touch released a new series of deep, piercing sobs. He removed his hand and kept the memory of his mother's hand, warm and rough. He kept his gaze lowered until the series of piercing sobs and repressed tears had passed. He waited. He thought. That's not what it is. Uncle Eddy and her pension wouldn't upset her that much. It's something completely different. And suddenly he knew it had to be something to do with him, and he could feel himself turning pale. Nothing would upset his mother this much unless it concerned him. He simply looked up. His mother pressed her lips together tightly, her eyes were moist, and now she forced out the words, opening her mouth tersely but firmly. She spoke haltingly. 'A postcard came for you, it's out there – in the hall . . .'

He put down his cup at once, got up and walked into the hall. He could see the card even at a distance; it was white and perfectly ordinary, a regulation-size card, three by five inches.

It lay innocently on the table beside the dark vase of spruce sprigs. He rushed over to it and picked it up, read the address, saw the red, white and black sticker with the red rectangle surrounding the thick black *R*, then turned the card over and looked first for the signature. It was scribbled illegibly above a long line that read: 'District Recruitment Commander'. The word 'Major' was typed beneath it.

Everything was quiet; nothing had changed. A simple postcard had arrived, a perfectly ordinary postcard, and the only handwritten word on it was the illegible scrawl of some major or other. The greenish light from the upper portion of the hall door made everything seem to float as if in an aquarium: the vase was still standing there, his coat hung on the wardrobe, his mother's coat hung there, her hat beside it – her Sunday hat with the dainty, white veil at the top, the hat she wore to church when she knelt beside him, quietly praying, while he slowly turned the pages of the missal. Everything was as it should be. Through the open kitchen door he heard the laughter of the carpenters in the courtyard outside, the sky was clear and bright again, the storm had passed, an ordinary postcard had arrived, hastily signed by some major who might have knelt not far from him in church on Sundays, who slept with his wife, reared his children to be decent Germans, and who signed stacks of postcards during the week. It was all quite harmless . . .

He didn't know how long he'd stood in the hall with the postcard, but when he returned, his mother was sitting there crying. She held her trembling head propped on one hand, the other hand lay motionless in her lap, as if it didn't even belong to her, flat, worn and forlorn . . .

He walked over to her, lifted her head, and tried to look her in the eyes, but he gave up immediately. His mother's face was distorted, foreign, a face he'd never seen before, a face that frightened him, to which he had no access, could claim none . . .

He sat down in silence, sipped his coffee, and pulled out a cigarette, but let it drop suddenly and stared straight ahead.

Then a voice came from behind the propped hand. 'You should eat something . . .'

'You mustn't be upset.'

He poured coffee, added milk and dropped in two sugar cubes. Then he lit his cigarette, took the postcard from his pocket, and read in a low voice, 'You are to report to the Bismarck barracks in Adenbrück at 7 a.m. on 4 July for eight weeks of military training.'

'For goodness sake,' he said loudly, 'be reasonable, Mother, it's only eight weeks.'

She nodded.

'It was bound to happen, I knew I'd be called up for eight weeks of training.'

'Yes, I know,' she said, 'eight weeks.'

They both knew they were lying, they were lying without knowing why. They couldn't know, but they lied and they knew it. They knew he wasn't leaving for just eight weeks.

She said again, 'You should eat something.'

He took a slice of bread, buttered it, added sausage and started chewing, very slowly and without appetite.

'Give me the card,' said his mother.

He gave it to her.

There was a strange look on her face. She was very calm. She examined the card carefully, reading through it quietly.

'What is today?' she asked as she laid the card on the table.

'Thursday,' he said.

'No,' she said, 'the date.'

'The third,' he said.

Only then did he realize the point of her question. That meant he had to leave that very day, he had to be 180 miles to the north by seven the next morning, in the barracks of a strange city . . .

He put down the half-finished slice of bread; there was no point in pretending to be hungry. His mother covered her face with her hand again and began crying harder, a strange, soundless weeping . . .

He went into his room and packed his briefcase. He stuffed a shirt inside, a pair of underpants and socks, writing paper, then he cleared out the drawer and threw everything in it into the stove without looking through it. He tore a sheet from a notebook, folded it, set it on fire and held it under the pile of paper. At first there was only thick, white smoke; slowly the fire ate its way through until it burst crackling and hissing out the stove top, a slender, strong flame surrounded by black fumes. As he rummaged through all the drawers and compartments again he caught himself thinking. Get going, just get away quick. Away from his mother, from the only human being he could say loved him.

He heard her taking the tray back to the kitchen; he crossed the hall, knocked hurriedly on the frosted glass pane, and called in to her: 'I'm going to the train station, I'll be right back.'

She didn't answer right away. He waited, and he could feel the small, white postcard in the pocket of his trousers. Then his mother called out, 'OK. Come back soon. Goodbye . . .'

'Goodbye,' he called, then stood quietly for a moment before he walked out . . .

When he came home it was twelve-thirty, and the meal was ready. His mother carried dishes, cutlery and plates into the living room . . .

Recalling this now, that first tormented afternoon seemed to him worse than the entire war. He stayed home another six hours. His mother kept trying to force things on him she thought he'd need: soft bath towels in particular, packages of food, cigarettes, soap. And the whole time she was crying. For his part he smoked, arranged his books; the table had to be set again, bread, butter, jam had to be carried into the living room, and coffee had to be brewed.

Then, after coffee, when the sun had already passed behind the building and an agreeable twilight reigned in the front of the house, he suddenly went into his room, put his briefcase under his arm, and stepped out into the hall . . .

'What is it?' asked his mother, 'do you have to . . .'

'Yes,' he said, 'I have to go,' even though his train didn't leave for another five hours.

He put his case down and embraced his mother with a

despairing tenderness. As she placed her arms around him, she felt the postcard in his hip pocket and pulled it out. She was suddenly calm, and her sobs ceased as well. The postcard in her hand looked entirely harmless; the only human thing about it was the major's scrawl, and even this could have been written by a machine, by a major's mechanical pen . . . The only menacing thing about it was the gleaming rectangular sticker, standing out in bright red with a thick, black *R* inside, a small scrap of paper of the kind pasted on letters daily, whole rolls of them, in every post office. But now beneath the *R* he discovered a number; it was his number, the only thing that distinguished this card from all others, the number 846, and now he knew that everything was in its place, that nothing could happen, that in some post office or other this number stood beside a column bearing his name. It was his number and he couldn't flee from it; he had to race toward this bold-faced *R*. He couldn't run away . . .

He was registration number 846, nothing else, and this small, white postcard, this trivial piece of cardboard of the lowest, cheapest quality, which even when printed cost at most three marks per thousand and was delivered post-free to his house, meant nothing but a major's scribble, a secretary who reached into a card file, and yet another scribble as a postal official entered it in his ledger . . .

His mother was totally calm when he left. She pushed the postcard back into his pocket, kissed him, and said softly, 'God bless you.'

He went out. His train didn't leave till midnight, and it was barely seven. He knew his mother was watching him, and he turned to wave from time to time as he walked toward the tram.

He was at the station five hours before departure. He strolled from counter to counter a few times, studied the timetables again. Everything was normal. People were returning from or leaving for vacations; most were laughing. They were happy, tanned, and carefree. It was warm and beautiful, vacation weather . . .

He walked out again, got on a tram that could have taken him home, jumped off on the way and went back to the station. He checked the train-station clock and discovered that only twenty minutes had passed. He wandered among the crowd again for a while, smoking, then got on another streetcar at random, jumped off again and rode back to the station, as if he knew that he would be spending eight years in train stations. It drew him like a magnet . . .

He went into the waiting room, drank a beer, wiped the perspiration from his forehead, and suddenly recalled the girl at the bookshop he'd walked home a few times. He looked up her number in his notebook, rushed to a pay phone, inserted a coin, and dialled, but when a voice answered on the other end, he couldn't utter a word and hung up. He put in another coin and redialled. Again he heard an unfamiliar voice say hello and a name, and he gathered up all his courage and stammered out, 'May I speak to Fräulein Wegmann? This is Herr Schnitzler . . .'

'One moment, please,' said the voice, and through the receiver he heard a baby whimpering, dance music and a man cursing, a door slamming shut. Sweat beaded his forehead. Then he heard her voice. She said, 'Yes?' and he stammered, 'It's me . . . Hans . . . can I see you again, I have to go away . . . to the army . . . today . . .'

He could tell she was surprised, and she said, 'Yes . . . but when . . . where . . .?'

'At the train station,' he said, 'right away . . . at the gate . . .'

She came quickly, a delicate, petite blonde with a round, very red mouth and a pretty nose. She greeted him with a smile. 'Now this is a surprise.'

'What would you like, what shall we do?'

'How much time do we have?'

'Till twelve.'

'Let's go to the cinema,' she said.

They went to a cinema near the train station, a small, dirty theatre at the back of a courtyard, and when they were sitting

140

together in the dark, he suddenly knew that he had to take her hand and hold it tight for as long as the film lasted. The air was warm, there was a stale odour, and most of the seats were empty. It bothered him somehow that she let him take her hand so matter-of-factly, but he held it firmly, almost desperately, for two hours, and when they came out of the theatre it was dark at last, and raining . . .

As he turned into the park with her, he put his briefcase under his right arm and drew her to him with his left. Once more she yielded. He felt the warmth of her small, fragrant body, inhaled the smell of her wet hair, and kissed her, on the throat, the cheeks, and he was startled as he brushed her soft mouth with his lips . . .

She had put her arms tightly and nervously around him; his briefcase slipped from his grasp, and as he kissed her he suddenly realized he was trying to make out the trees and bushes on both sides of the path. He saw the damp, silvery path, gleaming in the rain, the dripping bushes and black tree trunks, and the sky, where thick clouds were racing eastward . . .

They walked up and down the path a few times. They kissed, and at certain moments he thought he felt a tenderness toward her, something like pity, perhaps love as well, he didn't know. He delayed their return to the lighted streets until it was so quiet around the train station that he thought it must be time . . .

He showed his postcard at the barrier, had them punch her platform ticket, and was glad to see the train already standing in the empty hall, steaming and ready. He kissed her again and got on. As he leaned out to wave, he was afraid she would cry, but she smiled at him, waved for a long time, energetically, and he sensed his own relief that she wasn't crying . . .

Kay Boyle

DEFEAT

First published in 1941, Kay Boyle's miniature short story attempts to evoke the initial shock caused by the defeat of France in June 1940: a shock which was to become a national trauma.

TOWARDS THE END of June that year and through July, there was a sort of uncertain pause, an undetermined suspension that might properly be called neither an armistice nor a peace, and it lasted until the men began coming back from where they were. They came at intervals, trickling down from the north in twos or threes, or even one by one, some of them prisoners who had escaped and others merely a part of that individual retreat in which the sole destination was home. They had exchanged their uniforms for something else as they came along – corduroys, or workmen's blue, or whatever people might have given them in secret to get away in – bearded, singularly and shabbily outfitted men getting down from a bus or off a train without so much as a knapsack in their hands and all with the same bewildered, scarcely discrepant story to tell. Once they had reached the precincts of familiarity, they stood there a moment where the vehicle had left them, maybe trying to button the jacket that didn't fit them or set the neck or shoulders right, like men who have been waiting in a courtroom and have finally heard their names called and stand up to take the oath and mount the

142

witness stand. You could see them getting the words ready – revising the very quality of truth – and the look in their eyes, and then someone coming out of the post office or crossing the station square in the heat would recognize them and go toward them with a hand out, and the testimony would begin.

They had found their way back from different places, by different means, some on bicycle, some by bus, some over the mountains on foot, coming home to the Alpes-Maritimes from Rennes, or from Clermont-Ferrand, or from Lyons, or from any part of France, and looking as incongruous to modern defeat as survivors of the Confederate Army might have looked, transplanted to this year and place (with their spurs still on and their soft-brimmed, dust-whitened hats), limping wanly back, half dazed and not yet having managed to get the story of what happened straight. Only, this time, they were the men of that tragically unarmed and undirected force which had been the French Army once but was no longer, returning to what orators might call reconstruction but which they knew could never be the same.

Wherever they came from, they had identical evidence to give: that the German ranks had advanced bareheaded, in short-sleeved summer shirts – young blond-haired men with their arms linked, row on row, and their trousers immaculately creased, having slept all night in hotel beds and their stomachs full, advancing singing and falling singing before the puny coughing of the French machine-guns. That is, the first line of them might fall, and part of the second, possibly, but never more, for just then the French ammunition would suddenly expire and the bright-haired blond demi-gods would march on singing across their dead. Then would follow all the glittering display: the rust-proof tanks and guns, the chromium electric kitchens, the crematoriums. Legends or truth, the stories became indistinguishable in the mouths of the Frenchmen who returned – that the Germans were dressed as if for tennis that summer, with nothing but a tune to carry in their heads, while the French crawled out from under lorries where they'd slept maybe for every night for a week, going to meet them like crippled, encumbered miners emerging from the pit of a warfare fifty years interred with thirty-five kilos of kit and a change of shoes and a tin helmet left over from 1914 breaking them in two as they met the brilliantly nickelled Nazi dawn. They said their superiors were the first to run; they said their ammunition had been sabotaged; they said the ambulances had been transformed into accommodations for the officers' lady friends; they said *Nous avons été vendus* or *On nous a vendu* over and over, until you could have made a popular song of it – the words and the music of defeat. After their testimony was given, some of them added (not the young but those who had fought before) in grave, part embittered, part vainglorious voices, 'I'm ashamed to be a Frenchman' or 'I'm ashamed of being French today', and then gravely took their places with the others.

Jean-Louis Curtis

THE FORESTS OF THE NIGHT

*So painful were events in occupied France from 1940 to 1944
that it has taken more than 50 years of denial for the complex
truth to surface. While historians avoided the era, two novels
published in the late 1940s,* A Bon Beurre *by Jean Dutourd
and* The Forests of the Night *by Jean-Louis Curtis, gave early
and fair accounts of the many shades of opinion and degrees
of co-operation with the enemy.*

*In the first extract, Curtis struggles to dramatise a
popular pro-German, anti-Allied point of view, and the
characters are little more than mouthpieces for one opinion
or another. In the second extract, however, he is able to
make moral and comic capital out of the daily details of
collaboration.*

JACQUES SMILED. 'NEVERTHELESS, you must admit that
we are quite comfortable, you and I, and you, too, Mother, in
the middle of this leprosy. We haven't much difficulty in
resigning ourselves to the inevitable.'

'I don't understand what you mean, either of you,' Mme
Costellot protested with energy. 'Leprosy? What leprosy?
You're really priceless. I don't feel in the least leprous, I assure
you. My conscience is clear. Of course, if you are referring to
the general deterioration of morals and to twentieth-century
materialism, I agree with you. But only with reservations,
with one very important reservation. The world is mad, we

know that, and the part of the world infested by the Anglo-Saxons is particularly odious and particularly rotten, and what has rotted it is precisely the influence of the worst enemies of Christianity – the Jews. That part of the world should be shown on the map with the inscription *Hic sunt* and the Latin names for jackals and hyenas: I don't know Latin. But France, in my opinion, France, if I am not mistaken, if I am not deluding myself, is not as rotten as that today: or is she? We have raised ourselves up again since 1940, or haven't we? France today is the cleanest place on the earth. At least, we have a leader who is clean.'

The clasped hands, the old, puffy face, the high-pitched voice immediately expressed veneration and respectful emotion.

'Most certainly you are right, Marguerite. How right you are to remind me of the things that can sustain our hope and feed our courage. The Marshal* . . . A gift of God, a providential blessing to our unhappy country . . . As long as we have this man at the wheel of our ancient ship, this honest, upright man at the wheel of the ancient ship that is almost wrecked . . .'

'Shouldn't we sing *Maréchal, vous voilà?*' Jacques suggested briskly.

'Mock as much as you like!' cried Mme Costellot. 'That's easy. But stop to think for a moment where you would be at the present hour if the Marshal had not been here in 1940. And even if the Marshal were not here now. You might well find yourself in Hamburg or in Kiel, exposed to Anglo-American bombing. You know it, of course, but you don't want to admit it. I cannot understand your cynicism, your irony, your scorn . . . If one did not know you, one might sometimes take you for a Communist or . . . a Gaullist! But as you jeer at them too and despise them just as bitterly, one asks

* Marshal Henri Philippe Pétain (1856–1951) became a national hero for his defence of Verdun in 1916. When France collapsed in June 1940, he negotiated the armistice with Germany and became Chief of State, establishing his government at Vichy. After the liberation in 1944, he was tried and convicted of treason.

oneself what you really think and feel, what your guts are made of . . . Perhaps you consider yourself above the parties? Withdrawn into an ivory tower? That's all very fine, my boy. The only objection is that one has to make one's choice: nowadays one has to be on one side or the other. It is no longer a moral problem – although my choice, and I hope M. Lardenne's as well, is primarily dictated by moral considerations. It is above all a question of personal safety, of life and death, or very nearly. I talk realism to you. I am not afraid of words. So, my lad, you are clever enough to recognize which is the good side, the safe side, the side not only of the just but – let us be realistic, even cynical – the side of the astute. It is the side of the Marshal. The Marshal chose his side at Montoire* and has done so more and more clearly and openly ever since Montoire, and he has good reasons for it, you can be sure.'

'I have always admired your perspicacity, mother, but I must confess that you would really be quite extraordinary if you had complete insight into the reasons which govern the Marshal's behaviour. Supposing, of course, that he has reasons. There is no end to the senseless discussions as to whether he thinks this or that, whether he has been won over by Germany or whether he is playing a double game. But my personal opinion is that he does not think at all.'

'In other words, that he is in his dotage?'

'If you like to put it that way.'

M. Lardenne raised his hands to his face. 'Jacques!' he murmured reproachfully.

'And I would go further still,' continued the young man. 'Look at the maudlin comedy that is being played in France today: the visits of the victor of Verdun to the martyr cities: acclamations to order for the "grand old man", kids presenting him with posies, craftsmen with examples of their craft in wood or copper: idiotic refrains bleated in the schools: tricolour portraits: Frankish battle-axes in shop windows denuded of everything else: the opportune and comforting

* A town north of Tours where Marshal Pétain met Hitler on 24 October 1940.

147

revival of Péguy and of Corneille*, the whole sickening display of sentimentality, the maudlin comedy around an old fellow in his second childhood who imagines himself to be the Maid of Orleans – you will pardon me, but I find it grotesque and hypocritical, and I beg your permission to hold aloof.'

'Jacques!' said M. Lardenne again, genuinely distressed.

The restaurant was what one calls 'luxurious', and the affluence of a clientele which was too well dressed, too showy, too chic, made it appear vulgar; this was accentuated by the cinema décor of shining glass, nickel tubes and parchment-shaded lamps . . . On closer examination, the guests were frankly despicable, even more despicable than the waiters. Only the Germans, soldiers as well as officers, had some dignity. The women seemed all to be more or less *demi-mondaines*. The young people, both boys and girls, looked like illustrations in a fashion paper. All the men had the appearance of successful dagos, with their fat, flabby cheeks, their listless and yet rapacious air. For most of them, the end of 1940 had been the dawn of their Golden Age. Now they were living in the midst of it, and every little tart had become a Danaë. If you strayed into one of the eating houses *de luxe* or into a first-class compartment on one of the main railway-lines during the years 1942 and 1943, you could hardly escape the sudden revelation that France deserved to be destroyed. But unfortunately it was not quite as simple as all that: the modest and respectable old ladies wedged against the lavatories of third-class compartments in suburban trains and pressing a bottle of milk against their hearts, precious milk which they had obtained by dint of humble supplications from some millionaire peasant farmer in the Loiret or the Seine-et-Marne, did they not furnish a living proof that France did not deserve to be destroyed?

Gérard did not like the restaurant. But he had invited

* Charles Pierre Péguy (1873–1914), a poet who had died in the First World War; Pierre Corneille (1606–1684), popular dramatist.

Hélène to dinner and the only way of getting a decent meal was to take it in one of these night resorts. One cannot invite anyone to a meal consisting of boiled spinach and dry cheese. The young man disliked the idea of contributing to the prosperity of the black marketeers; on this question, his principles resembled those of Cato. But all the same, when one wanted to give a girl a treat, and besides, if one did not wish to appear a skinflint, one had to forget one's moral principles for the time being and accept a compromise with the indignities of the epoch. Finally there exist certain organic laws of a fairly intransigent nature concerning the minimum nourishment required to maintain human life. Cato would certainly have died of malnutrition in 1942–1943.

Hélène was consulting the menu. In a detached and epicurean manner, she announced her choice: precisely the least expensive items on the list of dishes. Gérard laughed: taking the menu card out of her hands, he ordered something more substantial. 'And a bottle of red Médoc,' he added to the *maître d'hôtel*. Hélène protested, alleging that she drank only water, but Gérard insisted. The *maître d'hôtel*, an old rascal who was not easily taken in, considered the two young people with affectionate contempt, his pencil poised in mid-air. When the Médoc had been definitely ordered, he bowed and said 'Oui, Monsieur.' Médoc at 250 francs a bottle decidedly called for deference. 'And see that it is well *chambré*,' added Gérard, in the tones of an old gastronome who is accustomed to having the best. The *maître d'hôtel* suppressed a smile and bowed once more: 'But naturally, Monsieur,' he said and walked away majestically.

Elizabeth Bowen

Everybody in London Was in Love

In her novel The Heat of the Day *(1949) Elizabeth Bowen describes that peculiar atmosphere in London during the bombing raids of the autumn of 1940, when a new intimacy evolved among the people of the city. While the 'Spirit of the Blitz' and the cockney resilience became self-advertising mechanisms of defence, there were more* louche, romantic *and desperate undercurrents.*

THEY HAD MET one another, at first not very often, throughout that heady autumn of the first London air raids. Never had any season been more felt; one bought the poetic sense of it with the sense of death. Out of mists of morning charred by the smoke from ruins each day rose to a height of unmisty glitter; between the last of sunset and first note of the siren the darkening glassy tenseness of evening was drawn fine. From the moment of waking you tasted the sweet autumn not less because of an acridity on the tongue and nostrils; and as the singed dust settled and smoke diluted you felt more and more called upon to observe the daytime as a pure and curious holiday from fear. All through London, the ropings-off of dangerous tracts of street made islands of exalted if stricken silence, and people crowded against the ropes to admire the sunny emptiness on the other side. The diversion of traffic out of blocked main thoroughfares into byways, the unstopping phantasmagoric streaming of lorries, buses, vans, drays, taxis past modest windows and quiet doorways set up an overpowering sense of London's organic power – somewhere here was a source from which heavy motion boiled, surged and, not to be damned up, forced for itself new channels.

The very soil of the city at this time seemed to generate more strength: in parks the outsize dahlias, velvet and wine, and the trees on which each vein in each yellow leaf stretched out perfect against the sun blazoned out the idea of the finest hour. Parks suddenly closed because of time-bombs – drifts of leaves in the empty deck chairs, birds afloat on the dazzlingly silent lakes – presented, between the railings which still girt them, mirages of repose. All this was beheld each morning more light-headedly: sleeplessness disembodied the lookers-on.

In reality there were no holidays; few were free however light-headedly to wander. The night behind and the night to come met across every noon in an arch of strain. To work or think was to ache. In offices, factories, ministries, shops, kitchens the hot yellow sands of each afternoon ran out slowly; fatigue was the one reality. You dared not envisage sleep. Apathetic, the injured and dying in the hospitals watched light change on walls which might fall tonight. Those rendered homeless sat where they had been sent; or, worse, with the obstinacy of animals retraced their steps to look for what was no longer there. Most of all the dead, from mortuaries, from under cataracts of rubble, made their anonymous presence – not as today's dead but as yesterday's living – felt through London. Uncounted, they continued to move in shoals through the city day, pervading everything to be seen or heard or felt with their torn-off senses, drawing on this tomorrow they had expected – for death cannot be so sudden as all that. Absent from the routine which had been life, they stamped upon that routine their absence – not knowing who the dead were you could not know which might be the staircase somebody for the first time was not mounting this morning, or at which street corner the newsvendor missed a face, or which trains and buses in the homegoing rush were this evening lighter by at least one passenger.

These unknown dead reproached those left living not by their own death, which might any night be shared, but by their unknownness, which could not be mended now. Who had the right to mourn them, not having cared that they had lived? So, among the crowds still eating, drinking, working, travelling, halting, there began to be an instinctive movement to break down indifference while there was still time. The wall between the living and the living became less solid as the wall between the living and the dead thinned. In that September transparency people became transparent, only to be located by the just darker flicker of their hearts. Strangers saying 'Good night, good luck', to each other at street corners, as the sky first blanched then faded with evening, each hoped not to die that night, still more not to die unknown.

That autumn of 1940 was to appear, by two autumns later, apocryphal, more far away than peace. No planetary round was to bring again that particular conjunction of life and death; that particular psychic London was to be gone for ever; more bombs would fall, but not on the same city. War moved from the horizon to the map. And it was now, when you no longer saw, heard, smelled war, that a deadening acclimatization to it began to set in. The first generation of ruins, cleaned up, shored up, began to weather – in daylight they took their places as a norm of the scene; the dangerless nights of September two years later blotted them out. It was from this new insidious echoless propriety of ruins that you breathed in all that was most malarial. Reverses, losses, deadlocks now almost unnoticed bred one another; every day the news hammered one more nail into a consciousness which no longer resounded. Everywhere hung the heaviness of the even worse you could not be told and could not desire to hear. This was the lightless middle of the tunnel. Faith came down to a slogan, desperately reworded to catch the eye, requiring to be pasted each time more strikingly on to hoardings and bases of monuments . . . No, no virtue was to be found in the outward order of theirs: happy those who could draw from some inner source.

For Stella, her early knowing of Robert was associated with the icelike tinkle of broken glass being swept up among the crisping leaves, and with the charred freshness of every morning. She could recapture that 1940 autumn only in sensations; thoughts, if there had been any, could not be found again. She remembered the lightness, after her son had left, of loving no particular person now left in London – till one morning she woke to discover that lightness gone. That was the morning when, in the instant before opening her eyes, she saw Robert's face with a despairing hallucinatory clearness. When she did open her eyes, it had been to stare round her room in sunshine certain that he was dead. *Something* final had happened, in any case. That autumn, she was living in lodgings in a house in a square: raising the sash of her bedroom window – which, glassless since two or three nights ago, ran up with a phantom absence of weight – she leaned out and called to the square's gardener, impassively at work just inside the railings with rake and barrow. Had he, had the old man, any idea where the bombs had fallen last night? He said, some said Kilburn, some King's Cross. She shouted, 'Then, not Westminster?' but he shrugged his shoulders, once again turned his back. The sun stood so high over the opposite roof-line that Stella looked at her watch – yes, the sun was right; she had overslept. So far, nothing had happened to anybody she knew, or even to anyone she knew knew – today, however, tingled all over from some shock which could be the breaking down of immunity. The non-existence of her window, the churchyard hush of the square, the grit which had drifted on to her dressing-table all became ominous for the first time. More than once she reached for the telephone which was out of order. Trying to dress in haste in the blinding sunshine, she threw away any time she had gained by standing still while something inside her head, never quite a thought, made felt a sort of imprisoned humming. Could this nervousness be really nothing more than fatigue?

More loss had not seemed possible after that fall of France. On through the rest of that summer in which she had not rallied from that psychological blow, and forward into this autumn of the attack on London, she had been the onlooker with nothing more to lose – out of feeling as one can be out of breath. She had had the sensation of being on furlough from her own life. Throughout these September raids she had been awed, exhilarated, cast at the very most into a sort of abstract of compassion – only what had been very small indeed, a torn scrap of finery, for instance, could draw tears. To be at work built her up, and when not at work she was being gay in company whose mood was at the pitch of her own – society became lovable; it had the temperament of the stayers-on in London. The existence, surrounded by one another, of these people she nightly saw was fluid, easy, holding inside itself a sort of ideality of pleasure. These were campers in rooms of draughty dismantled houses or corners of fled-from flats – it could be established, roughly, that the wicked had stayed and the good had gone. This was the new society of one kind of wealth, resilience, living how it liked – people whom the climate of danger suited, who began, even, all to look a little alike, as they might in the sun, snows, and altitude of the same sports station, or browning along the same beach in the south of France. The very temper of pleasures lay in their chanciness, in the canvas-like impermanence of their settings, in their being off-time – to and fro between bars and grills, clubs and each other's places moved the little shoal through the noisy nights. Faces came and went. There was a diffused gallantry in the atmosphere, an unmarriedness: it came to be rumoured about the country, among the self-banished, the uneasy, the put-upon and the safe, that everybody in London was in love – which was true, if not in the sense the country meant. There was plenty of everything in London – attention, drink, time, taxis, most of all space.

Into that intimate and loose little society of the garrison Stella and Robert both gravitated, and having done so could hardly fail to meet. They for the first time found themselves face to face in a bar or club – afterwards they could never remember which. Both were in their element, to which to have met instantaneously added more. It was a characteristic of that life in the moment and for the moment's sake that one knew people well without knowing much about them: vacuum as to future was offset by vacuum as to past; life-stories were shed as so much superfluous weight – this for different reasons suited both her and him. (Information, that he had before the war lived, worked abroad, in a branch of his father's or a friend of his father's business accumulated gradually, later on.) At the first glance they saw in each other's faces a flash of promise, a background of mystery. While his eyes, in which mirror-refracted lighting intensified a curious blue, followed the one white lock slowly back from her forehead, she found herself not so much beginning to study as in the middle of studying this person – communicative, excitable – from whom she only turned away to wave good-bye to the friend who had brought her across the room.

That gesture of good-bye, so perfunctory, was a finalness not to appear till later. It comprehended the room and everybody, everything in it which had up to now counted as her life: it was an unconscious announcement of the departure she was about to take – a first and last wave, across widening water, from a liner. Remembered, her fleeting sketch of a gesture came to look prophetic; for ever she was to see, photographed as though it had been someone else's, her hand up. The bracelet slipping down and sleeve falling back, against a dissolving background of lights and faces, were vestiges, and the last, of her solidity. She returned to Robert – both having caught a breath, they fixed their eyes expectantly on each other's lips. Both waited, both spoke at once, unheard.

Overhead, an enemy plane had been dragging, drumming slowly round in the pool of night, drawing up bursts of gunfire – nosing, pausing, turning, fascinated by the point for its intent. The barrage banged, coughed, retched; in here the lights in the mirrors rocked. Now down a shaft of anticipating silence the bomb swung whistling. With the shock of detonation, still to be heard, four walls of in here yawped in then bellied out; bottles danced on glass; a distortion ran through the view. The detonation dulled off into the cataracting roar of a split building: direct hit, somewhere else.

It was the demolition of an entire moment: he and she stood at attention till the glissade stopped. What they *had* both been saying, or been on the point of saying, neither of them ever now were to know. Most first words have the nature of being trifling; theirs from having been lost began to have the significance of a lost clue. What they next said, what they said instead, they forgot: there are questions which if not asked at the start are not asked later; so those they never did ask. The top had been knocked off their first meeting – perhaps later they exonerated themselves a little because of that. Nothing but the rising exhilaration of kindred spirits was, after all, to immortalize for them those first hours: and even forward into the time when meetings came to count for too much to be any more left to chance, they were still liking each other for their alikeness' sake. Into their attraction to one another entered their joy *in* attraction, in everything that was flattering and uncertain. There existed between them the complicity of brother and sister twins, counterpart flowerings of a temperament identical at least with regard to love. That unprecedented autumn, in which in everything round them feeling stood at full tide, made the movement of their own hearts imperceptible: in their first weeks of knowing each other they did not know how much might be the time, how much themselves. The extraordinary battle in the sky transfixed them; they might have stayed for ever on the eve of being in love.

Alistair MacLean

FIRE ON THE WATER

Alistair MacLean's novel HMS Ulysses *(1955) tells the story of Convoy FR77 to Murmansk, carrying supplies for the Russian allies. It is a voyage through bitter cold and storm, with the ships in permanent danger of being attacked by German U-boats lying in wait somewhere in the icy waters of the Arctic.*

As an adventure writer, MacLean found his natural readership among schoolboys, and literary critics have not been able to tolerate the strained and sometimes second-hand nature of his language. However, at its best – as in this memorable passage – MacLean's writing has a passionate authenticity.

THE *ULYSSES* WAS at dawn Action Stations as the shadowy shapes of the convoy, a bare mile ahead, lifted out of the greying gloom. The great bulk of the *Blue Ranger*, on the starboard quarter of the convoy, was unmistakable. There was a moderate swell running, but not enough to be uncomfortable: the breeze was light, from the west, the temperature just below zero, the sky chill and cloudless. The time was exactly 0700.

At 0702, the *Blue Ranger* was torpedoed. The *Ulysses* was two cable-lengths away, on her starboard quarter: those on the bridge felt the physical shock of the twin explosions, heard them shattering the stillness of the dawn as they saw two searing columns of flame fingering skywards, high above the *Blue Ranger*'s bridge and well aft of it. A second later they heard a signalman shouting something unintelligible, saw him pointing forwards and downwards. It was another torpedo, running astern of the carrier, trailing its evil phosphorescent wake across the heels of the convoy, before spending itself in the darkness of the Arctic.

Vallery was shouting down the voice-pipe, pulling round the *Ulysses*, still doing upwards of twenty knots, in a madly heeling, skidding turn, to avoid collision with the slewing carrier. Three sets of Aldis lamps and the fighting lights were already stuttering out the 'Maintain Position' code signal to ships in the convoy. Marshall, on the phone, was giving the standby order to the depth-charge LTO: gun barrels were already depressing, peering hungrily into the treacherous sea. The signal to the *Sirrus* stopped short, unneeded: the destroyer, a half-seen blue in the darkness, was already knifing its way through the convoy, white water piled high at its bows, headed for the estimated position of the U-boat.

The *Ulysses* sheered by parallel to the burning carrier, less than 150 feet away; travelling so fast, heeling so heavily and at such close range, it was impossible to gather more than a blurred impression, a tangled, confused memory of heavy black smoke laced with roaring columns of flame, appalling in that near-darkness, of a drunkenly listing flight-deck, of Grummans and Corstairs cartwheeling grotesquely over the edge to splash icy clouds of spray in shocked faces, as the cruiser slewed away; and then the *Ulysses* was round, heading back south for the kill.

Within a minute, the signal-lamp of the *Vectra*, up front with the convoy, started winking: 'Contact, Green 70, closing: Contact, Green 70, closing.'

'Acknowledge,' Tyndall ordered briefly.

The Aldis had barely begun to clack when the *Vectra* cut through the signal.

'Contacts, repeat contacts. Green 90, Green 90. Closing. Very close. Repeat contacts, contacts.'

Tyndall cursed softly.

'Acknowledge. Investigate.' He turned to Vallery. 'Let's join him, Captain. This is it. Wolf-pack Number One – and in force. No bloody right to be here,' he added bitterly. 'So much for Admiralty Intelligence!'

The *Ulysses* was round again, heading for the *Vectra*. It should have been growing lighter now, but the *Blue Ranger*, her squadron fuel tanks on fire, a gigantic torch against the eastern horizon, had the curious effect of throwing the surrounding sea into heavy darkness. She lay almost athwart of the flagship's course for the *Vectra*, looming larger every minute. Tyndall had his night glasses to his eyes, kept on muttering: 'The poor bastards, the poor bastards!'

The *Blue Ranger* was almost gone. She lay dead in the water, heeled far over to starboard, ammunition and petrol tanks going up in a constant series of crackling reports. Suddenly, a succession of dull, heavy explosions rumbled over the sea: the entire bridge island structure lurched crazily sideways, held, then slowly, ponderously, deliberately, the whole massive body of it toppled majestically into the glacial darkness of the sea. God only knew how many men perished with it, deep down in the Arctic, trapped in its iron walls. They were the lucky ones.

The *Vectra*, barely two miles ahead now, was pulling round south in a tight circle. Vallery saw her, altered course to intercept. He heard Bentley shouting something unintelligible from the fore corner of the compass platform. Vallery shook his head, heard him shouting again, his voice desperate with some nameless urgency, his arm pointing frantically over the windscreen, and leapt up beside him.

The sea was on fire. Flat, calm, burdened with hundreds of tons of fuel oil, it was a vast carpet of licking, twisting flames. That much, for a second, and that only, Vallery saw: then, with heart-stopping shock, with physically sickening abruptness, he saw something else again: the burning sea was alive with swimming, struggling men. Not a handful, not even dozens, but literally hundreds, soundlessly screaming, agonizingly dying in the barbarous contrariety of drowning and cremation.

'Signal from *Vectra*, sir.' It was Bentley speaking, his voice abnormally matter-of-fact. '"Depth-charging. 3, repeat 3 contacts. Request immediate assistance."'

Tyndall was at Vallery's side now. He heard Bentley, looked a long second at Vallery, following his sick, fascinated gaze into the sea ahead.

For a man in the sea, oil is an evil thing. It clogs his movements, burns his eyes, sears his lungs and tears away his stomach in uncontrollable paroxysms of retching; but oil on fire is a hellish thing, death by torture, a slow, shrieking death by drowning, by burning, by asphyxiation – for the flames devour all the life-giving oxygen on the surface of the sea. And not even in the bitter Arctic is there the merciful extinction by cold, for the insulation of an oil-soaked body stretches a dying man on the rack for eternity, carefully preserves him for the last excruciating refinement of agony. All this Vallery knew.

He knew, too, that for the *Ulysses* to stop, starkly outlined against the burning carrier, would have been suicide. And to come sharply round to starboard, even had there been time and room to clear the struggling, dying men in the sea ahead, would have wasted invaluable minutes, time and to spare for the U-boats ahead to line up firing-tracks on the convoy; and the *Ulysses*'s first responsibility was to the convoy. Again all this Vallery knew. But at that moment, what weighed most heavily with him was common humanity. Fine off the port bow, close in to the *Blue Ranger*, the oil was heaviest, the flames fiercest, the swimmers thickest: Vallery looked back over his shoulder at the Officer of the Watch.

'Port 10!'

'Port 10, sir.'

'Midships!'

'Midships, sir.'

'Steady as she goes!'

For ten, fifteen seconds the *Ulysses* held her course, arrowing through the burning sea to the spot where some gregariously atavistic instinct for self-preservation held two hundred men knotted together in a writhing, seething mass, gasping out their lives in hideous agony. For a second a great gout of flame leapt up in the centre of the group, like a giant, incandescent magnesium flare, a flame that burnt the picture into the hearts and minds of the men on the bridge with a permanence and searing clarity that no photographic plate could ever have reproduced: men on fire, human torches beating insanely at the flames that licked, scorched and then incinerated clothes, hair and skin: men flinging themselves almost out of the water, backs arched like tautened bows, grotesque in convulsive crucifixion: men lying dead in the water, insignificant, featureless little oil-stained mounds in an oil-soaked plain: and a handful of fear-maddened men, faces inhumanly contorted, who saw the *Ulysses* and knew what was coming, as they frantically thrashed their way to a safety that offered only a few more brief seconds of unspeakable agony before they gladly died.

'Starboard 30!' Vallery's voice was low, barely a murmur, but it carried clearly through the shocked silence on the bridge.

'Starboard 30, sir.'

For the third time in ten minutes, the *Ulysses* slewed crazily round in a racing turn. Turning thus, a ship does not follow through the line of the bows cutting the water; there is a pronounced sideways or lateral motion, and the faster and sharper the turn, the more violent the broadside skidding motion, like a car on ice. The side of the *Ulysses*, still at an acute angle, caught the edge of the group on the port bow: almost on the instant, the entire length of the swinging hull smashed into the heart of the fire, into the thickest press of dying men.

For most of them, it was just extinction, swift and glad and merciful. The tremendous concussion and pressure waves crushed the life out of them, thrust them deep down into the blessed oblivion of drowning, thrust them down and sucked them back into the thrashing vortex of the four great screws . . .

On board the *Ulysses*, men for whom death and destruction had become the stuff of existence, to be accepted with the callousness and jesting indifference that alone kept them sane – these men clenched impotent fists, mouthed meaningless, useless curses over and over again and wept heedlessly like little children. They wept as pitiful, charred faces, turned up towards the *Ulysses* and alight with joy and hope, petrified into incredulous staring horror, as realization dawned and the water closed over them; as hate-filled men screamed insane invective, both arms raised aloft, shaking fists white-knuckled through the dripping oil as the *Ulysses* trampled them under: as a couple of young boys were sucked into the mælstrom of the propellers, still giving the thumbs-up sign: as a particularly shocking case, who looked as if he had been barbecued on a spit and had no right to be alive, lifted a scorified hand to the blackened hole that had been his mouth, flung to the bridge a kiss in token of endless gratitude; and wept, oddly, most of all, at the inevitable humorist who lifted his fur cap high above his head and bowed gravely and deeply, his face into the water as he died.

Suddenly, mercifully, the sea was empty. The air was strangely still and quiet, heavy with the sickening stench of charred flesh and burning Diesel, and the *Ulysses*'s stern was swinging wildly almost under the black pall overhanging the *Blue Ranger* amidships, when the shells struck her.

The shells – three 3.7s – came from the *Blue Ranger*. Certainly, no living gun-crews manned these 3.7s – the heat must have ignited the bridge fuses in the cartridge cases. The first shell exploded harmlessly against the armour-plating: the second wrecked the bosun's store, fortunately empty: the third penetrated No. 3 Low Power Room via the deck. There were nine men in there – an officer, seven ratings and Chief Torpedo Gunner's Mate Noyes. In that confined space, death was instantaneous.

Only seconds later a heavy rumbling explosion blew out a great hole along the waterline of the *Blue Ranger* and she fell slowly, wearily right over on her starboard side, her flight-deck vertical to the water, as if content to die now that, dying, she had lashed out at the ship that had destroyed her crew.

On the bridge, Vallery still stood on the yeoman's platform, leaning over the starred, opaque windscreen. His head hung down, his eyes were shut and he was retching desperately, the gushing blood – arterial blood – ominously bright and scarlet in the erubescent glare of the sinking carrier. Tyndall stood there helplessly beside him, not knowing what to do, his mind numbed and sick. Suddenly, he was brushed unceremoniously aside by the Surgeon-Commander, who pushed a white towel to Vallery's mouth and led him gently below. Old Brooks, everyone knew, should have been at his Action Stations position in the Sick Bay: no one dared say anything.

Carrington straightened the *Ulysses* out on course, while he waited for Turner to move up from the after Director Tower to take over the bridge. In three minutes the cruiser was up with the *Vectra*, methodically quartering for a lost contact. Twice the ships regained contact, twice they dropped heavy patterns. A heavy oil-slick rose to the surface: possibly a kill, probably a ruse, but in any event neither ship could remain to investigate further. The convoy was two miles ahead now, and only the *Stirling* and *Viking* were there for its protection – a wholly inadequate cover and powerless to save the convoy from any determined attack.

It was the *Blue Ranger* that saved FR77. In these high latitudes, dawn comes slowly, interminably: even so, it was more than half-light, and the merchant ships, line ahead through that very gentle swell, lifted clear and sharp against a cloudless horizon, a U-boat commander's dream – or would have been, had he been able to see them. But, by this time, the convoy was completely obscured from the wolf-pack lying to the south: the light westerly wind carried the heavy black smoke from the blazing carrier along the southern flank of the convoy, at sea level, the perfect smoke-screen, dense, impenetrable. Why the U-boats had departed from their almost invariable practice of launching dawn attacks from the north, so as to have their targets between themselves and the sunrise, could only be guessed. Tactical surprise, probably, but whatever the reason it was the saving of the convoy. Within an hour, the thrashing screws of the convoy had left the wolf-pack far behind – and FR77, having slipped the pack, was far too fast to be overtaken again.

Robert Harris

ENIGMA

Robert Harris's novel Enigma *(1995) is set in Bletchley Park where throughout the war men and women worked night and day to break the German signal codes. Among them is the novel's hero, a Cambridge mathematician called Tom Jericho.*

When in March 1943 the Germans unaccountably change their U-boat code ('Shark'), the codebreakers in Hut 8 are desperate for U-boat signs from the Atlantic that they can decrypt to read the new code. They do know, however, that the U-boats will only break their radio silence when they have found and started hunting one of the convoys crossing the Atlantic on its way to Britain.

AT 5 A.M. GMT on Tuesday 16 March, some nine hours after Jericho had parked the Austin and walked into Hut 8, *U-653* was heading due east on the surface, returning to France. In the North Atlantic it was 3 a.m.

After ten days on station in the *Raubgraf* line, with no sign of any convoy, Feiler had finally decided to head for home. He had lost, along with Leutnant Laudon, four other ratings washed overboard. One of his petty officers was ill. The starboard diesel was still giving trouble. His one remaining torpedo was defective. The boat, which had no heating, was cold and damp, and everything – lockers, food, uniforms – was covered in a greenish-white mould. Feiler lay on his wet bunk, curled up against the cold, wincing at the irregular beat of the engine, and tried to sleep.

Up on the bridge, four men made up the night watch: one for each point of the compass. Cowled like monks in dripping black oilskins, lashed to the rail by metal belts, each had a pair of goggles and a pair of Zeiss binoculars clamped firmly to his eyes and was staring blindly into his own sector of darkness.

The cloud cover was ten-tenths. The wind was a steel attack. The hull of the U-boat thrashed beneath their feet with a violence that sent them skidding over the wet deck plates and knocking into one another.

Facing directly ahead, towards the invisible prow, was a young Obersteuermann, Heinz Theen. He was peering into such an infinity of blackness that it was possible to imagine they might have fallen off the edge of the world, when suddenly he saw a light. It flared out of nowhere, several hundred yards in front of him, winked for two seconds, then disappeared. If he hadn't had his binoculars trained precisely upon it, he would never have seen it.

Astonishing though it seemed, he realized he had just witnessed someone lighting a cigarette.

An Allied seaman lighting a cigarette in the middle of the North Atlantic.

He called down the conning tower for the captain.

By the time Feiler had scrambled up the slippery metal ladder to the bridge thirty seconds later the cloud had shifted slightly in the high wind and shapes were moving all around them. Feiler swivelled through 360 degrees and counted the outlines of nearly twenty ships, the nearest no more than 500 yards away on the port side.

A whispered cry, as much of panic as command: 'Alarrrmmm!'

The *U-653* came out of her emergency dive and hung motionless in the calmer water beneath the waves.

Thirty-nine men crouched silently in the semidarkness, listening to the sounds of the convoy passing overhead: the fast revs of the modern diesels, the ponderous churning of the steamers, the curious singing noises of the turbines in the warship escorts.

Feiler let them all go by. He waited two hours, then surfaced.

The convoy was already so far ahead as to be barely visible in the faint dawn light – just the masts of the ships and a few smudges of smoke on the horizon, and then, occasionally, when a high wave lifted the U-boat, the ironwork of bridges and funnels.

Feiler's task under standing orders was not to attack – impossible in any case, given his lack of torpedoes – but to keep his quarry in sight while drawing in every other U-boat within a radius of 100 miles.

'Convoy steering 070 degrees,' said Feiler. 'Naval grid square BD 1491.'

The first officer made a scrawled note in pencil then dropped down the conning tower to collect the Short Signal Code Book. In his cubbyhole next to the captain's berth the radioman pressed his switches. The Enigma came on with a hum.

At 7 a.m., Logie had sent Pinker, Proudfoot and Kingcome back to their digs to get some decent rest. 'Sod's law will now proceed to operate,' he predicted, as he watched them go, and sod's law duly did. Twenty-five minutes later, he was back in the Big Room with the queasy expression of guilty excitement which would characterize the whole of that day.

'It looks like it may have started.'

St Erith, Scarborough and Flowerdown had all reported an E-bar signal followed by eight Morse letters, and within a minute one of the Wrens from the Registration Room was bringing in the first copies. Jericho placed his carefully in the centre of his trestle table.

RGHC DMIG. His heart began to accelerate.

'Hubertus net,' said Logie. '4601 kilocycles.'

Cave was listening to someone on the telephone. He put his hand over the mouthpiece. 'Direction finders have a fix.' He clicked his fingers. 'Pencil. Quick.' Baxter threw him one.

'49.4 degrees north,' he repeated. '38.8 degrees west. Got it. Well done.' He hung up.

Cave had spent all night plotting the convoys' courses on two large charts of the North Atlantic – one issued by the Admiralty, the other a captured German naval grid, on which the ocean was divided into thousands of tiny squares. The cryptanalysts gathered round him. Cave's finger came down on a spot almost exactly midway between Newfoundland and the British Isles. 'There she is. She's shadowing HX-229.' He made a cross on the map and wrote 0725 beside it.

Jericho said: 'What grid square is that?'

'BD 1491.'

'And the convoy course?'

'070.'

Jericho went back to his desk and in less than two minutes, using the Short Signal Code Book and the current Kriegs-marine address book for encoding naval grid squares ('Alfred Krause, Blucherplatz 15': Hut 8 had broken that just before the blackout) he had a five-letter crib to slide under the contact report.

R G H C D M I G
D D F G R X ??

The first four letters announced that a convoy had been located steering 070 degrees, the next two gave the grid square, the final two represented the code name of the U-boat, which he didn't have. He circled R-D and D-R. A four-letter loop on the first signal.

'I get D-R/R-D,' said Puck a few seconds later.

'So do I.'

'Me too,' said Baxter.

Jericho nodded and doodled his initials on the pad. 'A good omen.'

After that, the pace of events began to quicken.

At 8.25, two long signals were intercepted emanating from Magdeburg, which Cave at once surmised would be U-boat headquarters ordering every submarine in the North Atlantic into the attack zone. At 9.20, he put down the telephone to announce that the Admiralty had just signalled the convoy commander with a warning that he was probably being shadowed. Seven minutes later, the telephone rang again. Flowerdown intercept station. A second E-bar flash from almost the same location as the first. The Wrens hurried in with it: KLYS QNLP.

'The same hearse,' said Cave. 'Following standard operating procedure. Reporting every two hours, or near as damn it.'

'Grid square?'

'The same.'

'Convoy course.'

'Also the same. For now.'

Jericho went back to his desk and manipulated the original crib under the new cryptogram.

$$K \; L \; Y \; S \; Q \; N \; L \; P$$
$$D \; D \; F \; G \; R \; X \; ?? $$

Again, there were no letter clashes. The golden rule of Enigma, its single, fatal weakness: *nothing is ever itself – A can never be A, B can never be B . . .* It was working. His feet performed a little tap dance of delight beneath the table. He glanced up to find Baxter staring at him and he realized, to his horror, that he was smiling.

'Pleased?'

'Of course not.'

But such was his shame that when, an hour later, Logie came through to say that a second U-boat had just sent a contact signal, he felt himself personally responsible.

SOUY YTRQ.

At 11.40, a third U-boat began to shadow the convoy, at 12.20, a fourth, and suddenly Jericho had seven signals on his desk. He was conscious of people coming up and looking over his shoulder – Logie with his burning hayrick of a pipe and the meaty smell and heavy breathing of Skynner. He didn't look round. He didn't talk. The outside world had melted for him. Even Claire was just a phantom now. There were only the loops of letters, forming and stretching out towards him from the grey Atlantic, multiplying on his sheets of paper, turning into thin chains of possibility in his mind.

They didn't stop for breakfast, nor for lunch. Minute by minute, throughout the afternoon, the cryptanalysts followed, at third hand, the progress of the chase two thousand miles away. The commander of the convoy was signalling to the Admiralty, the Admiralty had an open line to Cave, and Cave would shout each time a fresh development looked like affecting the hunt for cribs.

Two signals came at 13.40 – one a short contact report, the other longer, almost certainly originating from the U-boat that had started the hunt. Both were for the first time close enough to be fixed by direction finders on board the convoy's own escorts. Cave listened gravely for a minute, then announced that HMS *Mansfield*, a destroyer, was being dispatched from the main body of merchantmen to attack the U-boats.

'The convoy's just made an emergency turn to the southeast. She's going to try to shake off the hearses while *Mansfield* forces them under.'

Jericho looked up. 'What course is she steering?'

'What course is she steering?' repeated Cave into the telephone. 'I *said*,' he yelled, 'what fucking *course* is she steering?' He winced at Jericho. The receiver was jammed tight to his scarred ear. 'All right. Yes. Thank you. Convoy steering 118 degrees.' Jericho reached for the Short Signal Code Book.

'Will they manage to get away?' asked Baxter.

Cave bent over his chart with a ruler and protractor. 'Maybe. It's what I'd do in their place.'

A quarter of an hour passed and nothing happened.

'Perhaps they have done it,' said Puck. 'Then what do we do?'

Cave said: 'How much more material do you need?'

Jericho counted through the signals. 'We've got nine. We need another twenty. Another twenty-five would be better.'

'Jesus!' Cave regarded them with disgust. 'It's like sitting with a flock of carrion.'

Somewhere behind them a telephone managed half a ring before it was snatched out of its cradle. Logie came in a moment later, still writing.

'That was St Erith reporting an E-bar signal at 49.4 degrees north, 38.1 degrees west.'

'New location,' said Cave, studying his charts. He made a cross, then threw his pencil down and leaned back in his chair, rubbing his face. 'All she's managed to do is run straight from one hearse into another. Which is what? The fifth? Christ, the sea must be teeming with them.'

'She isn't going to get away,' said Puck, 'is she?'

'Not a chance. Not if they're coming in from all around her.'

A Wren moved among the cryptanalysts, doling out the latest cryptogram: BKEL UUXS.

Ten signals. Five U-boats in contact.

'Grid square?' said Jericho.

The ocean was alive with signals. They were landing on Jericho's desk at the rate of one every twenty minutes.

At 16.00 a sixth U-boat fastened on to the convoy and soon afterwards Cave announced that HX-229 was making another turn, to 028 degrees, in her latest and (in his opinion) hopeless attempt to escape her pursuers.

By 18.00 Jericho had a pile of nineteen contact signals, out of which he had conjured three four-letter loops and a mass of half-sketched bombe menus that looked like the plans for some complex game of hopscotch. His neck and shoulders were so knotted with tension he could barely straighten up.

The room by now was crowded. Pinker, Kingcome and Proudfoot had come back on shift. The other British naval lieutenant, Villiers, was standing next to Cave, who was explaining something on one of his charts. A Wren with a tray offered Jericho a curling Spam sandwich and an enamel mug of tea and he took them gratefully.

Logie came up behind him and tousled his hair.

'How are you feeling, old love?'

'Wrecked, frankly.'

'Want to knock off?'

'Very funny.'

'Come into my office and I'll give you something. Bring your tea.'

The 'something' turned out to be a large, yellow Benzedrine tablet, of which Logie had half a dozen in an hexagonal pillbox.

Jericho hesitated. 'I'm not sure I should. These helped send me funny last time.'

'They'll get you through the night, though, won't they? Come on, old thing. The commandos swear by them.' He rattled the box under Jericho's nose. 'So you'll crash out at breakfast? So what? By then we'll either have this bugger beaten. Or not. In which case it won't matter, will it?' He took one of the pills and pressed it into Jericho's palm. 'Go on. I won't tell Nurse.' He closed Jericho's fingers around it and said quietly: 'Because I can't let you go, you know, old love. Not tonight. Not you. Some of the others, maybe, but not you.'

'Oh, Christ. Well, since you put it so nicely.'

Jericho swallowed the pill with a mouthful of tea. It left a foul taste and he drained his mug to try and swill it away. Logie regarded him fondly.

'That's my boy.' He put the box back in his desk drawer and locked it. 'I've been protecting your bloody back again, incidentally. I had to tell him you were much too important to be disturbed.'

'Tell who? Skynner?'

'No. Not Skynner. Wigram.'

'What does he want?'

'You, old cock. I'd say he wants you. Skinned, stuffed and mounted on a pole somewhere. Really, I don't know, for such

171

a quiet bloke, you don't half make some enemies. I told him to come back at midnight. All right by you?'

Before Jericho could reply the telephone rang and Logie grabbed it.

'Yes? Speaking.' He grunted and stretched across his desk for a pencil. 'Time of origin 19.02, 52.1 degrees north, 37.2 degrees west. Thanks, Bill. Keep the faith.'

He replaced the receiver.

'And then there were seven . . .'

It was dark again and the lights were on in the Big Room. The sentries outside were banging the blackout shutters into place, like prison warders locking up their charges for the night.

Jericho hadn't set foot out of the hut for twenty-four hours, hadn't even looked out of the window. As he slipped back into his seat and checked his coat to make sure the crypto-grams were still there, he wondered vaguely what kind of day it had been and what Hester was doing.

Don't think about that now.

Already, he could feel the Benzedrine beginning to take effect. The muscles of his heart seemed feathery, his body charged. When he glanced across his notes, what had seemed inert and impenetrable a half-hour ago was suddenly fluid and full of possibility.

The new cryptogram was already on his desk: YALB DKYF.

'Naval grid square BD 2742,' called Cave. 'Course 055 degrees. Convoy speed nine and a half knots.'

Logie said: 'A message from Mr Skynner. A bottle of Scotch for the first man with a menu for the bombes.'

Twenty-three signals received. Seven U-boats in contact. Two hours to go till nightfall in the North Atlantic.

20.00: nine U-boats in contact.
20.46: ten.

'It's almost dark out there,' said Cave, looking at his watch. 'Not long now. How many have you had?'

'Twenty-nine,' said Baxter.

'I believe you said that would be enough, Mr Jericho?'

'Weather,' said Jericho, without looking up. 'We need a weather report from the convoy. Barometric pressure, cloud cover, cloud type, wind speed, temperature. Before it gets too dark.'

'They've got ten U-boats on their backs and you want them to tell you the *weather?*'

'Yes, please. Fast as they can.'

The weather report arrived at 21.31.

There were no more contact signals after 21.40.

Thus convoy HX-229 at 22.00:

Thirty-seven merchant vessels, ranging in size from the 12,000-ton British tanker *Southern Princess* to the 3,500-ton American freighter *Margaret Lykes*, making slow progress through heavy seas, steering a course of 055 degrees, direct to England, lit up like a regatta by a full moon to a range of ten miles visibility – the first such night in the North Atlantic for weeks. Escort vessels: five, including two slow corvettes and two clapped out, elderly ex-American destroyers donated to Britain in 1940 in exchange for bases, one of which – HMS *Mansfield* – had lost touch with the convoy after charging down the U-boats because the convoy commander (on his first operational command) had forgotten to signal her with his second change of course. No rescue ship available. No air cover. No reinforcements within a thousand miles.

'All in all,' said Cave, lighting a cigarette and contemplating his charts, 'what you might fairly call a bit of a cock-up.'

The first torpedo hit at 22.01.

At 22.32, Tom Jericho was heard to say, very quietly, 'Yes.'

The bombe was heavy – Jericho guessed it must weigh more than half a ton – and even though it was mounted on castors it still took all his strength, combined with the engineer's, to drag it away from the wall. Jericho pulled while the engineer went behind it and put his shoulder to the frame to heave. It came away at last with a screech and the Wrens moved in to strip it.

The decryptor was a monster, like something out of an H. G. Wells fantasy of the future: a black metal cabinet, eight feet wide and six feet tall, with scores of five-inch-diameter drum wheels set into the front. The back was hinged and opened up to show a bulging mass of coloured cables and the dull gleam of metal drums. In the place where it had stood on the concrete floor there was a large puddle of oil.

Jericho wiped his hands on a rag and retreated to watch from a corner. Elsewhere in the hut a score of other bombes were churning away on other Enigma keys and the noise and the heat were how he imagined a ship's engine room might be. One Wren went round to the back of the cabinet and began disconnecting and replugging the cables. The other moved along the front, pulling out each drum in turn and checking it. Whenever she found a fault in the wiring she would hand the drum to the engineer who would stroke the tiny brush wires back into place with a pair of tweezers. The contact brushes were always fraying, just as the belt which connected the mechanism to the big electric motor had a tendency to stretch and slip whenever there was a heavy load. And the engineers had never quite got the earthing right, so that the cabinets had a tendency to give off powerful electric shocks.

Jericho thought it was the worst job of all. A pig of a job. Eight hours a day, six days a week, cooped up in this windowless, deafening cell. He turned away to look at his watch. He didn't want them to see his impatience. It was nearly half past eleven.

His menu was at that moment being rushed into bombe bays all across the Bletchley area. Eight miles north of the Park, in a hut in a clearing in the forested estate of Gayhurst Manor, a clutch of tired Wrens near the end of their shift were being ordered to halt the three bombes running on Nuthatch (Berlin-Vienna-Belgrade Army administration), strip them and prepare them for Shark. In the stable block of Adstock Manor, ten miles to the west, the girls were actually sprawled with their feet up beside their silent machines, drinking

Ovaltine and listening to Tommy Dorsey on the BBC Light Programme, when the supervisor came storming through with a sheaf of menus and told them to stir themselves, fast. And at Wavendon Manor, three miles northeast, a similar story: four bombes in a dank and windowless bunker were abruptly pulled off Osprey (the low-priority Enigma key of the Organisation Todt) and their operators told to stand by for a rush job.

Those, plus the two machines in Bletchley's Hut 11, made up the promised dozen bombes.

The mechanical check completed, the Wren went back to the first row of drums and began adjusting them to the combination listed on the menu. She called out the letters to the other girl, who checked them.

'Freddy, Butter, Quagga . . .'

'Yes.'

'Apple, X-ray, Edward . . .'

'Yes.'

The drums slipped on their spindles and were fixed into place with a loud metallic click. Each was wired to mimic the action of a single Enigma rotor: 108 in all, equivalent to thirty-six Enigma machines running in parallel. When all the drums had been set, the bombe was trundled back into place and the motor started.

The drums began to turn, all except one in the top row which had jammed. The engineer gave it a whack with his spanner and it, too, began to revolve. The bombe would now run continuously on this menu – certainly for one day; possibly, according to Jericho's calculations, for two or three – stopping occasionally when the drums were so aligned they completed a circuit. Then the readings on the drums would be checked and tested, the machine restarted, and so it would go on until the precise combination of settings had been found, at which point the cryptanalysts would be able to read that day's Shark traffic. Such, at any rate, was the theory.

The engineer began dragging out the other bombe and Jericho moved forward to help, but was stopped by a tugging on his arm.

'Come on, old love,' shouted Logie above the din. 'There's nothing more we can do here.' He pulled at his sleeve again.

Reluctantly, Jericho turned and followed him out of the hut.

He felt no sense of elation. Maybe tomorrow evening or maybe on Thursday, the bombes would give them the Enigma settings for the day now ending. Then the real work would begin – the laborious business of trying to reconstruct the new Short Weather Code Book – taking the meteorological data from the convoy, matching it to the weather signals already received from the surrounding U-boats, making some guesses, testing them, constructing a fresh set of cribs . . . It never ended, this battle against Enigma. It was a chess tournament of a thousand rounds against a player of prodigious defensive strength, and each day the pieces went back to their original positions and the game began afresh.

Louis de Bernières

SEND IN THE CLOWNS

When Italian troops invade the Greek island of Cephallonia, the setting of Louis de Bernières's novel Captain Corelli's Mandolin *(1994), the islanders prepare themselves for resistance. Their initial encounter with the enemy, however, is not quite as they had expected.*

THERE IS A story that in the Royal Palace, which was so vast and empty that the Royal Family travelled within it on bicycles, and so derelict that its water-taps spewed cockroaches, a White Lady appears as an omen of disaster. Her footsteps make no sound, her face blazes with malevolence, and once, when two aides-de-camp attempted to arrest her for attacking the grandmother of Prince Christopher, she vanished into thin air. If she had wandered the palace on this day, she would have found it occupied not by King George, but by German soldiers. If she had gone outside the city, she would have found the swastika flying from the Acropolis, and she would have had to travel to Crete to find the King.

The Cephallonians needed no such malicious ghosts to warn them. Two days before, the Italians had taken Corfu under farcical circumstances which were to be repeated identically today, and there was no one on the island who did not anticipate the worst.

It was the waiting that was tormenting. A great nostalgia rose up like a palpable mist; it was like making love for the last time to someone who is adored but is leaving forever. Every last moment of freedom and security was rolled about on the tongue, tasted, and remembered. Kokolios and Stamatis, the Communist and the monarchist, sat together at a table cleaning the components of a hunting rifle that had gathered dust on a wall for fifty years. They were without ammunition, but, as it was to everyone on the island, it seemed important to be engaged upon some gesture of resistance. Their busy fingers sought to calm the storms of anxiety and speculation in their minds, and they talked in low voices with a mutual affection that belied their years of vehement ideological difference. Neither of them knew any more how long their lives would be, and they had become precious to each other at last.

Families embraced more than had been the habit; fathers who expected to be beaten to death stroked the hair of pretty daughters who expected to be raped. Sons sat with their mothers on doorsteps and talked gently of their memories. Farmers took their barrels of wine with the glint of sunlight in it, and buried them in the earth so that no Italian would have the pleasure of their drinking. Grandmothers sharpened their cooking knives, and grandfathers remembered old deeds, persuading themselves that age had not diminished them; in the privacy of sheds they practised the 'shoulder-arms' with shovels and sticks. Many people visited their favourite places as if for the last time, and found that stones and dust, pellucid sea and ancient rock, had taken on an air of sadness such as one finds in a room where a beautiful child is lying at the door of death.

Nothing was as anyone had anticipated. Those who had thought that they would be filled with rage were afflicted instead by sensations of wonder, curiosity, or apathy. Those who knew that they would be terrified felt an icy calm and a rush of grim determination. Those who had long felt a terrible anxiety became calm, and there was one woman who was visited by an almost venial apprehension of salvation.

Pelagia ran up the hill to be with her father, following the ancient instinct that decrees that those who love each other must be united when they die. She found him standing in his doorway, as everyone else stood in theirs, his hand shielding his eyes against the sun as he watched the paratroops descend. Out of breath, she flew into his arms, and felt him tremble. Could he be afraid? She glanced up at him as he stroked her hair, and realized with a small shock that his lips moved and his eyes gleamed, not with fear, but with excitement. He looked down at her, straightened his back, and waved one hand to the skies. 'History,' he proclaimed, 'all this time I have been writing history, and now history is happening before my very eyes. Pelagia, my darling daughter, I have always wanted to live in history.' He released her, went indoors, and returned with a notebook and a sharpened pencil.

The planes disappeared and there was a long silence. It seemed as though nothing was to happen.

Down in the harbours the men of the Acqui Division disembarked apologetically from their landing craft and waved cheerfully but diffidently to the people in their doorways. Some of them shook their fists in return, others waved, and many made the emphatic gesture with the palm of the hand that is so insulting that in later years its perpetration was to become an imprisonable offence.

In the village, Pelagia and her father watched the platoons of paratroopers amble by, their commanders consulting maps with furrowed brows and pursed lips. Some of the Italians seemed so small as to be shorter than their rifles. 'They're a funny lot,' observed the doctor. At the back of one line of soldiers a particularly diminutive man with cockerel feathers nodding in his helmet was goose-stepping satirically with one finger held under his nose in imitation of a moustache. He widened his eyes and explained, 'Signor Hitler,' as he passed Pelagia by, anxious that she should perceive the joke and share it.

In front of his house Kokolios defiantly raised a Communist salute, his arm outstretched, his fist clenched, only to be confounded completely when a small group without an officer cheered him as it passed by and returned the salute, *con brio* and with exaggeration. He dropped his arm and his mouth fell open with astonishment. Were they mocking him, or were there comrades in the Fascist army?

An officer looking for his men stopped and questioned the doctor anxiously, waving a map in his face. '*Ecco una carta della Cephallonia*,' he said, '*Dov'è Argostoli?*'

The doctor looked into the dark eyes set in a handsome face, diagnosed a terminal case of extreme amiability, and replied, in Italian, 'I don't speak Italian, and Argostoli is more or less opposite Lixouri.'

'You speak very fluently for one who doesn't,' said the officer, smiling, 'so where is Lixouri?'

'Opposite Argostoli. Find one and you find the other, except that you must swim between them.'

Pelagia nudged her father in the ribs, fearful on his behalf. But the officer sighed, lifted his helmet, scratched his forehead, and glanced sideways at them. 'I'll follow the others,' he said, and hurried away. He returned a moment later, presented Pelagia with a small yellow flower, and disappeared once more. 'Extraordinary,' said the doctor, scribbling in his notebook.

A column of men, much smarter than most of the others, marched by in unison. At their head perspired Captain Antonio Corelli of the 33rd Regiment of Artillery, and slung across his back was a case containing the mandolin that he had named Antonia because it was the other half of himself. He spotted Pelagia. '*Bella bambina* at nine o'clock,' he shouted, 'E-y-e-s left.'

In unison the heads of the troops snapped in her direction, and for one astonishing minute she endured a march-past of the most comical and grotesque antics and expressions devisable by man. There was a soldier who crossed his eyes and folded down his lower lip, another who pouted and blew her a kiss, another who converted his marching into a Charlie Chaplin walk, another who pretended at each step to trip over his own feet, and another who twisted his helmet sideways, flared his nostrils, and rolled his eyes so high that the pupils vanished behind the upper lids. Pelagia put her hand to her mouth.

'Don't laugh,' ordered the doctor, *sotto voce*. 'It is our duty to hate them.'

All over the island there was a burgeoning of graffiti that took merry or malicious advantage of the fact that the Italians could not decipher the Cyrillic script. They mistook Rs for Ps, did not know that Gs can look like Ys or inverted Ls, had no idea what the triangle was, thought that an E was an H, construed theta as a kind of O, did not appreciate that the letter in the shape of a tent was the same as the one that looked like an inverted Y, were baffled by the three horizontal strokes that could also be written as a squiggle, knew from mathematics that pi meant 22 divided by 7, were unaware that E the wrong way round was an S, that the Y could also be written as a V and was in fact an E, were confused by the existence of an O with a vertical stroke that was actually an F, did not understand that the X was a K, failed utterly to find anything that might be meant by the elegant trident, and found that the omega reminded them of an earring. Ergo, conditions were ideal for the nocturnal splashing of white paint in huge letters on all available walls, especially as the quirks of an individual's handwriting could render the letters even more completely inscrutable. ENOSIS fought for space with ELEPHTHERIA, 'Long Live The King' cohabited without apparent anomaly with 'Workers Of The World Unite', 'Wops Fuck Off' abutted with 'Duce, Eat My Shit'. An admirer of Lord Byron wrote, 'I dream'd that Greece might still be free' in wobbly Roman letters, and General Tsolakoglou, the new quisling leader of the Greek people, appeared everywhere as a cartoon figure, committing various obscene and unpleasant acts with the Duce.

In the *kapheneia* and fields the men related Italian jokes: How many gears does an Italian tank have? One forward and four in reverse. What is the shortest book in the world? *The*

Italian Book of War Heroes. How many Italians does it take to put in a lightbulb? One to hold the bulb and two hundred to rotate the room. What is the name of Hitler's dog? Benito Mussolini. Why do Italians wear moustaches? To be reminded of their mothers. In the encampments the Italian soldiers in their turn asked, 'How do you know when a Greek girl is having a period?' And the answer would be 'She is wearing only one sock.' It was a long interlude during which the two populations stood off from each other, defusing by means of jokes the guilty suspicion on the one side and the livid resentment on the other. The Greeks talked fierily in secret about the partisans, about forming a resistance, and the Italians confined themselves to camp, the only signs of activity being the setting up of batteries, a daily reconnaissance by amphibious aircraft, and a mounted curfew patrol that jogged about at dusk, its members more anxious to exercise charm on females than to enforce an early night. Then a decision was made to billet officers upon suitable members of the local population.

The first thing about it that Pelagia knew was when she returned from the well, only to find a rotund Italian officer, accompanied by a sergeant and a private, standing in the kitchen, looking around with an appraising expression, and making notes with a pencil so blunt that he was obliged to read what he had written by casting the indentations against the light.

Pelagia had already stopped fearing that she was going to be raped, and had become accustomed to scowling at leers and slapping at the hands that made exploratory pinches of the backside; the Italians had turned out to be the modest kind of Romeo that is resigned to being rebuffed, but does not abandon hope. Nonetheless, she felt a momentary leap of fear when she came in and found the soldiers, and, but for a moment of indecision, she would have turned tail and fled. The plump officer smiled expansively, raised his arms in a gesture that signified, 'I would explain if I could, but I don't speak Greek,' and said, 'Ah,' in a manner that signified, 'How delightful to see you, since you are so pretty, and I am

embarrassed to be in your kitchen, but what else can I do?'
Pelagia said, '*Aspettami, vengo*,' and ran to fetch her father
from the *kapheneion*.

The soldiers waited, as requested, and soon Pelagia
reappeared with her father, who was anticipating the
encounter with some trepidation. There was a lurch of dread
waiting to surge into his heart and weaken it, but also a cold
and detached courage that comes to those who are determined to resist oppression with dignity; he remembered his
advice to the boys in the *kapheneion* – 'Let us use our anger
wisely' – and squared his shoulders. He wished that he had
retained his moustache with the waxed tips, so that he might
twist its extremities balefully and censoriously.

'*Buon giorno*,' said the officer, holding out his hand hope-
fully. The doctor perceived the conciliatory nature of the
gesture and its lack of conqueror's hubris, and much to his
own surprise he reached out and shook the proffered hand.

'*Buon giorno*,' he replied. 'I do hope that you enjoy your
regrettably short stay on our island.'

The officer raised his eyebrows, 'Short?'

'You have been expelled from Libya and Ethiopia,' the
doctor said, leaving the Italian to extrapolate his meaning.

'You speak Italian very well,' said the officer, 'you are the
first one I have come across. We are very badly in need of
translators to work with the populace. There would be
privileges. It seems that no one here speaks Italian.'

'I think you mean that none of you speak Greek.'

'Just so, as you say. It was only an idea.'

'You are very kind,' said Dr Iannis acidly, 'but I think you
will find that those of us who do speak Italian will suddenly
lose our memory when required to do so.'

The officer laughed. 'Understandable under the circumstances. I meant no offence.'

'There is Pasquale Lacerba, the photographer. He is an
Italian who lives in Argostoli, but perhaps even he would not
like to co-operate. But he is young enough not to know better.
As for me, I am a doctor, and I have enough to do without
becoming a collaborator.'

'It's worth a try,' said the quartermaster, 'most of the time we don't understand anything.'

'It's just as well,' observed the doctor. 'Perhaps you could tell me why you're here?'

'Ah,' said the man, shifting uneasily, aware of the unpleasantness of his position, 'the fact is, I am sorry to say, and with great regret, that . . . we shall be obliged to billet an officer on these premises.'

'There are only two rooms, my daughter's and my own. This is quite impossible, and it is also, as you probably realize, an outrage. I must refuse.' The doctor bristled like an angry cat, and the officer scratched his head with his pencil. It was really very awkward that the doctor spoke Italian; in other houses he had avoided this kind of scene and left it to the unfortunate guests to explain the situation, by means of grunts and gesticulations, when they turned up unannounced with their kitbags and drivers. The two men looked at one another, the doctor tilting his chin at a proud angle, and the Italian searching for a form of words that was both firm and mollifying. Suddenly the doctor's expression changed, and he asked, 'Did you say that you are a quartermaster?'

'No, *Signor Dottore*, you seem to have worked it out for yourself. I am a quartermaster. Why?'

'So do you have access to medical supplies?'

'Naturally,' replied the officer, 'I have access to everything.' The two men exchanged glances, divining perfectly the train of the other's thought. Dr Iannis said, 'I am short of many things, and the war has made it worse.'

'And I am short of accommodation. So?'

'So it's a deal,' said the doctor.

'A deal,' repeated the quartermaster. 'Anything you want, you send me a message via Captain Corelli. I am sure you will find him very charming. By the way, do you know anything about corns? Our doctors are useless.'

'For your corns I would probably need morphia, hypodermic syringes, sulphur ointment and iodine, neosalvarsan, bandages and lint, surgical spirit, salicylic acid, scalpels, and collodion,' said the doctor, 'but I will need a great deal, if you

184

understand me. In the meantime get a pair of boots that fits you.'

When the quartermaster had gone, taking with him the details of the doctor's requirements, Pelagia took her father's elbow anxiously and asked, 'But *Papas*, where is he to sleep? Am I to cook for him? And what with? There is almost no food.'

'He will have my bed,' said the doctor, knowing perfectly well that Pelagia would protest.

'O no, *Papas*, he will have mine. I will sleep in the kitchen.

'Since you insist, *koritsimou*. Just think of all the medicine and equipment it will mean for us.' He rubbed his hands together and added, 'The secret of being occupied is to exploit the exploiters. It is also knowing how to resist. I think we shall be very horrible to this captain.'

John Fowles

FREEDOM

At the heart of John Fowles's novel The Magus *(1966) lies the following story, recounted by Conchis, the mysterious old man living on a small Greek island, to his young visitor, Nicholas Urfe.*

When during the German occupation of the island in the Second World War four German soldiers were killed, SS Colonel Wimmel not only captured the guerrillas responsible but took 80 islanders hostage. Staging a cruel show trial, he put the fate of the hostages into the hands of Conchis, the mayor.

WE WERE MARCHED to the harbour. The entire village was there, some four or five hundred people, black and grey and faded blue, crammed on to the quays with a line of *die Raben* watching them. The village priests, the women, even little boys and girls. They screamed as we came into sight. Like some amorphous protoplasm. Trying to break bounds, but unable to.

We went on marching. There is a large house with huge Attic acroteria facing the harbour – you know it? – in those days there was a taverna on the ground-floor. On the balcony above I saw Wimmel and behind him Anton, flanked by men with machine-guns. I was taken from the column and made to stand against the wall under the balcony, among the chairs and tables. The hostages went marching on. Up a street and out of sight.

It was very hot. A perfect blue day. The villagers were driven from the quay to the terrace with the old cannons in front of the taverna. They stood crowded there. Brown faces upturned in the sunlight, black kerchiefs of the women fluttering in the breeze. I could not see the balcony, but the colonel waited above, impressing his silence on them, his presence. And gradually they fell absolutely quiet, a wall of expectant faces. Up in the sky I saw swallows and martins. Like children playing in a house where some tragedy is taking place among the adults. Strange, to see so many Greeks . . . and not a sound. Only the tranquil cries of little birds.

Wimmel began to speak. The collaborationist interpreted.

'You will now see what happens to those . . . those who are the enemies of Germany . . . and to those who help the enemies of Germany . . . by order of a court martial of the German High Command held last night . . . three have been executed . . . two more will now be executed . . .'

All the brown hands darted up, made the four taps of the Cross. Wimmel paused. German is to death what Latin is to ritual religion – entirely appropriate.

'Following that . . . the eighty hostages . . . taken under Occupation law . . . in retaliation for the brutal murder . . . of four innocent members of the German Armed Forces . . .' and yet again he paused . . . 'will be executed.'

When the interpreter interpreted the last phrase, there was an exhaled groan, as if they had all been struck in the stomach. Many of the women, some of the men, fell to their knees, imploring the balcony. Humanity groping for the non-existent pity of a *deus vindicans*. Wimmel must have withdrawn, because the beseechings turned to lamentations.

Now I was forced out from the wall and marched after the hostages. Soldiers, the Austrians, stood at every entrance to the harbour and forced the villagers back. It horrified me that they could help *die Raben*, could obey Wimmel, could stand there with impassive faces and roughly force back people that I knew, only a day or two before, they did not hate.

The alley curved up between the houses to the square beside the village school. It is a natural stage, inclined slightly to the

187

north, with the sea and the mainland over the lower roofs. With the wall of the village school on the uphill side, and high walls to east and west. If you remember, there is a large plane tree in the garden of the house to the west. The branches come over the wall. As I came to the square that was the first thing I saw. Three bodies hung from the branches, pale in the shadow, as monstrous as Goya etchings. There was the naked body of the cousin with its terrible wound. And there were the naked bodies of the two girls. They had been disembowelled. A slit cut from their breastbones down to their pubic hair and the intestines pulled out. Half-gutted carcasses, swaying slightly in the noon wind.

Beyond those three atrocious shapes I saw the hostages. They had been herded against the school in a pen of barbed wire. The men at the back were just in the shadow of the wall, the front ones in sunlight. As soon as they saw me they began to shout. There were insults of the obvious kind to me, confused cries of appeal – as if anything I could say then would have touched the colonel. He was there, in the centre of the square, with Anton and some twenty of *die Raben*. On the third side of the square, to the east, there is a long wall. You know it? In the middle a gate. Iron grilles. The two surviving guerrillas were lashed to the bars. Not with rope – with barbed wire.

I was halted behind the two lines of men, some twenty yards away from where Wimmel was standing. Anton would not look at me, though Wimmel turned briefly. Anton – staring into space, as if he had hypnotized himself into believing that none of what he saw existed. As if he no longer existed himself. The colonel beckoned the collaborationist to him. I suppose he wanted to know what the hostages were shouting. He appeared to think for a moment and then he went towards them. They fell silent. Of course they did not know he had already pronounced sentence on them. He said something that was translated to them. What, I could not hear, except that it reduced the village to silence. So it was not the death sentence. The colonel marched back to me.

He said, 'I have made an offer to these peasants.' I looked

at his face. It was absolutely without nervousness, excitation; a man in complete command of himself. He went on, 'I will permit them not to be executed. To go to a labour camp. On one condition. That is that you, as mayor of this village, carry out in front of them the execution of the two murderers.'

I said, 'I am not an executioner.'

The village men began to shout frantically at me.

He looked at his watch, and said, 'You have thirty seconds to decide.'

Of course in such situations one cannot think. All coherence is crowded out of one's mind. You must remember this. From this point on I acted without reason. Beyond reason.

I said, 'I have no choice.'

He went to the end of one of the ranks of men in front of me. He took a sub-machine-gun from a man's shoulder, appeared to make sure that it was correctly loaded, then came back with it and presented it to me with both hands. As if it was a prize I had won. The hostages cheered, crossed themselves. And then were silent. The colonel watched me. I had a wild idea that I might turn the gun on him. But of course the massacre of the entire village would then have been inevitable.

I walked towards the men wired to the iron gates. I knew why he had done this. It would be widely publicized by the German-controlled newspapers. The pressure on me would not be mentioned, and I would be presented as the Greek who co-operated in the German theory of order. A warning to other mayors. An example to other frightened Greeks everywhere. But those eighty men – how could I condemn them?

I came within about fifteen feet of the two guerillas. So close, because I had not fired a gun for very many years. For some reason I had not looked them in the face till then. I had looked at the high wall with its tiled top, at a pair of vulgar ornamental urns on top of the pillars that flanked the gate, at the fronds of a pepper tree beyond. But then I had to look at them. The younger of the two might have been dead. His head

189

had fallen forward. They had done something to his hands, I could not see what, but there was blood all over the fingers. He was not dead. I heard him groan. Mutter something. He was delirious.

And the other. His mouth had been struck or kicked. The lips were severely contused, reddened. As I stood there and raised the gun he drew back what remained of those lips. All his teeth had been smashed in. The inside of his mouth was like a blackened vulva. But I was too desperate to finish to realize the real cause. He too had had his fingers crushed, or his nails torn out, and I could see multiple burns on his body. But the Germans had made one terrible error. They had not gouged out his eyes.

I raised the gun blindly and pressed the trigger. Nothing happened. A click. I pressed it again. And again, an empty click.

I turned and looked round. Wimmel and my two guards were standing thirty feet or so away, watching. The hostages suddenly began to call. They thought I had lost the will to shoot. I turned back and tried once more. Again, nothing. I turned to the colonel, and gestured with the gun, to show that it would not fire. I felt faint in the heat. Nausea. Yet unable to faint.

He said, 'Is something wrong?'

I answered, 'The gun will not fire.'

'It is a Schmeisser. An excellent weapon.'

'I have tried three times.'

'It will not fire because it is not loaded. It is strictly forbidden for the civilian population to possess loaded weapons.'

I stared at him, then at the gun. Still not understanding. The hostages were silent again.

I said, very helplessly, 'How can I kill them?'

He smiled, a smile as thin as a sabre-slash. Then he said, 'I am waiting.'

I understood then. I was to club them to death. I understood many things. His real self, his real position. And from that came the realization that he was mad, and that he was therefore innocent, as all mad people, even the most cruel, are innocent. He was what life could do if it wanted – an extreme possibility made hideously mind and flesh. Perhaps that was why he could impose himself so strongly, like a black divinity. For there was something superhuman in the spell he cast. And therefore the real evil, the real monstrosity in the situation lay in the other Germans, those less-than-mad lieutenants and corporals and privates who stood silently there watching this exchange.

I walked towards him. The two guards thought I was going to attack him because they sharply raised their guns. But he said something to them and stood perfectly still. I stopped some six feet from him. We stared at each other.

'I beg you in the name of European civilization to stop this barbarity.'

'And I command you to continue this punishment.'

Without looking down he said, 'Refusal to carry out this order will result in your own immediate execution.'

I walked back over the dry earth to that gate. I stood in front of those two men. I was going to say to the one who seemed capable of understanding that I had no choice, I must do this terrible thing to him. But I left a fatal pause of a second to elapse. Perhaps because I realized, close to him, what had happened to his mouth. It had been burnt, not simply bludgeoned or kicked. I remembered that man with the iron stake, the electric fire. They had broken in his teeth and branded his tongue, burnt his tongue right down to the roots with red-hot iron. That word he shouted must finally have driven them beyond endurance. And in those astounding five seconds, the most momentous of my life, I understood this guerilla. I mean that I understood far better than he did himself what he was. He helped me. He managed to stretch his head towards me and say the word he could not say. It was almost not a sound, but a contortion in his throat, a five-syllabled choking. But once again, one last time, it was unmistakably that word. And the word was in his eyes, in his being, totally in his being. What did Christ say on the cross? Why hast thou forsaken me? What this man said was something far less sympathetic, far less pitiful, even far less human, but far profounder. He spoke out of a world the very opposite of mine. In mine life had no price. It was so valuable that it was literally priceless. In his, only one thing had that quality of pricelessness. It was *eleutheria*: freedom. He was the immalleable, the essence, the beyond reason, beyond logic, beyond civilization, beyond history. He was not God, because there is no God we can know. But he was a proof that there is a God that we can never know. He was the final right to deny. To be free to choose. He, or what manifested itself through him, even included the insane Wimmel, the despicable German and Austrian troops. He was every freedom, from the very worst to the very best. The freedom to desert on the battlefield of Neuve Chapelle. The freedom to confront a primitive God at Seidevarre. The freedom to disembowel peasant girls and castrate with wire-cutters. He was something that passed beyond morality but sprang out of the very essence of things – that comprehended all, the freedom to do all, and stood against only one thing – the prohibition not to do all.

All this takes many words to say to you. And I have said nothing about how I felt this immalleability, this refusal to cohere, was essentially Greek. That is, I finally assumed my Greekness. All I saw I saw in a matter of seconds, perhaps not in time at all. Saw that I was the only person left in that square who had the freedom left to choose, and that the annunciation and defence of that freedom was more important than common sense, self-preservation, yes, than my own life, than the lives of the eighty hostages. Again and again, since then, those eighty men have risen in the night and accused me. You must remember that I was certain I was going to die too. But all I have to set against their crucified faces are those few transcendent seconds of knowledge. But knowledge like a white heat. My reason has repeatedly told me I was wrong. Yet my total being still tells me I was right.

I stood there perhaps fifteen seconds – I could not tell you, time means nothing in such situations – and then I dropped the gun and stopped beside the guerilla leader. I saw the colonel watching me, and I said, for him and so also for the remnant of a man beside me to hear, the one word that remained to be said.

Somewhere beyond Wimmel I saw Anton moving, walking quickly towards him. But it was too late. The colonel spoke, the sub-machine-guns flashed and I closed my eyes at exactly the moment the first bullets hit me.

Norman Mailer

WE YOU COMING-TO-GET, YANK

Norman Mailer's classic novel, The Naked and the Dead
*(1949), tells the story of a platoon of American soldiers
fighting the Japanese on a Pacific island. The following
extract shows the transformation of one of the soldiers when
he finds himself in the front line with just a river separating his
platoon from the enemy.*

CROFT SAT DOWN on the edge of the hole and peered
through the bushes at the river. The jungle completely surrounded him, and now that he was no longer active, he felt
very weary and a little depressed. To counteract this mood, he
began to feel the various objects in the hole. There were three
boxes of belt ammunition and a row of seven grenades lined
up neatly at the base of the machine-gun. At his feet were a
box of flares and a flare gun. He picked it up and broke open
the breech quietly, loaded it, and cocked it. Then he set it
down beside him.

A few shells murmured overhead and began to fall. He was
a little surprised at how near they landed to the other side of
the river. Not more than a few hundred yards away, the noise
of their explosion was extremely loud; a few pieces of
shrapnel lashed the leaves on the trees above him. He broke
off a stalk from a plant and put it in his mouth, chewing
slowly and reflectively. He guessed that the weapons platoon
of A Company had fired, and he tried to determine which trail

at the fork would lead to them in case he had to pull back his men. Now he was patient and at ease; the danger of their position neutralized the anticipation for some combat he had felt earlier, and he was left cool and calm and very tired.

The mortar shells were falling perhaps fifty yards in front of the platoon at his left, and Croft spat quietly. It was too close to be merely harassing fire; someone had heard something in the jungle on the other side of the river or they would never have called for mortars so close to their own position. His hand explored the hole again and discovered a field telephone. Croft picked up the receiver, listened quietly. It was an open line, and probably confined to the platoons of A Company. Two men were talking in voices so low that he strained to hear them.

'Walk it up another fifty and then bring it back.'

'You sure they're Japs?'

'I swear I heard them talking.'

Croft stared tensely across the river. The moon had come out, and the strands of beach on either side of the stream were shining with a silver glow. The jungle wall on the other side looked impenetrable.

The mortars fired again behind him with a cruel flat sound. He watched the shells land in the jungle, and then creep nearer to the river in successive volleys. A mortar answered from the Japanese side of the river, and about a quarter of a mile to the left Croft could hear several machine-guns spattering at each other, the uproar deep and irregular. Croft picked up the phone and whistled into it. 'Wilson,' he whispered. '*Wilson!*' There was no answer and he debated whether to walk over to Wilson's hole. Silently Croft cursed him for not noticing the phone, and then berated himself for not having discovered it before he briefed the others. He looked out across the river. Fine sergeant I am, he told himself.

His ears were keyed to all the sounds of the night, and from long experience he sifted out the ones that were meaningless. If an animal rustled in its hole, he paid no attention; if some crickets chirped, his ear disregarded them. Now he picked a muffled slithering sound which he knew could be made only by men moving through a thin patch of jungle. He peered across the river, trying to determine where the foliage was least dense. At the point between his gun and Wilson's there was a grove of a few coconut trees sparse enough to allow men to assemble; as he stared into that patch of wood, he was certain he heard a man move. Croft's mouth tightened. His hand felt for the bolt of the machine-gun, and he slowly brought it to bear on the coconut grove. The rustling grew louder; it seemed as if men were creeping through the brush on the other side of the river to a point opposite his gun. Croft swallowed once. Tiny charges seemed to pulse through his limbs and his head was as empty and shockingly aware as if it had been plunged into a pail of freezing water. He wet his lips and shifted his position slightly, feeling as though he could hear the flexing of his muscles.

The Jap mortar fired again and he started. The shells were falling by the next platoon, the sound painful and jarring to him. He stared out on the moonlit river until his eyes deceived him; he began to think he could see the heads of men in the dark swirls of the current. Croft gazed down at his knees for an instant and then across the river again. He looked a little to the left or right of where he thought the Japanese might be; from long experience he had learned a man could not look directly at an object and see it in the darkness. Something seemed to move in the grove, and a new trickle of sweat formed and rolled down his back. He twisted uncomfortably. Croft was unbearably tense, but the sensation was not wholly unpleasant.

He wondered if Wilson had noticed the sounds, and then in answer to his question, there was the unmistakable clicking of a machine-gun bolt. To Croft's keyed senses, the sound echoed up and down the river, and he was furious that Wilson should have revealed his position. The rustling in the brush became louder and Croft was convinced he could hear voices whispering on the other side of the river. He fumbled for a grenade and placed it at his feet.

Then he heard a sound which pierced his flesh. Someone

called from across the river, 'Yank, Yank!' Croft sat numb. The voice was thin and high-pitched, hideous in a whisper. 'That's a Jap,' Croft told himself. He was incapable of moving for that instant.

'Yank!' It was calling to him. 'Yank. We you coming-to-get, Yank.'

The night lay like a heavy stifling mat over the river. Croft tried to breathe.

'*We you coming-to-get, Yank.*'

Croft felt as if a hand had suddenly clapped against his back, travelled up his spine over his skull to clutch at the hair on his forehead. 'Coming to get you, Yank,' he heard himself whisper. He had the agonizing frustration of a man in a nightmare who wants to scream and cannot utter a sound. 'We you *coming-to-get*, Yank.'

He shivered terribly for a moment, and his hands seemed congealed on the machine-gun. He could not bear the intense pressure in his head.

'We you coming-to-get, Yank,' the voice screamed.

'COME AND GET ME, YOU SONSOFBITCHES,' Croft roared. He shouted with every fibre of his body as though he plunged at an oaken door.

There was no sound at all for perhaps ten seconds, nothing but the moonlight on the river and the taut rapt buzzing of the crickets. Then the voice spoke again. 'Oh, we come, Yank, we come.'

Croft pulled back the bolt on his machine-gun, and rammed it home. His heart was still beating with frenzy. 'Recon . . . RECON, UP ON THE LINE,' he shouted with all his strength.

A machine-gun lashed at him from across the river, and he ducked in his hole. In the darkness, it spat a vindictive white light like an acetylene torch, and its sound was terrifying. Croft was holding himself together by the force of his will. He pressed the trigger of his gun and it leapt and bucked under his hand. The tracers spewed wildly into the jungle on the other side of the river.

But the noise, the vibration of his gun, calmed him. He

197

directed it to where he had seen the Japanese gunfire and loosed a volley. The handle pounded against his fist, and he had to steady it with both hands. The hot metallic smell of the barrel eddied back to him, made what he was doing real again. He ducked in his hole waiting for the reply and winced involuntarily as the bullets whipped past.

BEE-YOWWWW! . . . BEE-YOOWWWW! Some dirt snapped at his face from the ricochets. Croft was not conscious of feeling it. He had the surface numbness a man has in a fight. He flinched at sounds, his mouth tightened and loosened, his eyes stared, but he was oblivious to his body.

Croft fired the gun again, held it for a long vicious burst, and then ducked in his hole. An awful scream singed the night, and for an instant Croft grinned weakly. Got him he thought. He saw the metal burning through flesh, shattering the bones in its path. 'AHYOHHHH.' The scream froze him again, and for an odd disconnected instant he experienced again the whole complex of sounds and smells and sighs when a calf was branded. 'RECON, UP . . . UP!' he shouted furiously and fired steadily for ten seconds to cover their advance. As he paused he could hear some men crawling behind him, and he whispered, 'Recon?'

'Yeah.' Gallagher dropped into the hole with him. 'Mother of Mary,' he muttered. Croft could feel him shaking beside him.

'Stop it!' He gripped his arm tensely. 'The other men up?'

'Yeah.'

Croft looked across the river again. Everything was silent, and the disconnected abrupt spurts of fire were forgotten like vanished sparks from a grindstone. Now that he was no longer alone, Croft was able to plan. The fact that men were up with him, were scattered in the brush along the bank between their two machine-guns, recovered his sense of command. 'They're going to attack soon,' he whispered hoarsely in Gallagher's ear.

Gallagher trembled again. 'Ohh. No way to wake up,' he tried to say, but his voice kept lapsing.

'Look,' Croft whispered. 'Creep along the line and tell them to hold fire until the Japs start to cross the river.'

'I can't, I can't,' Gallagher whispered.

Croft felt like striking him. 'Go!' he whispered.

'I can't.'

The Jap machine-gun lashed at them from across the river. The bullets went singing into the jungle behind them, ripping at leaves. The tracers looked like red splints of lightning as they flattened into the jungle. A thousand rifles seemed to be firing at them from across the river, and the two men pressed themselves against the bottom of the hole. The sounds cracked against their eardrums. Croft's head ached. Firing the machine-gun had partially deafened him. BEE-YOWWWW! A ricochet slapped some more dirt on top of them. Croft felt it pattering on his back this time. He was trying to sense the moment when he would have to raise his head and fire the gun. The firing seemed to slacken, and he lifted up his eyes cautiously. BEE-YOWWWW, BEE-YOWWWW! He dropped in the hole again. The Japanese machine-gun raked through the brush at them.

There was a shrill screaming sound, and the men covered their heads with their arms. BAA-ROWWMM, BAA-ROWWMM, ROWWMM, ROWWMM. The mortars exploded all about them, and something picked Gallagher up, shook him, and then released him. 'O God,' he cried. A clod of dirt stung his neck. BAA-ROWWMM, BAA-ROWWMM.

'Jesus, I'm hit,' someone screamed. 'I'm hit. Something hit me.'

BAA-ROWWMM.

Gallagher rebelled against the force of the explosions. 'Stop, I give up,' he screamed. 'STOP! . . . I give up! I give up!' At that instant he no longer knew what made him cry out.

BAA-ROWWMM, BAA-ROWWMM.

'I'm hit, I'm hit,' someone was screaming. The Japanese rifles were firing again. Croft lay on the floor of the hole with his hands against the ground and every muscle poised in its place.

BAA-ROWWMM. TEEEEEEEE! The shrapnel was singing as it scattered through the foliage.

199

Croft picked up his flare gun. The firing had not abated, but through it he heard someone shouting in Japanese. He pointed the gun in the air.

'Here they come,' Croft said.

He fired the flare and shouted, 'STOP 'EM!'

A shrill cry came out of the jungle across the river. It was the scream a man might utter if his foot was being crushed. 'AAAIIIIII, AAAIIIIII.'

The flare burst at the moment the Japanese started their charge. Croft had a split perception of the Japanese machine-gun firing from a flank, and then began to fire automatically, not looking where he fired, but holding his gun low, swinging it from side to side. He could not hear the other guns fire, but saw their muzzle blasts like exhausts.

He had a startling frozen picture of the Japanese running toward him across the narrow river. 'AAAAIIIIIIIIIH,' he heard again. In the light of the flare the Japanese had the stark frozen quality of men revealed by a shaft of lightning. Croft no longer saw anything clearly, he could not have said at that moment where his hands ended and the machine-gun began; he was lost in a vast moil of noise out of which individual screams and shouts etched in his mind for an instant. He could never have counted the Japanese who charged across the river; he knew only that his finger was rigid on the trigger bar. He could not have loosened it. In those few moments he felt no sense of danger. He just kept firing.

The line of men who charged across the river began to fall. In the water they were slowed considerably and the concentrated fire from recon's side raged at them like a wind across an open field. They began to stumble over the bodies ahead of them. Croft saw one soldier reach into the air behind another's body as though trying to clutch something in the sky and Croft fired at him for what seemed many seconds before the arm collapsed.

He looked to his right and saw three men trying to cross the river where it turned and ran parallel to the bluff. He swung the gun about and lashed them with it. One man fell, and the other two paused uncertainly and began to run back toward their own bank of the river. Croft had no time to follow them; some soldiers had reached the beach on his side and were charging the gun. He fired point blank at them, and they collapsed about five yards from his hole.

Croft fired and fired, switching targets with the quick reflexes of an athlete shifting for a ball. As soon as he saw men falling he would attack another group. The line of Japanese broke into little bunches of men who wavered, began to retreat.

The light of the flare went out and Croft was blinded for a moment. There was no sound again in the darkness and he fumbled for another flare, feeling an almost desperate urgency. 'Where is it?' he whispered to Gallagher.

'What?'

'Shit.' Croft's hand found the flare box, and he loaded the gun again. He was beginning to see in the darkness, and he hesitated. But something moved on the river and he fired the flare. As it burst, a few Japanese soldiers were caught motionless in the water. Croft pivoted his gun on them and fired. One of the soldiers remained standing for an incredible time. There was no expression on his face; he looked vacant and surprised even as the bullets struck him in the chest.

Nothing was moving now on the river. In the light of the flare, the bodies looked as limp and unhuman as bags of grain. One soldier began to float downstream, his face in the water. On the beach near the gun, another Japanese soldier was lying on his back. A wide stain of blood was spreading out from his body, and his stomach, ripped open, gaped like the swollen entrails of a fowl. On an impulse Croft fired a burst into him, and felt the twitch of pleasure as he saw the body quiver.

A wounded man was groaning in Japanese. Every few seconds he would scream, the sound terrifying in the cruel blue light of the flare. Croft picked up a grenade. 'That sonofabitch is makin' too much noise,' he said. He pulled the pin and lobbed the grenade over to the opposite bank. It dropped like a beanbag on one of the bodies, and Croft pulled Gallagher down with him. The explosion was powerful and yet empty like a blast that collapses window-panes. After a moment, the echoes ceased.

Croft tensed himself and listened to the sounds from across the river. There was the quiet furtive noise of men retreating into the jungle. 'GIVE 'EM A VOLLEY!' he shouted.

All the men in recon began to fire again, and Croft raked the jungle for a minute in short bursts. He could hear Wilson's machine-gun pounding steadily. 'I guess we gave 'em something,' Croft told Gallagher. The flare was going out, and Croft stood up. 'Who was hit?' he shouted.

'Toglio.'

'Bad?' Croft asked.

'I'm okay,' Toglio whispered. 'I got a bullet in my elbow.'

'Can you wait till morning?'

There was silence for a moment, then Toglio answered weakly, 'Yeah, I'll be okay.'

Croft got out of his hole. 'I'm coming down,' he announced. 'Hold your fire.' He walked along the path until he reached Toglio. Red and Goldstein were kneeling beside him, and Croft spoke to them in a low voice. 'Pass this on,' he said. 'We're all gonna stay in our holes until mornin'. I don't think they'll be back tonight but you cain't tell. And no one is gonna fall asleep. They's only about an hour till dawn, so you ain't got nothin' to piss about.'

'I wouldn't go to sleep anyway,' Goldstein breathed. 'What a way to wake up.' It was the same thing Gallagher had said.

'Yeah, well I just wasn't ridin' on my ass either, waitin' for them to come,' Croft said. He shivered for a moment in the early morning air and realized with a pang of shame that for the first time in his life he had been really afraid. 'The sonsofbitch Japs,' he said. His legs were tired and he turned to go back to his gun. I hate the bastards, he said to himself, a terrible rage working through his weary body.

'One of these days I'm gonna really get me a Jap,' he whispered aloud. The river was slowly carrying the bodies downstream.

'At least,' Gallagher said, 'if we got to stay here a couple of days, the fuggers won't be stinkin' up the joint.'

202

The Time Machine:

SAM CROFT
THE HUNTER

A lean man of medium height but he held himself so erectly he appeared tall. His narrow triangular face was utterly without expression. There seemed nothing wasted in his hard small jaw, gaunt firm cheeks and straight short nose. His gelid eyes were very blue . . . he was efficient and strong and usually empty and his main cast of mind was a superior contempt toward nearly all other men. He hated weakness and he loved practically nothing. There was a crude unformed vision in his soul but he was rarely conscious of it.

No, but why *is* Croft that way?

Oh, there are answers. He is that way because of the corruption-of-the-society. He is that way because the devil has claimed him for one of his own. It is because he is a Texan; it is because he has renounced God.

He is that kind of man because the only woman he ever loved cheated on him, or he was born that way, or he was having problems of adjustment.

Croft's father, Jesse Croft, liked to say, 'Well, now, my Sam is a mean boy. I reckon he was whelped mean.' And then Jesse Croft, thinking of his wife who was ailing, a weak woman sweet and mild, might add, ''Course Sam got mother's milk if ever a one did, but Ah figger it turned sour on him 'cause that was the only way his stomach would take it.' Then he would cackle and blow his nose into his hand and wipe it on the back of pale-blue dungarees. (Standing before his dirty wood barn, the red dry soil of western Texas under his feet.) 'Why, Ah 'member once Ah took Sam huntin', he was only an itty-bitty runt, not big enough to hold up the gun hardly . . . but he was a mean shot from the beginning. And Ah'll tell ya, he just didn't like to have a man interfere with him. That was one thing could always rile him, even when he was an itty-bitty bastard.

'Couldn't stand to have anyone beat him in anything'.

'Never could lick him. Ah'd beat the piss out o' him and he'd never make a sound. Jus' stand there lookin' at me as if he was fixin' to wallop me back, or maybe put a bullet in mah head.'

James Jones
No Choice

A novel of graphic realism, filmed by Terence Mallick in 1998, James Jones's The Thin Red Line *(1963) is the story of American soldiers fighting against the Japanese, in the Battle of Guadalcanal in 1942. The following episode describes in tragicomic fashion Private Bead's first encounter with a Japanese soldier – in quite unusual circumstances.*

AT JUST ABOUT five o'clock he had had to take a crap. And he had not had a crap for two days. Everything had quieted down on the line by five and at the aid station below them the last of the wounded were being cared for and sent back. Bead had seen other men taking craps along the slope, and he knew the procedure. After two days on these slopes the procedure was practically standardized. Because every available bit of level space was occupied, jammed with men and equipment, crapping was relegated to the steeper slopes. Here the process was to take along an entrenching shovel and dig a little hole, then turn your backside to the winds of the open air and squat, balancing yourself precariously on your toes, supporting yourself on the dirt or rocks in front of you with your hands. The effect, because of the men below in the basin, was rather like hanging your ass out of a tenth-floor window above a crowded street. It was an embarrassing position to say the least, and the men below were not above taking advantage of it with catcalls, whistles or loud soulful sighs.

Bead was shy. He could have done it that way if he'd had to, but because he was shy, and because now everything had quieted down to an unbelievable evening peace after the terror, noise and danger of the afternoon, he decided to have himself a pleasant, quiet, private crap in keeping with the peacefulness. Without saying anything to anyone he dropped all of his equipment by his hole and taking only his GI roll of toilet paper, he started to climb the twenty yards to the crest. He did not even take an entrenching tool because on the other side there was no need to bury his stool. Beyond the crest he knew that the slope did not drop precipitously as it did further to the left, but fell slowly for perhaps fifty yards through the trees before it plunged in a bluff straight down to the river. This was where D Company had caught the Japanese patrol earlier in the day.

'Hey, bud, where you going?' somebody from the 2nd Platoon called to him as he passed through.

'To take a shit,' Bead called back without looking around and disappeared over the crest.

The trees began three yards below the actual crest. Because the jungle was thinner with less undergrowth here at its outer edge, it looked more like the columnar, smooth-floored woods of home and made Bead think of when he was a boy. Reminded of times when as a Boy Scout he had camped out and crapped with peaceful pleasure in the summer woods of Iowa, he placed the roll of paper comfortably near, dropped his pants and squatted. Halfway through with relieving himself, he looked up and saw a Japanese man with a bayoneted rifle moving stealthily through the trees ten yards away.

As if feeling his gaze, the Japanese man turned his head and saw him in almost the same instant but not before, through the electrifying, heart stabbing thrill of apprehension, danger, disbelief, denial, Bead got a clear, burned in the brain impression of him.

He was a small man, and thin; very thin. His mudslicked, mustard-khaki uniform with its ridiculous wrap leggings hung from him in jungledamp, greasy folds. Not only did he not wear any of the elaborate camouflage Bead had been taught by movies to expect, he did not even wear a helmet. He wore a greasy, wrinkled, bent-up forage cap. Beneath it his yellow-brown face was so thin the high cheek-bones seemed about to come out through his skin. He was badly unshaven, perhaps two weeks, but his greasy-looking beard was as straggly as Bead's nineteen-year-old one. As to age, Bead could not form any clear impression; he might have been twenty, or forty.

All of this visual perception occurred in an eyewink of time, an eyewink which seemed to coast on and on and on, then the Japanese man saw him too and turning, all in one movement, began to run at him, but moving cautiously, the bayonet on the end of his rifle extended.

Bead, still squatting with his pants down, his behind still dirty, gathered his weight under him. He was going to have to try to jump one way or another, but which? Which side to jump to? Am I going to die? Am I really going to die now? He did not even have his knife with him. Terror and disbelief, denial, fought each other in him. Why the Japanese did not simply fire the rifle he did not know. Perhaps he was afraid of being heard in the American lines. Instead he came on, obviously meaning to bayonet Bead where he sat. His eyes were intent with purpose. His lips were drawn back from his teeth, which were large, but were well formed and not at all protruding as in the posters. Was it really true?

In desperation, still not knowing which way to try to jump, all in one movement Bead pulled up his pants over his dirty behind to free his legs and dived forward in a low, shoestring football tackle when the Japanese man was almost on him, taking him around the ankles, his feet driving hard in the soft ground. Surprised, the Japanese man brought the rifle down sharply, but Bead was already in under the bayonet. The stacking swivel banged him painfully on the collarbone. By clasping the mudcaked shins against his chest and using his head for a fulcrum, still driving hard with his feet, the Japanese man had no way to fall except backward, and Bead was already clawing up his length before he hit the ground. In the fall he dropped the rifle and had the wind knocked out of him. This gave Bead time to hitch up his pants again and spring upward once more until, kneeling on his upper arms and sitting on his chest, he began to punch and claw him in the face and neck. The Japanese man could only pluck feebly at his legs and forearms.

Bead heard a high, keening scream and thought it was the Japanese begging for mercy until finally he slowly became aware that the Japanese man was now unconscious. Then he realized it was himself making that animal scream. He could not, however, stop it. The Japanese man's face was now running blood from the clawing, and several of his teeth had been broken back into his throat from the punches. But Bead could not stop. Sobbing and wailing, he continued to belabour the unconscious Japanese with fingernail and fist. He wanted to tear his face off with his bare hands, but found this difficult. Then he seized his throat and tried to break his head by beating it on the soft ground but only succeeded in digging a small hole with it. Exhausted finally, he collapsed forward on hands and knees above the bleeding, unconscious man, only to feel the Japanese immediately twitch with life beneath him.

Outraged at such a display of vitality, alternately sobbing and wailing, Bead rolled aside, seized the enemy rifle and on his knees raised it above his head and drove the long bayonet almost full length into the Japanese chest. The Japanese man's body convulsed in a single spasm. His eyes opened, staring horribly at nothing, and his hands flipped up from the elbows and seized the blade through his chest.

Staring with horror at the fingers which were cutting themselves on the blade trying to draw it out, Bead leaped to his feet, and his pants fell down. Hiking his pants up and standing spraddlelegged to keep them from falling, he seized the rifle and tried to pull it out in order to plunge it in again. But the bayonet would not come loose. Remembering dimly something he had been taught in bayonet practice, he grabbed the small of the stock and pulled the trigger. Nothing happened. The gun was on safety. Fumbling with the unfamiliar, foreign safety, he released it and pulled again.

There was a flesh-muffled explosion and the bayonet came free. But the fool of a Japanese with his open eyes went on grasping at his chest with his bleeding fingers as if he could not get it through his thick head that the bayonet was out. My god, how much killing did the damned fool require? Bead had beaten him, kicked him, choked him, clawed him, bayoneted him, shot him. He had a sudden frantic vision of himself, by rights the victor, doomed forever to kill perpetually the same single Japanese.

This time, not intending to be caught in the same trap twice, instead of sticking him he reversed the rifle in his hands and drove the butt down full force into his face, smashing it. Standing above him spraddlelegged to keep his pants up, he drove the rifle butt again and again into the Japanese man's face, until all of the face and most of the head were mingled with the muddy ground. Then he threw the rifle from him and fell down on his hands and knees and began to vomit.

Bead did not lose consciousness, but he completely lost his sense of time. When he came to himself, still on hands and knees, gasping, he shook his hanging head and opened his eyes and discovered his left hand was resting in a friendly way on the Japanese man's still, mustard-khaki knee. Bead snatched it away as though he had discovered it lying across a burning stove. He had an obscure feeling that if he did not look at the corpse of the man he had killed or touch it, he would not be held responsible. With this in mind he crawled feebly away through the trees, breathing in long painful groans.

The woods were very quiet. Bead could not remember ever having heard such quiet. Then faintly, penetrating the immensity of this quiet, he heard voices, American voices, and the casual sound of a shovel scraped against a rock. It seemed impossible that they could be that close. He got shakily to his feet holding up his pants. It also seemed impossible that anything could ever again sound as casual as that shovel had. He knew he had to get back inside the lines. But first he would have to try to clean himself up. He was a mess. He had no desire to finish his crap.

209

First of all, he had to go back to the vicinity of the dead man to get his roll of toilet paper. He hated that but there wasn't any choice. His pants and his dirty behind were what bothered him most. Horror of that was inbred in him; but also he was terrified someone might think he had crapped his pants from fear. He used most of his roll of toilet paper on that, and in the end even sacrificed one of his three clean handkerchiefs which he was saving back for his glasses, moistening it with spittle. In addition he was spattered with blood and vomit. He could not remove every stain, but he tried to get enough so that nobody would notice. Because he had already decided he was not going to mention this to anybody.

Also, he had lost his glasses. He found them, miraculously unbroken, beside the dead man. Searching for his glasses, he had to go right up to the body, and to look at it closely. The faceless – almost headless – corpse with its bloody, cut fingers and the mangled hole in its chest, so short a time ago a living, breathing man, made him so dizzy in the stomach that he thought he might faint. On the other hand, he could not forget the intent look of deliberate purpose on the man's face as he came in with the bayonet. There didn't seem to be any reasonable answer.

The feet were the saddest thing. In their hobnailed infantry boots they splayed outward, relaxed, like the feet of a man asleep. With a kind of perverse fascination Bead could not resist giving one of them a little kick. It lolloped up, then flopped back. Bead wanted to turn and run. He could not escape a feeling that, especially now, after he'd both looked and touched, some agent of retribution would try to hold him responsible. He wanted to beg the man's forgiveness in the hope of forestalling responsibility. He had not felt such oppressive guilt over anything since the last time his mother had caught and whipped him for masturbating.

If he'd had to kill him, and apparently he had, at least he could have done it more efficiently and gracefully, and with less pain and anguish for the poor man. If he had not lost his head, had not gone crazy with fear, perhaps he might even have taken him prisoner and obtained valuable information from him. But he had been frantic to get the killing over with, as if afraid that as long as the man could breathe he might suddenly stand up and accuse him. Suddenly Bead had a mental picture of them both with positions reversed: of himself lying there and feeling that blade plunge through his chest; of himself watching that riflebutt descend upon his face, with the final fire-exploding end. It made him so weak that he had to sit down. What if the other man had got the bayonet down quicker? What if he himself had tackled a little higher? Instead of merely a bruise on his collarbone, Bead saw himself spitted through the soft of the shoulder, head on, that crude blade descending into the soft dark of his chest cavity. He could not believe it.

Settling his glasses on his face, taking a couple of deep breaths and a last look at his ruined enemy, he got up and started clumping up out of the trees toward the crest. Bead was ashamed and embarrassed by the whole thing, that was the truth, and that was why he didn't want to mention it to anybody.

He got back through the line all right, without questions. 'Have a good shit?' the man from the 2nd Platoon called to him. 'Yeah,' he mumbled and clomped on, down the slope toward the CP. But on his way he was joined by Pfc Doll, on his way down from 1st Platoon with a message to ask again about water. Doll fell in step with him, and immediately noticed his damaged hands and the blood spatters.

'Christ! What happened to your knuckles? You have a fight with somebody?'

Bead's heart sank. It would have to be Doll. 'No. I slipped and fell and skinned myself,' he said. He was as stiff and sore all over as if he *had* had a fistfight with somebody. Horror welled in him again, suddenly, ballooningly. He took several very deep breaths into a sore rib cage.

Doll grinned with frank but amiable scepticism. 'And I spose all them little blood spatters came from your knuckles?'

'Leave me alone, Doll!' Bead blazed up. 'I dont feel like talking! So just leave me alone, hunh? Will you?' He tried to put into his eyes all the fierce toughness of a man just returned from killing an enemy. He hoped maybe that would shut him up, and it did. At least for a while. They walked on down in silence, Bead aware with a kind of horrified disgust that already he was fitting the killing of the Japanese man into the playing of a role; a role without anything, no reality, of himself or anything else. It hadn't been like that at all.

Doll did not stay shut up, though. Doll had been a little taken aback by Bead's vehemence, a forcefulness he was not used to expecting from Bead. He could smell something when he saw it. And after he had delivered his message, receiving the answer he expected which was that Stein was doing everything he could to get them water, he brought it up again, this time by calling it to the attention of Welsh. Welsh and Storm were sitting on the sides of their holes matching pennies for cigarettes, which were already beginning to be precious. They would match four best out of seven, to lengthen the game and cut down the expense in cigarettes, then both pull out their plastic pack holders which everyone had bought to keep their butts dry and carefully pass the one tube between them. Doll went over to them grinning with his eyebrows raised. He did not feel, at least not at the time, that what he was doing had anything to do with ratting on someone or stooling.

'What the fuck happen to your boy there? Who the hell he beat up with them skinned knuckles and all them blood spatters on him? Did I miss somethin?'

Welsh looked up at him with that level gaze of his which, when he wasn't pretending to be crazy, could be so penetrating. Already, Doll felt he had made a mistake, and guilty. Without answering Welsh turned to look at Bead, who sat hunched up by himself on a small rock. He had put back on his equipment.

'Bead, come over here!'

Bead got up and came, still hunched, his face drawn. Doll grinned at him with his raised eyebrows. Welsh looked him up and down.

'What happened to you?'

'Who? Me?'

Welsh waited in silence.

'Well, I slipped and fell down and skinned myself, that's all.'

Welsh eyed him in silence, thoughtfully. Obviously he was not even bothering with that story. 'Where'd you go a while ago? When you were gone for a while? Where were you?'

'I went off to take a crap by myself.'

'Wait!' Doll put in, grinning. 'When I seen him, he was comin down from the 2nd Platoon's section of line on the ridge.'

Welsh swung his gaze to Doll and his eyes blazed murderously. Doll subsided. Welsh looked back at Bead. Stein, who had been standing nearby, had come closer now and was listening. So had Band and Fife and some of the others.

'Lissen, kid,' Welsh said. 'I got more problems than I know what to do with in this screwy outfit. Or how to handle. I got no time to fuck around with kid games. I want to know what happened to you, and I want the truth. Look at yourself! Now, what happened, and where were you?'

Welsh apparently, at least to Bead's eyes, was much closer to guessing the truth than the unimaginative Doll, or the others. Bead drew a long quavering breath.

'Well, I went across the ridge outside the line in the trees to take a crap in private. A Jap guy came up while I was there and he tried to bayonet me. And – and I killed him.' Bead exhaled a long, fluttering breath, then inhaled sharply and gulped.

Everyone was staring at him disbelievingly, but nevertheless dumbstruck. 'Goddam it, kid!' Welsh bellowed after a moment. 'I told you I wanted the goddam fucking *truth*! And not no kid games!'

It had never occurred to Bead that he would not be believed. Now he was faced with a choice of shutting up and being taken for a liar, or telling them where and having them see what a shameful botched-up job he'd done. Even in his upset and distress it did not take him long to choose.

213

'Then god damn you go and *look*!' he cried at Welsh. 'Dont take my word, go and look for your goddam fucking *self*!'

'I'll go!' Doll put in immediately.

Welsh turned to glare at him. 'You'll go nowhere, stooly,' he said. He turned back to Bead. 'I'll go myself.'

Doll had subsided into a stunned, shocked, whitefaced silence. It had never occurred to Doll that his joking about Bead would be taken as stoolpigeoning. But then he had never imagined the result would turn out to be what it apparently had. Bead killing a Jap! He was not guilty of stooling, and furiously he made up his mind that he was going along; if he had to crawl.

'And if you're lyin, kid, God help your fucking soul.' Welsh picked up his Thompson-gun and put on his helmet. 'All right. Where is it? Come on, show me.'

'I'm not going up there again!' Bead cried. 'You want to go, go by yourself! But I aint going! And nothin's gonna make me!'

Welsh stared at him narrowly a moment. Then he looked at Storm. Storm nodded and got up. 'Okay,' Welsh said. 'Where is it, then?'

'A few yards in the trees beyond the crest, at the middle of the 2nd Platoon. Just about in front of Krim's hole.' Bead turned and walked away.

Storm had put on his helmet and picked up his own Thompson. And suddenly, with the withdrawal of Bead and his emotion from the scene, the whole thing became another larking, kidding excursion of the 'Tommy-gun Club' which had held the infiltrator hunt that morning. Stein, who had been listening in silence nearby all the time, dampened it by refusing to allow any of the officers to leave the CP; but MacTae could go, and it was the three sergeants and Dale who prepared to climb to the crest. Bead could not resist calling a bitter comment from his rock. 'You wont need all the goddamned artillery, Welsh! There's nobody up there but him!' But he was ignored.

It was just before they departed that Doll, his eyes uneasy but nonetheless steady, presented himself manfully in front of

214

the First Sergeant and gazed at him squarely.

'Top, you wouldn't keep me from goin, would you?' he asked. It was not begging nor was it a try at being threatening, just a simple, level, straightforward question.

Welsh stared at him a moment, then without change of expression turned away silently. It was obviously a reprimand. Doll chose to take it as silent acquiescence. And with himself in the rear the five of them started the climb to the line. Welsh did not send him back.

While they were gone no one bothered Bead. He sat by himself on his rock, head down, now and then squeezing his hands or feeling his knuckles. Everyone avoided looking at him, as if to give him privacy. The truth was nobody really knew what to think. As for Bead himself, all he could think about was how shamefully he and his hysterical, graceless killing were going to be exposed. His memory of it, and of that resolute face coming at him, made him shudder and want to gag. More times than not he wished he had kept his mouth shut and let them all think him a crazy liar. It might have been much better.

When the little scouting party returned, their faces all wore a peculiar look. 'He's there,' Welsh said. 'He sure is,' MacTae said. All of them looked curiously subdued. That was all that was said. At least, it was all that was said in front of Bead. What they said away from him, Bead could not know. But he did not find in their faces any of the disgust or horror of him that he had expected. If anything, he found a little of the reverse: admiration. As they separated to go to their various holes, each made some gesture.

Doll had hunted up the Japanese rifle and brought it back for Bead. He had scrubbed most of the blood and matter from the butt-plate with leaves and had cleaned up the bayonet. He brought it over and presented it as if presenting an apology offering.

'Here, this is yours.'

Bead looked at it without feeling anything. 'I dont want it.'

'But you won it. And won it the hard way.'

'I don't want it anyway. What good's it to me.'

215

'Maybe you can trade it for whisky.' Doll laid it down. 'And here's his wallet. Welsh said to give it to you. There's a picture of his wife in it.'

'Jesus Christ, Doll.'

Doll smiled. 'There's pictures of other broads, too,' he hurried on. 'Filipino, it looks like. Maybe he was in the Philippines. That's Filipino writing on the back, Welsh says.'

'I don't want it anyway. You keep it.' But he took the proffered wallet anyway, his curiosity piqued in spite of himself. 'Well –' He looked at it. It was dark, greasy from much sweating. 'I don't feel good about it, Doll,' he said, looking up, wanting suddenly to talk about it to someone. 'I feel guilty.'

'Guilty! What the hell for? It was him or you, wasn't it? How many our guys you think maybe he stuck that bayonet in in the Philippines? On the Death March. How about those two guys yesterday?'

'I know all that. But I cant help it. I feel guilty.'

'But why?'

'Why! Why! How the fuck do I know why!' Bead cried. 'Maybe my mother beat me up too many times for jerking off when I was a kid!' he cried plaintively, with a sudden half-flashing of miserable insight. 'How do I know why!'

Doll stared at him uncomprehendingly.

'Never mind,' Bead said.

'Listen,' Doll said. 'If you really dont want that wallet.'

Bead felt a sudden clutching greed. He put the wallet in his pocket quickly. 'No. No, I'll keep it. No, I might as well keep it.'

'Well,' Doll said sorrowfully, 'I got to get back up to the platoon.'

'Thanks anyway, Doll,' he said.

'Yeah. Sure.' Doll stood up. 'I'll say one thing. When you set out to kill him, you really killed him,' he said admiringly.

Bead jerked his head up, his eyes searching. 'You think so?' he said. Slowly he began to grin a little.

Doll was nodding, his face boyish with his admiration.

'I aint the only one.' He turned and left, heading up the slope.

Bead stared after him, still not knowing what he really felt. And Doll had said he wasn't the only one. If they did not find it such a disgraceful, botched-up job, then at least he need not feel so bad about that. Tentatively he grinned a little wider, a little more expansively, aware that his face felt stiff doing it.

A little later on Bugger Stein came over to him. Stein had remained in the background up to now. The news of Bead's Japanese had of course spread through the whole company at once, and when messengers or ration details came down from the line, they looked at Bead as though he were a different person. Bead was not sure whether he enjoyed this or not but had decided that he did. He was not surprised when Stein came over.

Bead was sitting on the edge of his hole when Stein appeared, jumped down in and sat down beside him. Nobody else was around. Stein adjusted his glasses in that nervous way he had, the four fingers on top of one frame, the thumb beneath, and then put his hand on Bead's knee in a fatherly way and turned to look at him. His face was earnest and troubled-looking.

'Bead, I know you've been pretty upset by what happened to you today. That's unavoidable. Anybody would be. I thought perhaps you might like to talk about it, and maybe relieve yourself a little. I dont know that what I would have to say to you about it would be of any help, but I'm willing to try.'

Bead stared at him in astonishment, and Stein, giving his knee a couple of pats, turned and looked sadly off across the basin toward Hill 207, the command post of yesterday.

'Our society makes certain demands and requires certain sacrifices of us, if we want to live in it and partake of its benefits. I'm not saying whether this is right or wrong. But we really have no choice. We have to do as society demands. One of these demands is the killing of other humans in armed combat in time of war, when our society is being attacked and must defend itself. That was what happened to you today. Only most men who have to do this are luckier than you. They do their first killing at a distance, however small. They have a chance, however small, to get used to it before having to kill hand to hand and face to face. I think I know what you must have felt.'

Stein paused. Bead did not know what to say to all this, so he did not say anything. When Stein turned and looked at him for some answer, he said, 'Yes, sir.'

'Well, I just want you to know that you were morally justified in what you did. You had no choice, and you mustn't worry or feel guilty about it. You only did what any other good soldier would have done, for our country or any other.'

Bead listened incredulously. When Stein paused again, he did not know what to say so he didn't say anything. Stein looked off across the basin.

'I know it's tough. You and I may have had our little differences, Bead. But I want you to know' – his voice choked slightly – 'I want you to know that after this war is over, if there is anything I can ever do for you, just get in touch with me. I'll do everything I possibly can to help you.'

Without looking at Bead he got up, patted him on the shoulder and left.

Bead stared after him, as he had done after Doll. He still did not know what he really felt. Nobody told him anything that made any sense. But he realized now, quite suddenly, that he could survive the killing of many men. Because already the immediacy of the act itself, only minutes ago so very sharp, was fading. He could look at it now without pain, perhaps even with pride, in a way, because now it was only an idea like a scene in a play, and did not really hurt anyone.

Shusaku Endo

WE ARE ABOUT TO KILL A MAN

In his novel The Sea and the Poison *(1957), Shusaku Endo describes the personal disintegration of Suguro, a young Japanese doctor who was forced to assist in a cruel experiment – the vivisection of American prisoners of war.*

WHEN THE RECEPTION was over, my sister-in-law and her husband left for the station. The relatives and I saw them off there. Rain had begun to fall throughout the city. As soon as the honeymooners had departed, everyone began to feel ill at ease. The family invited me to a restaurant with them; but I told them I was tired, and I returned to my inn. There were scarcely any guests there. After the chambermaid had laid out my bedding, I sat for a long time cross-legged, thinking – thinking and smoking one cigarette after another. After I had slipped under the thick quilted spread, I couldn't sleep. I kept on thinking about what the bridegroom's cousin at the reception had told me about Dr Suguro in such a stealthy voice. I could hear the sound of falling rain on the roof. From somewhere far away inside the hotel a group of maids with nothing to do were laughing and talking.

If I dozed off, I soon awoke. In the darkness the image of Dr Suguro would loom up and disappear again and again, his grey, puffy face, his thick caterpillar fingers. Once more I felt the chilling touch of those fingers on the skin of my right side.

There was more rain the next day. In the afternoon I went

out in the midst of it to visit a newspaper office in the city.

'Excuse me, but I was wondering if it would be all right to take a look at some back numbers of your paper.'

The girl at the receptionist's desk gave me a suspicious look, but she put through a call to the archives for me.

'An article from about what time?'

'Right after the war. There was a trial wasn't there, about the vivisections at Fukuoka Medical School?' I asked.

'Do you have any kind of authorization?'

'No, no, nothing like that.'

Finally I got the necessary permission. In a corner of the third floor archives, I read through the back numbers covering that period for about an hour. It was the affair involving the staff of the Medical School during the war. Eight captured American airmen had been used for medical experiments. In general the purpose of the experiments had been to obtain such information as how much blood a man could lose and remain alive, how much salt water in place of blood could safely be injected into a man's veins, and up to what point a man could survive the excision of lung tissue. There were twelve medical personnel involved in the vivisections, two of them nurses. The trial opened in Fukuoka but was later transferred to Yokohama. Towards the end of the list of defendants, I found Dr Suguro's name. There was nothing in the articles about his part in the experiments. The professor of medicine who had been in charge of the experiments committed suicide at the first opportunity. The principal defendants received long prison terms. Three, however, got off with light sentences of two years. Dr Suguro was one of the latter.

From the window of the newspaper office, I looked out at the clouds, the colour of soiled cotton wool, which hung low over the city. From time to time I'd look up from the articles to gaze at that dark sky. I left the newspaper office and walked through the streets. The thin, slanting rain struck my face. The passing cars, buses, lorries and street-cars made the same noises as they did in Tokyo. Young girls in raincoats of red and blue and other vivid shades walked along the sidewalk, which was streaming with rain. From the coffee shops came the sound of pleasant, titillating music. The singer Chiemi Eri was soon coming to town it seemed. Her face with its open, laughing mouth lent gaudy colour to the front of a cinema.

'Hey, Mister! How about a lottery ticket?' A woman in a full length apron accosted me from a doorway.

I felt tired and somehow out of sorts. I dropped into a coffee shop and had some coffee and a roll. Parents with their children and young men with their girlfriends came and went in and out through the door. I saw among them shrewd, long, narrow faces like that of the gas station owner. And square-jawed farmer faces with prominent cheek bones like that of the men's wear proprietor were frequent enough too. What was the gas station owner doing now, about this time of day? In his white uniform, was he filling the tank of a truck? Behind his dust covered show window, was the men's wear proprietor bent over his sewing machine? When one thought of it, both of them alike were men with murder in their pasts. So even in this West Matsubara to which I had moved, no matter how few its shops and houses, I had got to know two men who had tasted the experience of killing a man. And I could count Dr Suguro as a third.

Something, somehow, I could not figure out. How strange, I thought, that up to today, I had hardly reflected at all upon this. Now, this father of a family coming in through the door, perhaps during the war he killed a man or two. But now his face as he sips his coffee and scolds his children is not the face of a man fresh from murder. Just as with the show window in West Matsubara, past which the trucks rumble, the dust of the years settles on our faces too.

I left the shop and got on a streetcar. Fukuoka University Medical School was the stop at the end of the line. A light rain had begun to fall again, and water was dripping from the pagoda trees which stood in neatly ordered ranks across the wide campus.

I soon found the wing containing the First Surgical Department, where the vivisection had been performed. Pretending to be someone visiting a patient, I climbed to the third floor.

Up to the third floor, the wing consisted entirely of wards. In the corridors the smell of grime mingled with the permeating odour of disinfectant. There could be no doubt about it. This is what I had smelled in Dr Suguro's examination room – the same odour coming from the same poisonous source.

No one was in the operating theatre. Two leather-covered operating tables had been rolled over next to the window ledge. I squatted down on the floor and remained still for some time. Why had I come all the way up here I myself didn't know. I was thinking that somewhere in this dark room, some years before, Dr Suguro's grey, bloated face had had its due place. All at once I realized with a shock of surprise that I wanted to see him here.

I felt the start of a headache, so I went up to the roof. Fukuoka seemed to be crouching before me like a huge grey beast. Beyond the city I could see the ocean. The sea was a piercingly vivid blue, which I could feel, even at that distance, blurring my vision.

All through the day up to three o'clock, Toda and Suguro hardly spoke a word. While Toda was making ward rounds, Suguro, with nothing else to do, stayed at his desk. On other days when he arrived at the laboratory, there were always all sorts of odd jobs clamouring to be attended to. Why on this day was there such a feeling of everything being settled and in order? There was nothing to be done, nothing to engage him at all, he felt, other than what was to happen at three o'clock in the afternoon. So when Toda came back to the laboratory, Suguro got up and went out into the hall, as though he had thought of something. When after a while he came back, he found that Toda had left his notebook face down on the desk and gone off somewhere. They were avoiding each other and the chance of having to exchange words.

But, finally, close to three o'clock, as Suguro was about to go out, Toda blocked his way at the door.

'Hey, why have you been avoiding me?'

'I haven't been avoiding you.'

'There's no way out. That's for sure, isn't it?'

He stared hard at Suguro's face for a few moments. Then realizing the ineptness of his own question, he gave a twisted, bitter smile. And they both stood like this before the door. There was an uncanny silence throughout the hospital wing. The patients were waiting for the end of the quiet period, no concern of theirs what was to happen within half an hour. There was not a sound from the nurses' room either.

However, when the two of them climbed the stairs to the second floor operating room a bit later, the painfully oppressive atmosphere was unexpectedly shattered. The corridor, in fact, echoed with laughter. Four or five officers, whom Suguro and Toda had never seen, were leaning against the window ledges and puffing cigarettes while telling jokes in loud voices. It was as though they were waiting to be served lunch at the Officers Club.

'It's after two-thirty, isn't it? And the prisoners aren't here yet.'

The chubby little medical officer who had been in Dr Shibata's room that day clucked his tongue, as he opened his camera case.

'According to the order they were to be taken from the compound thirty minutes before. So they ought to be here before long,' an officer sporting an under-developed moustache answered, consulting his watch.

'I think I'm going to get some good pictures today,' said the medical officer, spitting on the floor and rubbing the spot with his boot.

'You really know how to handle one of those, don't you, Sir? That's a fine camera,' said the officer with the moustache, ingratiating himself as best he might.

'Oh, the camera. It's German made. After this there's going to be a farewell party for Lieutenant Omori in the hospital dining room. They say the experiment is going to be over at five o'clock. So we made it five-thirty.'

'How about the food?'

'Well whatever else, thanks to the prisoners, we'll be able to dine on a bit of American liver.'

With not a glance in the direction of Toda and Suguro, the officers laughed uproariously. The door of the operating theatre stood open, but the Old Man and Doctor Shibata and Asai were not there yet.

'You know in China . . .' The medical officer, scratching his buttock, began a story. 'No joke. I heard in my outfit there was a bunch who opened up a Chink and tried his liver.'

'They say it goes down surprisingly well,' said the officer with the moustache, his face aglow with knowing complacency.

'Well, what do you say? Let's give it a try at dinner today!'

At that moment Asai came slowly down the corridor, his rimless glasses catching the light as always. With the officers he turned on his customary charm.

'The prisoners have just come, gentlemen.' His feminine tones assured them that all was well.

'Yeah, but Shibata, where is Shibata?'

'He'll be here in a moment. No need for hurry, gentlemen.'

With that, he gestured with both hands to Suguro and Toda who were leaning against the wall as though to gain support against the oppression weighing upon them.

'Come here a minute, both of you.'

After he had called them into the operating theatre, he shut the door.

'They had to come, *that* bunch! The patients are going to sense that something is up. But anyway, first of all, the prisoners haven't been warned at all about what's going to happen. They think they were brought here to get a medical check up before being sent to the camp at Oita.' After he said this, his thin voice betraying his uneasiness, he took an ether container from the shelf. 'I want you to take care of the anaesthetic. OK? Today there are two prisoners. One of them has been wounded in the shoulder. With him, there'll be no trouble. We're giving him an anaesthetic in order to treat him. But it'll be awkward if we do anything to alarm the other one. So when they come, I'll pretend that I'm giving them an examination, you see. Finally, I'll ask them to lie down on the table so that I can check their hearts.'

'We'll have to strap them down, won't we? Otherwise during the initial anaesthetic period, they're liable to start resisting.'

'Of course, of course. Suguro, you're familiar too, aren't you, with the anaesthetic stages?'

'Yes, Doctor.'

There were three stages before the patient was fully anaesthetized. Furthermore, since the patient was easily roused from this kind of anaesthetic, it was essential throughout the operation to keep a careful watch.

This was the task entrusted to Suguro and Toda.

'The Old Man and Doctor Shibata?'

'They are putting on their surgical gowns in the room below. Once the anaesthetic takes effect, I'll call them. If everybody is here from the beginning, you see, the prisoners are liable to get alarmed.'

As he listened, Suguro had the impression that there was nothing unusual about the operation he was about to take part in. It was only the word *prisoner* that jolted him out of that illusion. He found himself oppressed by the realization that he had at last come to the point where it was irrevocably a matter of going ahead or turning aside.

'We are about to kill a man.' All at once a dark wave of fear and dismay began to flood through him. He grasped the handle of the door of the operating theatre. He could hear the echoing laughter of the officers on the other side. Their laughing voices seemed to thud against Suguro's heart, to block off his way of escape, a massive, thick wall in his path. Soon the stream of water, gleaming in the light from the ceiling lamp, would begin to flow across the floor of the operating theatre, with a light trickle, ready to wash away the patient's blood. Asai and Toda took off their jackets and shoes in silence and began to put on their surgical gowns and wooden sandals.

The door opened and Chief Nurse Oba, her Noh mask expression fixed as always, came in with a nurse called Ueda. The women too had a sombre air as they opened the cabinets and began to lay out the scalpels, scissors, oiled paper, and absorbent cotton, on top of the glass table next to the operating table. No one said a word. All that could be heard now were the voices of the officers talking in the corridor and the trickle of the water, which had just begun.

Suguro wondered why, besides Chief Nurse Oba, the nurse Ueda was taking part in the vivisection. She had not been at the hospital long, and Suguro had seldom had anything to do with her while making his rounds; but he had a distinct impression of her as a woman of dark mood, forever staring at something far in the distance.

Suddenly the laughter in the corridor stopped. Suguro looked to one side at Toda, his eyes fearful. Toda was Toda, and though his expression was shot through with pain for an instant, he gave a mocking smile as though in challenge.

The door of the operating theatre opened, and the officer with the under-developed moustache, who had been officiously consulting his watch before, poked his shaven head into the room.

'Is everything ready here?'

'Bring one in please,' Asai answered in a strained voice. 'How many are there? Are there two?'

'Two.'

Suguro sagged back against the wall. And then he saw a tall, thin prisoner come into the room as though he had been pushed. Just like the other prisoners Suguro had seen outside the entrance of Second Surgery, this man was dressed in a loose, ill-fitting green fatigue uniform. When he looked around at Suguro and the others in their surgical gowns, he smiled in a flustered way. Then he gazed at the white walls of the room.

'Sit here.' Addressing him in English, Asai pointed to a chair; and the man, awkwardly bending his long legs, sat down trustingly.

Suguro had seen many movies starring Gary Cooper. This American prisoner – his face, his way of moving – somehow resembled the actor. When Chief Nurse Oba had taken off his jacket, Suguro saw that he was wearing a torn, Japanese made vest. Through the rips in his vest, the thick, chestnut coloured hair of his chest was visible. When Dr Asai reached for his stethoscope, the prisoner shut his eyes as though dismayed, but then suddenly he became aware of the odour which floated through the room.

'Say, that's ether, isn't it?' he exclaimed.

'That's right. It's to cure you.' As well it might, Asai's voice shook slightly, and his hand trembled as it held the stethoscope.

The patient seemed to become more relaxed as the examination progressed and followed all Asai's directions obediently. It was evident from his gentle blue eyes and the frequency of his friendly smile, that he had not the slightest misgivings about Suguro and the others. It seemed that the confidence that men have in doctors as a profession was quite enough to put the prisoner at ease. While giving him the explanation about the heart examination, Asai indicated the operating table, and the prisoner readily lay down upon it.

'The straps?' Toda quickly asked.

'In a minute, in a minute,' Asai answered keeping his voice low. 'If you do it now, it will seem funny. When the second stage comes or if there are any spasms, then do it right away.'

'The medical officers have asked if it's all right if they come in,' said Chief Nurse Oba, putting her head in from the anteroom.

'No, not yet. I'll let you know later. Suguro, have the anaesthetic mask ready.'

'No, I can't, Doctor Asai.' Suguro's voice was almost breaking. 'Let me go. I want to get out.'

Asai, over his rimless glasses, looked up searchingly, but he said nothing.

'I'll do it, Doctor Asai.' Taking Suguro's place, Toda put layers of oiled paper and cotton on the mask which lay on a wire screen.

When he saw this, the prisoner looked as though he were about to ask something, but Dr Asai quickly put on a smile and gestured with his hand. Then he put the mask over the prisoner's face. The liquid ether began to drip upon it. The prisoner moved his head from side to side as though trying to dislodge the mask.

'Fasten the straps! The straps!'

The two nurses, bending over, fastened the straps of the operating table to the prisoner's legs and body.

'First stage,' Nurse Ueda whispered, looking at the dial. During this stage a patient, feeling his consciousness slipping away, struggles instinctively.

'Stop the ether flow,' ordered Asai, pressing the hand of the prisoner.

A low animal-like groan began to come from beneath the mask. It was the second stage of the anaesthetic. During this stage, some patients roar angrily or sing. But this prisoner, in a voice like that of a dog howling far off, did nothing but utter drawn out, intermittent groans.

'Ueda, bring the stethoscope.'

Taking the stethoscope from Nurse Ueda, Asai hurriedly placed it upon the prisoner's hairy chest.

'Ueda, start the ether again.'

'All right, Doctor.'

'The pulse is slower.'

Asai released the prisoner's hands and they flopped back on to the operating table on either side of him. Then Asai began to examine his eyes with a flashlight the chief nurse had given him.

'No reflex in the cornea. All right, that does it. I'll go and call the Old Man and Dr Shibata.' Asai took away his stethoscope and put it into the pocket of his gown. 'Stop the ether for now. If you give too much, he'll die, and that would be awkward. Miss Oba, get all the instruments ready please.'

Casting a cold glance in Suguro's direction, he went out of the operating theatre. The two nurses went back to the anteroom and did as Asai had directed. The bluish shine from the ceiling lamp was reflected from the walls. As Suguro leaned against the wall, the transparent stream of water flowed relentlessly around his sandals. Toda stood by himself beside the prisoner on the operating table.

'Come over here.' Toda suddenly spoke in a low voice. 'You won't come and help?'

'It's no use, no use at all. I can't,' Suguro muttered. 'I . . . I should have refused before.'

'You're a fool. And what do you have to say for yourself?' Toda turned, glaring at Suguro. 'If it were a matter of refusing, yesterday or even this morning would have been time enough. But now, having come this far, you're already more than half way, Suguro.'

'Half way? What do you mean, half way?'

'You're already tarred with the same brush as the rest of us.' Toda spoke quietly. 'From now on, there's no way out, none at all.'

Martin Booth

Hiroshima Joe

Set in the Far Eastern theatre of war, Martin Booth's novel Hiroshima Joe (1985) tells the story of Captain Joseph Sandingham who after the fall of Hong Kong in 1941 is taken prisoner by the Japanese. After years in a PoW camp, he is transferred towards the end of the war to a slave labour camp in Japan. There he is present outside Hiroshima on the day when the nuclear bomb is dropped. When the guards abandon the camp, Joe makes his way into the city to look for a friend he has made among the Japanese workers.

THE BICYCLE WAS old and heavy and his legs were not strong enough to propel it forward at any speed. At first he had wobbled: it was six years since he had last ridden a bike. This one was plainly a poor man's model, for it lacked gearing and there was a metal-framed shelf behind the saddle for the carriage of packages and boxes.

The road wound through paddyfields and vegetable farms, many of them partially harvested. The few hamlets he pedalled through contained knots of people talking excitedly to each other. Everyone was facing the city.

The nearer he came to the city limits the more people he found to be travelling with him. Some were on cycles, some on foot, a few in cars or on lorries. As he came alongside the railway line to Kure the road took a bend. Here he decided to stop, to regain his breath. He squeezed on the brake levers and halted by the kerb under the shade of a tree that grew over a stone wall.

From around the corner he could hear a mysterious sound. More accurately, it was a great number of disparate sounds melding together to make one orchestration, much as many notes join in unison to make a complex chord. He tried, leaning over the handlebars, to recognize any one of the noises but he was unable to do so, for whatever they were they registered in his brain as unlikely to unite. They did not fit into a pattern – much as a cawing crow would not be expected to join in harmony with a harpsichord.

His breath regained, Sandingham shifted the pedals and took the pressure of the chain. He rode away from the kerb and around the corner.

Ahead of him on the road, half a mile away, there was what appeared to be a tide coming in his direction. As he pedalled on and approached it, he saw it was a multitude of people. Behind them was the smoke of what Sandingham took to be the burning city.

When he caught sight of them he assumed the crowd he was riding up to was made of refugees from the air raid. He had seen Chinese in droves leaving a district under fire in Hong Kong. As he got closer, he saw that he was only partly right.

Within easy sight of them, he stopped again. He could not quite believe what he witnessed in front of him.

The crowd was silent except for the shuffling of their feet and the creaking of the axles on their handcarts. A few moaned but none spoke. Many of them were injured. Cuts about the face and hands had bled into streaks upon their clothing. Some limped, while others were riding on the handcarts, sitting on an assortment of mundane household belongings. As they passed by, he saw that they were all stunned, bemused even. Refugees were usually more alert than this, eager in their escape. These people were strangely apathetic.

He was about to set off the way they had come when an elderly man in a dirtied *ukata* – a light indoor kimono used by Japanese much as Europeans might use a cotton dressing-gown – touched his arm. Sandingham looked down at the man's hand. It was badly grazed as if he had rubbed it along a rough surface. Straw-coloured plasma was weeping from the wound.

The man said nothing but looked Sandingham straight in the face, then shifted his eyes to the bicycle. He pleaded through the telepathy that pain brings to the injured. Without a thought Sandingham lifted his leg over the saddle and relinquished his machine. The old man said nothing at all; he did not even smile his thanks. He steered the bicycle through the crowd and, propping it by a pedal to the opposite kerb, helped a middle-aged woman on to the saddle, precariously balancing a child on the crossbar between her arms.

Sandingham watched them rejoin the crowd.

Walking was easier for him than cycling. His legs, after initially feeling weakened as he dismounted, set back into the stride to which they were accustomed.

It was not long before he reached the outer limits of the blast damage. House walls were askew, trees leafless: windows were blown out and fences down. Debris littered the road.

The more he walked, the worse the damage became.

All the while, from the city, there rose the vast pall of smoke and dust. It was so wide and huge now that it entirely cut off the sun. The head of the tree-cloud over-toppled him and was widening its branches.

Sounds increased. From the city came the noise of human turmoil, of burning, of disintegration and the musical tinkling of metal bending or breaking, glass shattering. In the fire-storm were the popping detonations of houses igniting in an instant and exploding. It was the symphony of destruction.

He walked with his head lowered, his brain struggling to recall the instructions from Mishima on reaching his Japanese friend's home. If he looked up, what he spied wiped his thoughts clean with horror.

Around him, few buildings stood. They were heaps of wood and tiles, cloth and glass and metal. Some smouldered. Brick or stone edifices were cracked and leaning. Everything had collapsed. The narrower sidestreets between the houses were filled with rubble. Further on, the sides of buildings were burned as if scorched. Telegraph and power poles were charred down one side. Flimsy upright objects, like some of the street lamp-posts, were bent over. The air was filled with the acrid stink of the ruination of war.

Everywhere, there were the people. Or what was left of the people.

The tram was gutted. Only a steel skeleton remained. The side-panelling had warped, fractured and prised loose. The glass that had been the windows had melted and run down the sides, cooling like a coating of speckled sugar on the wheels and road surface. The paint was seared off.

Sandingham walked up to the tram, not knowing why he did so. Nothing was making sense to him. Inside, the seats had disappeared and only the frameworks remained in their original rows, twisted crookedly. On the floor of the tram cabin was a partly congealed liquid slush of greyish-brown matter in which lay some broken branches, stripped bare of their bark.

It was more than a minute before he realized that the floor-covering had been people, the branches nude bones.

He did not vomit at this realization. His stomach did not even lurch towards his throat. There was nothing left to throw up – not food nor bile nor rage. He was growing devoid of new emotion, his inner store insufficient for what he was experiencing.

He simply cried. It was not a loud venting of tears but a gradual, miserable sobbing, such as a child might make when its toy was irretrievably lost.

Their hair, eyebrows and eyelashes had been scorched off and, when they closed their eyes, the upper lids snagged under the lower. Few had skin left on the fronts of their bodies. Some were smeared with vomit that had stuck to their chests and breasts. Some walked with their arms held out before them, as if in supplication to a greater power for a hint of mercy. Many were naked and, of those, some had even their pubic hairs singed short.

They all moved with their heads hung, not speaking, not complaining. Their submission chilled Sandingham even more than their hideous wounds.

As he studied them shuffling past him, he saw upon the backs of a few the patterns of straps or elastics, of flowers or birds or delicate designs printed indelibly upon their skin.

A boat was being punted across a river by a Japanese man. Helping him was a priest. He was European. His soutane was besmirched and stiff with sweat and grime.

Sandingham watched them guiding wounded over the water. They worked with little conversation, passing instructions to each other but saying little else. He thought at once that he should give them assistance, to help them as any man might another in a crisis, and began gingerly to step over the debris to where a flight of stairs was cut into the bank.

As he neared them the punter spoke to the priest in German.

'*Da ist nichts zu machen.*'

Joe thought better of offering his assistance and turned aside, keeping his face to the rubble-strewn ground.

'*Wakarimasen*,' the old man uttered.

The teenage boy lifted his index finger to the smoke as if instructing his elder on one of the finer points of warfare.

'*Molotoffano hanakago.*'

He overheard this as he shuffled by the pair. They were sitting on an inverted and much-dented trader's tricycle. No other words passed between them.

Hanakago, Sandingham knew, meant flower-basket. He wondered how a bomb could bear blossoms.

In the middle channel of the river there sailed a gunboat of the Imperial Japanese Navy. It made slow headway. In the bows stood an officer. He was holding a megaphone through which he shouted unintelligibly.

The marvel to Sandingham was not that the gunboat had appeared but that it was trim and tidy, so unadulterated, its shape clean and purposeful, deliberate and ordered. And the officer was so neat in his uniform, so dispassionate. He was almost serene.

It was nearly evening and the fires were dying in the city centre. Against a wall that had withstood the blast because it had been end-on the epicentre, Sandingham paused. He was utterly tired but unable to consider sleep quite yet. He slid down to a sitting position against the wall and hunched his knees to his chin, hugging his calves with his arms. So far, no one had recognized him as a foreigner. Few people were in a position to care.

Wherever he went there were bodies. He had never seen such carnage. In Hong Kong at the fall, when someone died, they just – died. The bullet that did for them might make a small hole going in and a large hole coming out, but that was all. Someone freshly shot in the head was not mutilated but simply broken. Those caught in the ambush at Wong Nai Chung Gap had lain on the road looking like humans that were now ceased. Even those caught in a crossfire of mortars were still recognizably human until the flies and the ants started their forays.

The dead he now saw littering the wreckage of the city were not like that at all. Many were as unlike to human form as was conceivably possible. They were not necessarily dismembered, but hideously disfigured. Sandingham was used to seeing the dead lying in grotesquely contorted positions, but not like these.

He found a man bent backwards over a post, his head touching the backs of his knees, his stomach unsplit but stretched so tight it had contouring under it the coiled map of gut. The man's skin was maroon and his arms hung back against the shoulder sockets.

At one point in the afternoon, he had paused by a water butt to drink. His throat was parched from retching and swallowing smoke. He also wanted to try to wash off the blotches the rain had given him.

He reached into the water. It was cool, indescribably cool. It was luxurious. He slopped water on his arms and rubbed at them. The rain spots did not even smudge let alone show signs of washing clean.

Resigned to leaving himself dirty, Sandingham leaned over the edge of the barrel to press his face into the surface and suck up the water. His reflection stared back at him. Beside his face was another. It was floating a foot under the surface. The eyes were holes. The mouth was a slit cavern of darkness. The hair willowed around the scalp. He did not drink but watched. The face folded up in the water. He was dreaming. It was the effects of exhaustion. He thrust his fingers into the clear jet-black of the water and felt for the face. There was nothing hard there. No skull. No corpse. Yet something soft brushed against the back of his hand and his forearm. As he brought his arm clear, something clung to it. It was light and wrapped itself on to his arm like algae. He straightened his arm. Clinging to it was the face: no features, just a flat mask of skin, peeled from its owner and cast into the water.

Sandingham screamed. He flicked and threshed his arm trying to dislodge it, but it would not move. It was glued to him by the water and its own grossness. He could not bear to touch it: instead, grabbing a piece of wood, he scraped it off, all the time hollering. The face fragmented and came away like curds off milk.

In a temper of panic, he toppled the butt over, the water soaking invisibly into the dry ground.

By the time he reached the river again it had become a tide of dead. The once-living wallowed to and fro in the wash, rising and falling with the slow motion of obscene lovers. Old men, young women, children. For fifteen minutes, Sandingham had blankly watched a baby floating next to its mother, her hand entangled forever in the infant's clothing. Between the bodies, where they were not log-jammed together against the shore or a collapsed waterfront building, hundreds of tiny fish floated belly-up. An occasional seabird filled in the occasional space. In death, they were all equal.

He found himself talking quite loudly to himself in English

and instantly jammed his mouth with his fingers. This slip of concentration brought him out in a cold sweat of fear, for leaning against the wall a few feet away was a young Japanese man.

Sandingham glanced sideways to see if he had been overheard.

The man was bruised all over his side and was nursing a broken left arm. The shattered bone was protruding not just through the skin but also through the shreds of clothing he was wearing. He was moaning.

Sandingham edged along the ground to the man's side.

'*Doshita no desuka?*' he asked.

The man raised his face to Sandingham but made no reply. His open eyes saw nothing. It was quite obvious that he was blind.

Finally he mumbled a reply. Sandingham, not understanding it, said, '*Doshite agema shoka? Nanio motte kimashoka?*'

'*Mizu,*' answered the man, his fingers pressing to his arm. Then, again, '*Mizu. Mizu.*'

Sandingham could do nothing. There was no water.

After a while the young man got to his feet, rubbing his back up the wall. He staggered off in the direction of the river but, after going about a hundred yards, he fell on to his side, gave a yodelling howl and lay still.

All through the late afternoon, wounded figures had been continuously going by him, walking aimlessly, stumbling, tottering, lurching, feeling their way, crawling even. For the last half-hour, however, this traffic of pain and despair had eased.

The evening sun was trying to sever the clouds and smoke. It was weak and lifeless.

Leaning now against the wall, Sandingham sensed he was not on his own. He looked around him. No one alive was in sight. The dead youth lay in the road. The dead girl opposite was still there, partially covered by ash that had drifted against her like snow. The little group of dead by the remains of the food shop was unchanged. The dead cat beside the burnt-out car had not moved. Yet he felt he was with someone.

237

His eyes focused on a section of wall to his right. There was someone there. They were standing in the centre of the street. Their shadow was plainly outlined on the plaster of the wall. Sandingham gazed at it. Yet in the street there was no one.

He stood up hurriedly and ran to the point where the person should be. Still no living person in sight; yet the shadow was still there, imprinted on the wall.

He took two quick strides and his own shadow merged with the other. He was where the person had been, should still be. If that person had had a soul and that soul had had a shadow it would be inhabiting his body now. They would be in him, safe in the deep recesses of his marrow. He heard himself shout – a shriek, his dry throat ripping apart as the sound rose to a whistling falsetto.

He ran, his own shadow flitting over the rubble of the houses and the bodies of the dead; his voice he left behind in the air, hanging there like the shadow that had lost its owner.

He was worn out, totally enervated. All he wanted to do was sleep, lose consciousness forever, just as Mishima had chosen to do.

After leaving the shadow he had fled along a maze of streets and, as darkness fell, found himself on the edge of what appeared to be a public park. There was a mass of people on the ground within it, lying or squatting upon the grass. Their silence shocked him deeply. Some were moaning or wheezing, some keening in undertones of anguish, but no one was speaking.

From a gate pillar there hung a gate. It was still, miraculously, on its hinges. Pointlessly, for the second half of the twin gate had disappeared, he pushed it open and stepped on to a pathway.

As soon as he passed a group of people on the ground, and they noticed that he was unhurt and standing upright, they begged water of him, or help, or comfort. They did not clamour or shout or demand. Nor did they really ask. They merely said it in soft, lover-like voices.

'. . . *awaremi tamai*,' they pleaded. '. . . *awaremi tamai*.'

He had no pity left to offer.

An old woman was going from one corpse to another, skilful in her ability to distinguish between the living and the non-living: there was often little apparent difference. From any corpse that wore spectacles she helped herself to them, trying on pair after pair before discarding them. Sandingham followed her movements until she discovered some that suited her vision and disappeared behind a clump of trees.

One man lying beside a split tree trunk captured Sandingham's attention. He sat cross-legged on the ground, stark-naked like a grotesque holy man. His body was covered with dancing stars. He was muttering something to himself, over and over. Curious, Sandingham went up to him and listened to his liturgy.

'*Tenno heika, banzai, banzai, banzai, banzai.*'

The stars around his body were made by the brittle evening light splitting apart in the hundreds of glass splinters that were embedded in his skin.

Towards the centre of the park the people thinned out and the shrubbery that had survived the blast rustled in the hot night breezes. Behind him, the pitiful congregation were illuminated by the dying fires in the city.

The bushes offered Sandingham the shelter and protection he needed to sleep. His eyes were leaden and his brain numbed by all he had seen. He pressed the branches aside and entered the cavern of the undergrowth.

The men were sitting in a row, their legs stretched out before them.

Sandingham eased himself on to the earth, not noticing them. Gradually, he felt their presence. He looked up at them.

They were all alike. Their faces were entirely burned and the frail skin hung from their cheeks and foreheads like the flaking surfaces of the hoods of ripe mushrooms. Their sockets were red voids and the mucus of their melted eyes shone glutinously on the raw, hanging flesh of their faces, like the glass from the tram windows. Their lips were gross, swollen slits surrounded by creamy pus and plasma.

He jerked back. They heard his movement and whispered

through the cracks of their mouths. They hissed like creatures of the underworld. They spoke as insects might.

One of them tried to get up, rocking himself from side to side on his buttocks. Another raised his arms very slowly towards Sandingham. As he did so, Sandingham could hear the tissues in the man's armpits tearing.

He grunted with fear, with ultimate horror. He wanted to scream but could not.

The dead were coming to life.

He picked up a clod of dried earth and hurled it at the man with the crackling arms. The ball of soil hit him on the chest and disintegrated like a tiny grenade. The earth made a radiant pattern on the man's flayed skin which darkened as the blood soaked into the dirt, absorbing it into the meat.

Sandingham ran pell-mell through the park, standing on people's hands, tripping over their prostrate bodies, oblivious of everything. He ran until there was nothing in his life but the next step following the last step and the cartoon strip of all he had witnessed that day flickering in an endless loop through his brain.

He was lying in a ditch. Over his head, thin leaves were shifting in a breeze. A bird was cheeping somewhere, readying itself for dawn. Far off, a dog was howling and barking.

Opening his eyes, he stared upwards at the pattern of the tree against the vaguely lightening sky. Mud was caking on his chest and his left cheek. His right cheek was cushioned by wet clay. As he lifted his left arm to pull himself upright, the dried mud cracked. He shuddered and checked that it was just mud and not his flesh.

He took a deep breath and slapped his hand on the mud to reassure himself. The grimy splash spattered his soiled skin.

'I'm alive,' he said to the tufts of grass by his face. 'Filthy, agreed. But alive. Definitely!' He raised his eyes. 'But why? Why on earth me?'

Louis Begley

Wartime Lies

Wartime Lies (1991) tells the story of an orphaned Jewish boy who, together with his aunt Tania, lives in hiding under assumed Polish identity to escape the Nazi death camps. When they are caught up in the Warsaw uprising, the desperate attempt by the Polish Home Army to liberate the city in the autumn of 1944, they hope that their days in hiding will soon be over.

ONE AFTERNOON, AN AK* officer came to speak to the people in the cellar. He said that the AK would have to withdraw at once from the neighbourhood through the sewers; the Germans could be expected within a few hours. We should stay calm and, when the Germans did come, follow their orders promptly and without argument. They would make us leave the building; it was a good idea to gather whatever clothes we needed and have a little suitcase ready. The Germans had Ukrainian guards with them. The Ukrainians were like wild animals. It would be best if young women put shawls over their heads and faces and tried to be inconspicuous. He saluted and wished us all luck. Soon afterwards, a bomb fell on the building next to us; another made a hole in the street. People from the building that had

* *Armia Krajowa* (Home Army), the main branch of the Polish resistance directed by the government in London.

241

been hit came to our cellar. There was less gunfire, and after a while both the gunfire and the bombs began to seem more distant. It was already dark, and the Germans had not come. Few people slept that night. Families sat together talking. Some people prayed aloud.

Tania told me to lie down on our mattress. She lay down too, put her arms around me and talked to me in a whisper. She said it was lucky that we had not forgotten for a moment we were Catholic Poles and that nobody seemed to suspect us. Our only hope was to be like all the others. The Germans weren't going to kill every Pole in Warsaw; there were too many of them, but they would kill every Jew they could catch. We would make ourselves very small and inconspicuous, and we would be very careful not to get separated in the crowd. If something very bad happened and she was taken away, I wasn't to try to follow: it wouldn't help her and I might even make things worse for both of us. If possible I should wait for her. Otherwise, I should take the hand of whatever grown-up near me had the nicest face, say I was an orphan, and hope for the best. I shouldn't say I was a Jew, or let myself be seen undressed if I could avoid it. She had me repeat these instructions and told me to go to sleep.

We were awake when they arrived late the next morning. It was the same bellowing as for Jews in T., the same pounding of rifle butts on the gate and then on the cellar door and the apartment doors and people trying to hurry and stumbling on the stairs. A Wehrmacht officer and a couple of German soldiers stood on the sidewalk in a little group apart while the work was done by Ukrainians: they rushed around, pushing and hitting people as they came out into the street. Some of them had whips and some had dogs. A woman just ahead of us did not move fast enough to satisfy a Ukrainian. He hit her with his whip. Her husband pushed his way in front of her. Two Ukrainians beat him. Many people from other buildings were already assembled in a column, four abreast, ready to march. A Ukrainian called for silence and asked that all the women in our group immediately give up their jewellery. He pointed to a bucket. Then he told us to pass by it one by one.

When our turn came, Tania took off her bracelet and ring and threw them in. He asked to see her hands and waved us ahead. I looked at Tania. She had put a kerchief over her head and tied it under her chin; her face was smeared black with coal dust; she was walking bent over like an old woman. When we reached the column she said she wanted to be in the middle of a row; I could be on the outside. The column seemed ready to march when another squabble erupted: a woman had not thrown anything into the bucket; the Ukrainian in charge of it grabbed her hand, saw a ring, beat her on the face and with an easy, fluid gesture, just like a butcher, cut off her finger. He held it up for all to see. There was a ring on it. The finger and ring both went into the bucket.

The march began. Tania had manœvred us both into the middle of the row, with a man on either side. We no longer saw familiar faces. People from our building had drifted away; much rearranging had to be done before the German officer gave the order for departure. The column went down Krakowskie Przedmieście, turned right on Aleje Jerozolimskie, but it was difficult to recognize in the smouldering ruins the street we had tried to memorize. Tania said she thought they were taking us to the Central Station. We were a sea of marchers. Tania and I had no possessions; our hands were free. I was walking with a light and bouncy step. Was it fear or the strange parade we were a part of after the weeks spent in cellars? Around us, people were staggering under huge valises; some were transporting a piece of furniture or a rug. Many had children in their arms. Directly in front of us was a man with a large grey-and-red parrot in a cage; every few minutes the bird screamed. The man had the cage door open, and he would put his hand in to quiet the bird.

As in T., when I watched the final departure of the ghetto Jews, but on a vaster scale suited to the breadth of the avenues we were walking on and the enormous length of the column, the crowd was contained on both sides by Ukrainians, SS and Wehrmacht. Many of the Germans were officers. The Ukrainians and their dogs walked with us, while the

Germans, immobile on the ruined sidewalks, were like green-and-black statues. From time to time, a Ukrainian would plunge into the column and beat a marcher who was not keeping up with the others or had stopped to shift his load. They beat marchers whose children were crying; we were to make no noise. And they dragged out of the column women who had attracted their attention. They beat them, beat men who tried to shield them, and then led the women to the side, beyond the line held by the Germans. They possessed them singly, in groups, on the ground, leaning them against broken walls of houses. Some women were made to kneel, soldiers holding them from the back by the hair, their gaping mouths entered by penis after penis. Women they had used were pushed back into the column, reeling and weeping, to resume the march. Others were led toward the rubble and bayoneted or shot.

Occasionally, the column halted. Tania and I remained standing; people foolish enough to sit down on a suitcase or a parcel were beaten to the ground and then kicked and shoved till they were properly upright again. During these stops, the selection of women for Ukrainians was most active. Just ahead of us stood a tall and strikingly beautiful young woman with a baby in her arms. I had noticed both her beauty and her elegance; she wore a beige tweed suit with a dark zigzag pattern that reminded me of Tania's old suits. A Ukrainian grabbed her by the arm and was pulling her out of the column. At first she followed without protest, but then she broke away from him and ran toward a German officer standing some two metres away. I had also noticed this officer before. He had a distinguished, placid face and a very fresh uniform. The boots hugging his calves were polished to a high shine that seemed impossible to maintain in this street covered with chalky dust and debris. His arms were crossed on his chest. Could the young woman also have been dazzled by the boots? When she reached the officer, she threw herself on her knees at his feet, held the baby up with one arm, and with the other encircled these superb black tubes. A cloud of annoyance mixed with disdain moved across the officer's face.

He gestured for the Ukrainians to stand back; a silence fell as he decided on the correct course of action. What followed the moment of reflection was precise and swift. The officer grasped the child, freed his boots from the young woman's embrace and kicked her hard in the chest. With a step or two he reached an open manhole. There was no lack of these, because the A.K. had used the sewers as routes of attack and escape. He held up the child, looked at it very seriously, and dropped it into the sewer. The Ukrainians took away the mother. In a short while, the column moved forward.

It was late in the afternoon when we reached the great square adjoining the Central Station. The space was divided into two unequal parts. The much larger one was where we and, we supposed, the rest of the remaining population of Warsaw were now gathered. People were lying down, with their heads in the laps of companions; others were sitting on their possessions or crouching on the ground. Alleys kept free for access, like lines of a crossword puzzle, traversed the multitude. On the perimeter Ukrainian guards paced back and forth. The smaller part of the square had become a military encampment, crowded with trucks and armoured cars.

Tania and I sat down on the ground, leaning against each other, back to back. Our neighbours, who had been there since the day before, said there was no food and no water to drink except what one could get from people who had a canteen or something to eat in their bundles. Apparently, there was no lack of such clever people among us. We also learned that in the morning and during the previous day parts of the square had been emptied; whole sections had been taken to the station. New arrivals like ourselves had taken their place. The night had been worse than the march and the waiting: the Ukrainians and the Germans were drunk. They roamed through the access alleys, chose women to take to the encampment. There had been screams, probably they tortured as well as raped. Tania asked if anyone knew where the trains would take us. Opinions were divided. Some thought it was just a short ride to some forests where we would be machine-gunned; others talked of concentration camps or work in factories in Germany. Tania also asked about latrines. It turned out there were several points that served that purpose. They were easy to find: one followed the smell. That was, Tania decided, where we would now have to go; we should not wait until the night.

We picked our way among the crowd; there was a long line to use the place. Tania said that after we finished she would somehow buy food and water; we had to keep up our strength. She would do it without me, it would be easier, but first we would choose a place that I would keep for us in one of these clusters. She wanted to find one without crying children or wailing sick: they attracted misfortune. And she wanted us to be in the middle of the group. People trying to be on the outside, to get more air and to be able to get around, were wrong. She didn't care about fresh air; she wanted to live through the night. We did as she said. In a little while she returned. She whispered that she had bread and chocolate. We had not eaten chocolate since the beginning of the uprising. She also had a bottle of water. She had traded her earrings for them; earrings, she informed me, had never been more useful; she had been right to hide them. Best of all, from her point of view, she had also been able to acquire a small mirror, a comb, a lipstick and a blanket. The blanket was for the night, the rest was for the morning. Tania didn't let the food be seen until our neighbours began to eat. She thought it was difficult, and in some degree dangerous, for a woman and a small boy to eat in a hungry crowd without sharing. Then she divided the bread into evening and morning portions. She allowed us each one gulp of water. The rest, and especially the chocolate, were also for the morning. We wrapped ourselves in the blanket and lay down. It was getting dark; all around us people were clinging to one another for warmth and comfort. Tania told me she was afraid of this night, but we had to make ourselves sleep; if we were exhausted we would make mistakes. For instance, she said, that young woman with a child made a terrible mistake when she knelt down before the officer. She should have stood as straight as she could, looked him in the eye, and demanded that he make the Ukrainians behave like disciplined soldiers. Germans, said Tania, cannot bear the feeling of pity; they prefer pain. If you ask for pity, you get the devil that is inside them, worse than the Ukrainians.

The day finally departed. I fell into a dead sleep. Shouts and curses awoke me. Beams of electric torches criss-crossed the night. Just as we had been warned, Ukrainians and Germans were hunting for women. Tania said, Quick, cover me with the blanket and lie on top of me; pretend I am a bundle. Around us, soldiers were wading among the sleepers, looking them over, rejecting some, hauling away others. Then they were gone.

Peace, disturbed only by sighs, laments and moans had barely settled on us when we heard a new and improbable noise: the loudspeaker the Germans had used to give orders during the day was now filling the square with familiar Wehrmacht songs. Some soldier had brought a gramophone and was playing background music for a field brothel. But fornication apparently did not preclude other amusements. Soon, a sound like very loud static was interfering with the ninth or tenth rendition of 'Lili Marlene'. It was a machine-gun. Cries of wounded replied. Perhaps a soldier thought it disorderly for prisoners to scurry about in the night. The way to end any such unauthorized activity was to aim the fire directly above the heads of people quietly squatting or lying on the ground: anyone who stood up would be mowed down, which was good for discipline. Alas, not everybody could crouch or sit or, better yet, lie face down. The wounded were begging for help, disembodied voices called for doctors to make themselves known, and doctors who were brave enough to respond became new moving targets.

That night, in turn, departed. It was followed by yet another sparkling and cloudless day. Autumn is the sweetest season in Poland, redolent of harvest smells and promise, a time to pick mushrooms in the moist shade of giant trees. But neither the morning hour nor the season brought with it hope. The loudspeaker began braying lengthy instructions about going to the right and going to the left, forming in groups of fifty, forming in groups of one hundred, leaders responsible for order, picking up trash, sitting, standing and waiting. Since we were thought incapable of comprehending, Ukrainians with their dogs and whips came again into our midst to help us form satisfactory columns. By noon, Tania and I were marching in step in the rear of such a column. The Central Station was before us, oddly unmarked by the fighting. I was very afraid: our destination was about to be revealed.

I could not tell whether Tania was as afraid as I. We had eaten the rest of our bread and chocolate as soon as the sun rose. Unlike most of our neighbours, Tania did not need the help of the Ukrainians to fathom the meaning of the loud-speaker, and the moment it was clear that we were leaving, she had become very busy. Long before the Ukrainians began charging the crowd and one had to stand in ranks at rigid attention, over my tearful protests she had used our remaining water to wash our faces and hands. She brushed the dust off her clothes and mine and straightened them. Then she combed my hair and, with great concentration, peering into the pocket mirror, combed her own hair and put on lipstick, studied the result, and made little corrections. I was astonished to see how she had transformed herself. The stooped-over, soot-smeared old woman of the march from the Old Town had vanished. Instead, when we entered the station, I was holding the hand of a dignified and self-confident young matron. Unlike the day before, she was not hanging back, trying to lose us in the crowd; she pushed her way to the outside row and, holding my hand very tight, to my horror, led me away from the column so that we were standing, completely exposed, in the space on the platform between the rest of the people and the train. Despite my panic, I began to understand that Tania was putting on a very special show. Her clear blue eyes surveyed the scene before her; it was as if she could barely contain her impatience and indignation. I thought that if she had had an umbrella she would be tapping the platform with it. And, indeed, what a tableau was there to contemplate! Two long trains of cargo and passenger cars, one on each side of the platform, group after group of Poles in the column being pushed and beaten by the Ukrainians, then shoved toward the trains, old people falling on the platform, some slipping off the platform on to the tracks as they tried to hoist themselves into the freight cars, suitcases judged too large by the Ukrainians torn open and their contents scattered on the ground, howling dogs pulling on their leashes, Ukrainians yelling in their mixture of broken Polish and German, people weeping and sometimes embracing each other.

Also surveying the scene, with an air of contempt that matched Tania's indignation, was a fat middle-aged Wehrmacht captain, standing alone a few metres from us, in the middle of the platform. I realized that Tania was including him in her outraged stare and that her show seemed particularly directed at him. All at once, I felt her pulling me behind her again. With a few rapid strides she reached the officer. Addressing him in her haughtiest tone, she asked if he would be kind enough to tell her where these awful trains were going. The answer made my legs tremble: Auschwitz. Completely wrong destination, replied Tania. To find herself with all these disreputable-looking people, being shouted at by drunk and disorderly soldiers, and all this in front of a train going to a place she had never heard of, was intolerable. She was a doctor's wife from R., about two hours from Warsaw; she had come to Warsaw to buy dresses and have her son's eyes examined; of course, everything she bought had been lost in this dreadful confusion. We had nothing to do with whatever was going on here. Would he, as an officer, impose some order and help us find a train to R.? We had spent almost all our money, but she thought she had enough for a second-class compartment. The captain burst out laughing. My dear lady, he said to Tania, not even my wife orders me about quite this way. Could Tania assure him her husband would be glad to have her return? And where had she learned such literary turns of expression? After he had an answer to these basic questions he would see about this wretched train business. Tania blushed. Should I tell you the truth, even though you won't like it? Naturally, replied the captain. I think my husband doesn't mind my being sometimes hot tempered. I learned German in school and probably I managed to improve it by reading, especially everything by Thomas Mann I can find in the original – not much in R., but quite a lot in Warsaw. It's a good way for a provincial housewife to keep occupied. I know Mann's work is forbidden in the Reich, but that is the truth. I am not a party member, merely a railroad specialist, announced the captain still laughing. I am glad you have chosen a great stylist. Shall I get someone to carry your suitcases while we look for transportation to R.?

The captain was a man of the world. He did not feel compelled to introduce himself and gave no sign of being discouraged or startled by our lack of luggage. Having handed Tania into a first-class compartment of a train waiting at a distant platform, he clicked his heels. Tania was not to worry. He was signing a pass to R.; it was not necessary to buy tickets; the German reservist in charge of this military train would see to it that she was not disturbed.

The train remained in the station for some hours after he left us. Slowly, it filled up with soldiers; noisy groups of officers were in the compartments on both sides of ours. Meanwhile, Tania's excitement left her and with it her boldness: her face turned haggard, it was the face of the night before. She could not stop shivering or talking about our being doomed because the train had not left. She was sure the captain would mention the amusing little shrew from R. with an interest in Mann to some officer whose understanding extended beyond railway trains, and they would immediately send the Gestapo to get us. Once again, she had gone too far with her lies; we would pay for it. But no one came. The officers who glanced at us curiously as they passed in the corridor continued on their way. A whistle blew, the train started, and soon the elderly reservist came to tell us that the next stop would be G., more than halfway to R.

Italo Calvino

WHY ARE THE MEN FIGHTING?

Italo Calvino's first novel, The Path to the Spiders' Nests
*(1947), draws on the author's own experience in the Italian
partisan war against the Germans. In the following extract,
Ferriera and Kim, the commander and the commissar of the
partisan brigade, discuss the motivation of their men and why
they have decided to fight.*

*It is an intriguing meditation on both the making of moral
judgements and the historical importance of the actions of
men fighting in a war – because, as Calvino writes in his
introduction, 'for many of my contemporaries it had been
solely a question of luck which determined what side they
should fight on'.*

KIM AND FERRIERA are walking along the dark mountain-
side towards another encampment.

'Surely you see now it was a mistake, Kim?' says Ferriera.

Kim shakes his head. 'No, it's not a mistake,' he says.

'But it is,' says the commander, 'it was a mistaken idea of
yours to make up a detachment entirely of men who can't be
trusted, with a commander who can be trusted even less. You
see what happens. If we'd divided them up among the good
ones it might have kept them on the right lines.'

Kim continues to chew his moustache. 'For my part,' he
says, 'this is the detachment I'm most pleased with.'

At this Ferriera nearly loses his calm; he raises his ice-cold

251

eyes and rubs his forehead. 'But Kim, when will you realize that this is a fighting brigade, not an experimental laboratory? I can understand your getting a scientific satisfaction from watching the reactions of these men, all arranged as you wanted them, proletariat in one part, peasants in another, then "sub-proletariat", as you call it . . . The political work you ought to be doing, it seems to me, is mixing them all up together and giving class-consciousness to those who haven't got it, so as to achieve this blessed unit we hear so much about . . . Apart from the military value, of course . . .'

Kim, who has difficulty in expressing himself, shakes his head.

'Nonsense,' he says. 'Nonsense. The men all fight with the same sort of urge in them . . . well, not quite the same, . . . each has an urge of his own . . . but they're all fighting in unison now, each as much as the other. Then there's Dritto, there's Pelle . . . You don't understand what it costs them . . . Well, they too have the same urge . . . Any little thing is enough to save or lose them . . . That's what political work is . . . to give them a sense . . .'

When Kim talks to the men and analyses the situation for them, he is absolutely clear and dialectical. But when he is talking like this just for one other person to hear him, it makes one's head spin. Ferriera sees things more simply. 'All right, let's give them this sense, let's organize them the way I say.'

Kim breathes through his moustache. 'This isn't an army, you see, they aren't soldiers to whom one can say: this is your duty. You can't talk about duty here, you can't talk about ideals like country, liberty, communism. The men don't want to hear about ideals, anyone can have those, they have ideals on the other side too. You see what happens when that extremist cook begins his sermonizing? They shout at him and knock him about. They don't need ideals, myths, or to shout "Long live . . ." They fight and die without shouting anything.'

'Why do they fight, then?' asks Ferriera. He knows why he does, everything is perfectly clear to him.

'Well,' says Kim, 'at this moment the various detachments

are climbing silently up towards their positions. Tomorrow many of them will be wounded or dead. They know that. What drives them to lead this life, what makes them fight? Well, first, the peasants who live in these mountains, it's easier for them. The Germans burn their villages, take away their cattle. Theirs is a basic human war, one to defend their own country, for the peasants really have a country. So they join up with us, young and old, with their old shot-guns and corduroy hunting-jackets; whole villages of them; they're with us as we're defending their country. And defending their country becomes a serious ideal for them, transcends them, as an end in itself; they sacrifice even their homes, even their cattle, to go on fighting. Then there are other peasants for whom "country" remains something selfish; *their* cattle, *their* home, *their* crops. And to keep all that they become spies, Fascists . . . there are whole villages which are our enemies. Then there are the workers. The workers have a background of their own, of wages and strikes, work and struggle elbow to elbow. They're a class, the workers are. They know there's something better in life and they fight for that something better. They have a "country" too, a "country" still to be conquered, and they're fighting here to conquer it. Down in the town there are factories which will be theirs; they can already see the red writing on the factory walls and the banners flying on the factory chimneys. But there's no sentimentality in them. They understand reality and how to change it. Then there is an intellectual or a student or two, very few of them though, here and there, with ideas in their heads that are often vague or twisted. Their "country" consists of words, or at the most of some books. But as they fight they find that those words of theirs no longer have any meaning, and they make new discoveries about men's struggles, and they just fight on without asking themselves questions, until they find new words and rediscover the old ones, changed now, with unsuspected meanings. Who else is there? Foreign prisoners, who've escaped from concentration camps and joined us; they're fighting for a real proper country, a distant country which they want to get back to and which is theirs just because it is distant. But, after all, can't you see that this is only a struggle between symbols? that to kill a German, a man must think not of that German but of another German, with a substitution technique which is enough to turn his brain? that everything and everybody must become a Chinese shadow-play, a myth?'

Ferriera strokes his blond beard; he doesn't see any of these things.

'It's not like that,' he says.

'No, it's not like that,' Kim goes on, 'I know that too. It's not like that. Because there's something else, common to all of them: an inner frenzy. Take Dritto's detachment; petty thieves, *carabinieri*, ex-soldiers, black marketeers, down-and-outs; men on the fringes of society, who got along somehow despite all the chaos around them, with nothing to defend and nothing to lose; either that, or they're defective physically, or they have fixations, or they're fanatics. No revolutionary idea can ever appear in them, tied as they are to the millstones grinding them. Or if it does it will be born twisted, the product of rage and humiliation, like that cook's extremism. Why do they fight, then? They have no "country", either real or invented. And yet you know there's courage, there's a frenzy in them too. It comes from the squalor of their streets, the filth of their homes, the obscenities they've known ever since childhood, the strain of having to be bad. And any little thing, a false step, a momentary impulse, is enough to send them over to the other side, to the Black Brigade, like Pelle, there to shoot with the same frenzy, the same hatred, against either side, it doesn't matter which.'

Ferriera mutters into his beard: 'So you think the spirit of our men . . . and the Black Brigade's . . . the same thing?'

'The same thing, the same thing . . . but, if you see what I mean . . .' Kim has stopped, with a finger pointing as if he were keeping the place in a book. 'The same thing but the other way round. Because here we're in the right, there they're in the wrong. Here we're achieving something, there they're just reinforcing their chains. That age-old resentment which weighs down on Dritto's men, on all of us, including you and me, and which finds expression in shooting and killing enemies, the Fascists have that too: it forces them to kill with the same hope of purification and of release. But then there is also the question of history. The fact is that on our side nothing is lost, not a single gesture, not a shot, though each may be the same as theirs – d'you see what I mean? – they will all serve if not to free us then to free our children, to create a world that is serene, without resentment, a world in which no one has to be bad. The others are on the side of lost gestures, of useless resentment, which are lost and useless even if they should win, because they are not making positive history, they are not helping to free themselves but to repeat and perpetuate resentment and hatred, until in another twenty or a hundred or a thousand years it will begin all over again, the struggle between us and them; and we shall both be fighting with the same anonymous hatred in our eyes, though always, perhaps without knowing it, *we* shall be fighting for redemption, *they* to remain slaves. That is the real meaning of the struggle now, the real, absolute meaning, beyond the various official meanings. An elementary, anonymous urge to free us from all our humiliations; the worker from his exploitation, the peasant from his ignorance, the petty bourgeois from his inhibitions, the outcast from his corruption. This is what I believe our political work is, to use human misery against itself, for our own redemption, as the Fascists use misery to perpetuate misery and man fighting man.'

Only the blue of Ferriera's eyes and the yellow glimmer of his beard can be seen in the dark. He shakes his head. He does not feel this resentment; he is precise as a mechanic and practical as a mountain-peasant; for him the struggle is a precise machine of which he knows the workings and purpose.

'It seems impossible,' he says, 'it seems impossible that with all that balls in your head you can still be a good commissar and talk clearly to the men.'

Kim is not displeased at Ferriera not understanding him; men like Ferriera must be talked to in exact terms; 'a, b, c,' one must say, things are either definite or they're 'balls', for them there are no ambiguous or dark areas. But Kim does not reason that way because he believes himself to be superior to Ferriera; no, his aim is to be able to think like Ferriera, to see no other reality but Ferriera's, nothing else matters.

'Well, I'll say good-bye.' They have reached a parting in the path. Now Ferriera will go on to Gamba's detachment and Kim to Baleno's. They have to separate in order to be able to inspect every detachment that night, before the battle.

Nothing else matters. Kim walks on alone, the slim Sten-gun hanging from his shoulder like a broken walking-stick. Nothing else matters. The tree trunks in the dark take on strange human shapes. Man carries his childhood fears with him for his whole life long. 'Perhaps,' thinks Kim, 'I'd be frightened, if I wasn't brigade commissar. Not to be frightened any more, that's the final aim of man.'

Kim is logical when he is analysing the situation with the detachment commissars, but when he is walking along alone and reasoning with himself things become mysterious and magical again, and life seems full of miracles. Our heads are still full of magic and miracles, thinks Kim. Sometimes he feels he is walking amid a world of symbols, like his namesake, little Kim in the middle of India, in that book of Kipling's which he had so often reread as a boy.

'Kim . . . Kim . . . Who is Kim . . .?'

Why is he walking over the mountains that night, getting ready for a battle, with power over life and death, after that gloomy childhood of his as a rich man's son, and his shy adolescence? At times he feels at the mercy of crazy swings of mood, as if he's acting hysterically, but no, his thoughts are logical, he can analyse everything with perfect clarity. And yet, he's not serene. His parents were serene, those parents from the great middle class which created their own riches. The proletariat is serene for it knows what it wants, so are the peasants who are now doing sentry duty over their own villages. The Soviets are serene, they have made their minds up about everything and are now fighting with both passion and method, not because war is a fine thing but because it is necessary. The Bolsheviks! The Soviet Union is perhaps already a serene country, perhaps there is no more poverty there. Will Kim ever be serene? One day perhaps, we will all achieve serenity and will not understand so much because we will have understood everything.

Here men still have troubled eyes and haggard faces. Kim has become fond of these men, though. That little boy in Dritto's detachment, for instance. What's his name? With that rage eating up his freckly face, even when he laughs . . . He's said to be the brother of a prostitute. Why is he fighting? He doesn't know it's so that he should no longer be the brother of a prostitute. And those Calabrian brothers-in-law. They're fighting so as not to be despised folk from the south any more, poor immigrants, looked down on as foreigners in their own country. And that *carabiniere* is fighting so that he won't feel a *carabiniere* any more, always spying on his fellow man. Then there's Cousin, the good, gigantic, ruthless Cousin . . . They say he's out for revenge on a woman who betrayed him . . . We all have a secret wound which we are fighting to avenge. Even Ferriera? Yes, perhaps even Ferriera; the frustration of not being able to get the world to go as he wants it. Not Red Wolf, though. Because everything that Red Wolf wants is possible. He must be made to want the right thing, that is political work, commissar's work. And learn that what he wants is right; that too is political work, commissar's work.

Perhaps, one day, thinks Kim, I won't understand these things any more. I'll be serene, and understand men in a completely different way, a juster way, perhaps. Why perhaps? Well, I shan't say 'perhaps' any more then, there won't be any more 'perhaps' in me. And I'll have Dritto shot. Now I'm too linked to them and all their twists. To Dritto too. I know that Dritto must suffer a lot for always being determined to behave badly. Nothing in the world hurts so much as behaving badly. One day as a child I shut myself up for two days in my room without eating. I suffered terribly but would not open the door and they had to come and fetch me by ladder through the window. I longed to be consoled and understood. Dritto is doing the same. But he knows we'll shoot him. He wants to be shot. That longing gets hold of men sometimes. And Pelle, what is Pelle doing at this moment?

Kim walks on through a larch wood and thinks of Pelle down in the town going round on curfew patrol with the death's head badge on his cap. Pelle must be alone, alone with his anonymous mistaken hatred, alone with his betrayal gnawing at him and making him behave worse than ever to justify it. He'll shoot at the cats in the black-out, even, from rage, and the shots will wake the bourgeoisie nearby, and make them start up in their beds.

Kim thinks of the column of Germans and Fascists who are perhaps at that moment advancing up the valley, towards the dawn which will bring death pouring down on their heads from the crests of the mountains. It is the column of lost gestures. One of the soldiers, waking up at a jolt of the truck is now thinking 'I love you, Kate.' In six or seven hours he'll be dead, we'll have killed him; even if he hadn't thought 'I love you, Kate,' it would have been the same; everything that he does or thinks is lost, cancelled from history.

I, on the other hand, am walking through a larch wood and every step I take is history. I think 'I love you, Adriana' and that is history, will have great consequences. I'll behave tomorrow in battle like a man who has thought tonight 'I love you, Adriana.' Perhaps I may not accomplish great deeds but history is made up of little anonymous gestures; I may die tomorrow even before that German, but everything I do before dying and my death too will be little parts of history, and all the thoughts I'm having now will influence my history tomorrow, tomorrow's history of the human race.

Now, instead of escaping into fantasy as I did when I was a child I could be making a mental study of the details of the attack, the dispositions of weapons and squads. But I am too fond of thinking about those men, studying them, making discoveries about them. What will they do 'afterwards' for instance? Will they recognize in post-war Italy something made by them? Will they understand what system will have to be used then in order to continue our struggle, the long and constantly changing struggle to better humanity? Red Wolf will understand, I think; I wonder how he'll manage to put his understanding into practice, how will he use that adventurous, ingenious spirit of his when there are no more daring deeds or escapes to be made? They should all be like Red Wolf. We should all be like Red Wolf. There'll be some, on the other hand, whose anonymous resentment will continue, who will become individualists again, and thus sterile; they'll fall into crime, the great outlet for dumb resentments; they'll forget that history once walked by their side, breathed through their clenched teeth. The ex-Fascists will say: 'Oh, the partisans! I told you so! I realized it at once!' And they won't have realized anything, either before or after.

One day Kim will be serene. Everything is clear with him now. Dritto, Pin, the Calabrian brothers-in-law. He knows how to behave towards each of them, without fear or pity. Sometimes when he is walking at night the mists of souls seem to condense around him like the mists in the air; but he is a man who analyses; 'a, b, c,' he'll say to the commissars; he's a Bolshevik, a man who dominates situations. 'I love you, Adriana.'

The valley is full of mist, and Kim is walking along a slope which is as stony as a lakeside. The larches appear out of the mist like mooring-poles. *Kim . . . Kim . . . Who is Kim?* He feels like the hero of that novel read in his childhood; the half-English half-Indian boy who travels across India with the old Red Lama looking for the river of purification.

Two hours ago he was talking to that liar Dritto, to the prostitute's brother, and now he is reaching Baleno's detachment, the best in the brigade. There is a squad of Russians with Baleno, ex-prisoners who had escaped from the fortification works on the border.

'Who goes there?'

It's the sentry; a Russian.

Kim gives his name.

'Bring news, Commissar?'

It's Aleksjéi, the son of a *moujik*, an engineering student.

'Tomorrow there will be a battle, Aleksjéi.'

'Battle? Hundred Fascists *kaput*?'

'I don't know how many *kaput*, Aleksjéi. I don't even know how many alive.'

'*Sale e tabacchi*, Commissar.'

Sale e tabacchi, is the Italian phrase which has made most impression on Aleksjéi, he repeats it all the time, like a refrain, a talisman.

'*Sale e tabacchi*, Aleksjéi.'

Tomorrow there will be a big battle. Kim is serene. 'A, b, c,' he'll say. Again and again he thinks: 'I love you, Adriana.' That, and that alone, is history.

Joseph Heller
They Were Trying to Kill Me

Drawing on his experiences as a bombardier during the Second World War, Joseph Heller's Catch-22 *is one of the most famous novels of the century. In his memoir,* Now and Then: From Coney Island to Here, *published in 1998, Heller writes for the first time about the people and events he was eventually to translate into the memorable characters of* Catch-22.

REMARKABLY, THROUGH ALL his unlucky series of mishaps the pilot Ritter remained imperviously phlegmatic, demonstrating no symptoms of fear or growing nervousness, even blushing with a chuckle and a smile whenever I gagged around about him as a jinx, and it was on these qualities of his, his patient genius for building and fixing things and these recurring close calls in aerial combat, only on these, that I fashioned the character of Orr in *Catch-22*. (I don't know if he's aware of that. I don't know if he's even read the book, for I've never been in touch with him or almost any of the others.)

In a nearby tent just across a railroad ditch in disuse was the tent of a friend, Francis Yohannon, and it was from him that I nine years later derived the unconventional name for the heretical Yossarian. The rest of Yossarian is the incarnation of a wish. In Yohannon's tent also lived the pilot Joe Chrenko, a pilot I was especially friendly with, who later, in several skimpy ways, served as the basis for the character

261

Hungry Joe in *Catch-22*. In that tent with them was a pet dog Yohannon had purchased in Rome, a lovable, tawny cocker spaniel he bought while others were purchasing and smuggling back contraband Italian pistols, Berettas. In my novel I turned the dog into a cat to protect its identity.

Except for the insertion into the novel of a radio gunner who is mortally wounded, the incidents I actually experienced in my plane on this second mission to Avignon were very much like those I related in fictional form. A co-pilot panicked and I thought I was doomed. By that time I had learned through experience that this war was perilous and that they were trying to kill me. The earlier cluster of missions I had flown to Ferrara when first overseas had assumed in my memory the character of a fantasy nightmare from which I had luckily escaped without harm in my trusting innocence, like an ingenuous kid in a Grimm fairy tale. And I also knew from the serious tone in the briefing room and from an earlier mission to Avignon that this target was a dangerous one.

All four squadrons in the group were involved, flying into southern France in a single large bunch, then separating near the city to simultaneously attack three separate targets that were several miles apart. My plane was in the last of the three elements turning in, and as we neared our IP, the initial point from which we would begin our bomb run, I looked off into the distance to see what was taking place with the other formations. The instant I looked, I glimpsed far off amid black bursts of flak a plane in formation with an orange glow of fire on its wing. And the instant I spied the fire, I saw the wing break off and the plane nose over and fall straight down, like a boulder – rotating slowly with its remaining wing, but straight down. There was no possibility of parachutes. Then we made the turn toward our target and we were in it ourselves.

The very first bursts of flak aimed at us were at an accurate height, and that was a deadly sign. We could hear the explosions. I have since read of the tactic developed by the

Germans of sending a monitor plane out to fly alongside our bombers and radio our exact altitude and speed to the anti-aircraft batteries below, and it's possible they were doing it that day. Soberly and tensely, I did what I had to – we all did. When I observed the bomb-bay doors of the lead bombardier opening, I opened mine; when I saw his bombs begin to go, I toggled away mine; when the indicator on my dial registered that all our bombs were away, I announced on the intercom that our bombs were away. When a gunner in the rear looking down into the bomb-bay announced that the bomb-bay was clear, I flipped the switch that closed the doors. And then our whole formation of six planes wrenched away upward at full throttle into a steep and twisting climb. And then the bottom of the plane just seemed to drop out: we were falling, and I found myself pinned helplessly to the top of the bombardier's compartment, with my flak helmet squeezed against the ceiling. What I did not know (it was reconstructed for me later) was that one of the two men at the controls, the co-pilot, gripped by the sudden fear that our plane was about to stall, seized the controls to push them forward and plunged us into a sharp descent, a dive, that brought us back down into the level of the flak.

I had no power to move, not even a finger. And I believed with all my heart and quaking soul that my life was ending and that we were going down, like the plane on fire I had witnessed plummeting only a few minutes before. I had no time for anything but terror. And then just as suddenly – I think I would have screamed had I been able to – we levelled out and began to climb away again from the flak bursts, and now I was flattened against the floor, trying frantically to grasp something to hold on to when there was nothing. And in another few seconds we were clear and edging back into formation with the rest of the planes. But as I regained balance and my ability to move, I heard in the ears of my headphones the most unnatural and sinister of sounds: silence, dead silence. And I was petrified again. Then I recognized, dangling loosely before me, the jack to my headset. It had torn free from the outlet. When I plugged myself back in, a shrill bedlam of voices was clamouring in my ears, with a wail over all the rest repeating on the intercom that the bombardier wasn't answering. 'The bombardier doesn't answer!' 'I'm the bombardier,' I broke in immediately. 'And I'm all right.' 'Then go back and help him, help the gunner. He's hurt.'

It was our top gunner who was wounded, and his station was in the front section of the plane just behind the pilot's flight deck. But so deeply, over time, have the passages in the novel entrenched themselves in me that I am tempted even now to think of the wounded man as the radio gunner in the rear. Our gunner was right there on the floor in front of me when I moved back through the crawlway from my bombardier's compartment, and so was the large oval wound in his thigh where a piece of flak – a small one, judging from the entrance site on the inside – had blasted all the way through. I saw the open flesh with shock. I had no choice but to do what I had to do next. Overcoming a tremendous wave of nausea and revulsion that was close to paralysing, I delicately touched the torn and bleeding leg, and after the first touch, I was able to proceed with composure.

Although there was a lot of blood puddling about, I could tell from my Boy Scout days – I had earned a merit badge in first aid – that no artery was punctured and thus there was no need for a tourniquet. I followed the obvious procedure. With supplies from the first-aid kit, I heavily salted the whole open wound with sulphanilamide powder. I opened and applied a sterile compress, maybe two – enough to close and to cover everything injured. Then I bandaged him carefully. I did the same with the small hole on the inside of his thigh. When he exclaimed that his leg was starting to hurt him, I gave him a shot of morphine – I may have given him two if the first didn't serve quickly enough to soothe us both. When he said he was starting to feel cold, I told him we would soon be back on the field and he was going to be all right. Truthfully, I hadn't the slightest idea where we were, for my attention had been totally concentrated on him.

With a wounded man on board, we were given priority in

landing. The flight surgeon and his medical assistants and an ambulance were waiting to the side at the end of the runway. They took him off my hands. I might have seemed a hero and been treated as something of a small hero for a short while, but I didn't feel like one. They were trying to kill me, and I wanted to go home. That they were trying to kill all of us each time we went up was no consolation. They were trying to kill *me*.

I was frightened on every mission after that one, even the certified milk runs. It could have been about then that I began crossing my fingers each time we took off and saying in silence a little prayer. It was my private ritual.

Michael Ondaatje

THE LAST MEDIEVAL WAR

The following extract, taken from Michael Ondaatje's novel
The English Patient *(1992), describes that peculiar war fought
against the retreating German troops in Italy, and shows the
perspective of a young Sikh sapper with the Eighth Army,
who in the middle of war and destruction is fascinated by the
achievements of Western civilization.*

    *Anthony Minghella's 1996 film of Ondaatje's novel ampli-
fied the themes of internationalism in the book and made
memorable pictures of the scene described here, particularly
when the sapper repeats the trick for a Canadian nurse.*

THE LAST MEDIEVAL war was fought in Italy in 1943 and
1944. Fortress towns on great promontories which had been
battled over since the eighth century had the armies of new
kings flung carelessly against them. Around the outcrops of
rocks were the traffic of stretchers, butchered vineyards,
where, if you dug deep beneath the tank ruts, you found
blood-axe and spear. Monterchi, Cortona, Urbino, Arezzo,
Sansepolcro, Anghiari. And then the coast.

Cats slept in the gun turrets looking south. English and
Americans and Indians and Australians and Canadians
advanced north, and the shell traces exploded and dissolved
in the air. When the armies assembled at Sansepolcro, a town
whose symbol is the crossbow, some soldiers acquired them
and fired them silently at night over the walls of the untaken

city. Field Marshal Kesselring of the retreating German army seriously considered the pouring of hot oil from battlements.

Medieval scholars were pulled out of Oxford colleges and flown into Umbria. Their average age was sixty. They were billeted with troops, and in meetings with strategic command they kept forgetting the invention of the airplane. They spoke of towns in terms of the art in them. At Monterchi there was the *Madonna del Parto* by Piero della Francesca, located in the chapel next to the town graveyard. When the thirteenth-century castle was finally taken during the spring rains, troops were billeted under the high dome of the church and slept by the stone pulpit where Hercules slays the Hydra. There was only bad water. Many died of typhoid and other fevers. Looking up with service binoculars in the Gothic church at Arezzo soldiers would come upon their contemporary faces in the Piero della Francesca frescoes. The Queen of Sheba conversing with King Solomon. Nearby a twig from the Tree of Good and Evil inserted into the mouth of the dead Adam. Years later this queen would realize that the bridge over the Siloam was made from the wood of this sacred tree.

It was always raining and cold, and there was no order but for the great maps of art that showed judgement, piety and sacrifice. The Eighth Army came upon river after river of destroyed bridges, and their sapper units clambered down banks on ladders of rope within enemy gunfire and swam or waded across. Food and tents were washed away. Men who were tied to equipment disappeared. Once across the river they tried to ascend out of the water. They sank their hands and wrists into the mud wall of the cliff face and hung there. They wanted the mud to harden and hold them.

The young Sikh sapper put his cheek against the mud and thought of the Queen of Sheba's face, the texture of her skin. There was no comfort in this river except his desire for her, which somehow kept him warm. He would pull the veil off her hair. He would put his right hand between her neck and olive blouse. He too was tired and sad, as the wise king and guilty queen he had seen in Arezzo two weeks earlier.

He hung over the water, his hands locked into the mud-bank. Character, that subtle art, disappeared among them during those days and nights, existed only in a book or on a painted wall. Who was sadder in that dome's mural? He leaned forward to rest on the skin of her frail neck. He fell in love with her downcast eye. This woman who would someday know the sacredness of bridges.

At night in the camp bed, his arms stretched out into distance like two armies. There was no promise of solution or victory except for the temporary pact between him and that painted fresco's royalty who would forget him, never acknowledge his existence or be aware of him, a Sikh, halfway up a sapper's ladder in the rain, erecting a Bailey bridge for the army behind him. But he remembered the painting of their story. And when a month later the battalions reached the sea, after they had survived everything and entered the coastal town of Cattolica and the engineers had cleared the beach of mines in a twenty-yard stretch so the men could go down naked into the sea, he approached one of the medievalists who had befriended him – who had once simply talked with him and shared some Spam – and promised to show him something in return for his kindness.

The sapper signed out a Triumph motorbike, strapped a crimson emergency light on to his arm, and they rode back the way they had come – back into and through the now innocent towns like Urbino and Anghiari, along the winding crest of the mountain ridge that was a spine down Italy, the old man bundled up behind him hugging him, and down the western slope towards Arezzo. The piazza at night was empty of troops, and the sapper parked in front of the church. He helped the medievalist off, collected his equipment and walked into the church. A colder darkness. A greater emptiness, the sound of his boots filling the area. Once more he smelled the old stone and wood. He lit three flares. He slung block and tackle across the columns above the nave, then fired a rivet already threaded with rope into a high wooden beam. The professor was watching him bemused, now and then peering up into the high darkness. The young sapper circled him and knotted a sling across his waist and shoulders, taped a small lit flare to the old man's chest.

He left him there by the communion rail and noisily climbed the stairs to the upper level, where the other end of the rope was. Holding on to it, he stepped off the balcony into the darkness, and the old man was simultaneously swung up, hoisted up fast until, when the sapper touched ground, he swung idly in midair within three feet of the frescoed walls, the flare brightening a halo around him. Still holding the rope the sapper walked forward until the man swung to the right to hover in front of *The Flight of Emperor Maxentius*.

Five minutes later he let the man down. He lit a flare for himself and hoisted his body up into the dome within the deep blue of the artificial sky. He remembered its gold stars from the time he had gazed on it with binoculars. Looking down he saw the medievalist sitting on a bench, exhausted. He was now aware of the depth of this church, not its height. The liquid sense of it. The hollowness and darkness of a well. The flare sprayed out of his hand like a wand. He pulleyed himself across to her face, his Queen of Sadness, and his brown hand reached out small against the giant neck.

John Horne Burns

MY HEART FINALLY BROKE IN NAPLES

Set in Naples towards the end of the Second World War, John Horne Burns's novel The Gallery *(1948) portrays life in the city after its liberation by the US Army. The following extract describes the disillusionment of an American soldier whose ideals have been destroyed by the behaviour of the liberators towards the Italian people.*

I REMEMBER THAT my heart finally broke in Naples. Not over a girl or a thing, but over an idea. When I was little, they'd told me I should be proud to be an American. And I suppose I was, though I saw no reason I should applaud every time I saw the flag in a newsreel. But I did believe that the American way of life was an idea holy in itself, an idea of freedom bestowed by intelligent citizens on one another. Yet after a little while in Naples I found out that America was a country just like any other, except that she had more material wealth and more advanced plumbing. And I found that outside of the propaganda writers (who were making a handsome living from the deal) Americans were very poor spiritually. Their ideals were something to make dollars on. They had bankrupt souls. Perhaps this is true of most of the people of the twentieth century. Therefore my heart broke.

I remember that this conceit came home to me in crudest black and white. In Naples of 1944 we Americans had everything. The Italians, having lost their war, had nothing.

And what was this war really about? I decided that it was because most of the people of the world didn't have the cigarettes, the gasoline, and the food that we Americans had.

I remember my mother's teaching me out of her wisdom that the possession of Things implies a responsibility for Their use, that They shouldn't be wasted, that Having Things should never dominate my living. When this happens, Things become more important than People. Comfort then becomes the be-and-end-all of human life. And when other people threaten your material comfort, you have no recourse but to fight them. It makes no difference who attacks whom first. The result is the same, a killing and a chaos that the world of 1944 wasn't big enough to stand.

Our propaganda did everything but tell us Americans the truth: that we had most of the riches of the modern world, but very little of its soul. We were nice enough guys in our own country, most of us; but when we got overseas, we couldn't resist the temptation to turn a dollar or two at the expense of people who were already down. I can speak only of Italy, for I didn't see France or Germany. But with our Hollywood ethics and our radio network reasoning we didn't take the trouble to think out the fact that the war was supposed to be against fascism – not against every man, woman, and child in Italy . . . But then a modern war is total. Armies on the battlefield are simply a remnant from the old kind of war. In the 1944 war everyone's hand ended by being against everyone else's. Civilization was already dead, but nobody bothered to admit this to himself.

I remember the crimes we committed against the Italians, as I watched them in Naples. In the broadest sense we promised the Italians security and democracy if they came over to our side. All we actually did was to knock the hell out of *their* system and give them nothing to put in its place. And one of the most tragic spectacles in all history was the Italians' faith in us – for a little while, until we disabused them of it. It seemed to me like the swindle of all humanity, and I wondered if perhaps we weren't all lost together. Collective and social decency didn't exist in Naples in August, 1944. And I used to laugh at our attempts at relief and control there, for we undid with one hand what we did with the other. What we should have done was to set up a strict and square rationing for all goods that came into Italy. We should have given the Neapolitans co-operative stores.

I remember watching the American acquisitive sense in action. We didn't realize, or we didn't want to realize, that we were in a poor country, now reduced to minus zero by war. Nearly every GI and officer went out and bought everything he could lay hands on, no matter how worthless it was; and he didn't care how much he paid for it. They'd buy all the bamboo canes in a little Neapolitan shop, junk jewellery, worthless art – all for the joy of spending. Everywhere we Americans went, the prices of everything sky-rocketed until the lira was valueless. And the Italians couldn't afford to pay these prices, especially for things they needed just to live on. For all the food we sent into Italy for relief, we should have set up some honest American control by honourable and incorruptible Americans. Instead we entrusted it to Italians who, nine times out of ten, were grafters of the regime we claimed to be destroying.

I remember too that an honest American in August, 1944, was almost as hard to find as a Neapolitan who owned up to having been a Fascist. I don't know why, but most Americans had a blanket hatred of all Italians. They figured it this way: these Ginsoes have made war on us; so it doesn't matter what we do to them, boost their prices, shatter their economy, and shack up with their women. I imagine there's some fallacy in my reasoning here. I guess I was asking for the impossible. This was war, and I wanted it to be conducted with honour. I suppose that's as phony reasoning as talking about an honest murder or a respectable rape.

I remember that the commonest, and the pettiest, crime we did against the Neapolitans was selling them our PX rations. We paid five lire a package for cigarettes, which was a privilege extended to us by the people of the United States. To a Neapolitan we could sell each package for three hundred lire. Really big business. A profit of 6,000 per cent. Of course the Neapolitans were mad to pay this price for them, but I don't see that it made our selling any the righter. I don't believe that these cigarettes were legally ours – ours, that is, to sell at a profit. They were only ours if we wanted to smoke them. If we didn't smoke, we had no right to buy them. Though there was no harm in *giving* these cigarettes away.

I remember that we went the next step in vulturism and sold our GI clothes to the Neapolitans. Then we could sign a statement of charges and get new ones, having made meanwhile a small fortune out of the deal. This was inexcusable on any grounds whatever. There are loopholes in my cigarette syllogism, but none that I see on the clothes question.

Then I remember that there were not a few really big criminals who stole stuff off the ships unloading in Naples harbour, stuff that didn't belong to them by *any* stretch of the imagination. For all this that I saw I could only attribute a deficient moral and humane sense to Americans as a nation and as a people. I saw that we could mouth democratic catchwords and yet give the Neapolitans a huge black market. I saw that we could prate of the evils of fascism, yet be just as ruthless as Fascists with people who'd already been pushed into the ground. That was why my heart broke in Naples in August, 1944. The arguments that we advanced to cover our delinquencies were as childishly ingenious as American advertising.

– If a *signorina* comes to the door of my mess hall, the mess sergeant said, making a salad, an she says she's hungry, why, I give her a meal . . . But first I make it clear to her Eyetie mind that I'm interested in somethin she's got . . . If she says ixnay I tell her to get the hell out.

– Of course the only reason I sell my cigarettes, the corporal said, is because we're gettin creamed on the rate of exchange for the lira . . . What can I buy in Naples on the seventy bucks a month I'm pullin down?

– You've got enough to eat and a place to sleep, said the Pfc with the glasses. That's better than most of the world is doing in 1944.

273

– I didn't ask for this war, the sergeant major said. I didn't ask to be sent overseas. Guess I've got a right to turn a buck when I see the chance, ain't I?

– You must make the distinction, said the Pfc, between so-called honest business tactics and making money out of human misery.

But he was only a Jewish Communist; so no one paid any attention to him.

Yes, I remember that being at war with the Italians was taken as a licence for Americans to defecate all over them. Even though most of us in the base section at Naples had never closed with an Italian in combat. Our argument was that we should treat the Neapolitans as the Neapolitans would have treated our cities presumably if they'd won the war. I watched old ladies of Naples pushed off the sidewalks by drunken GIs and officers. Every Italian girl was fair prey to propositions we wouldn't have made to a streetwalker back home. Those who spoke Italian used the *tu* on everyone they met. And I remember seeing American MPs beating the driver of a horse and wagon because they were obstructing traffic on Via Roma. I don't think the Germans could have done any better in their concentration camps. I thought that all humanity had gone from the world, and that this war had smothered decency forever.

– These Eyeties, the mess sergeant said, ain't human beins. They're just Gooks, that's all.

– All I know, the corporal said doggedly and worriedly, is that they ain't Americans . . . They don't see things the way we do.

– They'd steal anything, the mess sergeant said, stuffing a turkey, his mouth crammed with giblet leavings.

I remember that other arguments against the Neapolitans, besides the cardinal one, that they'd declared war on us, were that they stole and were filthy-dirty. I only know that no Neapolitan ever stole anything from me, for I took pains to see that no temptation was put in their way. Though once my wallet was lifted in a New York subway. And for those Neapolitans to whom I sometimes gave an extra bar of soap,

I noticed that they used this soap joyfully on themselves, their children, their clothes. I've buried my face in the hair of Neapolitan girls. It was just as sweet as an American girl's if the *Napoletana* had the wherewithal to wash it.

I remember that in Naples after my heart broke I decided that a strictly American point of view in itself offered no peace or solution for the world. So I began to make friends with the Neapolitans. And it didn't surprise me to find that, like everyone else in the world, they had their good and their bad and their admixtures of both. To know them, I'd been working on my Italian. That lovely supple language was kind to my tongue. The Neapolitans were gracious in helping me with it.

I met agile dapper thieves who'd steal the apple out of my eye if they could sell it on the black market. But this tribute I must pay even to the crooks: when I answered them in Italian, they'd laugh and shake my hand and say they were going to try someone else who didn't know their language quite so well.

I met *studenti* and young soldiers just fled from the army, baffled and bitter, with nothing but a black bottomless pit of despair for their future. Perhaps I'd have been like them if I'd been on the losing side?

I met Neapolitan whores who charged a rate a countess couldn't have earned from her favours in the old days.

And I met *ragazze* and *mamme* so warm and laughing that in Neapolitan dining rooms I thought I was back in my own house, hearing the talk of my mother with my sisters.

This forced me to the not original conclusion that the Neapolitans were like everybody else in the world, and in an infinite variety. Because I was an *americano* the Neapolitans treated me with a strange pudding of respect, dismay, and bewilderment. A few loathed me. But from most Italians I got a decency and a kindness that they'd have showered on any other American in Naples who'd made up his mind to treat them like human beings. I'm not bragging. I'm not unique. I'm not Christlike. Many other Americans in Naples made friends they'll never forget. Thus I remember that in Naples, though my heart had broken from one idea, it mended again when I saw how good most human beings are if they have enough to eat and are free from imminent annihilation.

I remember that I came to love the courtesy and the laughter and the simplicity of Italian life. The compliment I pay to most Italians who haven't too much of this world's goods is that they love life and love. I don't know what else there is, after all. Even in their frankness the Italians were so seldom offensive. An Italian mother told a friend of mine that he could never marry her daughter because he had the face of a whoremaster. And we all laughed. No one was hurt.

I remember the passion and the understanding of Italian love. There's no barrier between the lovers. Everything is oxidized at the moment, without rancour or reservation.

– *Fammi male, amore mio . . . Fammi godere da movire . . .*

And I remember the storms and quarrels of Italian love, mostly rhetorical. The going to bed is all the sweeter for the reconciliation.

For I thought that to this people, broken and saddened and dismayed, there yet remained much of that something which had made Italy flower – though not as a nation of warriors. To this day I'm convinced of Italy's greatness in the world of the spirit. In war she's a tragic farce. In love and sunlight and music and humanity she has something that humanity sorely needs. It's still there. Something of this distillation of noble and gentle grandeur seeps down through most of Italy's population, from *contessa* to *contadina*. I don't think I'm romanticizing or kidding myself. In the middle of the war, in August, 1944, with my heart broken for an ideal, I touched the beach of heaven in Naples. At moments.

I remember how the children of Naples pointed my dim conception of American waste. They'd stand about our mess hall quiet or noisy, watching the glutted riches from our mess kits being dumped into the garbage cans. I remember the surprise and terror in their faces. We were forbidden to feed them, though I heard that combat soldiers, gentler and more determined than we, took the law into their hands and were much kinder to Italian children than we were allowed to be. When I watched the bitten steaks, the nibbled lettuce, the half-eaten bread go sliding into the swill cans in a spectrum of waste and bad planning, I realized at last the problem of the modern world, simple yet huge. I saw then what was behind the war. I'll never forget those Neapolitan children whom we were forbidden to feed. After a while many of us couldn't stand it any longer. We'd brush past the guard with our mess kit full of supper and share it with Adalgisa and Sergio and Pasqualino. They were only the *scugnizz'* of Napoli, but they had mouths and stomachs just like us. I remember the wild hungry faces of those kids diving into cold Spam. But our orders were that since America was in no position to feed all the Italians, we were not to feed any. Just dump your waste in the GI cans, men.

But I remember even then thinking and fearing that we'd come to a day when we too, we rich rich rich Americans, would pay for this mortal sin of waste. We've always thought that there was no end to our plenty, that the horn would never dry up. Already I seem to hear the menacing rumblings, like a long-starved stomach. But in Naples in August 1944, we were on the crest of the wave. We? We were Americans, from the best little old country on God's green earth. And if you don't believe me, mister, I'll knock your teeth in . . .

And I remember well our first facing of the problem that we couldn't live in Naples as though there were a wall between us and the Neapolitans. There were American clubs and American movies, but only a blind man can carry his life around with him quite that much. Perhaps in Washington the generals had their doubts about the perfect probity of the American way of life and wished to make sure that overseas we wouldn't come in contact with any other. Consequently we were flooded with American movies and with Coca-Cola to distract our wandering attention and to ensure that we shouldn't fall into dangerous furren ways of thinking. But some of us wondered none the less.

The main leak, I remember, was in sex. It just isn't possible to take millions of American men and shut them off from love for years on end – no, not with a thousand other American distractions. Sooner or later every man's thoughts start centring around his middle. The cold and scientific solution would have been to have brothels attached to all our armies overseas, as other nations of the world have always done. But the American people wouldn't have stood for that. I mean the American people back home. Too many purity lobbies from old ladies who have nothing else to do but form pressure groups to guard other people's morals. And there were few women in our army as compared to our own percentage. There were WACs, to be sure, but in such a tiny ratio to us. And with the nurses we couldn't go out because they were officers. Thus our perfect chastity was theoretically assured. From the hygienic point of view there were pro stations on every corner of Naples. This was a nice paradox in that every interesting alley was off limits. The army took the point of view: you absolutely must not. But if by chance you do . . . Finally they had a restriction on marrying overseas.

Then we started casting our eyes on the Neapolitan girls.

– These Gook wimmin, the mess sergeant said. It's so easy with em. You just walk down Via Roma an some *signorina* does all the rest.

– But, the corporal said, dreamy in his shorts, I don't wanna hafta pay for it. I just wanna little girl all my own to love.

– There's something very nice about Italian women, the Pfc with spectacles said. No funny ideas about fur coats and higher income brackets and silk stockings, like American girls. And they don't feel they have to discuss books with you that they haven't read . . . not that women shouldn't be emancipated . . . to a certain degree, as companion to man and as his helpmate . . . But the Neapolitan women are so down to earth. First they cook you a spaghetti dinner . . . Then . . .

I remember that we GIs were used to women in a different tradition. American women, with their emancipation, had imposed their own standards on us. In America most Nice Girls Would . . . if you knew them well enough. Nearly all college girls Would, and waitresses too, if they thought there

278

was a reasonable chance of your eventually getting spliced. And as for the separate career women of America, with their apartments – well, they'd abrogated to themselves all the freedom of single men. A Career Girl would keep you, or you kept her, depending on the financial status of one or both. And in America there were lots of rich middle-aged ladies who liked their young chauffeurs or gardeners, but didn't dare marry them for fear of what Cousin Hattie would say.

But to us GIs the girls of southern Italy fell into two tight classes only. That's where we got stymied. There were the girls of Via Roma, whom the Neapolitans, mincing no words, called *puttane*. These girls asked fixed prices in either lire or PX rations. They satisfied for a while as long as we had money, but their fee was steep for a GI unless he were a big operator in the black market. And then too something in a man's vanity craves something other than a girl who's shacking with Tom, Dick, and Harry. American men are so sentimental that they refuse to have a whore for their girl – if they can help it. That's the schizophrenia of our civilization, with its sharp distinction between the Good Girl and the Bad Girl.

Consequently after a few tries, with the fear of VD always suspended over our heads, we began to look at the Good Women of Naples. And here entered the problem of the GI Italian bride. I remember that Italian girls began to look sweet to us early. Perhaps because their virginity was put on such a pedestal. There were few of us who didn't have access to some Neapolitan home, where we were welcomed, once our entrée was definite and our purposes above-board. We usually got in through a Neapolitan brother. Then we discovered that there were girls in the family, carefully kept and cherished as novices in a nunnery. It was obvious that these girls were interested in us . . . if we proposed marriage to them.

– I don't get a minute alone with Rosetta, the corporal said. They treat me swell at her *casa*, but Mamma doesn't trust Rosetta out her sight for one minnit. An after midnight Papa's always remindin me what time it is . . . as if I didn't have a wrist watch.

– Ah, I keep to Via Roma, the mess sergeant said. Ya can't lay a finger on the others.

– But north of Rome, said the Pfc with the spectacles, a girl once she's engaged will do anything to satisfy her fiancé . . . short of the real McCoy. I don't get these fine distinctions in tribal ethics.

– These Ginso girls, the sergeant major said, never forget that they're women. That's their strongest and weakest point. They know how to get in ya hair and under ya skin with wantin em till ya have ta slide that gold ring on their finger.

– Onelia told me quite frankly, the corporal said, that she was interested in a passport to the States as my wife . . . I liked that honesty in her. I guess she likes me too.

– Us GIs is so hot, the mess sergeant said, that once we leave Italy, these *signorinas* will never be satisfied with the Eytie men . . . never again . . .

I remember that we Americans brought heartbreak to Neapolitan girls in many instances. There were Negroes who told their shack-jobs that they weren't really black, just stained that way for camouflage and night fighting. There were mess sergeants who told nice Neapolitan girls that they owned chains of restaurants back in the States. I've often wondered at the face of some of those girls of good faith, arriving in the States to discover they'd live in one cabbage-smelling room over the stairs.

There were, I remember, American GIs and officers who most cruelly betrayed and seduced Neapolitan girls, conceal-ing from them and their families that back in the States they'd a wife and kids. These girls weren't in the position of an American girl, who knows the language and can make her own investigations. For the heartless deceit of such as these I sometimes felt shame that I was an American because the life of a pure woman is like a mirror, and can be smashed but once.

But I also remember instances of love and good faith on both sides. GIs and officers met Neapolitan girls, fell in love with them, and married them. I see no reason why such marriages shouldn't be happy and lasting, once the girls have learned English and made the not easy adjustment to American wifehood.

I remember Lydia, the gay shy mouse who sang in the chorus of the Teatro Reale di San Carlo. She was courted and won by our medic. I remember their wedding at Sorrento and their honeymoon at Taormina in Sicilia. Unless the world falls apart, I think that little Lydia and her *capitano medico* will be as happy in their lives together as human beings ever are outside of fairy tales.

I remember Laura, to whom a GI killed at Cassino made two presents. He gave her a baby and a white spirochete. When I see flowers lying crushed in a muddy street, I think of Laura.

I remember plump and smiling Emilia, who thought she'd married an MP. The MP disappeared forever after the wedding, and Emilia just sat in the kitchen night after night and wept so bitterly that her heart would have broken if it hadn't already been in tiny pieces. Her mother kept cursing her and asking where were all those allotment checks from America? And her brother yelled that he'd put a razor into the first *americano* he met on a dark night.

And I remember Wanda, stately and blonde, who used to sit by the stove and feel the life stirring within her. We all said she was too big to be having just one. And sure enough she came out with twins whom she christened Mario and Maria. They were brilliant gay babies, the way Italian children know how to be. Wanda hoped they'd grow up strong in St. Louis. She got me to point out that city for her on the map of America.

I remember that in Naples in August, 1944, for all the red tape and the army regulations and the blood tests and the warning talks by chaplains, there was still a great deal of human love. And this rejoiced me. For all the ruin and economic asphyxiation we'd brought the Neapolitans, we also in some cases gave them a new hope. They'd been like Jews standing against a wall and waiting to be shot for something they'd never done. And I began to think that perhaps something good might emerge or be salvaged from the abattoir of the world. Though in the main all national decency and sense of duty might be dead, I saw much individual goodness and loveliness that reassured me in my agony. I saw it in some Neapolitans. I saw it in some Americans. And I wondered if perhaps the world must eventually be governed by individuality consecrated and unselfish, rather than by any collectivism of the propagandists, the students, and the politicians. In Naples in August, 1944, I drowned in mass ideologies, but was fished out by separate thinking and will. I remember watching the mad hordes in the street of Naples and wondering what it all meant. But there was a certain unity in the bay, in the August moon over Vesuvius. Then humanity fell away from me like the rind of an orange, and I was something much more and much less than myself . . .

Wolfgang Koeppen

A SERVANT OF DEATH

Wolfgang Koeppen's novel A Death in Rome *(1954) describes the reunion of a German family in Rome a few years after the end of the Second World War, and forms a scathing attack on the postwar Germany of the* Wirtschaftswunder. *The following extract portrays the black sheep of the family, Gottlieb Judejahn, a former SS General. Unreconstructed and unrepentant, he is angered by the hypocrisy of his family who have become 'respectable people once more'.*

HE WENT DOWN. He went down the Spanish Steps, climbed down into picturesque Italy, into the idling population that was sitting on the steps, lying, reading, studying, chatting, quarrelling or embracing one another. A boy offered Judejahn some maize, yellow roasted kernels of maize. He held out a paper cornet to the foreigner, to the barbarian from the north, said '*cento lire*' in a wheedling voice, and Judejahn knocked the bag out of his hand. The maize scattered over the steps, and Judejahn trod it underfoot. He hadn't meant it. It was clumsiness. He felt like giving the boy a thrashing.

He crossed the square and reached the Via Condotti, panting. The pavement was narrow. People squeezed together in the busy shopping street, squeezed in front of the shop windows, squeezed past each other. Judejahn jostled and was jostled back. He didn't understand. He was surprised that no one made way for him, that no one got out of his road. He was surprised to find himself being jostled.

He looked for the cross street, looked for it on the map – but was he really looking? His years on the fringe of the desert seemed to him like time spent under anaesthetic, he had felt no pain, but now he felt sick, he felt fever and pain, felt the cuts that had pruned his life to a stump, felt the cuts that severed this stump from the wide flourishing of his power. What was he? A shadow of his former self. Should he rise from the dead, or remain a spook in the desert, a ghost in the Fatherland's colour magazines? Judejahn was not afraid to keep the world at bay. What did it want with him, anyway? Let it come, let it come in all its softness and venality, all its dirty, buzzard lusts, concealed under the mask of respectability. The world should be glad there were fellows like himself. Judejahn wasn't afraid of the rope. He was afraid of living. He feared the absence of commands in which he was expected to live. He had issued any number: the higher he'd been promoted, the more he'd issued, and the responsibility had never bothered him; he merely said, 'That's on my say-so,' or 'I'm in command here,' but that had been a phrase, an intoxicating phrase, because in reality he had only ever followed orders himself. Judejahn had been mighty. He had tasted power, but in order to enjoy it, he required it to be limited, he required the Führer as an embodiment and visible god of power, the commander who was his excuse before the Creator, man and the Devil: I only did what I was told, I only obeyed orders. Did he have a conscience then? No, he was just afraid. He was afraid it might be discovered that he was little Gottlieb going around in boots too big for him. Judejahn heard a voice, not the voice of God nor the voice of conscience, it was the thin, hungry, self-improving voice of his father, the primary schoolteacher, whispering to him: You're a fool, you didn't do your homework, you're a bad pupil, a zero, an inflated zero. And so it was as well that he had stayed in the shadow of a greater being, stayed a satellite, the shining satellite of the most powerful celestial body, and even now he didn't realize that this sun from whom he had borrowed light and the licence to kill had himself been nothing but a cheat, another bad pupil, another little Gottlieb who happened to be the Devil's chosen tool, a magical zero, a chimera of the people, a bubble that ultimately burst.

Judejahn felt a sudden craving to fill his belly. Even in his Freikorps days he had had bouts of gluttony, and shovelled ladles of peas from the field-kitchen down his throat. Now, at the corner of the street he was looking for, he scented food. A cheap eating-place had various dishes on display in its windows, and Judejahn went inside and ordered fried liver, which he had seen in the window under a little sign, '*Fritto scelto*'. And so now Judejahn ordered the liver by asking for '*fritto scelto*', but that means 'fried food on request', and so, at a loss what to do, they brought him a plate of sea-creatures fried in oil and batter. He gulped them down; they tasted like fried earthworms to him, and he felt nauseated. He felt his heavy body turning into worms, he felt his guts squirming with putrescence, and in order to fight off his disintegration, and in spite of his nausea, he polished off everything on the plate. Then he drank a quarter-litre of wine, this too, standing up, and then he was able to go on

no more than a few paces, and there was the German hotel where his in-laws were staying. Cars bearing 'D' licence plates stood in tidy ranks outside the hotel. Judejahn saw the emblems of German recovery, the sleek metal of the German economic miracle. He was impressed. He was attracted. Should he go inside, click his heels together and rap out, 'At your service!'? They would receive him with open arms. Would they? But there was also something that repelled him about these shiny cars. Recovery, life going on, going on fatly and prosperously after total war, total battle and total defeat, it was betrayal, betrayal of the Führer's plans and his vision for the future, it was disgraceful collaboration with the arch-enemy in the West, who needed German blood and German troops to ward off its former Eastern allies and sharers in the stolen victory. What to do? Already the lights were going on in the hotel. One window after another was lit up, and behind one of them Eva would be sitting and waiting. Her letters, with their obscure turns of phrase that spoke of the disappointment that awaited him, the degeneracy and the shame, allowed him no hope of finding Adolf his son there. Was it worth going home? The desert was still open to him. The net of the German bourgeoisie had not yet been thrown over the old warrior. Hesitant, uncertain, he strode in through the door, came into the wood-panelled lobby, and there he saw German men, his brother-in-law, Friedrich Wilhelm Pfaffrath, was among them, he had hardly changed at all, and the German men stood facing one another in the German fashion; they were holding glasses in their hands, not mugs of German barley brew, but glasses of Italian swill, but then he Judejahn drank swill like that himself and God knows what else besides, no blame attached to that away from home. And these men, they were strong and stout, he could hear that, they were singing 'A Fortress Sure', and then he felt himself being observed, not by the singers, he felt himself being observed from the doorway, it was a serious, a seeking, an imploring, a desperate look that was levelled at him.

He retreated, with his angular skull between his hunched shoulders – retreat or tactical withdrawal, the way a patrol between the lines in no man's land retreats or withdraws when they feel they've been spotted; no shots are fired, no flares light the night sky, fate hangs in the balance, but they withdraw, creep back through barbed wire and vegetation, back to their own position, and conclude for the moment that the enemy position is impregnable. And the murderer too, the hunted criminal, presses back into the shadows, the jungle, the city, when he senses the bloodhounds are near by, when he knows he's in the policeman's field of vision. Likewise the sinner flees the eye of the Lord. But what of the godless man who doesn't know himself to be a sinner, where does he turn? Straight past God, and into the desert! Judejahn didn't know who was watching him. He saw no spies. There was only a priest in the lobby – Rome was crawling with religious brethren – standing strangely transfixed and staring like Judejahn through the glazed double door at the animated company sitting at the table, drinking and talking. It was a German *Stammtisch*, a table established in the German way but transported provisionally to a southern latitude; and, objectively speaking, there was only the wood and glass of the double door to separate Judejahn and his brother-in-law, Friedrich Wilhelm Pfaffrath, but he had remained seated: whether he was holding forth here or in front of the town council at home, he had remained seated, whereas Judejahn had strode boldly on, boldly and blindly on with the watchword that God is dead. He had gone further than the burghers in the hall, but it was they who had made it possible for him to go so far. They had underwritten his wanderings with their lives. They had invoked blood, they had summoned him, exhorted him, the world will be won by the sword, they had made speeches, there was no death to compare with death in battle, they had given him his first uniform, and had cowered before the new uniform he had made for himself, they had praised his every action, they had held him up as an example to their children, they had summoned the 'Reich' into being, and endured death and injury and the smoke from burning bodies all for the sake of Germany. But they themselves had remained seated at their table in the old German beer hall, German slogans on their garrulous tongues, Nietzsche clichés in their brains, and even the Führer's words and the Rosenberg myth had only been exhilarating clichés for them, while for Judejahn they had been a call to arms: he had set out, little Gottlieb wanted to change the world, well well, so he was a revolutionary, and yet he detested revolutionaries and had them flogged and hanged. He was stupid, a dim little Gottlieb, worshipping punishment, little Gottlieb afraid of a beating and desiring to beat, powerless little Gottlieb, who had gone on a pilgrimage to power, and when he had reached it and had seen it face to face, what had he seen? Death. Power was Death. Death was the true Almighty. Judejahn had accepted it, he wasn't frightened, even little Gottlieb had guessed that there was only this one power, the power of death, and only one exercise of power, which was killing. There is no resurrection. Judejahn had served Death. He had fed plentiful Death. That set him apart from the burghers, the Italian holiday-makers, the battlefield tourists; they had nothing, they had nothing except that nothing, they sat fatly in the midst of nothing, they got ahead in nothing, until finally they perished in nothing and became part of it, as they always had been. But he, Judejahn, he had his Death and he clung to it, only the priest might try to steal it from him. But Judejahn wasn't about to be robbed. Priests might be murdered. Who was the fellow in the black frock? A pimply face, a haggard youth seething with lust under the womanish robes. The priest too was looking at the assembly in the lobby, and he too seemed to be repulsed by it. But he was no ally for Judejahn. Judejahn was equally revolted by the priest and the burghers. He recognized that the burghers' position was impregnable for today. But time was in Judejahn's favour, and so he would return to the desert, drill recruits for Death, and one day, when battlefields were more than tourist attractions, then Judejahn would be on the march again.

Kurt Vonnegut

A NAZI CITY MOURNED AT SOME PROFIT

As a prisoner of war in Germany, Kurt Vonnegut witnessed the destruction of Dresden by Allied bombers in 1944, an experience which inspired his classic novel, Slaughterhouse-Five. *The following extract, written in 1976 and taken from his 'auto-biographical collage',* Palm Sunday, *is a sharp and witty reflection on the 'hidden benefits' of a wartime tragedy.*

I HAVE NOT only praised a Nazi sympathizer, I have expressed my sorrow at the death of a Nazi city as well. I am speaking of Dresden, of course. And I have to say again that I was an American soldier, a prisoner of war there, when the city was simultaneously burned up and down. I was not on the German side.

I mourned the destruction of Dresden because it was only temporarily a Nazi city, and had for centuries been an art treasure belonging to earthlings everywhere. It could have been that again. The same was true of Angkor Wat, which military scientists have demolished more recently for some imagined gain.

Being present at the destruction of Dresden has affected my character far less than the death of my mother, the adopting of my sister's children, the sudden realization that those children and my own were no longer dependent on me, the breakup of my marriage, and on and on. And I have not been encouraged to go on mourning Dresden – even by Germans.

Even Germans seem to think it is not worth mentioning any-more.

So I myself thought no more about Dresden until I was asked by Franklin Library in 1976 to write a special intro-duction to a deluxe edition they were bringing out of my novel, *Slaughterhouse-Five*.

I said this:

This is a book about something that happened to me a long time ago (1944) – and the book itself is now something else that happened to me a long time ago (1969).

Time marches on – and the key event in this book, which is the fire-bombing of Dresden, is now a fossilized memory, sinking ever deeper into the tar pit of history. If American school children have heard of it at all, they are surely in doubt as to whether it happened in World War One or Two. Nor do I think they should care much.

I, for one, am not avid to keep the memory of the fire-bombing fresh. I would of course be charmed if people continued to read this book for years to come, but not because I think there are important lessons to be learned from the Dresden catastrophe. I myself was in the midst of it, and learned only that people can become so enraged in war that they will burn great cities to the ground, and slay the inhabitants thereof.

That was nothing new.

I write this in October of 1976, and it so happens that only two nights ago I saw a screening of Marcel Ophul's new documentary on war crimes, 'The Memory of Justice', which included movies, taken from the air, of the Dresden raid – at night. The city appeared to boil, and I was down there somewhere.

I was supposed to appear onstage afterwards, with some other people who had had intimate experiences with Nazi death camps and so on, and to contribute my notions as to the meaning of it all.

Atrocities celebrate meaninglessness, surely. I was mute. I

did not mount the stage. I went home.

The Dresden atrocity, tremendously expensive and meticulously planned, was so meaningless, finally, that only one person on the entire planet got any benefit from it. I am that person. I wrote this book, which earned a lot of money for me and made my reputation, such as it is.

One way or another, I got two or three dollars for every person killed. Some business I'm in.

James Salter

THE HUNTERS

Drawing on his own experience as a fighter pilot in the Korean War, James Salter's novel The Hunters *(1956) is the story of Cleve Connell, leader of a flight of jet fighters striking at enemy MiGs along the Yalu river. His dreams of becoming an ace seem to be slipping out of reach when weeks pass without a single engagement. Meanwhile the competition among the pilots grows as they all hope to encounter 'Casey Jones', the elusive enemy with black bars painted on his plane.*

FLASHING LIKE FISH silver, they broke through a low, billowing surf of clouds and into unmarked sky. They climbed. They crossed the Han and into enemy territory, passing the invisible line beyond which little was forgiven. Time seemed to be going quickly. The tempo of landmarks was greater than usual. The compounding hands of the altimeter seemed to be moving more rapidly. Over the radio, nothing except for routine traffic. The fight had not started. Cleve felt elated. He had not hoped for such luck.

He looked back towards Hunter, and his courage and pride swelled. There was nothing to compare with the happiness of leading. Towards the final test and winnowing they flew together, and though a man on the ground could neither see nor hear them, they were up, specks of metal moving through a prehistoric sky, contaminating an ocean of air with only their presence, electrifying the heavens. Cleve felt a distilled fulfilment. For these moments, no price could be too high.

As they neared the Yalu, the cloudiness increased, and above a spotty floor of white there was one huge cumulus build-up, a towering mushroom of brightness as big as a country. It looked like a cosmic fungus, like layers of wrath. They were at forty thousand feet then and climbing. The river was still five minutes away. Suddenly, cutting through the lesser voices, there was Colonel Imil's.

'Dust on the runway at Antung, boys,' he called. 'Heads up.'

It was as if they had waited for him, Cleve thought slowly. He tried to see the reddish plumes rising, but the cumulus was in the way. Beyond that vast cloud and beneath it, they were taking off to fight. He began searching the sky with the intensity of a man who has lost a diamond on a public beach.

The first train was called out, a confirmation of the colonel's sighting. Less than a minute later, they were announcing a second. Then a third.

'They're climbing to altitude north of the river,' Imil said. 'It won't be long.'

As Cleve reached the river, they were up to five bandit trains. He turned northeast, towards the dam and reservoir already marked by noiseless explosions that seemed as small as those made by stones dropped into lake silt. He watched as they appeared irregularly in unexpected places. Smoke from a big fire was starting to rise. He looked behind. Hunter was in good position, steady as a shadow. Over the radio an unemotional voice was tolling again:

'Bandit trains numbers six and seven leaving Antung, heading north. Trains six and seven leaving Antung.'

He reached the reservoir and turned back towards the southwest, high, higher than the others, climbing very gradually all the time. There was a brittle expectancy running through the flights. Urgent, confused calls came continually over the radio, but nobody had made definite contact. Nobody was in a fight yet. The eighth and ninth trains were announced. It would all happen at once. He felt himself living

293

by individual seconds. He flew along the river, turning at the mouth.

'Bandit train number ten is on a heading of three three zero. Train number ten heading three three zero.'

Ten was more than he remembered ever having heard. The eleventh was called, and twelve, like compartments filling in a stricken ship. It was a flood. He could feel the skin all over his shoulders and back, as if there were eyes staring at it. His sensitivity was almost unbearable. Then he heard Hunter's quick voice:

'Bogies high at ten o'clock!'

He looked up into the vacant sky to his left.

'Five, six of them,' Hunter called.

Six. That number made it a certainty. Cleve started a gentle turn to the left, trying to locate them as he did.

'I don't have them.'

'They're at ten o'clock, high, way out, passing to nine now!'

Cleve looked. The sky was bright, empty blue. He stared hard at it, fighting to see, working painfully across it.

'Do you have them?' Hunter cried anxiously.

Surely they would appear at any second. The effort made his eyes water.

'No,' he said at last. 'I don't have them. Go ahead, you take them.'

Hunter did not turn. Cleve watched him and waited.

'Go ahead. Take them.'

There was still a pause.

'Aw,' Hunter said, 'I've lost them now.'

In silence they took up a track along the river again. The last of the fighter-bombers were going in towards the dam, serenely, he knew how they must feel. Everybody was uneasy. It was unbelievable that the MiGs would not strike, but slowly, as the minutes sank away, he began to accept it. Flights were starting to leave the area, low on fuel. He heard Imil turning towards home. He checked his own gauge: twenty-one hundred pounds.

They were going up the river, throttled back now for economy and descending slightly all the while to maintain good speed. They reached the reservoir and flew about twenty miles past it before turning towards Antung again. Halfway there, he called Hunter.

'How much do you have, Billy?'

'Eighteen hundred pounds.'

One more time, he thought. He listened impassively to more and more flights starting their withdrawals, intact, unsuccessful. In roughly the same order that they had arrived in, their fuel dropped to the minimum, and they departed. Fortune was a matter to be measured in minutes. At Antung, as he swung around towards the northeast, he had sixteen hundred pounds.

'Just once more,' he said. 'How much do you have now?'

'Fifteen hundred.'

They started up the river. It was like swimming alone far out to sea. The minutes were a tide they were moving against. His eyes kept coming back to the fuel gauge. He knew it would be motionless for as long as he could look at it, like a clock. They were at the reservoir. The radio was almost silent. They were among the last ones remaining within fifty miles. They made a large orbit to the left and encountered nothing. They had stayed too long. Turning south, Cleve had twelve hundred pounds. He started climbing for home.

He looked in Hunter's direction, back, over his shoulder. A memorial smoke hung over Sui Ho. He stared for a few moments. On the other side, as he turned his head, the great cumulus still rose near Antung, but now it seemed as inanimate and fading as an extinct volcano. It was a relic, enormous in a lonely sky. His gaze moved slightly. Something that could not be seen had drawn it, a force beyond all things sensory. He continued to watch idly, without a motive. Then, as if from out of nothing, so far off and delicate that if he were to move his eyes even slightly or blink he would not be able to pick them up again, aeroplanes appeared. He could not glance into the cockpit to check his fuel. He called Hunter instead, as he began turning towards them.

'How much fuel, Green Two?'

295

'I'm down to eleven hundred. What are you turning north again for?'

Cleve did not answer. He maintained his focus. The ships slowly grew to be unmistakable specks. They were still miles away, becoming not so much bigger as a little darker. A minute later, Hunter called them out.

'Four bogies off at one o'clock, Lead!'

'I have them.'

'They're crossing to two now. They're starting in!'

'What?' Cleve said. The ships he was looking at were no more than decimal points.

'Four of them coming down from three o'clock, Cleve!'

Then, 'Get ready to break!'

He looked quickly up to his right. There were MiGs, four of them. He had not even seen them, concentrating as he had been on the ones out ahead.

'Take it around to the right, Billy!'

They turned into the attacking ships. The MiGs did not continue in, then, but pulled back up. Cleve watched them flash overhead. He reversed his turn to follow. He watched with chilling recognition as they did something he had never seen before. They split into pairs.

'We've got some cool ones this time, Billy.'

'Cleve?'

'Roger.'

'Did you get a good look at them?'

'Yes. Why?'

'The leader has black stripes.'

His heart became audible. Something opened within him, full and frightening. He watched them as they swung apart, trying to pick the one out. Of all the times to have his chance. He came close to laughing, but he was too electrified.

'Are you sure?'

'Absolutely.'

Yes, absolutely. Finally to meet him, this far north with this much fuel. He looked at his gauge now: nine hundred pounds. He could almost feel the tanks draining as he flew. It was like blood from his own arteries.

'Let's keep working south,' he said.

They were not to do it that easily, though. The MiGs started back in, working in coordinated pairs: two first, with two more timing their pass so that they would be coming in behind Cleve as he met the others. It took skill to operate that way. It was difficult, and murderous if expertly done. He waited as long as he could before turning into the nearest ones. He wanted to carry the fight as far south as possible. The MiGs might be low on fuel, too.

'Around to the left,' he said.

The first two were already in close. He strained to watch them over his shoulder, the Gs tugging at his head. They were firing. The cannon tracers were streaming by, just behind and below him, like dashes of molten ore.

They did not follow in the turn, but began climbing right back up, to achieve position and come in again. The two teams of them were going to work like that. As the MiGs went by behind him the first time, he called, 'Reverse it!' to Hunter, hoping to get a shot in as they went away from him. He was not able to. He was behind them, but too far back and out of line. He stole a glance over his shoulder. He could not see Hunter.

'You with me, Billy?'

There was no answer.

'Billy!'

'I'm all right.'

Cleve looked back again, on both sides. He still could not see him.

'Break right!' he heard Hunter call.

It was the second pair. Cleve turned into them as hard as he could. He caught sight of Hunter then a little below him, turning too. The MiGs fired and passed behind him. Cleve rolled out of the turn immediately. He was heading west. He turned back towards the south. As he did, he saw the first two coming in again, but not from so good a position this time. They were too far forward. Cleve was going to be able to meet them almost head on. He turned into them and, at the last second, was able to fire as they came. Hunter was firing, too.

They passed the MiGs in a brief instant, and Cleve turned hard after them, without hesitation, caught up in the blood lust, brimming with lunacy. He was fighting for any advantage, and the MiGs were not climbing away. They were turning, too. He was astonished to see it. He recognized the chance.

He was not completely conscious of what he was doing or even planning. A hand that had done this for years was guiding his ship. He was merely riding along, it seemed, striving to see better, to see everything; and he was cutting the MiGs off in the turn, getting inside them. He could distinguish the black markings on the leader. He pulled after him, distended. As he did, still far from being in a position to shoot, he was stricken with a sense of resignation and fear. They went around and around in this silent, unyielding circle. His fuel was getting lower and lower. He glanced quickly at it: seven hundred pounds. They were going down steadily; they had passed through twenty thousand. The airspeed was building. He had lost sight of the other two MiGs, of Hunter, of everything but the winding earth and the lead ship turning with him, motionless as the world spun about them.

They were passing fourteen thousand. They might go all the way, to the deck. Every minute made fuel more critical, and at full throttle in the lower altitudes they were using it prodigiously. It was a devouring circle. He could not break out of it without being in a worse position in a running fight if they followed him, but he did not have fuel enough to continue, either. He needed every remaining pound just to get back.

'You st . . . have me, Billy?' He spoke with difficulty. The words came out distorted by Gs.

'Roger. You're clear.'

He could hear Hunter's breath over the radio, being forced out of him.

They kept turning, fighting for position. He was not gaining now. He was a quarter of the circle behind holding that spot, turning, turning, turning while the MiG held still ahead of him. They were struggling for the slightest change. The aeroplanes no longer seemed involved. It was a battle of wills, of the strength to hang on, as if by the teeth alone. To let up meant to lose, and it was Cleve's advantage. He was rigid with the determination to stay there.

Suddenly the MiG rolled over and started down. For an endless part of a second Cleve hesitated, surprised. They were very low. He was not sure he could follow him through and clear the ground. He was almost certain the MiG could not make it. He knew an instant of awful decision, and then rolled and followed. They were going straight down, in a split S, wide open. They burst through the level of clouds. The earth was shooting up at him. The stick seemed rigid. He trimmed and pulled back as hard as he could, popping the speed brakes to help pitch him through. Everything faded into grey and then black. When it began to be grey again, he saw that they had made it. He was right behind Casey, on the deck. The hills and trees were whipping past just beneath them. His ship slammed and jolted crazily against ripples of air.

Casey broke left. French curves of vapour trailed from his wingtips. Cleve was behind him, on the inside, turning as hard as he could. The bright pipper of his sight was creeping up on the MiG, jerkily, but moving slowly up to the tail, the fuselage, the wing root. He squeezed the trigger. The tracers arced out, falling mostly behind. There were a few strikes near the tail. He could hardly hold the wild pipper where it was, but somehow he moved it forward, it seemed only inches more.

They were just above the trees. He could not take his eyes off the MiG to look, but he saw from their corners an avalanche of green and brown flashing fatally by. He fired again. His heart ballooned into his throat. He shouted into the mask, not words, but a senseless cry. Solid strikes along the fuselage. There was a burst of white flame and a sudden flood of smoke. The MiG pulled up sharply, climbing. It was slipping away from him, but as it did, he laced it with hits. Finally, trailing a curtain of fire, it rolled over on one wing and started down.

'There he goes!'

Cleve could not answer.

'Head south,' he finally said. 'Do you have the other ones in sight?'

'Not now.'

'All right. Let's go.'

They turned for home, climbing, too low on fuel to make it, Cleve was certain. The other MiGs had vanished. They were alone in the sky. He checked his fuel: three hundred and fifty pounds.

'How much do you have?' he asked Hunter.

'Say again, Cleve.'

'What state fuel?'

'I'm down to . . . down to three hundred now.'

'We'll climb as high as we can.'

The engines drank as they climbed. It was a haemorrhage. They were paying for altitude with an open-throated flow. It poured away. The needle of the gauge seemed to fail as Cleve looked at it. The minutes were endless. He suffered through them, trying not to think, restraining himself. He looked out to sea, where they would probably end up. It had always seemed a sanctuary. Now it was unnerving, a place to drown in. He thought of the bailing out. He had never left an aeroplane before, and the moment of abandoning that close cockpit for sheer, climactic space chilled him.

They were climbing fast. The ships performed better the emptier they became, and the black-faced dial then showed just less than one hundred pounds. It was hardly enough to wet the bottom of the tank. They were past Sinanju, but with more than a hundred miles to go.

'What do you have now, Billy?'

'Not enough to mention.'

'Empty?'

'Almost,' Hunter said. 'Do you think we'll make it?'

'Well,' Cleve began. He was interrupted.

'Oh, oh! There it is,' Hunter said.

'Did you run out?'

'Yes.'

Cleve looked at his own gauge. It read zero, although the

engine was still running. He shut it off. There could not be more than a minute or two of fuel left, anyway.

It was almost absolutely silent, gliding evenly together. They were at thirty-eight thousand feet. It was all up to the winds aloft and the exact number of miles remaining. He looked out ahead. They still had a long way to go. The altimeter unwound: thirty-seven thousand.

They glided south, descending steadily as the unyielding miles fell behind them. The altimeter surrendered feet mechanically: thirty-six thousand five hundred. Thirty-six thousand. He watched it creep and then hurry, like a nightmare's clock, as slowly, gently, they fell from grace. He listened to the valves in his mask open and close to his breathing. Thirty-five thousand. It all had to happen at the most regulated pace. The airspeed was important. A few knots too high or low meant miles. He guarded it carefully. Thirty-four thousand. Thirty-three thousand five hundred.

He reassessed the chances constantly, checking the altitude against his map. There were things that had to be guessed, but he computed over and over. Thirty-two thousand. The moment he dreaded was when he would have to decide between heading for the water or continuing towards the Han, trying to make it all the way. That was the final commitment. He kept waiting, hoping to be sure. Thirty-one thousand. Finally the time came.

He did not really have to choose. He continued south. Afraid or not, he had decided beforehand. The feeling in his stomach was heavy as mercury. Perhaps he had not decided really, but only failed to decide. It did not matter. The hand of the altimeter was moving a little faster.

At twenty-five thousand, with the field far off, not yet visible, he heard somebody calling. It was Imil, back at the base.

'. . . now, Green Lead?'

'I can't read you. Say again.'

'What's your position? Where are you now, Green Lead?'

'We're about forty miles north.'

'How much fuel do you have?'

'None.'

'What?'

'We're both empty.'

There was a thoughtful silence.

'Do you have enough altitude to make it across the Han?'

'I think so,' Cleve answered. 'It's going to be close.'

'Get out if you can't make the field. Don't ride it down.'

'Understand.'

'But try and make it.'

They were passing through seventeen thousand. The air grew thicker all the way down, more viscous, so that they had to keep lowering the nose slightly to maintain speed. The ship felt heavier and heavier as it passed from the abstraction of deep air and slipped closer to the solid, irresistible ground. The field was in sight now. Fifteen thousand.

'Did you get any?' the colonel asked abruptly.

'Roger.'

'How many?'

'One.'

There was no reply.

At eleven thousand feet they were gliding across the mouth of the Han. The water bore the flat gleam of daylight. The backs of the hills were edged with shadows. In the cockpit with the engine dead, the silence was cruel as Cleve alternately abandoned and then retook hope. He altered course slightly to line up better with the runway. If they were able to reach the field they would have to land straight in.

'If it looks like we won't make it,' Cleve said, 'get out at two thousand feet. Don't wait any longer than that, Billy.'

'Roger. I think we're going to be all right, though.'

'Maybe.'

Cleve was slightly in front. When he passed through eight thousand feet he was still not absolutely certain, but shortly after that he knew. He could make it. The last thousand feet, coming easily down the path of the final approach he knew so well, was overwhelmingly fulfilling. Dead-sticking it in, he landed a little long but smoothly in the stillness. He felt an emptying relief as his wheels touched the runway. He cracked the canopy open. The fair wind came in to cool him.

Hunter misjudged. He had been off to one side and a little lower than Cleve, and when he saw that he was going to be short, he tried to stretch his glide, turning very low at the last with not enough speed left. There was that moment of immense awkwardness, as when a wall begins to fall outwards into a crowd. He crashed just north of the field. There was no fire. It was a dry, rending disintegration that ploughed up a storm of dust.

They towed Cleve's ship in from the end of the runway. Halfway back, Colonel Imil came driving up. He jumped on to the wing.

'Well, you made it, anyway,' he said.

'Is Hunter all right?'

'They're out there now. I haven't heard.'

'I thought he was going to make it,' Cleve said.

'He was half a mile short. It wasn't even close.'

In the parking area they were gathered, pilots and crewmen. They pressed close as the plane came to a stop. Cleve looked out at the rash of faces. He recognized some. Others were like those at a station, seen from a moving train. He could hear the armourers clearing his guns. The bolts clapped forward.

'How did it happen?' the colonel asked.

'We were jumped on the way back,' Cleve said. They were all listening. He was conscious of that. They were stretching their necks to hear. 'There were four of them, tough babies. They finally ran us out of fuel.'

'You got one, though?'

He felt his heart skip and his hands become weightless from what he was about to cast before them, to hold high like a severed head. One? He was not in complete control of himself. He could have laughed with tears running from his eyes. Had he gotten one? They were all packed close, looking up, the strong and the slight, the famous and the unfulfilled. He opened his mouth a little to prevent the words from forming there and bursting out. He knew how to say it, the phrase that stilled trumpets, that fell like a great tree; but he had to wait. He gazed out over their open faces.

Somebody was pushing through to the aeroplane. Cleve watched. He saw Pell just below, his hands in his hip pockets, his expression querulous. Somebody squeezed past Pell. It was Colonel Moncavage. He had come from the wreck.

'Is he all right?'

Moncavage was trying to get up on the wing.

'Is Hunter all right?'

Imil took his arm and pulled him up.

'He's dead,' Moncavage said.

'Nice going,' Pell's voice rose piercingly.

Cleve stepped slowly over the side of the ship down to the wing. Suddenly he was tired, not physically; his whole body was still quickened with what had been done and the accident of being alive, but he was tired of everything else.

'You got one of them, anyway,' Imil said flatly.

'Yes.'

Below, near the nose of the ship, there was an exclamation.

'The film didn't run, Colonel,' somebody called.

The magazine was handed up. Imil turned it over, inspecting it. He scratched at the little green footage window with his thumbnail several times.

'Not a foot,' he said, passing it to Moncavage. 'There goes the damned confirmation.'

'It doesn't matter,' Cleve said.

'Don't be so goddamned casual. Of course it matters.'

'Not this time.'

'What are you talking about?' Imil asked sharply.

'It was Casey Jones.'

There was a moment of catastrophic silence, and as Cleve watched, he knew it was one for which he would not be forgiven.

'Are you sure?'

Cleve nodded. He hardly heard the words. He was listening to the murmur that had started to run like wind through deep grass.

'Are you sure?' Imil repeated.

Pell interrupted.

'There's no film, Colonel,' he cried.

'That's right,' Imil said uncertainly. He looked at Moncavage, who shrugged.

'There's no one to confirm it now, either,' Pell said.

'No,' Imil agreed. He decided quickly. That was certain enough. 'There's not.'

Cleve looked at them, one by one. Nothing was real. He heard a short, insane cough of contempt leave his lips. He did not know what he was thinking, only that he was far removed, farther than he had ever believed possible.

'Oh yes, there is,' he said.

'Who?'

'I can confirm it.' He drew a sudden breath. 'Hunter got him.'

It had come out almost subconsciously. Malice had brought it, and protest, and the sweeping magnanimity that accompanies triumph, but, as soon as he said the words, he realized there were no others that would have made it right.

Billy Hunter would have his day as a hero, and in memory be never less of a man than he had been on his last flight. Cleve could give him that, at least – a name of his own. It was strange. In all that had passed, he had never imagined anything faintly like it, to have searched the whole heavens for his destiny and godliness, and in the end to have found them on earth.

He had kept a pledge. His heart cried out to go among them and tell them how he had fulfilled whatever promise he had, how in the clean sky he had met and conquered a legend. He lay on his cot that night, the draining finally effective, unable to move. He was conscious of nothing except his weakness and surrender to a great fatigue. With his eyes closed to make a double darkness, he lay awake in the still summer night, victorious at last and feeling as little a desire to live as he had ever known.

Tim O'Brien

HOW TO TELL A TRUE WAR STORY

*As well as posing the perennial questions of motive, politics,
humanity and barbarism, the Vietnam War offered the United
States military a novel experience: defeat. Domestic opinion
was heavily influenced by the development of instant television reportage, while the media presence and abundance of
information raised new problems for writers.*

*Tim O'Brien's short story, published in 1990, is both a
powerful depiction of how American soldiers experienced
Vietnam and a meditation on the difficulty of telling the truth
about war.*

THIS IS TRUE.

I had a buddy in Vietnam. His name was Bob Kiley, but
everybody called him Rat.

A friend of his gets killed, so about a week later Rat sits
down and writes a letter to the guy's sister. Rat tells her what
a great brother she had, how together the guy was, a number
one pal and comrade. A real soldier's soldier, Rat says. Then
he tells a few stories to make the point, how her brother
would always volunteer for stuff nobody else would volunteer
for in a million years, dangerous stuff, like doing recon or
going out on these really badass night patrols. Stainless-steel
balls, Rat tells her. The guy was a little crazy, for sure, but
crazy in a good way, a real daredevil, because he liked the
challenge of it, he liked testing himself, just man against gook.
A great, great guy, Rat says.

Anyway, it's a terrific letter, very personal and touching.

Rat almost bawls writing it. He gets all teary telling about the good times they had together, how her brother made the war seem almost fun, always raising hell and lighting up villes and bringing smoke to bear every which way. A great sense of humour, too. Like the time at this river when he went fishing with a whole damn crate of hand grenades. Probably the funniest thing in world history, Rat says, all that gore, about twenty zillion dead gook fish. Her brother, he had the right attitude. He knew how to have a good time. On Halloween, this real hot spooky night, the dude paints up his body all different colours and puts on this weird mask and hikes over to a ville and goes trick-or-treating almost stark naked, just boots and balls and an M-16. A tremendous human being, Rat says. Pretty nutso sometimes, but you could trust him with your life.

And then the letter gets very sad and serious. Rat pours his heart out. He says he loved the guy. He says the guy was his best friend in the world. They were like soul mates, he says, like twins or something, they had a whole lot in common. He tells the guy's sister he'll look her up when the war's over.

So what happens?

Rat mails the letter. He waits two months. The dumb cooze never writes back.

A true war story is never moral. It does not instruct, nor encourage virtue, nor suggest models of proper human behaviour, nor restrain men from doing the things men have always done. If a story seems moral, do not believe it. If at the end of a war story you feel uplifted, or if you feel that some small bit of rectitude has been salvaged from the larger waste, then you have been made the victim of a very old and terrible lie. There is no rectitude whatsoever. There is no virtue. As a first rule of thumb, therefore, you can tell a true war story by its absolute and uncompromising allegiance to obscenity and evil. Listen to Rat Kiley. Cooze, he says. He does not say bitch. He certainly does not say woman, or girl. He says cooze. Then he spits and stares. He's nineteen years old – it's too much for him – so he looks at you with those big sad gentle killer eyes and says *cooze*, because his friend is dead, and because it's so incredibly sad and true: she never wrote back.

You can tell a war story if it embarrasses you. If you don't care for obscenity, you don't care for the truth; if you don't care for the truth, watch how you vote. Send guys to war, they come home talking dirty.

Listen to Rat: 'Jesus Christ, man, I write this beautiful fuckin' letter, I slave over it, and what happens? The dumb cooze never writes back.'

The dead guy's name was Curt Lemon. What happened was, we crossed a muddy river and marched west into the mountains, and on the third day we took a break along a trail junction in deep jungle. Right away, Lemon and Rat Kiley started goofing. They didn't understand about the spookiness. They were kids; they just didn't know. A nature hike, they thought, not even a war, so they went off into the shade of some giant trees – quadruple canopy, no sunlight at all – and they were giggling and calling each other yellow mother and playing a silly game they'd invented. The game involved smoke grenades, which were harmless unless you did stupid things, and what they did was pull out the pin and stand a few feet apart and play catch under the shade of those huge trees. Whoever chickened out was a yellow mother. And if nobody chickened out, the grenade would make a light popping sound and they'd be covered with smoke and they'd laugh and dance around and then do it again.

It's all exactly true.

It happened, to *me*, nearly twenty years ago, and I still remember that trail junction and those giant trees and a soft dripping sound somewhere beyond the trees. I remember the smell of moss. Up in the canopy there were tiny white blossoms, but no sunlight at all, and I remember the shadows spreading out under the trees where Curt Lemon and Rat Kiley were playing catch with smoke grenades. Mitchell Sanders sat flipping his yo-yo. Norman Bowker and Kiowa and Dave Jensen were dozing, or half dozing, and all around us were those ragged green mountains.

Except for the laughter things were quiet.

At one point, I remember, Mitchell Sanders turned and looked at me, not quite nodding, as if to warn me about something, as if he already *knew*, then after a while he rolled up his yo-yo and moved away.

It's hard to tell you what happened next.

They were just goofing. There was a noise, I suppose, which must've been the detonator, so I glanced behind me and watched Lemon step from the shade into bright sunlight. His face was suddenly brown and shining. A handsome kid, really. Sharp grey eyes, lean and narrow-waisted, and when he died it was almost beautiful, the way the sunlight came around him and lifted him up and sucked him high into a tree full of moss and vines and white blossoms.

In any war story, but especially a true one, it's difficult to separate what happened from what seemed to happen. What seems to happen becomes its own happening and has to be told that way. The angles of vision are skewed. When a booby trap explodes, you close your eyes and duck and float outside yourself. When a guy dies, like Curt Lemon, you look away and then look back for a moment and then look away again. The pictures get jumbled; you tend to miss a lot. And then afterward, when you go to tell about it, there is always that surreal seemingness, which makes the story seem untrue, but which in fact represents the hard and exact truth as it *seemed*.

In many cases a true war story cannot be believed. If you believe it, be sceptical. It's a question of credibility. Often the crazy stuff is true and the normal stuff isn't, because the normal stuff is necessary to make you believe the truly incredible craziness.

In other cases you can't even tell a true war story. Sometimes it's just beyond telling.

I heard this one, for example, from Mitchell Sanders. It was near dusk and we were sitting at my foxhole along a wide muddy river north of Quang Ngai. I remember how peaceful the twilight was. A deep pinkish red spilled out on the river, which moved without sound, and in the morning we would cross the river and march west into the mountains. The occasion was right for a good story.

'God's truth,' Mitchell Sanders said. 'A six-man patrol goes up into the mountains on a basic listening-post operation. The idea's to spend a week up there, just lie low and listen for enemy movements. They've got a radio along, so if they hear anything suspicious – anything – they're supposed to call in artillery or gunships, whatever it takes. Otherwise they keep strict field discipline. Absolute silence. They just listen.'

Sanders glanced at me to make sure I had the scenario. He was playing with his yo-yo, dancing it with short, tight little strokes of the wrist.

His face was blank in the dusk.

'We're talking regulation, by-the-book LP. These six guys, they don't say boo for a solid week. They don't got tongues. *All* ears.'

'Right,' I said.

'Understand me?'

'Invisible.'

Sanders nodded.

'Affirm,' he said. 'Invisible. So what happens is, these guys get themselves deep in the bush, all camouflaged up, and they lie down and wait and that's all they do, nothing else, they lie there for seven straight days and just listen. And man, I'll tell you – it's spooky. This is mountains. You don't *know* spooky till you been there. Jungle, sort of, except it's way up in the clouds and there's always this fog – like rain, except it's not raining – everything's all wet and swirly and tangled up and you can't see jack, you can't find your own pecker to piss with. Like you don't even have a body. Serious spooky. You just go with the vapours – the fog sort of takes you in . . . And the sounds, man. The sounds carry forever. You hear stuff nobody should *ever* hear.'

Sanders was quiet for a second, just working the yo-yo, then he smiled at me.

'So after a couple of days the guys start hearing this real soft, kind of wacked-out music. Weird echoes and stuff. Like a radio or something, but it's not a radio, it's this strange gook music that comes right out of the rocks. Faraway, sort of, but right up close, too. They try to ignore it. But it's a listening post, right? So they listen. And every night they keep hearing that crazyass gook concert. All kinds of chimes and xylophones. I mean, this is wilderness – no way, it can't be real – but there it *is*, like the mountains are tuned in to Radio fucking Hanoi. Naturally they get nervous. One guy sticks Juicy Fruit in his ears. Another guy almost flips. Thing is, though, they can't report music. They can't get on the horn and call back to base and say, "Hey, listen, we need some firepower, we got to blow away this weirdo gook rock band." They can't do that. It wouldn't go down. So they lie there in the fog and keep their mouths shut. And what makes it extra bad, see, is the poor dudes can't horse around like normal. Can't joke it away. Can't even talk to each other except maybe in whispers, all hush-hush, and that just revs up the willies. All they do is listen.'

Again there was some silence as Mitchell Sanders looked out on the river. The dark was coming on hard now, and off to the west I could see the mountains rising in silhouette, all the mysteries and unknowns.

'This next part,' Sanders said quietly, 'you won't believe.'

'Probably not,' I said.

'You won't. And you know why?' He gave me a long, tired smile. 'Because it happened. Because every word is absolutely dead-on true.'

Sanders made a sound in his throat, like a sigh, as if to say he didn't care if I believed him or not. But he did care. He wanted me to feel the truth, to believe by the raw force of feeling. He seemed sad, in a way.

'These six guys,' he said, 'they're pretty fried out by now, and one night they start hearing voices. Like at a cocktail party. That's what it sounds like, this big swank gook cocktail party somewhere out there in the fog. Music and chitchat and stuff. It's crazy, I know, but they hear the champagne corks. They hear the actual martini glasses. Real hoity-toity, all very civilized, except this isn't civilization. This is Nam.

311

'Anyway, the guys try to be cool. They just lie there and groove, but after a while they start hearing – you won't believe this – they hear chamber music. They hear violins and cellos. They hear this terrific mama-san soprano. Then after a while they hear gook opera and a glee club and the Haiphong Boys Choir and a barbershop quartet and all kinds of weird chanting and Buddha-Buddha stuff. And the whole time, in the background, there's still that cocktail party going on. All these different voices. Not human voices, though. Because it's the mountains. Follow me? The rock – it's *talking*. And the fog, too, and the grass and the goddamn mongooses. Everything talks. The trees talk politics, the monkeys talk religion. The whole country. Vietnam. The place talks. It talks. Understand? Nam – it truly *talks*.

'The guys can't cope. They lose it. They get on the radio and report enemy movement – a whole army, they say – and they order up the firepower. They get arty and gunships. They call in air strikes. And I'll tell you, they fuckin' crash that cocktail party. All night long, they just smoke those mountains. They make jungle juice. They blow away trees and glee clubs and whatever else there is to blow away. Scorch time. They walk napalm up and down the ridges. They bring in the Cobras and F-4s, they use Willie Peter and HE and incendiaries. It's all fire. They make those mountains burn.

'Around dawn things finally get quiet. Like you never even *heard* quiet before. One of those real thick, real misty days – just clouds and fog, they're off in this special zone – and the mountains are absolutely dead-flat silent. Like Brigadoon – pure vapour, you know? Everything's all sucked up inside the fog. Not a single sound, except they still *hear* it.

'So they pack up and start humping. They head down the mountain, back to base camp, and when they get there they don't say diddly. They don't talk. Not a word, like they're deaf and dumb. Later on this fat bird colonel comes up and asks what the hell happened out there. What'd they hear? Why all the ordnance? The man's ragged out, he gets down tight on their case. I mean, they spent six trillion dollars on firepower, and this fatass colonel wants answers, he wants to know what the fuckin' story is.

'But the guys don't say zip. They just look at him for a while, sort of funny like, sort of amazed, and the whole war is right there in that stare. It says everything you can't ever say. It says, man, you got *wax* in your ears. It says, poor bastard, you'll never know – wrong frequency – you don't *even* want to hear this. Then they salute the fucker and walk away, because certain stories you don't ever tell.'

You can tell a true war story by the way it never seems to end. Not then, not ever. Not when Mitchell Sanders stood up and moved off into the dark.

It all happened.

Even now, at this instant, I remember that yo-yo. In a way, I suppose, you had to be there, you had to hear it, but I could tell how desperately Sanders wanted me to believe him, his frustration at not quite getting the details right, not quite pinning down the final and definitive truth.

And I remember sitting at my foxhole that night, watching the shadows of Quang Ngai, thinking about the coming day and how we would cross the river and march west into the mountains, all the ways I might die, all the things I did not understand.

Late in the night Mitchell Sanders touched my shoulder.

'Just came to me,' he whispered. 'The moral, I mean. Nobody listens. Nobody hears nothin'. Like that fatass colonel. The politicians, all the civilian types. Your girlfriend. My girlfriend. Everybody's sweet little virgin girlfriend. What they need is to go out on LP. The vapours, man. Trees and rocks – you got to *listen* to your enemy.'

And then again, in the morning, Sanders came up to me. The platoon was preparing to move out, checking weapons, going through all the little rituals that preceded a day's march. Already the lead squad had crossed the river and was filing off toward the west.

'I got a confession to make,' Sanders said. 'Last night, man, I had to make up a few things.'

313

'I know that.'

'The glee club. There wasn't any glee club.'

'Right.'

'No opera.'

'Forget it, I understand.'

'Yeah, but listen, it's still true. Those six guys, they heard wicked sound out there. They heard sound you just plain won't believe.'

Sanders pulled on his rucksack, closed his eyes for a moment, then almost smiled at me. I knew what was coming.

'All right,' I said, 'what's the moral?'

'Forget it.'

'No, go ahead.'

For a long while he was quiet, looking away, and the silence kept stretching out until it was almost embarrassing. Then he shrugged and gave me a stare that lasted all day.

'Hear that quiet, man?' he said. 'That quiet – just listen. There's your moral.'

In a true war story, if there's a moral at all, it's like the thread that makes the cloth. You can't tease it out. You can't extract the meaning without unravelling the deeper meaning. And in the end, really, there's nothing much to say about a true war story, except maybe 'Oh.'

True war stories do not generalize. They do not indulge in abstraction or analysis.

For example: War is hell. As a moral declaration the old truism seems perfectly true, and yet because it abstracts, because it generalizes, I can't believe it with my stomach. Nothing turns inside.

It comes down to gut instinct. A true war story, if truly told, makes the stomach believe.

This one does it for me. I've told it before – many times, many versions – but here's what actually happened.

We crossed that river and marched west into the mountains. On the third day, Curt Lemon stepped on a booby-trapped 105 round. He was playing catch with Rat

Kiley, laughing, and then he was dead. The trees were thick; it took nearly an hour to cut an LZ for the dustoff.

Later, higher in the mountains, we came across a baby VC water buffalo. What it was doing there I don't know – no farms or paddies – but we chased it down and got a rope around it and led it along to a deserted village where we set up for the night. After supper Rat Kiley went over and stroked its nose.

He opened up a can of C rations, pork and beans, but the baby buffalo wasn't interested.

Rat shrugged.

He stepped back and shot it through the right front knee. The animal did not make a sound. It went down hard, then got up again, and Rat took careful aim and shot off an ear. He shot it in the hindquarters and in the little hump at its back. He shot it twice in the flanks. It wasn't to kill; it was to hurt. He put the muzzle up against the mouth and shot the mouth away. Nobody said much. The whole platoon stood there watching, feeling all kinds of things, but there wasn't a great deal of pity for the baby water buffalo. Curt Lemon was dead. Rat Kiley had lost his best friend in the world. Later in the week he would write a long personal letter to the guy's sister, who would not write back, but for now it was a question of pain. He shot off the tail. He shot away chunks of meat below the ribs. All around us there was the smell of smoke and filth and deep greenery, and the evening was humid and very hot. Rat went to automatic. He shot randomly, almost casually, quick little spurts in the belly and butt. Then he reloaded, squatted down, and shot it in the left front knee. Again the animal fell hard and tried to get up, but this time it couldn't quite make it. It wobbled and went down sideways. Rat shot it in the nose. He bent forward and whispered something, as if talking to a pet, then he shot it in the throat. All the while the baby buffalo was silent, or almost silent, just a light bubbling sound where the nose had been. It lay very still. Nothing moved except the eyes, which were enormous, the pupils shiny black and dumb.

Rat Kiley was crying. He tried to say something, but then

315

cradled his rifle and went off by himself.

The rest of us stood in a ragged circle around the baby buffalo. For a time no one spoke. We had witnessed something essential, something brand-new and profound, a piece of the world so startling there was not yet a name for it.

Somebody kicked the baby buffalo.

It was still alive, though just barely, just in the eyes.

'Amazing,' Dave Jensen said. 'My whole life, I never seen anything like it.'

'Never?'

'Not hardly. Not once.'

Kiowa and Mitchell Sanders picked up the baby buffalo. They hauled it across the open square, hoisted it up, and dumped it in the village well.

Afterward, we sat waiting for Rat to get himself together.

'Amazing,' Dave Jensen kept saying. 'A new wrinkle. I never seen it before.'

Mitchell Sanders took out his yo-yo. 'Well, that's Nam,' he said. 'Garden of Evil. Over here, man, every sin's real fresh and original.'

How do you generalize?

War is hell, but that's not the half of it, because war is also mystery and terror and adventure and courage and discovery and holiness and pity and despair and longing and love. War is nasty; war is fun. War is thrilling; war is drudgery. War makes you a man; war makes you dead.

The truths are contradictory. It can be argued, for instance, that war is grotesque. But in truth war is also beauty. For all its horror, you can't help but gape at the awful majesty of combat. You stare out at tracer rounds unwinding through the dark like brilliant red ribbons. You crouch in ambush as a cool, impassive moon rises over the night-time paddies. You admire the fluid symmetries of troops on the move, the harmonies of sound and shape and proportion, the great sheets of metal-fire streaming down from a gunship, the illumination rounds, the white phosphorus, the purply orange glow of napalm, the rocket's red glare. It's not pretty, exactly.

It's astonishing. It fills the eye. It commands you. You hate it, yes, but your eyes do not. Like a killer forest fire, like cancer under a microscope, any battle or bombing raid or artillery barrage has the aesthetic purity of absolute moral indifference – a powerful, implacable beauty – and a true war story will tell the truth about this, though the truth is ugly.

To generalize about war is like generalizing about peace. Almost everything is true. Almost nothing is true. At its core, perhaps, war is just another name for death, and yet any soldier will tell you, if he tells the truth, that proximity to death brings with it a corresponding proximity to life. After a firefight, there is always the immense pleasure of aliveness. The trees are alive. The grass, the soil – everything. All around you things are purely living, and you among them, and the aliveness makes you tremble. You feel an intense, out-of-the-skin awareness of your living self – your truest self, the human being you want to be and then become by the force of wanting it. In the midst of evil you want to be a good man. You want decency. You want justice and courtesy and human concord, things you never knew you wanted. There is a kind of largeness to it, a kind of godliness. Though it's odd, you're never more alive than when you're almost dead. You recognize what's valuable. Freshly, as if for the first time, you love what's best in yourself and in the world, all that might be lost. At the hour of dusk you sit at your foxhole and look out on a wide river turning pinkish red, and at the mountains beyond, and although in the morning you must cross the river and go into the mountains and do terrible things and maybe die, even so, you find yourself studying the fine colours on the river, you feel wonder and awe at the setting of the sun, and you are filled with a hard, aching love for how the world could be and always should be, but now is not.

Mitchell Sanders was right. For the common soldier, at least, war has the feel – the spiritual texture – of a great ghostly fog, thick and permanent. There is no clarity. Everything swirls. The old rules are no longer binding, the old truths no longer true. Right spills over into wrong. Order blends into chaos, love into hate, ugliness into beauty, law into anarchy, civility into savagery. The vapours suck you in. You can't tell where you are, or why you're there, and the only certainty is overwhelming ambiguity.

In war you lose your sense of the definite, hence your sense of truth itself, and therefore it's safe to say that in a true war story nothing is ever absolutely true.

Often in a true war story there is not even a point, or else the point doesn't hit you until twenty years later, in your sleep, and you wake up and shake your wife and start telling the story to her, except when you get to the end you've forgotten the point again. And then for a long time you lie there watching the story happen in your head. You listen to your wife's breathing. The war's over. You close your eyes. You smile and think, Christ, what's the *point*?

This one wakes me up.

In the mountains that day, I watched Lemon turn sideways. He laughed and said something to Rat Kiley. Then he took a peculiar half step, moving from shade into bright sunlight, and the booby-trapped 105 round blew him into a tree. The parts were just hanging there, so Dave Jensen and I were ordered to shinny up and peel him off. I remember the white bone of an arm. I remember pieces of skin and something wet and yellow that must've been the intestines. The gore was horrible, and stays with me. But what wakes me up twenty years later is Dave Jensen singing 'Lemon Tree' as we threw down the parts.

You can tell a true war story by the questions you ask. Somebody tells a story, let's say, and afterward you ask, 'Is it true?' and if the answer matters, you've got your answer.

For example, we've all heard this one. Four guys go down a trail. A grenade sails out. One guy jumps on it and takes the blast and saves his three buddies.

Is it true?

The answer matters.

You'd feel cheated if it never happened. Without the

grounding reality, it's just a trite bit of puffery, pure Holly-wood, untrue in the way all such stories are untrue. Yet even if it did happen – and maybe it did, anything's possible – even then you know it can't be true, because a true war story does not depend upon that kind of truth. Absolute occurrence is irrelevant. A thing may happen and be a total lie; another thing may not happen and be truer than the truth. For example: Four guys go down a trail. A grenade sails out. One guy jumps on it and takes the blast, but it's a killer grenade and everybody dies anyway. Before they die, though, one of the dead guys says, 'The fuck you do *that* for?' and the jumper says, 'Story of my life, man,' and the other guy starts to smile but he's dead.

That's a true story that never happened.

Twenty years later, I can still see the sunlight on Lemon's face. I can see him turning, looking back at Rat Kiley, then he laughed and took that curious half step from shade into sunlight, his face suddenly brown and shining, and when his foot touched down, in that instant, he must've thought it was the sunlight that was killing him. It was not the sunlight. It was a rigged 105 round. But if I could ever get the story right, how the sun seemed to gather around him and pick him up and lift him high into a tree, if I could somehow recreate the fatal whiteness of that light, the quick glare, the obvious cause and effect, then you would believe the last thing Curt Lemon believed, which for him must've been the final truth.

Now and then, when I tell this story, someone will come up to me afterward and say she liked it. It's always a woman. Usually it's an older woman of kindly temperament and humane politics. She'll explain that as a rule she hates war stories, she can't understand why people want to wallow in all the blood and gore. But this one she liked. The poor baby buffalo, it made her sad. Sometimes, even, there are little tears. What I should do, she'll say, is put it all behind me. Find new stories to tell.

I won't say it but I'll think it.

I'll picture Rat Kiley's face, his grief, and I'll think, *You dumb cooze.*

Because she wasn't listening.

It *wasn't* a war story. It was a *love* story.

But you can't say that. All you can do is tell it one more time, patiently, adding and subtracting, making up a few things to get at the real truth. No Mitchell Sanders, you tell her. No Lemon, no Rat Kiley. No trail junction. No baby buffalo. No vines or moss or white blossoms. Beginning to end, you tell her, it's all made up. Every goddamn detail – the mountains and the river and especially that poor dumb baby buffalo. None of it happened. *None* of it. And even if it did happen, it didn't happen in the mountains, it happened in this little village on the Batangan Peninsula, and it was raining like crazy, and one night a guy named Stink Harris woke up screaming with a leech on his tongue. You can tell a true war story if you just keep on telling it.

And in the end, of course, a true war story is never about war. It's about sunlight. It's about the special way that dawn spreads out on a river when you know you must cross the river and march into the mountains and do things you are afraid to do. It's about love and memory. It's about sorrow. It's about sisters who never write back and people who never listen.

Philip Caputo

BE LIKE THE FOREST

In Philip Caputo's novella 'In the Forest of the Laughing Elephant' (1998), the soldiers who fight their way through the jungle are in pursuit of an unusual enemy: a tiger has killed an American soldier and disappeared with the body, and the platoon has been sent out to bring the corpse back to camp.

The following extract suggests that sense of otherworldliness felt by the men who fought in the jungles of Vietnam.

THEY HAD BEEN six, now they were five, and none of them could see the sun. Three of the men, standing on one side of a deep, fast river, were looking up at the forest canopy, thick as thatch but green and wet and higher overhead than any thatch roof could be. A hundred feet at least, maybe two. Above it hung a dense ceiling of monsoon clouds. Turning their heads quickly side to side, like bird-watchers trying to spot some rare and elusive parrot, the men looked for the sun, the guiding light. They had no idea where they were.

Neither did the fourth man, who was on the other side of the river; but he was not trying to find the sun. Sitting naked at one end of the rope-and-plank bridge from which he'd jumped, attempting to rescue the radioman, he was wringing out his wet clothes. His rifle and his rucksack, lumpy with rations and coiled rope and other gear, lay on the grass where he'd tossed them before he'd leaped after his radioman, who had fallen from the bridge and went twirling and tumbling down the river like a broken branch.

The fifth man squatted nearby. He was the smallest and

dressed only in shorts, sandals, and a cork helmet that had once been green but was now faded almost to white. It was difficult to tell his age, because his skin, the colour of slightly overdone toast, was deeply creased on his face but as smooth and taut as a youth's on his arms and torso. He himself did not know how old he was in years; he had no idea what a year was. He measured his life by the rises and falls of the sun, the phases of the moon, the rhythms of the two seasons, wet and dry. His name was Han, and he was a hill tribesman and a hunter, a very good one. A quiver bristling with arrows hung from his belt, a leather pouch filled with krait poison from his neck, and a crossbow lay in his lap. It had been his father's – a beautiful weapon carved from mahogany, its stock bearing his father's talisman: three rings cut with a tiger's tooth and inlaid with mother-of-pearl. The three rings held the tiger's power. Han had killed more deer and birds with the crossbow than he could remember; with it and its arrows tipped in the venom of the krait, he had killed Tiger three times and Panther five. He rubbed the mother-of-pearl as he squatted, waiting for the tall *trung-si* to finish drying his clothes. Like him, Han was not looking for the sun; unlike him, he knew where he was.

The tall man stood and gave his trousers a last twist before putting them on. His black hair was cut very short – it looked as if a three-day growth of beard had migrated from his face to his skull – and the sooty wings of a luxuriant moustache swooped under his long, narrow nose. From the waist up, his body appeared to have been painted, so sharp were the lines between his browned arms, face, and neck and the white of his shoulders and chest. It was a sickly white, a pallor suggesting malaria or dengue, but Lincoln Coombes was far from sickly. The muscles in his abdomen were as ribbed as beach sand after a tide's run out, while those in his arms were long and tightly braided. He'd killed several men in hand-to-hand combat; he'd strangled them or broken their necks or crushed their skulls with blows from a rifle butt.

He tucked in his shirt, aligning the buttons with the buckle of his web belt, his movements slow and mechanical, as though he were just learning to dress himself. *Don't rush things*, he said silently as he looked into the forest, where vines hung in the shadowy, twisting corridors between the trees like electrical conduit in some unfinished construction project. He was not gazing idly but in a way meditating upon the forest's infinite patience, and trying to draw with each breath some of that patience into himself, for in that fecund world, time wasn't measured by man's petty instruments of gear and jewels, but by nature's clocks. The forest did things at its own slow, inexorable pace; some of its great trees had been saplings when Columbus sailed from Spain. *Don't rush things; be like the forest.*

He had been. Until last night, he had learned to live outside time, like the tiger, like Han. Yes, his military calling required him to keep a watch and maintain certain schedules, but he had freed himself from *caring* what day or month or even year it was. This land of jungles old as the earth had been the ally of his liberation. Its temporal landscape was barren of prominent features, its weeks unmarked by Sabbaths; its numberless years had names like Pig, Snake, and Monkey, the names repeating themselves in an endless cycle, and its two seasons joined like the halves of a circle, each day of the Dry fusing into the next without seam or weld, the nights of the Wet flowing smoothly into one another. And the war. The war, too, had helped Coombes unshackle himself. Monday or Friday, January or June, it was all the same to him, because the war was all the same: a stalemate without advances or retreats, triumphs or defeats. It just went on, the events of one month or year near-perfect copies of those from the month or year before. By his own choice, he'd been in it for so long even he'd forgotten how long, or thought he had. The firefights and pitched battles had become laminated in his mind into one continuous battle, as the seasons and the hot days and wet nights had merged into a constant, dateless *now*. And there was this too, this above all: Coombes' indifference to time had made him indifferent to death – the end of time for each human being – and that indifference had given him mastery over fear . . . until last night. Now he had but one aim – to return to that calm space where no clocks ticked, no calendars turned, and he was not afraid.

Be patient; be like the forest, he said to himself once again. Impatience had caused Gauthier's death. He'd hurried Gauthier across the rickety bridge, and now he was drowned and the radio drowned with him, although, Coombes realized, the radio's loss was not the disaster it had seemed at first.

Han thought the *trung-si* was, in his motionless silence, mourning the man taken by the river. It was bad luck to disturb someone mourning the dead, so Han said nothing about the pawprint. He had spotted it as soon as he'd crossed the bridge, and had been about to yell to the *trung-si* when the man with the talkingbox fell into the river. Since then, Han had been squatting beside the print, not moving an inch, as if he were afraid it would walk away if he let it out of his sight. He had seen only faint sign since leaving the soldier-camp, but this print was fresh and clear. Twice now he'd measured its depth with his thumb, its width with the span of his hand, and both times his heart rolled over from an excitement mingled with fear, but more from excitement than fear. A male, bigger than the one he and his father had killed long ago, when Han was no longer a boy but not yet a man, and that one was huge. Spread out, its coat had made a blanket four people could sleep under shoulder-to-shoulder.

Out of the corner of his eye, Han caught the flare of a match. The *trung-si* was smoking a cigarette; his mourning must be over. Han hissed to gain his attention.

He came over, rifle flat on one shoulder, his hand on the barrel. Han pointed to the pawprint.

'Jesus.'

'This is the one,' said Han, speaking in his tribal tongue, which the *trung-si* understood. 'A big male, moving fast.'

'Jesus.'

The smoke from the *trung-si*'s cigarette hung like campsmoke in the hotwetquiet air.

'He isn't running. Walking, but fast.'

'Jesus Christ.'

All the *My* said that all the time. The white *My*, the black *My*. A word from their tongue. Han had no idea what it meant, had never asked. Jesus. Jesus Christ.

The *trung-si* bent down and, spreading his fingers wide, laid his hand in the print.

'How can you tell it's walking?'

'If running, tracks would be more far apart.'

'What else?'

'He's carrying his kill. In his teeth. Look.' Han pointed to the long, shallow drag marks in the mud. 'Those are made by the kill's feet. Tiger is carrying him in his teeth. I don't know why. Tiger kills, Tiger eats close to where he kills, but now Tiger is carrying his kill to someplace far, walking, but fast.'

'How big?'

'Very big.'

'I mean, how much weight do you think it has?'

Han turned to him with truth in his small, earthbrown eyes. 'In all my hunting, *trung-si*, I've never tracked one this big.'

That wasn't much help. Coombes already knew that the cat was very big, for he was the only one of the five to have seen it. What he needed now was its weight and length, its speed of travel, the number of its teeth and claws and stripes, every last little concrete fact that could be ascertained. Coombes always made it a point to know his enemy; the more he knew, the more likely he was to win, but in this case, knowledge had a value beyond the practical. He hoped that facts would help dispel the mythic power of the awesome phantom that now stalked his memory with eyes glowing like the eyes in a jack-o'-lantern, only they were yellow-green instead of orange. He could see them still, as he'd seen them the night before, burning with no expression in them except serenity. Yes, serene, and malignant in their serenity, looking at him as *he* might at an ant or a worm. He'd never seen anything so terrible, for he could not believe there was anything in creation capable of looking upon him as if he were an ant or a worm.

A numbness began to spread through his legs. He stood to restore feeling in their nerves, strength to their sinews; he was afraid they would crumple the way they had last night, when the tiger, after staring at him impassively for a few seconds, padded off with Valesquez in its jaws, as effortlessly as a house cat with a mouse.

He needed facts.

'Han, how did it cross the river?'

'It swam. Tiger can swim. Or it jumped. Tiger can jump very far.'

'Nothing could swim that river, and it's thirty metres across. He's carrying a man weighing one hundred kilos.'

Han was silent, irritated by all the talk about metres and kilos. The *My* always spoke about kilos and metres and the time on their watches. Kilos. Metres. Hours. Jesus.

'Answer me, Han. What tiger could jump thirty metres with a big man in its jaws?'

'This tiger, *trung-si.*'

'What are you saying?' asked Coombes with a sardonic laugh. 'That it flew?'

'If it is a Ghostiger, yes.'

'*What?*'

Han explained. Sometimes, when Tiger turned man-eater, it ate a man's soul as well as his flesh. If the soul was angry, it possessed Tiger, giving it extraordinary powers. Powers to fly. To be in two places at once. Ghostiger sustained itself by devouring other souls.

'And that's what you think this is?' Coombes asked, rolling his eyes.

'I hope not. If it's Ghostiger, then we must not kill it.'

'We're going to kill it, all right.'

'Not if Ghost. The angry spirit will find a new Tiger to make its home in, and the new Ghostiger will kill the man who killed its brother. In revenge, it will devour his body and his soul, and the bodies and souls of his wife, his children, his children's children. So Ghostiger must be left alone.' Han traced the outline of the pawprint with his finger. 'That is why I hope Tiger is not Ghost. If we leave it alone, you will not pay me.'

'I'll do worse than that,' Coombes muttered in English.

He looked at his watch. Eleven o'clock. They'd been tracking for almost six hours and had another six or seven hours of daylight left. Hightower had given them until noon tomorrow to find Valesquez, or whatever was left of him, and bring him back. *Be patient; be like the forest.* Tomorrow noon. What was so magical about that hour? Coombes unbuckled the watch and, with a casual movement, flipped it into the river. Instantly, he felt lighter, and he rubbed the band's impression on his wrist like a prisoner when the cuffs are taken off. He waved to the others to come across.

Larry Heinemann

PACO'S STORY

Larry Heinemann's novel Paco's Story, *published in 1986,
describes the attempts of a Vietnam veteran to settle down
'back in the world' after the end of the war. In a small town
in the Midwest, where he has found a job washing dishes,
Paco realizes that for the people around him he is a curiosity,
a relic from a war they have already forgotten about.*

*Paco, however, cannot forget, and in the following extract
recalls his days in hospital as the only survivor of a night-
marish massacre.*

PACO REMEMBERS ALL right, and vividly.

There was the big red cross on the white field on the bottom
of the medevac chopper when it came to get him, and nearly
the instant he was aboard the chopper rose with a swoop,
making speed and altitude swiftly. Paco's stomach fluttered
and he felt mighty dizzy, and he thought he was going to
throw up. He remembers the healthy, browned faces of the
medics, and their gossip about the filthy debris in Paco's
wounds – the maggots in the running sores (almost the feeling
of an enticing caress), the soft, spongy scabs on burst blisters,
and the crusts of dirt. He remembers the peculiar sensation
(this through several quarter-grain doses of morphine) when
the boldest of the medics – an earnest-looking guy with a firm,
light touch and cool fingers – started picking at strips of cloth
and splinters of wood, bits of blackened, brittle skin as long
and curled as razor-clam shells (the pink, raw skin burning) –
the medics thinking it was like picking chips of old paint from

a thick coat of new paint, still tacky. All the while, the other medics soothed Paco, petting him, saying, 'Gonna be okay, hey! You gonna be cool in another ten minutes. Okay! Can't fuck up a tough motherfucker like you, now can they?' And they kept saying okay to him, as though it was part of their work. And they'd ask him, 'Who *are* you, Jack? What's your *name*? What *happened* there?' shouting over the whining, rushing engine noises. And all that time Paco kept one thought in his head as distinct as a colourful dream – I must not die – each word reverberating as though said out loud, the crisp pronunciation tingling the sore flesh of his mouth – *I must not die* – like the litany of an invocation, as though he felt his body shrink each instant he did not say it. And he remembers being overwhelmed with tears (though half the medics expected a wan, plucky smile), his swollen mouth watering and his eyes and nose burning with tears, again and again – because he *was* alive; because he had made it (thanks to God's luck, James) – the moisture cold on his face in the brisk rotor wash of the chopper blades. He remembers flying at a solid thousand feet, making a beeline for the western perimeter at Phuc Luc (so they could turn straight to the hospital dust-off pad without having to circle about the wards to come into the wind) – the young chopper pilot turning his head now and again, asking how the wounded guy was, and the medics telling him, 'Just keep hauling ass, Jack!' And the pilot swerved this way and that among the huge monsoon thunderheads to avoid their fierce weather, flying full-bore flat-out, James, just as fast as that machine would fly.

Paco stretched his neck and looked out the wide chopper doorway, and it was noon, remember, and there before him was a brilliant panorama of thunderheads in every direction – fleece-white and gunmetal-grey, and black as thick as night. They rose thousands of feet into the air, billowing up majestically, the same as Spanish dancers rising out of a deep curtsy, sweeping open their arms (an overpowering image of God's power shown to us in a small way, James). The slow-motion billows towered up and up above Paco and the others; some sailed serenely on; others rained hard, pounding down-

329

pours of monsoon storms, soaking the ground to mush. All the many storms drifted like sleepwalkers climbing a broad balcony stairway, Paco thought as he looked out the chopper – the lilting rain cascaded down like the lacy trains of airy ballgowns, trailing behind the dreamlike sleepers. And then it seemed to him that the thunderheads looked like plain, stern young women with long, loosened hair, standing here and there and yonder on a smooth stone quay, waiting for a dream death ship, say; each woman with her small clean hands folded lightly across a hard, swollen belly; each standing well away from the others, while pigeons pecked about underfoot, swarming for crumbs, and a hot, breathtaking sun beat down over all.

Well below the chopper the jungle looked spongy soft, as though Paco could have reached down into it – like reaching into the rich suds of a green bubble bath – and scooped up a frothy handful; Paco was sure it would be the most fragrant foam. Here and there the brilliant sunlight caught patches of water – rice paddies and irrigation ditches, ordinary hooch-yard puddles and snatches of some river or other through the jungle canopy, and bomb craters as big as house lots – the reflections caught his eye like a fierce light through the chinks in a wood fence, more stunning and fantastic than muzzle flashes. Paco saw the broad swaths of water-filled craters, the truck convoys making headway among the woods and curves and storms – dust rising above the dry sections of roadway – the old tank laagers where the tank treads had dug furrows in the thick, squishy turf.

Paco and the medics floated through that bizarre, horrific gloom in the broad light of day, with the air smelling of damp electricity. The rain slanted one way (the spray sucked into the rotor wash), indistinct and misted; the scorching midday sun slanted another, the colours and shadows crisp and vivid, as radiant and sharp as a bright and interesting face seen in a clean mirror.

The dust-off flew, pounding, over the perimeter at Phuc Luc above the sweltering bunker line bristling with guns, then banked downwind, eastward, making for the sandbagged hospital compound (you could see the huge red crosses on the many compound rooftops) – the air in the chopper suddenly hot and bright above the bare ground and tin roofs. Nearly everyone in the chopper's path looked up from his work to watch it cruise overhead – every man understanding full well that the one survivor of the Alpha Company holocaust massacre was aboard, half wrapped in a body bag and still alive (Can you beat that!), otherwise the pilot would not still be flying so hard. The chopper came swiftly, steeply in, making directly for that bit of tarmac at the end of the duckboard walkway outside the awning of the hospital triage. It settled quickly and firmly on the chopper pad. The triage medics, the zonked-out Graves Registration slick-sleeve privates, and other passersby and hangers-on hustled out to help – to gawk, too, no doubt; to touch luck, we might think, James – and brought Paco into the stuffy shade of the triage tent and laid him on one of those waist-high litter racks for the duty officer to inspect – everyone talking at once, taking pictures.

A triage is the place in the back of a hospital where the litter bearers line up the wounded brought in from the field; first come first served, you understand. A doctor examines them, culling through the wounds, comparing and considering, then picks who's first in the operating room, who's second, who's last – and who gets written off. In extreme emergencies the worst hopeless cases are drugged, usually with healthy doses of morphine, shunted off to the Moribund Ward, and allowed to die among themselves with only one another for comfort. And once you are taken into the Moribund Ward, James, you are as good as dead – no matter how long it takes. But Paco, by then famous as the nameless wounded man from Alpha Company's massacre, got every consideration.

The doctor, a pasty-faced major with a fresh pair of operating greens bloused sloppily into his jungle boots, swaggered into the open-air triage, wiping his hands on a mildly bloody apron like a fishmonger's wife. He took one look at Paco and saw immediately that he was unfit to take into the operating room. He knew also that they would be swamped with equally serious wounded, and plenty of them, from the bloodbath firefight at Fire Base Francesca as soon as a chopper could make it through the withering ground fire and RPGs, and that they – the doctors and nurses and medics – might well work through the night. Indeed, James, that was pretty much what happened. The doctor unzipped Paco's body bag – the sharp raw stench of Paco's wounds, Paco's bowels, rising fully in his face. He turned the bloody zippered flaps of the bag this way and that, reaching in to lift a scrap of cloth to inspect the festering wounds and the bone fragments that stuck through the skin. 'Christ Jesus on a bloody fuckin' crutch,' he said under his breath, 'how long was this guy left like this? – what's his name?'

'Almost two days,' said the medic with the good hands. 'This is that Alpha Company guy and he ain't said who he is yet, sir.'

(It must have been one motherfucker of a firefight, the medics and nurses said among themselves as they looked on, and ended the night steeped in blood.)

The major looked over at Paco again and said, 'Right.' And then, because Paco was stinking filthy and peppered with minute flakes and slivers of shrapnel, he said, 'Take this man into a side room here and scrub him up,' dropped the flaps of the body bag, and wiped his hands on his apron – his nose smarting the same as everyone else's – 'Then we'll take a look at him and start to work.' So the triage medics shot Paco another quarter-grain of morphine, grabbed a couple bottles of Phisohex surgical soap and a handful of scrub brushes, jerked him and his litter up, and hustled him into a side cubicle.

Paco remembers the stiff, greasy canvas drapes the medics pulled to, the hot light bulb with the jerry-rigged wires hanging in his face, the medics pouring sweat, the collapsed garbage bag of rotted field dressings in the corner – that oppressive and fetid, suffocating air. He remembers, too, oddly, the sweet and medicinal smell of the soap, and the sloppy, squishy sound of the lather.

Paco was warm and numb from the morphine (as though

332

tucked up snugly in stiff, thick blankets) when they smeared the first doses of surgical soap on his chest and arms, then commenced to scrub him raw. When the shot finally took full effect, Paco felt only a vague grinding sensation, that was all, as though someone were gouging the stringy meat and seeds from a ripe pumpkin with a blunt wooden spoon; it sounded as though they were scrubbing coarse cloth, bearing down with great vigour. He remembers lolling his head back on the small, flat pillow (a burlap sandbag stuffed with loose dressings), and finally, the welcome ease of sleep that came over him after nearly two days of his earnest and stoic, watchful anticipation of death. (It was something the same as the first moment you slipped off your 60–80–100-pound rucksack pack – that instantly dumb, numb, inexpressible relief when your shoulders, your lungs, your kidneys seemed to float upward, and your whole torso tingled and throbbed, ached and itched – like a foot and leg asleep. It felt like a hard task finally ended; not done well, mind you, James, simply done with.)

Now scrubbing out the shrapnel with Phisohex and surgical scrub brushes was a common first-aid procedure – comfort of the wounded had nothing to do with it, and most never got the consideration of morphine, 'Waste of good dope, Jack!' – more common certainly than having some first-of-May, fucking-new-guy rookie triage medic sit there picking at a million slivers of shrapnel with a manicure scissors, a magnifying glass, and a bottle of hydrogen peroxide. So the medics, wearing surgical masks and gagging at the stench, peeled back the black rubber body bag bit by bit and cut off the remains of Paco's clothes with surgical scissors as they went about the business of cleaning him up for his first surgery.

Paco awoke in what must have been the middle of the night in the stifling heat of a squalid little Quonset hut, the Recovery Ward, coming out of the anaesthetic with his legs and back itchy and prickly, feeling as though someone were chopping into them with a tailor's scissors as big as a shears –

skrit, skrit, skrit (the bosomy night nurse sitting at the nurses' station scribbling notes on charts with a bit of pencil in a small circle of harsh light) – Paco thinking that when an arm or leg is amputated you often have the sensation, later, that the amputated part itches or feels hot or cold. He felt the bedsheets tighten and slacken against his chest; felt his own breathing. He heard the bugs banging on the coppery screen of the door under the porch light, the hiss coming in over a radio receiver somewhere (white noise, we called it), someone walking on the duckboard outside, the duckboard slapping into shallow puddles. All of that immediate and simultaneous with someone's endless moaning, rhythmic and sustained – another of the wounded men in the ward letting go, breath by breath, of some deep and woeful hurt. Paco opened his eyes with a blink and whispered, 'Hey,' just to hear the sound of his own voice – the same as you might pinch yourself, James, to prove that you are substance, and awake and alive, after all. And the bosomy night nurse snapped her head around and looked across the way, quickly searching a roomful of vigorously healthy bodies suddenly extremely ill (instant amputations and cracked skulls, shredded organs and disembowelments, faces destroyed by close-in AK rifle fire – the slugs still embedded in the heads – the smell of heavy, foul sweat); the many IV bottles and the many drooping amber tubes; a huge pedestal fan whirring like crazy in the corner; the stainless-steel trays arranged just so in the nightstands; and the sparkles of light arching across the curved Quonset ceiling. The instant the woman turned her attention to the room, everything was chugging and ticking, hissing and thunking, rasping shrilly, and the men were jerking and gasping, but sleeping hard. They were so whacked out on painkillers they could not see and could not feel and could not smell anything except the sickly, rank medicinal odour of the bandages and the bloody slop of their own body rot, scabbing over – everything seemed a million miles below them, behind them, around back of them or up on the eight hundredth shelf and unfathomly, unreachably beyond them; as good as echoes. One man gritted his teeth and grimaced, rolling his eyes. Another man stretched and curled his toes, wrinkled his brow, squinched and blinked his eyes, as though he were counting the freight cars of a passing train. Another man pumped his legs as if he were pedalling a bike, and squirmed as though his bed were spread with rock salt, steam puffing out the holes in his oxygen mask in quick steady chugs. The night nurse saw Paco stretching and rustling around, pulling at the sheets gathered in his fists, trying to glimpse the end of his bed where his legs were, plastered and bandaged, as thick as bedposts. She dropped her paperwork and went immediately to him and sat lightly on the very edge of his bed. At first she reassured him, telling him where he was: 'The post-op ward of the evac hospital, and you've had an operation, and you'll have more, but you're okay,' she said, and gave him a drink of tepid water, holding the tall Styrofoam cup steady while he sipped deeply through the plastic straw; Paco always especially remembered her rich, feminine voice. 'What is your name?' she said. 'Tell me your name, say your name.' So he told her, though he discovered he could barely speak, and in that same instant he tried to take hold of her jungle trousers with the very tips of his fingers – his hands deeply cut, bruised, burned, heavily bandaged. He wanted to ask her who all these men were; if there was *anyone* from Alpha Company, *anyone* else from Fire Base Harriette? 'No,' she said clearly, anticipating him, 'these are from Fire Base Francesca. You're the *only* one from Harriette.' And Paco eased back on the bed, lapsing into thought about that, absorbing it. She gave him another shot of morphine – the surgeon had left orders to give him plenty, but not *too* much, because if the kid croaked he'd hear about it from every son-of-a-bitch in the chain of command and his career would be up shit creek. Then the woman pulled the sheet back (the smell of clean meat there) – Paco remembered always the smell of her Ivory soap and her face shining in the low light, and how her blouse clung to her body as she moved. She peeled back the stiff bandages (Paco mesmerized by the crackle of them, so many bandages) and then gave him a sponge bath with a soft hand towel rinsed in a shallow basin of water fetched from the ward's water cooler. The nurse went about her work with that calm and soothing patience some women have who understand full well the need for physical kindness and its effect – a fondness for the warm touch of care that is just as often a caress – she daubing his body clean bit by bit with a cool cloth and warm hands. Soon after she commenced, Paco got an erection (not as uncommon as you might think, James; after all, we'd been in the field for nearly forty-five days and Paco hadn't been with a woman for months before that). The nurse washed Paco's belly and watched his cock stand fully erect (a dozen or so knotted stitches pinching; Paco mightily embarrassed – the woman a nurse, a stranger after all, an officer, for Christ's sake!), but she discouraged the hard-on with a half-dozen hard flicks of her fingernail – the same as she would tap the morphine syringe to get rid of air bubbles, only harder. She washed his face and ears, combing back his hair with her hands and fingers. She redressed his wounds, pulled the sheet back to his chin, and soon he was fast asleep. Later that morning, before breakfast, the major (looking plainly exhausted) made the rounds of the wards – coming along first thing, in clean operating greens, to check on Paco and the other dozen wounded. The blousy night nurse stood with a hand on Paco's bed rail and casually mentioned that she thought the guy from the Alpha Company massacre would make it fine (none of the hospital staff ever did call him by his name). And bit by bit, day by day, he did get better, though he shit blackish, pasty stool for weeks.

Some smart-ass put the snips of shrapnel (hard metal shavings the colour of coconut flakes), the misshapen rifle slugs, the sharply jagged pieces of brass shell casings, the pieces of bones which they couldn't fit – all that – into a petri dish and slipped it in with Paco's other meagre belongings (fetched from his gear at Alpha Company) stashed under the nightstand. And weeks later, when Paco first saw the dish while he was sorting through his gear, it reminded him of those chintzy little souvenir saucers filled with pins and buttons and other trivial oddments that folks keep out of sheer sentimentality. Paco kept that petri dish, of course.

The night nurse tended him carefully, talking with him, protecting him from the Red Cross do-gooders and the brigade chaplain. She watched him sleep from her chair at the nurses' station across the room, bathed him every night with that same soft cloth and warm efficiency. Then one night while she bathed him, not long after he arrived, she wiped her hands of soap and encouraged an erection. His cock, dotted with stitching, rose from between his thighs with quick jerks – a fine, firm hard-on, though all he felt through the dazzling morphine was a peculiar fullness. The woman took hold of it with one hand and, caressing his belly with the other, leaned down and licked the head (shining like an oiled plum) with her swirling tongue, and gingerly caressed it more and more with her warm fingertips (the stitches stretching, stinging). He put his hands on her head and worked his fingers into her short hair – astonished, luxuriating in the wonderful pleasure (a sweet, toothache pain). A good long time she masturbated him, sucking languorously, and soon enough he felt the pause and urge of terrific inevitability. She sensed it, too (the muscles of his buttocks hunching under the bandages), reached for a large bandage, and clapped it over the head of his cock. And when he climaxed he went on and on. She cleaned him up, dusted his crotch with talc, and Paco felt fine, considering the stitches – just fine.

Then one night Paco was softly, abruptly awakened by two strapping medics, doped with an unscheduled shot of morphine, laid on a litter from the triage, loaded on a regular Huey chopper waiting at the dust-off pad with its running lights blinking, and brought – plaster casts, IV bottles, tubes, and all – to Tan Son Nhut Air Base on the outskirts of Saigon. Paco and several other deathly wounded, plus a couple of guys they waited better than two hours for, were strapped to tiered racks in the dim, reddish light of the spartan cargo bay, given another healthy dose of morphine, and flown to hospitals in Japan where they could get better treatment, prosthetics and skin grafts, and whatnot; where they could convalesce in heightened comfort and superb peace. During the flight, metal cabinets slammed open and shut, and the plane jerked and swung and vibrated like a thousand needles. Paco lay on his litter in the rack with his arms squeezed against his sides, holding clenched fists over his groin. He gritted his teeth, rolled his head back and forth to assuage the pain, and endured it as best he could (along with the other wounded) in gripping silence. Travel time was every minute of five solid hours. Two of the several wounded brought in from the bitter fighting around Ban Me Thuot bled to death, whimpering, because the medics could not staunch their wounds, which soaked through everything – field dressings and hospital dressings, skimpy blankets and litter canvas – the blood glistening.

One evening at the hospital in Japan a pasty-faced full-bird colonel from Westmoreland's MACV headquarters in Saigon arrived in Paco's room with a retinue of curious staff doctors and well-behaved nurses to give Paco his medals – a Purple Heart and a Bronze Star. The colonel wore a fat wedding ring, his sleeves crisply folded above the crook of his elbow, and jungle trousers tailored nicely and bloused neatly into his immaculately spit-shined jungle boots. Paco was still wrapped in bandages head to toe, his legs and hips packed in solid plaster casts. The colonel leaned over the head of the bed – the doctors horning in to clear away some of the bandages around Paco's head right and proper – and a keen startled look came into his eyes as the doctors unravelled more and more dressings and the colonel encountered Paco's wounds. Suddenly awkward, he opened his musette bag and laid the medal cases on the night table. He pinched some of the material of Paco's hospital pyjamas together above the breast pocket, slipped the pin of the Purple Heart through, and clasped it. His clean, well-manicured hands smelled of expensive, woodsy pipe tobacco. 'For wounds suffered,' he said in a low and steady voice, whispering just loud enough for everyone in the room to hear. Then he took up the Bronze Star. 'For particular bravery,' he said, repeating a key phrase in the citation, pinning the medal crooked and close to the other so that there was a mumbling buzz of comment in the softly lit room because the medals were draped oddly across his bandages. The colonel leaned over even farther, pressing Paco into the mattress somewhat, and whispered something in his ear. And Paco can never remember what it was the man said, as many times as he has puzzled over it, but *always* recalls the warm breath on the side of his head and in his hair. (Paco had the distinct memory *then* of when he was a small boy and his father would come into his darkened bedroom some evenings, in his rawhide slippers and baggy pants, sit down lightly on the edge of his bed, and sing him to sleep in that whispering, croaking voice of his:

> *Here comes the sandman,*
> *Stepping so softly,*
> *Stealing around on the tips of his toes,*
> *As he scatters the sand with his sure little hand,*
> *In the eyes of sleepy children.*

Paco remembered the warm, firm caresses of his father rubbing his back, and how the song always provoked yawns, and how his father would lean down and kiss his face when he had finished.)

The colonel fumbled with the ribbons and the cases and the tissue-paper citations, a sheen of tears welling in the man's eyes as he straightened up and left the room, saying to Paco, 'Goodbye, young sergeant,' with the doctors and nurses right behind.

That was the reason Paco never threw away the medals, or pawned them, as many times as he was tempted and as stone total worthless as the medals were – the Army gave them out like popcorn, you understand, like rain checks at a ball park. It is the kiss he cherishes and the memory of the whispered word. He has the medals still, packed in the shaving kit of his AWOL bag under the seat of that done-up tow truck from the Texaco station – the medal cases smeared with shaving soap and soaked with dimestore aftershave, and the citations folded up as small as matchbooks.

Christopher J. Koch

WELCOME TO SAIGON

The war in Vietnam ended with the fall of Saigon in April 1995. With North Vietnamese troops on the outskirts of the city, US Marine helicopters evacuated the last remaining American citizens. The atmosphere of initial chaos and then quiet resignation is suggested here in an extract from Christopher J. Koch's novel about war correspondents in Indochina, Highways to a War *(1995).*

BY MONDAY THE 28th, there were sixteen North Vietnamese divisions around Saigon, some of them only eight kilometres away.

Tan Son Nhut airport was being rocketed, and although many South Vietnamese pilots went on fighting, going up in gunships to hit the Communist positions, others now fought each other for the possession of planes. They made their escape in these, flying them out to Thailand.

There were thunderstorms that day, I remember: the noise mingling with the sound of shelling. Mike and I moved about the city, getting pictures and film. Restaurants and shops were still open, but thousands of people were streaming out to the airport in cars, lorries and on foot, still hoping that they could somehow get on planes.

The Army of South Vietnam continued to defend the city's perimeter. It had fought with great bravery in these last stages, but now it was falling into panic. The South had put all its hopes on the military aid promised by the Americans: now the news had come through that there would be no more aid. The last shipment of artillery had been sent, and there were no shells. The Government and the ARVN troops knew now that there was nothing more to hope for.

The end came the next day: on Tuesday the 29th. That morning, the US embassy began its evacuation. Americans in Saigon had been told to listen for a coded message on US Armed Forces Radio as the signal that evacuation had begun; it would come every fifteen minutes, followed by Bing Crosby singing 'White Christmas'. When this was heard, all the remaining foreign media offices began packing up – in the Eden Building, the Caravelle Hotel and elsewhere. The Telenews staff had gone the week before, taking their equipment to Bangkok, abandoning the office, and leaving me the keys. London was happy for me to cover since I chose to do it, I was told, but Telenews took no responsibility for me.

Despite the rocketing of Tan Son Nhut, Marine helicopters were being sent there from the US fleet off the coast to ferry out all remaining American citizens in Saigon. They were also to take Vietnamese who worked for American agencies. But fixed-wing aircraft could no longer fly because the bombardment had closed down the airport, and this meant that fewer Vietnamese could now be taken out than the Americans had planned. The people in the city knew this, and panic grew. The Americans had told Western correspondents that places would be found for them on the choppers; special buses were picking their people up from prearranged points around the city, and journalists were told to go to these points. Only a very small number of journalists and photographers decided to stay, as Mike and I were doing.

We had made our base in the deserted Telenews office in the Eden Building. The AP office was on the floor above, and at around 11 A.M., after we'd loaded and checked our cameras, we decided to look in there and say goodbye.

Nobody had much time to speak to us. The scene was frantic, like an out-of-control schoolroom. Phones were ringing and not being answered, an American voice was coming over a radio, and all over the room people were emptying desks and files and stuffing things into bags, moving very fast. Most of them were sweating a lot; some were laughing and joking; some looked pale and scared.

One of them glanced up at us from an airways bag he was packing: he was a staff writer with a blond moustache, whose name I've forgotten. You guys coming? he said. Better move your asses.

No, we said, we were staying.

And we gave him some film to take out and deliver for us. He did it, too, and Telenews were very happy with what I sent; it was shown in a great number of countries.

You're lunatics, he said. Crazy as Ed Carter. You're gonna die.

In the middle of the jerking and hurrying and shouting figures, Ed was sitting at his desk with his feet up, reading a newspaper. Ed was always very calm.

We went over to him, and he looked up over his glasses. I figured somebody should be around to welcome General Giap, he said. You guys gonna keep me company? I've got transport.

And he held up a bunch of keys.

The correspondents going out on the choppers had only been allowed to take one bag each; they had to leave everything else. One AP staff writer had been forced to leave a beautiful Ford Mustang, and he'd given the keys to Ed, with instructions that Ed was eventually to sell the car and send the money, if the Communists spared his life. So we went out to the man's house and picked up his Mustang, and drove in it around the city.

The crowds in the streets were huge, surging everywhere. Everyone carried bags or children. Many were running in a sort of hysteria: but I don't think they knew any longer where they were running to. I saw one little grey-haired man in a white canvas hat, a small suitcase in one hand, who was actually running in circles, in the middle of Nguyen Hue: I think he'd lost his wits. The White Mice had now disappeared, and we realized there was no law and order any more: no one was in charge of the city. There was supposed to be a curfew, but that meant nothing now. It was like a crazy carnival: but not a carnival of happiness.

The American buses for Tan Son Nhut were moving about the city to their special pickup points, collecting their passengers; and the people in the streets were following these buses in tens of thousands, begging and screaming to be let on. They saw the buses as their last hope, and they were right. The drivers were fighting them off when they opened the doors, not always successfully. Most of the windows were protected with heavy-duty mesh, but some people got in through sliding windows at the back; others pushed their babies in. Cars stood abandoned, keys still hanging in the dashboards: if you wanted a car, you just had to steal one. In many side streets, we saw ARVN uniforms lying in the gutter; the soldiers were changing into civilian clothes, and melting into the crowd. Looting had begun: people were breaking into rich villas, and the streets were getting dangerous. Many now hated the Americans for deserting them, and as we went by, and they saw the white faces of Mike and Ed Carter, they shouted: Go home, Yankees. The Saigon Cowboys were out on their Honda motor scooters, looking for what they could steal. We also saw people who did nothing; who stood crying on the pavements like lost children.

Taking the Mustang, Mike and Ed and I went around to the American embassy that evening. Mike and I shot film of the Marine Corps Sikorsky and Sea Knight helicopters landing inside the compound and on the roof, taking out the embassy staff while Marines stood guard on top of the walls. The Jolly Green Giants and the smaller Sea Knights had been coming and going since late afternoon, and it was now around seven-thirty. They would keep on coming at intervals until dawn. We got hold of an American newspaper journalist by the gates who was going out on one of the choppers, and gave him our film to deliver. You'll have seen the pictures – including the shots Mike took that were published in his American news-weekly, and which now appear in books on the war.

Thousands of people were hammering at the closed gates and on the walls with their fists, demanding, pleading, weeping, many of them holding up documents. A lot of the time it was raining, and very dark: the city's power supply had cut out at seven o'clock. The whirring and beating of twin rotors filled the blackness, and the choppers hovered and tilted, the glaring white lights in their noses guiding them down. Young Vietnamese climbed the walls and made it to the top, but the big Marine guards kicked and fought them off. Other Marines lobbed tear gas canisters into the crowd. What are you doing? I thought. You came here long ago to help them against their enemies; how can you do this to them now? And I felt ashamed to be filming.

There were some ARVN soldiers there, full of anger against the Americans for deserting them, and shouting up at the Marines. *Du-ma*, they called – meaning 'mummyfucker'. Yet some of the people around the walls were actually in a cheerful mood, knowing that we who were staying behind faced a new situation together, and that there was nothing more to be done. There's a sort of excitement in such disaster: a comradeship which most of us don't admit. And these people had now faced the fact that what they most wanted they were never going to have: they would never be lifted out by one of those giant green choppers that were the only things that could save them. All they could do now was to watch the white lights that kept on coming down through the dark, like lights from another world.

I won't forget those scenes; but what I find hardest to forget are certain other rooftops in the city, which we passed later in the evening. The Americans had sent some helicopters to these buildings in midafternoon, to pick up Vietnamese who'd been promised evacuation. Now, although many were still left, the choppers did not reappear. Yet little groups of people stood on those rooftops in the dark, quiet and patient, their luggage beside them. The throbbing of the choppers was gone from the air, except in the direction of the embassy; the evacuation was over. But still these people could not believe that the Americans would not come back. I heard that they were still there at dawn, watching the sky. They were waiting for helicopters that were only in their minds, coming to rescue them from tomorrow.

*

When tomorrow came, Saigon was very quiet. All the noise had stopped: it was the strangest quiet I've ever known.

Mike and Ed Carter and I sat at breakfast in the restaurant of the Continental: orange juice, croissants and coffee. There were only about half a dozen others there: some Italians, two French journalists from Le Monde, and a Japanese photographer. It was a hot morning, calm and pleasant. The power was working again, the big ceiling fans turned, and the Chinese waiters in their starched white jackets stood by the yellow pillars.

The whole city seemed silent, and the streets were half empty. Out on the square, some military trucks went by, and a few refugees still trudged through the streets with their possessions. But there were no ARVN troops; no black market operators; no Saigon Cowboys on Hondas; no White Mice. The blue haze of exhaust fumes was dissolving, and the air was almost clean. After the din and fear of the day before, waking to this silence had been like waking from a fever to find yourself well. Saigon was waiting for the victors to arrive.

Sure is peaceful, Ed said. I can handle plenty of this. The only thing is: who's in charge?

No one's in charge, Mike told him. I never thought I'd miss those little White Mice – but not having them around's a bit creepy.

We laughed, and Ed signalled for more coffee. One of the old Chinese waiters came shuffling forward, carrying the tall silver coffee pot. He had a dignified expression, but I detected a faint frown of worry. I wondered what would become of him after today. He'd probably been at the Continental for forty years: could he even understand what was happening?

We began to discuss where we should position ourselves, to be ready for the NVA's arrival. No one could know when that would be, or where they'd head for first when they came into the city.

Right here in the middle of town seems best to me, Ed said. We might as well make ourselves comfortable. I don't want any dealings with the South Vietnamese Army, either: they're pretty mad at Americans today. Yesterday on the sidewalk an ARVN sergeant spat at me, and told me we were running out on them. I told him I was staying, and then he shook my hand. They're feeling pretty emotional.

Can you blame them? Mike asked. His face grew set and bitter, and Ed looked at him.

I guess not, he said.

We were quiet for a moment; then Ed said: The NVA are going to want to hoist their flag somewhere significant, when they come into town. Maybe at the Palace. I guess Big Minh's sitting in his office out there, waiting to surrender. But my bet is they'll go just around the corner here, to City Hall.

You take City Hall, Mike told Ed. Jim and I will go to the Palace. And twenty dollars says we're right.

We shook hands on it, and Mike grinned. He still had a little of his old spirit; but he seldom smiled. His mind was always on Ly Keang.

So he and I went to the Presidential Palace, driving the Mustang again, which had survived the night in the Continental without being stolen.

It was now eleven-thirty, and the sun was growing hot. The streets were still very quiet, and out by the Palace it was quieter still. The big wrought-iron gates in front were locked as usual, and we drove down a side street to the service entrance, where journalists had always entered in the past. This gate was open, and there was no sign of the guards who used to be posted there. We walked into the grounds and around to the front of the long white building with its flight of marble steps going up to the entrance.

Here we found an even bigger quiet than the one in the city. The Palace stands in a wide parkland enclosed by iron railways, where spreading tamarinds and other trees stand in open, grassy spaces. These spaces were empty, all the way to the road and the railings a hundred metres or so away, and the quiet here was like sleep. Nothing but bird calls, and the whirring of cicadas. There seemed to be an unusual number of dragonflies in the air, hovering and shimmering, and I wondered what this signified. They must be a sign, I thought.

But of what? I guess I'm superstitious; and I was now very keyed up.

The only people we found at the entrance of the Palace were some South Vietnamese troops: members of the palace guard. They were sitting and lying on the grass near the marble steps in a way that was very unmilitary, their automatic rifles stacked beside them, many of them with their helmets off. It looked almost like a picnic.

They no longer consider themselves soldiers, I thought. It's over for them.

When we went up to them, we spoke to them in Vietnamese. I was concerned they might be hostile to us, like those Ed Carter had encountered, but they smiled back, and were quite friendly. Most of them were young, but there was a sergeant of middle age.

What are you doing? I asked.

Waiting to surrender, the sergeant said. Nothing more to do, now.

I guess that's right, Mike said, and offered him a cigarette.

We sat down in the grass, and talked with them. Many ARVN troops had thrown away their uniforms today, they told us; but they thought it better to go on guarding the Palace until they were told to do otherwise. They wanted to do their duty. Then they would surrender their weapons.

It was very still, and getting much hotter; soon we spoke only in snatches, lying there in the grass. The whirring of the insects began to sound to me like some mechanical alarm system, warning us of what was to come.

Then I saw the tank.

I could not believe what I was seeing, at first. I don't know what I'd expected, but it hadn't been this; I squinted at it through the shimmer of the heat for a number of seconds, before I called out to Mike. It was a green, Soviet-made tank, and it was moving down the road outside the railings. It flew a huge National Liberation Front flag on a pole – blue and red, with a yellow star – and the number on the side of it was 843. A North Vietnamese trooper was looking out from its turret; others, in their sun helmets and familiar green cotton uniforms, were riding on the front. I glimpsed people running behind it; one of them was a British correspondent, and I recognized some French correspondents and photographers. As we watched, flame shot from the barrel of its cannon and there was a report; then it turned towards the closed Palace gates, and Mike and I stood up. The soldiers were standing up too, and raising their hands.

The tank smashed into the gates, and one of them came half off its hinges. Mike ran towards it across the lawn, his Leica at the ready. I had my CP16 Commag, a sound-on-film camera: I hoisted it on to my shoulder and started after him.

The tank stopped, like a big slow animal, and seemed to consider; then it reversed and charged the gates again, and I saw Mike raise his camera. This time the tank smashed straight through the gates and rolled on, lumbering across the lawn. I was still running, the camera slowing me down. I was checking my light meter as I went, my face pouring with sweat, my heart pounding. I knew only one thing: this was film I must get no matter what happened to me.

Mike was still taking pictures when the tank stopped again. Some of the soldiers were pointing at us, and beginning to climb down, and I became aware that Mike and I were alone in this space of grass; none of the palace guard had followed us. But I was shooting film now; everything else was vague: the drilling of the cicadas inside my head, the dragonflies dancing around me. Looking at the soldiers through the lens, I was seeing their faces clearly, and they suddenly seemed very familiar to me. They were very young, mostly just boys, and they reminded me of Captain Danh's unit; I almost thought I recognized Doc and Weary and Prince among them, but of course I didn't. And in that instant, I saw a soldier in a sun helmet running towards us and shouting, his AK-47 cocked. He was telling us to put our hands up.

He reached Mike first, and Mike raised his hands, his camera held in the right. I did the same: it took all my strength to suspend that heavy Commag. The soldier was standing close to Mike, the AK levelled, shouting in Vietnamese.

American! he shouted. You are American!

348

He had a broad brown country face, and his eyes had a fierce, hard shine: the killing shine.

Mike answered in Vietnamese, his hands still high. No, he said. Australian. Welcome to Saigon.

The soldier frowned and looked puzzled; then I saw the shine go out of his eyes. He lowered his gun, and I knew we were going to live.

Bao Ninh

THE JUNGLE OF SCREAMING SOULS

Bao Ninh's The Sorrow of War *(1991) is one of the first novels about the war written from a Vietnamese point of view. Being part of a team that collects and buries corpses after the war has ended, the novel's narrator returns to a place where he once took part in a terrible battle – the Jungle of Screaming Souls.*

ON THE BANKS of the Ya Crong Poco River, on the northern flank of the B3 battlefield in the Central Highlands, the Missing In Action body-collecting team awaits the dry season of 1976.

The mountains and jungles are water-soaked and dull. Wet trees. Quiet jungles. All day and all night the water steams. A sea of greenish vapour over the jungle's carpet of rotting leaves.

September and October drag by, then November passes, but still the weather is unpredictable and the night rains are relentless. Sunny days but rainy nights.

Even into early December, weeks after the end of the normal rainy season, the jungles this year are still as muddy as all hell. They are forgotten by peace, damaged or impassable, all the tracks disappearing, bit by bit, day by day, into the embraces of the coarse undergrowth and wild grasses.

Travelling in such conditions is brutally tough. To get from Crocodile Lake east of the Sa Thay River, across District 67 to the crossroads of Cross Hill on the west bank of the Poco River – a mere fifty kilometres – the powerful Russian truck has to lumber along all day. And still they fall short of their destination.

Not until after dusk does the MIA Zil truck reach the Jungle of Screaming Souls, where they park beside a wide creek clogged with rotting branches.

The driver stays in the cabin and goes straight to sleep. Kien climbs wearily into the rear of the truck to sleep alone in a hammock strung high from cab to tailgate. At midnight the rains start again, this time a smooth drizzle, falling silently.

The old tarpaulin covering the truck is torn, full of holes, letting the water drip, drip, drip through on to the plastic sheets covering the remains of soldiers laid out in rows below Kien's hammock.

The humid atmosphere condenses, its long moist, chilly fingers sliding in and around the hammock where Kien lies shivering, half-awake, half-asleep, as though drifting along on a stream. He is floating, sadly, endlessly, sometimes as if on a lorry driving silently, robot-like, somnambulantly through the lonely jungle tracks. The stream moans, a desperate complaint mixing with distant faint jungle sounds, like an echo from another world. The eerie sounds come from somewhere in a remote past, arriving softly like featherweight leaves falling on the grass of times long, long ago.

Kien knows the area well. It was here, at the end of the dry season of 1969, that his Battalion 27 was surrounded and almost totally wiped out. Ten men survived from the Unlucky Battalion, after fierce, horrible, barbarous fighting.

That was the dry season when the sun burned harshly, the wind blew fiercely, and the enemy sent napalm spraying through the jungle and a sea of fire enveloped them, spreading like the fires of hell. Troops in the fragmented companies tried to regroup, only to be blown out of their shelters again as they went mad, became disoriented and threw themselves into nets of bullets, dying in the flaming inferno. Above them the helicopters flew at tree-top height and shot them almost one by one, the blood spreading out, spraying from their backs, flowing like red mud.

The diamond-shaped grass clearing was piled high with bodies killed by helicopter gunships. Broken bodies, bodies blown apart, bodies vaporised.

No jungle grew again in this clearing. No grass. No plants.

'Better to die than surrender my brothers! Better to die!' the Battalion commander yelled insanely; waving his pistol in front of Kien he blew his own brains out through his ear. Kien screamed soundlessly in his throat at the sight, as the Americans attacked with sub-machine-guns, sending bullets buzzing like deadly bees around him. Then Kien lowered his machine-gun, grasped his side and fell, rolling slowly down the bank of a shallow stream, hot blood trailing down the slope after him.

In the days that followed, crows and eagles darkened the sky. After the Americans withdrew, the rainy season came, flooding the jungle floor, turning the battlefield into a marsh whose surface water turned rust-coloured from the blood. Bloated human corpses, floating alongside the bodies of incinerated jungle animals, mixed with branches and trunks cut down by artillery, all drifting in a stinking marsh. When the flood receded everything dried in the heat of the sun into thick mud and stinking rotting meat. And down the bank and along the stream Kien dragged himself, bleeding from the mouth and from his body wound. The blood was cold and sticky, like blood from a corpse. Snakes and centipedes crawled over him, and he felt Death's hand on him. After that battle no one mentioned Battalion 27 any more, though numerous souls of ghosts and devils were born in that deadly defeat. They were still loose, wandering in every corner and bush in the jungle, drifting along the stream, refusing to depart for the Other World.

From then on it was called the Jungle of Screaming Souls. Just hearing the name whispered was enough to send chills down the spine. Perhaps the screaming souls gathered together on special festival days as members of the Lost Battalion, lining up on the little diamond-shaped grass plot, checking their ranks and numbers. The sobbing whispers were heard deep in the jungle at night, the howls carried on the wind. Perhaps they really were the voices of the wandering souls of dead soldiers.

Kien was told that passing this area at night one could hear birds crying like human beings. They never flew, they only cried among the branches. And nowhere else in these Central Highlands could one find bamboo shoots of such a horrible colour, with infected weals like bleeding pieces of meat. As for the fireflies, they were huge. Some said they'd seen firefly lights rise before them as big as a steel helmet – some said bigger than helmets.

Here, when it is dark, trees and plants moan in awful harmony. When the ghostly music begins it unhinges the soul and the entire wood looks the same no matter where you are standing. Not a place for the timid. Living here one could go mad or be frightened to death. Which was why in the rainy season of 1974, when the regiment was sent back to this area, Kien and his scout squad established an altar and prayed before it in secret, honouring and recalling the wandering souls from Battalion 27 still in the Jungle of Screaming Souls.

Sparkling incense sticks glowed night and day at the altar from that day forward.

'Kien, Kien, what the hell makes you cry so loudly?'

The truckdriver's beefy hand pushed through the hammock on to Kien's shoulder, shaking him awake.

'Get up! Get ready! Quick!'

Kien slowly opened his eyes. The dark rings under them revealed his deep exhaustion. The painful memory of the dream throbbed against his temples. After some minutes he got up, then slowly climbed down from the hammock and dropped from the back of the truck to the ground.

Seeing how sluggishly Kien ate, the driver sighed and says, 'It's because you slept back there, with nearly fifty bodies. You'll have had nightmares. Right?'

'Yes. Unbelievably horrible. I've had nightmares since joining this team, but last night's was the worst.'

'No doubt,' the driver said, waving his hand in a wide arc.

'This *is* the Jungle of Screaming Souls. It looks empty and innocent, but in fact it's crowded. There are so many ghosts and devils all over this battleground! I've been driving for this corpse-collecting team since early '73 but I still can't get used to the passengers who come out of their graves to talk to me. Not a night goes by without them waking me to have a chat. It terrifies me. All kinds of ghosts, new soldiers, old soldiers, soldiers from Division 10, Division 2, soldiers from the provincial armed forces, the Mobile Forces 320, Corps 559, sometimes women, and every now and again, some southern souls, from Saigon.' The driver spoke as though it was common knowledge.

'Met any old friends?' asked Kien.

'Sure! Even some from my own village. Blokes from my first unit. Once I met a cousin who died way back in sixty-five.'

'Do you speak to them?'

'Yes, but . . . well, differently. The way you speak in hell. There are no sounds, no words. It's hard to describe. It's like when you're dreaming – you know what I mean.'

'You can't actually do anything to help each other?' asked Kien. 'Do you talk about interesting things?'

'Not very. Just sad and pitiful things, really. Under the ground in the grave human beings aren't the same. You can look at each other, understand each other, but you can't do anything for each other.'

'If we found a way to tell them news of a victory would they be happier?' Kien asked.

'Come on! Even if we could, what would be the point? People in hell don't give a damn about wars. They don't remember killing. Killing is a career for the living, not the dead.'

'Still, wouldn't peacetime be an ideal moment for the resurrection of all the dead?'

'What? Peace? Damn it, peace is a tree that thrives only on the blood and bones of fallen comrades. The ones left behind in the Screaming Souls battlegrounds were the most honourable people. Without them there would be no peace,' the driver replied.

'That's a rotten way to look at it. There are so many good people, so many yet to be born, so many survivors now trying to live decent lives. Otherwise it's not been worth it. I mean, what's peace for? Or what's fighting for?' Kien asked.

'Okay, I'll grant you we have to have hope. But we don't even know if the next generation will get a chance to grow up, or if they do, how they'll grow up. We do know that many good people have been killed. Those of us who survived have all been trying to make something of ourselves, but not succeeding.

'But look at the chaotic post-war situation in the cities, with their black markets. Life is so frustrating, for all of us. And look at the bodies and the graves of our comrades! The ones who brought the peace. Shameful, my friend, shameful.'

'But isn't peace better than war?'

The driver seemed astonished. 'This kind of peace? In this kind of peace it seems people have unmasked themselves and revealed their true, horrible selves. So much blood, so many lives were sacrificed for what?'

'Damn it, what are you trying to say?' Kien asked.

'I'm not trying to say anything. I'm simply a soldier like you who'll now have to live with broken dreams and with pain. But, my friend, our era is finished. After this hard-won victory fighters like you, Kien, will never be normal again. You won't even speak with your normal voice, in the normal way again.'

'You're so damn gloomy. What a doom-laden attitude!'

'I am Tran Son, a soldier. That's why I'm a bit of a philosopher. You never curse your luck? Never feel elated? What did the dead ones tell you in your dreams last night? Call that normal?' he asked.

On the way out the Zil truck moves in slow, jerky movements. The road is bumpy, muddy and potholed. Son stays in first gear, the engine revving loudly as if about to explode. Kien looks out of the window, trying to lighten his mood.

The rain stops, but the air is dull, the sky lead-grey. Slowly they move away from the Screaming Souls Jungle and the whole forest area itself. Behind them the mountains, the streams, all drop away from view.

355

But strangely, Kien now feels another presence, feels someone is watching him. Is the final scene, the unfinished bloody dream of this morning, about to intrude itself in his mind? Will the pictures unfold against his wishes as he sits staring at the road?

Kien called to Son over the roar of the engine, asking if he'll be finished with MIA work after this tour of duty.

'Not sure. There's a lot of paperwork to do. What are your plans?'

'First, finish school. That means evening classes. Then try the university entrance exams. Right now my only skills are firing sub-machine-guns and collecting bodies. What about you, will you keep driving?'

The truck reached a drier section of road and Son was able to go up a gear, dropping the loud engine revs.

'When we're demobbed, I'll stop driving. I'll carry my guitar everywhere and be a singer. Sing and tell stories. "Gentlemen, brothers and sisters, please listen to my painful story, then I'll sing you a horror song of our times."'

'Very funny,' said Kien. 'If you ask me we'd do better to tell them to forget about the war altogether.'

'But how can we forget? We'll never forget any of it, never. Admit it. Go on, admit it!'

Christopher John Farley

MY FAVOURITE WAR

The Gulf War of 1991 will always be remembered as a media paradox – no other war in this century could be followed on television for twenty-four hours; yet nobody, least of all the press, seemed to know what was really going on.

Christopher John Farley's satirical novel, My Favourite War *(1997), tells the story of a young black newspaper reporter who is unexpectedly sent to the Gulf to cover the war.*

NEVER HAVE SO many known so little about so much. I had finally arrived at the bureaucracy of dunces that was the media community of the Persian Gulf War. When I stepped off the plane at the airport in Dhahran, I was hit by a blast of light and heat; the desert sun was unblinking, unforgiving. I had read that the temperature was supposed to drop to something manageable during the winter months here, but that certainly wasn't the case today. It would be hard for me to get my bearings in this draining desert heat, in a country I knew next to nothing about, and in wartime no less.

After Sojourner and I arrived at the Dhahran International Hotel, I realized I wasn't alone in my confusion and bewilderment. The five-star hotel was packed with reporters from all over America, journalists from small papers and large papers, TV crews and radio announcers. None of them had a clue either. They couldn't speak this country's language, they didn't know about the customs, they were all complaining bitterly about the relentless heat.

As a reporter, I knew firsthand that journalists weren't gods, that they weren't superheroes, that the stories they filed were patch jobs, hastily arranged, usually riddled with errors. But I guess in wartime that last little scrap within me that was optimistic and idealistic expected something different. I expected a press corps filled with grizzled supersleuths, willing to go anywhere and brave anything to get to the sludge at the bottom of the barrel of this war. But here they all were. Some of them were twentysomethings like me, waiting expectantly to see their first war. Others were fat, soft forty-year-olds, finally freed from their desks and hoping for a taste of action.

What disturbed me most was that these reporters wanted war. They were impatient for the action to start. They were tired of this foreign minister meeting that foreign minister, of the UN issuing resolutions, of the pollsters taking polls showing support for the use of force. They had come too far and had been waiting too long. They were tired of the sun and the sand and the prospect of stumbling upon the six-inch scorpions said to be somewhere in that sand. They were tired of the restrictions on alcohol and drugs. They had seen war in movies, read about it in books, heard the bitching about war from their draft-dodging Vietnam-era fathers and uncles, and now they wanted their own war. Covering a war was the culmination of any reporter's career and they wanted the culmination to begin. The diddling, the foreplay, the sloppy deep-throated kissing, the nipple-tweaking had all been going on for months. They were hot, sweaty, bothered, and they were ready to come, shouting 'Hallelujah,' and bucking their hips while simultaneously popping quarters into the vibrator bed. They wanted a wargasm and they wanted it now.

The hotel was overbooked. Sojourner and I would have to shar~ room.

we got to the room, we realized we'd have to share a ll. A very small bed. It was more of a cot, actually. t this was a five-star hotel, I said.

war brewing,' said Sojourner, tossing her luggage

on the bed. 'You want me to call room service, see if they can send up a more comfortable war?'

On-site media coverage of the Gulf War was organized into a pool system. The US military claimed it couldn't accommodate the flood of media people, so members of the press were forced into a cooperative in which rotating groups of reporters would be allowed to go out into the field with troops, each group accompanied by a military guide. The reporters would then file pool reports that would be shared by the whole cooperative.

The pool system was a perfect fit for a generation of reporters weaned on corporate newspapers, press-release reporting, and celebrity press junkets where ten reporters sat around a table interviewing one Hollywood star and then called it journalism. The pool system was part of what helped Bush sell the war; it effectively castrated the press. Reporters would think twice about risking their lives or reputations to get a story when it was just gonna be part of a pool report anyways. Pool reporting was notoriously slipshod. No gain, no pain, was the operative philosophy for many of the journalists involved.

In Vietnam, reporters roamed the countryside freely, hunting down stories, exposing atrocities. That kind of coverage, the ability to expose the war's horrors, helped shape public opinion and put a stop to Vietnam. In the Persian Gulf, the post-Vietnam military wasn't about to make that same mistake. All reporters were to be accompanied by military-provided press representatives, chaperons for this Prom Date from Hell, supposedly to look out for the safety of reporters and show them around, but in truth, these press officers were passive-aggressive censors. They weren't always blatant about shaping coverage, but it was hard to write a story that was critical of the war when your guide was one of the warriors.

There were four main pools – the TV pool, the radio pool, the photo pool, and the print pool.

The head of the print pool was a guy named Nick Adams. Back in the States he was a small-time editor for the *Chicago Tribune*. Running the print pool involved pushing a lot of papers, stroking a lot of erect egos until they spurted out contentment. It was a thankless, time-consuming job that paid nothing. Adams volunteered for the position and took to it as eagerly as a televangelist at a hookers' convention. You just know that back in high school, Adams was one of those slimeballs in the safety patrol – the losers with the orange sashes that told other kids to stop running in the halls and gave them a ticket when they failed to comply. In the States, Adams was a small-fry journalist; here, he was a big shot, in control, wearing the metaphorical orange sash.

Every day a list was posted containing the names of the reporters allowed to go into the field and the military units they would be assigned to. It was a long list, a rotating list, and it took a while to ascend to the top. That is, unless you got to know Nick Adams. If he knew you, if he liked you, Adams could hook you up with field slot, and you could finally get out of the hotel and do some real reporting. If he didn't like you, you might as well hang a 'Do Not Disturb' sign on your hotel-suite doorknob, 'cause it was going to be a long, indoor war for you.

Sojourner and I went to talk to the print-pool czar. Adams was a small pimply man, dressed from head to toe in Banana Republic pseudo safari gear and a cowboy hat. When he took off his hat you could see he was a hopelessly balding man, with just a few Charlie Brown/Homer Simpson strands of hair stretched and spun and teased across his bald pate.

Sojourner didn't have much luck trying to get herself inserted on to the list. Adams didn't like her. He was familiar with her columns in the *Post* and he didn't like her attitude, didn't think her perspective would be one that would really contribute to the field. After all, she was into black issues, women's issues, human-interest stories. He didn't come right out and say it, but Adams thought this was a man's war, and it should be covered by men. It was bad enough that the military had women in probable combat zones, but he wouldn't make the same mistake with the print corps. He wanted the pool reports that came back to have a hard, male, five-o'clock-shadow, big-swinging-hairy-brass-balls, Y-chromosome edge. He knew the way men like that thought. He knew the kind of stories they'd bring back. The kind of stories he could predict.

'Listen, I think I get your gist here,' said Sojourner. 'It seems to me that you want me to prove I can hack it out in the field. I'm a reporter for the *Washington Post*. You've got a male reporter from *GQ* filing stories from the *front*, for Christ's sake.'

'L-l-l-listen,' said Adams, who had a stutter. 'I-I-I-I have two reporters from the *Post* out in the field already. W-w-w-what can I do? If a slot comes up, I'll call you. That's the best I can d-d-d-do.'

'Goddamn military doesn't need to censor the press,' Sojourner muttered as we took the elevator downstairs to grab a bite to eat. 'We're censoring our own goddamn selves.'

How so?

'The guy knows I'm the shit,' she said, lighting a cigarette. 'He doesn't want any real reporters in the field. Just his buddies, the men, the ones who are gonna play by the rules and do the stories that don't rock the boat, or that rock it in a way everyone can anticipate. So the public gets bland coverage and General One-hundred-and-seventy-IQ Pinpoint doesn't have to raise a finger to enforce the homogeneity.'

Clark Gorrelesmen, a.k.a. 'the Girly-Man', was a reporter for the *Los Angeles Times*. He wasn't gay or effeminate, but everyone called him the Girly-Man because there was just something about the guy that called for it. He was a redhead, but he was considered the *Los Angeles Times*'s Golden Boy. Here he was, just twenty-six years old, fresh out of Stanford, and he was covering a war, with real bullets and everything. One look at him and I was disgusted. Here he was, in the desert, wearing a blue blazer, a button-down white shirt, striped tie, khaki designer pants, and Dock-Sider shoes.

'Just work within the pool system and you'll be okay,' the Girly-Man told me.

Are you one of the pool coordinators?

'No, I just like to let the new people know that there is a pool and that people need to abide by the rules. If one person goes unilateral and breaks the pool and gets a scoop, the system breaks down.'

'Oh, I see,' said Sojourner, elbowing me in the side as if to say, 'What an asshole dweeb!'

'If I'm going to forsake scoops to work with the system, I think we all have to do it,' explained the Girly-Man.

Sojourner was ticked about our meeting with Adams. We sat in the snackbar of the hotel drinking sodas.

'See, this is what happens when you have gutless bureaucrats running news organizations instead of people who have some sort of moral centre, some sort of aggressive, transgressive take on the world.'

Sojourner said newspapers had been co-opted by big money, corporate interests. There were fewer newspapers in America today than at any time in modern American history. Ten companies controlled more than half of all the newspaper business in America and the media was growing more oligarchic every year. the *New York Times* owns the *Sarasota Herald-Tribune*. The *Washington Post* owns *Newsweek*. Time-Warner owns Warner Bros., *Time* magazine, and *Life* magazine. Knight-Ridder owns the *Miami Herald*, the *Philadelphia Inquirer*, and the *San Jose Mercury News*. The big companies that run these media outlets weren't concerned with truth or justice or news, they were concerned with the bottom line, with profit margins, with purchasing other news organizations.

So they hire gutless editors to staff their papers, I said.

'Exactly. And only a gutless wonder would agree to a pool system. It goes against everything journalism is about! Can you imagine Watergate being cracked under a goddamn pool? The My Lai massacre? I mean, instead of just being out there and getting a story, we got to be dealing with this whole system, with personalities, and pencil pushers and acne-faced assholes like Nick Adams. That bastard! It's a waste of my time. I should be out there reporting.'

What we need to do is go over Adams's head, I said. Right over his bald little head.

Colonel George Willard was director of the military's Joint Information Bureau. He was the guy that actually, physically matched reporters with military units in the field. Adams really just did the paperwork.

The Colonel was a public-relations flack down to the bone. He would answer questions fully and completely and say absolutely nothing. He would promise you the moon with a smile and stall you and stall you and act like he was moving heaven and earth to get you what you wanted when actually he was doing absolutely zero. This guy was adept at screwing people over and making them like it. The guy would blow smoke up your ass and make you think he had transformed you into a fire-breathing dragon. And you, completely bamboozled as to what was going on, totally ignorant of the fact you'd just been fucked by this flack, would say, 'Thank you, sir, thank you for transforming me into this flame-throwing, legendary, mythical flying lizard. Thank you.'

Colonel Willard's office was on the very top floor of the hotel. The shades were drawn, so you couldn't see inside – I was told he spent most of his time behind closed doors, at his desk, quietly running things. It was a tastefully decorated office, like a room at an Ivy League club. He had a small bar in the corner of the room with miniature liquor bottles, like the ones they serve on airplanes. Behind his desk, on the wall, there was a sign that read: 'Salus Populi Suprema lex.' My high school Latin was rusty, but it meant either 'The safety of the people is the supreme law' or 'Time to make the doughnuts.'

And the Colonel had eaten his share of doughnuts. He was a large man, a fat man, which probably explained why he liked to keep to his desk. Unlike some of the other ya-hoos in the service, however, Willard struck me as very cultured, as well-read as some of my friends from college.

'Bismarck once said that fools learn by experience, but wise men learn by the experience of others,' Colonel Willard was saying. He had a voice that was a subtle cross between Thurston Howell III and William F. Buckley. 'It's good advice.'

'Be that as it may, I still want to get out in the field,' said Sojourner. 'Can you make it happen?'

'Sure, we can get you out into the field, Ms Zapader,' the Colonel said. 'And I'm sure there won't be a problem finding a slot for your assistant either. Just tell me when and where you want to go.'

'Today. Anywhere,' said Sojourner immediately.

'Ooooo, today might be tough,' he said.

'Okay then. Anytime, anywhere.'

'I'm gonna get back to you all on this. But I think it's a doer,' said the Colonel.

A friendly, talkative private named Thelonious Webster picked Sojourner and me up at the hotel and drove us out to visit the 2nd Infantry Division of the Army's XI Corps. Lying on his dashboard was a tin bugle with a mute in it that rattled as he drove. 'My real first name is Walter,' Thelonious confided amiably. 'But I like jazz, so there you go.' The public-relations officer who met us once we arrived wasn't so friendly. His name was Captain Bardman and he was a bitter man. He had so much nose hair it was a wonder he could breathe and so much ear hair I was surprised he wasn't deaf. Curiously, he had no eyebrows, which made his eyes look mean. He appeared to be about forty years old. The word was that he was stuck, careerwise, angry about it, and taking it out on the world. He was always grinding and clicking his teeth together in frustration. People called him Cap'n Crunch behind his back. He was not exactly pleased to be taking non-Army folks on a sightseeing trip.

'I don't want you people wandering around,' said Cap'n

Crunch to us as soon as we stepped out of the jeep. 'You go where I show you. I say, "Jump," you say, "How high?" Got it?' He turned around and began to walk briskly toward the encampment.

'Can you tell us a bit about the 2nd Infantry?' said Sojourner, pulling out her notepad and walking alongside him.

'Hey, I'm not here to hold your hand. We're here to prosecute a war, all right? I'm gonna walk you to where you need to go, show you what you need to see, and then Private Webster will take you back. Are we clear?'

He continued his fast-paced walk, grinding his teeth all the way.

Public affairs officer Cap'n Crunch was true to his word. He was helpful not one little bit. He stood around as Sojourner and I talked to troops. He interrupted questions that seemed to be even remotely controversial. He finished other soldiers' sentences during interviews. He didn't let us talk to any officers.

'They're too busy,' said Cap'n Crunch. 'We got a war to prepare for, got a problem with that?'

Sojourner spotted one soldier who looked like he had lost a finger. His sleeve was drenched with blood. He was waiting for medics or something. Cap'n Crunch wouldn't let us speak to him. I decided that this had gone far enough.

Where's the bathroom? I said.

'I'll have to come with you,' said Cap'n Crunch.

What, do you want to hold my fucking cock while I piss? I said, hoping this was the kind of gutter language a career Army man could understand.

That gave me a chance to wander off. I walked in a generally straight line to the latrines, but, unencumbered by the evil Cap'n, I got a few quotes on the way. The troops I talked to were itchy to start the fighting. Most of them were really down on the living conditions; it was a lot worse than what was being printed in the papers. They wanted the war to begin and to go home. Poor saps. It was gonna be a bloodbath for them. And it wasn't gonna be quick.

Cap'n Crunch was watching us. Occasionally his head would tilt back sharply and he'd throw down a gulp of some sort of pinkish liquid he kept in a small bottle, and then his mean eyes would refocus on us. Now and again, when we'd talk to soldiers, he'd pull out a tape recorder and start taping.

'What's that for?' said one spooked nineteen-year-old private from Tennessee.

'It's for the fucking Secretary of Defense,' said Cap'n Crunch.

The private didn't say much of anything after that. The whole trip was a waste in terms of getting some good raw-meat copy. So Sojourner and I decided to go back to the hotel and plan our next move.

'Okay, I got a column out of that, but not a very good column,' said Sojourner, smoking and flipping through her reporter's pad. 'I tried to talk to this private and Crunch pulled out a piece of paper and read a very long warning to the guy that essentially said he didn't have to say word one to me.'

That's standard practice. They call it the Miranda warning. These Army flacks read the soldiers their rights and then make it impossible for reporters to get candid quotes out of them.

'This war is no easy walk.' She exhaled a column of smoke. 'We gotta dig deeper.'

What's on your mind?

'The deadline's soon, day after tomorrow. January fifteen. I want to cover this war, I don't want a press release.'

I'm with you so far.

'Here's the thing then, honey. Tomorrow we break the pool. Go off on our own. You and I have to find the war. We're not gonna find it in the damn hotel room. And we're not gonna find it with Cap'n Crunch hovering over our shoulders.'

*

Lying awake in the hotel room. Tomorrow, the real war would begin for me. The UN deadline was almost up. I wondered if Bush would really do it. Was he really crazy enough to start bombing Iraq? It was going to be such a disaster. Saddam had mined all the oilfields; everyone was saying it was going to be a huge ecological mess, that the clouds of smoke rising from the burning oilfields in Kuwait could trigger a planet-wide climate shift, perhaps a new ice age. This was all biblical stuff, end-of-the-world stuff. Leaders today had too much power. Back in the days of, say, Napoleon, power-drunk leaders could only mess up things for a decade or so, and then the grass would grow back over all the bodies, the battlefields would become cornfields, and everyone would forget what all the fighting was about in the first place. Today, people like Bush and Saddam Hussein had the power to wreck things forever, to destroy the world, to screw up oceans and wipe out species.

The thought of danger was starting to become real to me. I had gone through life, as most noncombatants do, feeling as if great personal, physical harm happened to other people. But that bleeding soldier with the missing finger made me feel otherwise. People could bleed here. People could die. We could get hit by one of those Scud missiles, die from a poison gas attack, get hit by friendly fire. This was no longer a game, or just a job, or some ridiculous *National Now!* story on big vegetables. If I broke the pool with Sojourner tomorrow, it was all for real. And it was real enough to get my ass killed. A Nikki Giovanni poem was running through my mind: 'We kill for UN & NATO & USA and everywhere for all alphabet but BLACK. Can we learn to kill WHITE for BLACK? Learn to kill, niggers.'

That night I had a dream. No, it wasn't really a dream. It was an image that floated into my mind before I fell completely asleep. It applied too literally to my situation to be a dream. I was thinking about *Ascending and Descending*, a lithograph by M.C. Escher. It was a picture of monks trudging eternal loops in a monastery. Twenty-six monks walk up and walk down forty-five stairs only to find themselves back where they started, prisoners and participants in one of Escher's optical illusions. Were they going up or going down? Down or up? I guess the point was that these truth seekers had found a path but lost their goal.

BIOGRAPHICAL NOTES

Isaac Babel was born in Odessa in 1894, the son of a Jewish tradesman. At the age of twenty-one he went to St Petersburg, where he had to avoid the Tsarist police because he lacked the residence certificate required of all Jews. Maxim Gorky was the first to encourage Babel by printing two of his stories in his magazine. During the First World War, Babel fought with the Tsarist army and in 1917 went over to the Bolsheviks.

In 1923 he returned to literature with a number of short stories printed in periodicals. An instant literary success, these formed the nucleus of the *Odessa Stories*, a group of vivid sketches of Russian Jewish life, and *Red Cavalry* (1926), written out of his experiences with Budyonny's cavalry in the Polish campaign of 1920. Other stories, scenarios and plays followed. Unable to respond to the demands of political conformism that were being made on him, however, Babel was arrested suddenly in 1939. He died, possibly in 1941.

Pat Barker was born in Thornaby-on-Tees in 1943. She was educated at the London School of Economics and has been a teacher of history and politics. Her books include *Union Street* (1982), which has been filmed as *Stanley and Iris*; *Blow Your House Down* (1984); *Liza's England* (1986), formerly *The Century's Daughter*; *The Man Who Wasn't There* (1989); *Another World* (1998); and her acclaimed *Regeneration* trilogy: *Regeneration* (1991), which was filmed in 1997, *The Eye in the Door* (1993), and *The Ghost Road*, winner of the 1995 Booker Prize.

Louis Begley lives in New York City. He is the author of two novels, *Wartime Lies* and *About Schmidt*. *Wartime Lies* won the Pen Hemingway Foundation Award and the *Irish Times*/Aer Lingus International Fiction Prize.

Louis de Bernières is the author of *The War of Don Emmanuel's Nether Parts* (1990), *Señor Viva and the Coca Lord* (1991), *The Troublesome Offspring of Cardinal Guzman* (1992), and *Captain Corelli's Mandolin* (1994). He lives in London.

Heinrich Böll was born in Cologne in 1917 and brought up in a liberal Catholic pacifist family. Drafted into the Wehrmacht, he served on the Russian and French fronts and was wounded four times before he found himself in an American prisoner-of-war camp. After the war he enrolled at the University of Cologne, but dropped out to write about his experiences as a soldier. His first novel, *The Train Was on Time*, was published in 1949, and he went on to become one of the most prolific and important of postwar German writers. In 1972 he was awarded the Nobel Prize for Literature.

His best-known novels include *Billiards at Half-Past Nine*, *The Clown*, *The Lost Honour of Katharina Blum* and *Group Portrait with Lady*. He is also famous as a writer of short stories. Böll served for several years as president of the International PEN and was a leading defender of the intellectual freedom of writers throughout the world. He died in July 1985.

Martin Booth is a poet, novelist and critic. His novels include *Black Chameleon*, *The Jade Pavilion*, *Hiroshima Joe*, *Dreaming of Samarkand* and, most recently, *The Industry of Souls*, which was shortlisted for the 1998 Booker Prize.

Elizabeth Bowen was born in Dublin in 1899, the only child of an Irish lawyer and landowner, and was educated at Downe House School in Kent. She travelled a good deal, dividing most of her time between London and her family home in County Cork.

Her first book, a collection of short stories, *Encounters*, appeared in 1923, followed by another, *Ann Lee's*, in 1926. *The Hotel* (1927) was her first novel, and was followed by *The Last September* (1929), *Joining Charles* (1929), another book of short stories, *Friends and Relations* (1931), *To the North* (1932), *The Cat Jumps* (short stories, 1934), *The House in Paris* (1935), *The Death of the Heart* (1938), *Look at All the Roses* (short stories, 1941), *The Demon Lover* (short stories, 1945), *The Heat of the Day* (1949), *Collected Impressions* (essays, 1950), *The Shelbourne* (1951), *A World of Love* (1955), *A Time in Rome* (1960), *Afterthought* (essays, 1962), *The Little Girls* (1964), *A Day in the Dark* (1965), and her last book, *Eva Trout* (1969).

She was awarded the CBE in 1948, and received the honorary degree of Doctor of Letters from Trinity College, Dublin, in 1949 and from Oxford University in 1956. In the same year she was appointed Lacy Martin Donnelly Fellow at Bryn Mawr College in the United States. In 1965 she was made a Companion of Literature by the Royal Society of Literature. Elizabeth Bowen died in 1973.

William Boyd was born in 1952 in Accra, Ghana, and was brought up there and in Nigeria. He was educated at Gordonstoun School and at the universities of Nice, Glasgow and Oxford. Between 1980 and 1983 he was a lecturer in English literature at St Hilda's College, Oxford.

His novels include *A Good Man in Africa* (1981), *An Ice-Cream War* (1982), *Stars and Bars* (1984), *The New Confessions* (1987), *Brazzaville Beach* (1990), *The Blue Afternoon* (1993) and *Armadillo* (1998). Eight of his screenplays have been filmed, including *A Good Man in Africa*, based on his first novel. William Boyd lives in London.

Kay Boyle (1903–1992) was a novelist, short-story writer and poet. Born in Minnesota, her expatriate years in France before her return to the United States in 1941 provided her with much of the material for her fiction. Her novels include *Gentlemen, I Address You Privately* (1933), *Primer for Combat* (1942), *A Frenchman Must Die* (1946), *Generation Without Farewell* (1960) and *The Underground Woman* (1974).

John Horne Burns was born in Boston, Massachusetts in 1916. He was educated at Harvard and for five years worked as an English teacher in Connecticut. In 1942 he was drafted, and spent the war as an intelligence officer in North Africa and Italy, reading prisoner-of-war mail.

After the war he returned to America and to teaching for a year. In 1947 his first novel, *The Gallery* – loosely based on the author's wartime experience in Naples – was published to great critical acclaim. The success of *The Gallery* immediately established John Horne Burns's reputation, and he abandoned teaching to become a full-time writer. He wrote two other novels, *Lucifer with a Book* (1949) and *A Cry of Freedom* (1951). In 1949 he left America and settled in Italy, where he died in 1953 at the age of thirty-seven. At the time of his death he was working on a novel based on the life of St Francis of Assisi.

Italo Calvino was born in Cuba in 1923 and grew up in San Remo, Italy. He was an essayist and a journalist, and among his best-known works of fiction are *Invisible Cities*, *If on a winter's night a traveller*, *Marcovaldo* and *Mr Palomar*. He died in 1985.

Philip Caputo served with the Marines in Vietnam. After mustering out in 1967, he went on to a prize-winning career as a journalist for the *Chicago Tribune*, covering the war in Beirut and the fall of Saigon. In 1975 he was wounded in Beirut and, during his convalescence, completed the manuscript for *A Rumor of War*, his acclaimed Vietnam memoir. In 1977 he left the *Tribune* to devote himself to writing full-time. His novels are *Horn of Africa*, *DelCorso's Gallery*, *Indian Country* and *Equation for Evil*. He is also the author of a collection of novellas, *Exiles*, and a second volume of memoir, *Means of Escape*.

Louis-Ferdinand Céline, born in 1894, was one of the most controversial French writers of the century. *Journey to the End of the Night*, first published in 1932, became an instant bestseller and was followed by a string of other books, all based on the experience of his own life, written in the vernacular of his day and with a frankness of description that is still remarkable today.

His descriptions of war and poverty would seem to come from a man on the Left, but he was to turn to the Right after a visit to the Soviet Union in 1936. He became a rabid anti-Semite and a supporter of the German occupation of France. He was sentenced to death *in absentia* in 1945 and escaped to Denmark where he lived under police guard until 1951. Pardoned in 1952 he returned to Paris where he died in 1961.

Bruce Chatwin was born in Sheffield in 1940. After attending Marlborough College he began work as a porter at Sotheby's. Eight years later, having become one of Sotheby's youngest directors, he abandoned his job to pursue his passion for world travel. Between 1972 and 1975 he worked for the *Sunday Times*, before announcing his departure in a telegram: 'Gone to Patagonia for six months.'

This trip inspired the first of Chatwin's books, *In Patagonia*. Two of his books have been made into feature films: *The Viceroy of Ouidah* (retitled *Cobra Verde*), directed by Werner Herzog, and the British Film Institute's *On the Black Hill*. On publication *The Songlines* went straight to No. 1 in the *Sunday Times* bestseller list and stayed in the top ten for nine months. His novel, *Utz*, was shortlisted for the 1988 Booker Prize. He died in January 1989.

Jean-Louis Curtis was born in 1917 at Orthez in the Basses-Pyrenees. He was educated at a local college and the Sorbonne in Paris. Afterwards he spent a considerable time in England, where he made a particular study of the works of Huxley.

As Professor of English at Bayonne he wrote his first novel *Alceste Pas Perdu* (1943), followed by *Les Jeunes Hommes* (1945) which was awarded the Prix Cazes.

During 1944–5 he joined the Pyrenean *Corps Franc*, and as a member of the Army he later fought in Alsace and Germany and spent some time in Württemberg and in the Palatinate with the occupation forces. *Siegfried* was the result of this experience, published in 1946. *The Forests of the Night* was first published in France in 1947. His other novels include *Les justes causes* (1954), *La parade* (1960), *Un jeune couple* (1967) and *L'étage noble* (1978).

Shusaku Endo was born in Tokyo in 1923. He graduated in French Literature from Keio University, then studied for several years in Lyons on a scholarship from the French government.

Widely regarded as the leading writer in Japan, he has won a series of outstanding literary awards and his work has been translated into seventeen languages. His books include *The Samurai, The Sea and the Poison* and *Stained Glass Elegies*.

Christopher John Farley has worked as a journalist for the *Boston Globe, Chicago Tribune* and *USA Today*. He is a staff writer for *Time* magazine where he reports on national affairs and popular culture. Born in Kingston, Jamaica in 1966, he was raised in upstate New York. *My Favourite War* is his first novel.

John Fowles is the author of *The Collector* (1963), *The Aristos* (1964), *The Magus* (1966), *The French Lieutenant's Woman* (1969), *The Ebony Tower* (1974), *Daniel Martin* (1977), *Mantissa* (1982) and *A Maggot* (1985). He lives in Dorset.

A.D. Gristwood was born in Catford, south London in 1893. He volunteered in the summer of 1915 and served as Rifleman 302064, 2/5th London Rifle Brigade in France, where he was wounded twice. Encouraged by H.G. Wells, he wrote *The*

Somme which was published in 1927. He died in 1933 as a result of his war injuries.

Robert Harris was a reporter on the BBC's *Panorama* and *Newsnight* programmes before becoming Political Editor of the *Observer* in 1987, and then a columnist on the *Sunday Times*. His five non-fiction books include *Selling Hitler* (1986), an account of the forging of Hitler's diaries. His first novel, *Fatherland* (1992), was shortlisted for the Whitbread First Novel Prize, and was followed by *Enigma* (1995) and *Archangel* (1998).

Larry Heinemann was born in 1944 in Chicago, where he now lives with his wife and two children. In 1966 he was inducted into the army and served a tour of duty with the 25th Division in Vietnam as a combat infantryman. He is the author of two novels, *Close Quarters* (1977) and *Paco's Story* (1986).

Joseph Heller was born in 1923 in Brooklyn, New York. He served as a bombardier in the Second World War, afterwards attending the colleges of New York University and Columbia University and then Oxford, the last on a Fulbright scholarship. He then taught for two years at Pennsylvania State University before returning to New York, where he began a successful career in advertising. It was during this time that he had the idea for *Catch-22*. Working on the novel in spare moments and evenings at home, it took him eight years to complete and was first published in 1961.

Heller's second novel, *Something Happened*, was published in 1974, and was followed by *Good as Gold* (1979), *God Knows* (1984) and *Closing Time* (1994). His memoir, *Now and Then: From Coney Island to Here*, was published in 1998.

Ernest Hemingway was born in 1899. His father was a doctor and he was the second of six children. Their home was at Oak Park, a Chicago suburb.

In 1917 Hemingway joined the Kansas City *Star* as a cub reporter. The following year he volunteered to work as an ambulance driver on the Italian front where he was badly wounded but twice decorated for his services. He returned to America in 1919 and married in 1921. In 1922 he reported on the Greco-Turkish war, then two years later resigned from journalism to devote himself to fiction and settled in Paris.

Hemingway's first two published works were *Three Stories and Ten Poems* and *In Our Time*, but it was the satirical novel, *The Torrents of Spring*, which established his name more widely. His international reputation was firmly secured by his next three books: *Fiesta*, *Men Without Women* and *A Farewell to Arms*. He was passionately involved with bullfighting, big-game hunting and deep-sea fishing, and his writing reflected this. He visited Spain during the Civil War and described his experience in the bestseller, *For Whom the Bell Tolls*.

Recognition of his position in contemporary literature came in 1954 when he was awarded the Nobel Prize for Literature, following the publication of *The Old Man and the Sea*. Ernest Hemingway died in 1961.

Sebastien Japrisot was born in Marseilles and was already a published writer at the age of seventeen. He received early recognition as a crime novelist, and is now one of France's most popular writers. His novels have all been made into motion pictures, and he has himself written several screenplays.

In Great Britain he built up a reputation with his crime stories, among them *The Lady in the Car with Glasses and a Gun* and *The 10.30 from Marseilles*. Japrisot won the Prix Interallié with *A Very Long Engagement*.

James Jones was born in Robinson, Illinois, in 1922. He joined the army in 1939, rose to the rank of sergeant, and won a Purple Heart and a Bronze Star. He was discharged from the army in 1944 and went on to study at the University of New York.

His first novel, *From Here to Eternity*, was published in 1951 and became an instant bestseller. His other novels include *Some Came Running* (1957), *The Pistol* (1959), *The Thin Red Line* (1962), *Go to the Widow Maker* (1967), *The Merry Month of May* (1971) and *A Touch of Danger* (1973). James Jones died in 1977.

Christopher J. Koch was born and educated in Tasmania. For a good deal of his life, he was a broadcasting producer. He worked for UNESCO in Indonesia, and has travelled extensively in Asia.

Koch has been a full-time writer since 1972. He is the author of five novels – *The Boys in the Island*, *Across the Sea Wall*, *The Year of Living Dangerously*, *The Doubleman* and *Highways to a War* – and one collection of essays, *Crossing the Gap*. The screenplay of *The Year of Living Dangerously*, co-written by Koch, was nominated for an Academy Award. He now lives in Sydney.

Wolfgang Koeppen was born in 1906 in Greifswald on the Baltic Coast. He had a career as a writer and journalist in Berlin before the Second World War, but his reputation is based essentially on the trilogy of novels he published shortly after it: *Pigeons in the Grass* (1951), *The Hothouse* (1953) and *Death in Rome* (1954). These books remain unequalled in postwar German fiction for their combination of stylistic innovation and trenchant political criticism. Subsequently, Koeppen has published travel books and a short memoir of his childhood, but no further fiction. He lives in Munich.

Laurie Lee was born in Stroud, Gloucestershire, and educated at Slad village school and Stroud Central School. At the age of nineteen he walked to London and then travelled on foot through Spain, where he was trapped by the outbreak of the Civil War – to which he later returned by crossing the Pyrenees, as described in his book *As I Walked Out One Midsummer Morning*.

He published five books of poems: *The Sun My Monument*

(1944); *The Bloom of Candles* (1947); *My Many-Coated Man* (1955), *Pocket Poems* (1960); and *Selected Poems* (1983). His other works include a verse play for radio, *The Voyage of Magellan* (1948); a record of his travels in Andalusia, *A Rose for Winter* (1955); *The Firstborn* (1964); a collection of his occasional writing, *I Can't Stay Long* (1975); *Two Women* (1983); and three bestselling volumes of autobiography, *Cider with Rosie* (1959), which has sold over five million copies worldwide, *As I Walked Out One Midsummer Morning* (1969), and *A Moment of War* (1991), now published together in one volume as *Red Sky at Sunrise* (1992). Laurie Lee died in 1998.

Alistair MacLean, the son of a Scots Minister, was brought up in the Scottish Highlands. In 1941, at the age of eighteen, he joined the Royal Navy; two and a half years spent aboard a cruiser were later to give him the background for *HMS Ulysses*, his first novel. He went on to write twenty-nine bestselling novels, many of which have been filmed, including *The Guns of Navarone*, *Force 10 from Navarone*, *Where Eagles Dare* and *Bear Island*. He died in 1987.

Norman Mailer was born in New Jersey in 1923. He grew up in Brooklyn and entered Harvard University to study engineering when he was only sixteen. During the Second World War, Mailer served in the Philippines, an experience which formed the basis of his debut novel, *The Naked and the Dead*.

A major figure in postwar American literature, his other works include *Barbary Shore*, *The Deer Park*, *Advertisements for Myself* (for which he was awarded both the Pulitzer Prize and the National Book Award), *Ancient Evenings*, *Harlot's Ghost* and, most recently, *The Gospel According to the Son*.

David Malouf is recognized as one of Australia's finest writers. His novels include *Johnno*, *An Imaginary Life*, *Harland's Half Acre*, *The Great World*, *Remembering Babylon* and *The Conversations at Curlow Creek*. He has also written five collections of poetry and three opera libretti. He lives in Sydney.

André Malraux was born in France in 1901 and educated in Paris where he studied archaeology and orientalism. His first visit to Asia was in 1923, when he became involved in revolutionary activities in China. The visit resulted in his book *Les Conquérants* (1928). This was followed by *La Voie royale* (1930) and *La Condition humaine* (1933), which won the Prix Goncourt.

In the middle and late 1930s Malraux became one of France's leading anti-Fascists, and organized a volunteer air squadron to fight for the Republicans in Spain. His novel dealing with the early part of the war in Spain, *Days of Hope* (1938), was written close to the events.

After a distinguished career in the Second World War, Malraux became involved in the Gaullist movement. He was Minister of Information from 1945–6 and became Minister of State at the inception of the Fifth Republic in 1959. After de Gaulle's withdrawal from politics in 1969, Malraux continued to be active both in the intellectual and the international fronts. He was a member of the American Academy of Arts and Sciences, an Honorary Doctor of Civil Law at Oxford, an Officier de la Légion d'Honneur and a Compagnon de la Libération. Malraux died in 1976.

Stratis Myrivilis was born in Sykamia, Lesbos in 1892. He wrote his first novel, *Life in a Tomb*, in journal form as a sergeant in the trenches of the Macedonian front. It became one of the most successful and widely read works of fiction in Greece since its publication in serial form in 1923–4, despite its inclusion on the list of censored books under both Metaxas and the German occupation. It is the first volume in a trilogy containing *The Mermaid Madonna* and *The Schoolmistress with the Golden Eyes*.

A prolific author, Myrivilis was also an active journalist and broadcaster, being General Programme Director for the Greek National Broadcasting Institute from 1936 to 1951 (excluding the period of German occupation, when he was dismissed because of a broadcast he gave calling on Greeks to resist). After the war he was elected President of the National Society of Greek Writers. He died in 1969.

Bao Ninh was born in Hanoi in 1952. During the Vietnam War he served in the Glorious 27th Youth Brigade. Of the five hundred who went to war with the brigade in 1969, he is one of the ten who survived. A huge bestseller in Vietnam, *The Sorrow of War* is his first novel.

Tim O'Brien served as an infantryman in Vietnam and later worked as a national affairs reporter for the *Washington Post*. Born in Minnesota, he now lives in Boston, Massachusetts.

When *If I Die in a Combat Zone*, his first book, was published in 1973, it established him as one of the leading American writers of his generation, a status that was confirmed when his novel *Going After Cacciato* won the 1979 National Book Award. His other books include *The Things They Carried* (1990), *In the Lake of the Woods* (1994) and *Tomcat in Love* (1999).

Michael Ondaatje was born in Sri Lanka and lives in Toronto. His books include *Coming Through Slaughter*, *The Collected Works of Billy the Kid*, *The Cinnamon Peeler*, *Running in the Family*, *In the Skin of a Lion* and *The English Patient*.

Erich Maria Remarque was born in Osnabrück in 1898. Exiled from Nazi Germany, and deprived of his citizenship, he lived in America and Switzerland. His novels include *All Quiet on the Western Front*, *The Road Back*, *Three Comrades*, *The Sparkling of Life* and *A Time to Love and a Time to Die*. Remarque died in 1970.

James Salter was born in New Jersey in 1925. He is the author of *The Hunters* (1957), *The Arm of Flesh* (1961), *A Sport and a Pastime* (1967), *Light Years* (1975), *Solo Faces* (1981),

Dusk and Other Stories (1988) and his memoirs, *Burning the Days* (1997). He won the PEN/Faulkner Award for Fiction in 1989.

Siegfried Sassoon was born at Brenchley, Kent, in 1886. He was educated at Marlborough Grammar School and Clare College, Cambridge. After university, he lived at home and wrote poems which were privately printed.

He enlisted at the outbreak of the First World War and was sent to France as a second lieutenant where he won the Military Cross. In 1917 he threw his MC into the Mersey and publicly announced his refusal to go back to the front. He expected to be court-martialled but was sent to Craiglockart Hospital near Edinburgh, thanks to the intervention of his friend Robert Graves. There he befriended and encouraged the poet Wilfred Owen, before returning to his regiment, with whom he served in Palestine and France until July 1918.

His attitude towards the war found fierce expression in his poetry, including the collections *Counterattack* (1918) and *Satirical Poems* (1926). His fiction includes the autobiographical trilogy, *The Complete Memoirs of George Sherston*, containing *Memoirs of a Fox-Hunting Man* (1928), *Memoirs of an Infantry Officer* (1930) and *Sherston's Progress* (1936). He was awarded the CBE in 1951 and the Queen's Medal for Poetry in 1957. Sassoon died in Heytesbury, Wiltshire, in 1967.

Kurt Vonnegut was born in Indianapolis in 1922 and studied biochemistry at Cornell University. During the Second World War he served in Europe and, as a prisoner of war in Germany, witnessed the destruction of Dresden by Allied bombers, an experience which inspired his classic novel *Slaughterhouse-Five*. He is the author of fourteen other novels, most recently *Timequake*, a collection of stories and three non-fiction books. He lives in New York City.

SELECT BIBLIOGRAPHY

This is a list of some of the titles we considered. In many cases we wanted to include extracts but found none sufficiently representative and/or self-contained.

First World War

ALDINGTON, RICHARD, *Death of a Hero* (London: Chatto & Windus 1929)

ALVERDES, PAUL, *Changed Men* (London: Martin Secker 1933)

BARBUSSE, HENRI, *Under Fire* (1916; trans. London: J.M. Dent 1917)

BARKER, PAT, *Regeneration* (London: Viking 1991)

BARKER, PAT, *The Eye in the Door* (London: Viking 1993)

BARKER, PAT, *The Ghost Road* (London: Viking 1995)

BARNES, JULIAN, 'Evermore', in: *Cross Channel* (London: Jonathan Cape 1996)

BOYD, WILLIAM, *An Ice-Cream War* (London: Hamish Hamilton 1982)

BOYD, WILLIAM, *The New Confessions* (London: Hamish Hamilton 1987)

BRIFFAULT, ROBERT, *Europa* (London: Robert Hale 1936)

BRIFFAULT, ROBERT, *Europa in Limbo* (London: Robert Hale 1937)

CÉLINE, LOUIS-FERDINAND, *Journey to the End of the Night* (1932; trans. London: John Calder 1988)

CHATWIN, BRUCE, *On the Black Hill* (London: Jonathan Cape 1982)

DOS PASSOS, JOHN, *Three Soldiers* (New York: Viking Penguin 1921)

EDRIC, ROBERT, *In Desolate Heaven* (London: Duckworth 1997)

FAULKNER, WILLIAM, *Soldiers' Pay* (London: Chatto & Windus 1926)

FAULKNER, WILLIAM, 'The Wasteland' (comprising 'Ad Astra', 'Victory', 'Crevasse', 'Turnabout' and 'All the Dead Pilots'), in *Collected Stories* (London: Chatto & Windus 1951)

FORD, FORD MADDOX, *Parade's End* (London: The Bodley Head 1924–8)

GLAESER, ERNST, *Class 1902* (1928; trans. London: Martin Secker 1929)

GRISTWOOD, A.D., *The Somme*, including also *The Coward* (London: Jonathan Cape 1927)

HAŠEK, JAROSLAV, *The Good Soldier Švejk* (1921–3; trans. London: William Heinemann 1973)

HEMINGWAY, ERNEST, 'Soldier's Home', in *In Our Time* (London: Jonathan Cape 1926)

HEMINGWAY, ERNEST, *A Farewell to Arms* (London: Jonathan Cape 1929)

INGRAM, KENNETH, *Out of Darkness* (Chatto & Windus 1927)

JAPRISOT, SEBASTIEN, *A Very Long Engagement* (1991; trans. London: Harvill 1993)

JONES, DAVID, *In Parenthesis* (London: Faber and Faber 1937)

KEABLE, ROBERT, *Simon Called Peter* (London: Constable 1921)

MALOUF, DAVID, *Fly Away Peter* (London: Chatto & Windus 1982)

MANNING, FREDERIC, *The Middle Parts of Fortune* (1929; second edition: *Her Privates We*, London: Peter Davies 1930)

MAXWELL, W.B., *We Forget Because We Must* (London: Hutchinson 1928)

MYRIVILIS, STRATIS, *Life in the Tomb* (1924; trans. London:

Quartet 1987)

O'FLAHERTY, LIAM, *The Return of the Brute* (London: Mandrake Press 1929)

READ, HERBERT, *Ambush* (London: Faber and Faber 1930)

RENN, LUDWIG, *War* (1928; trans. London: Martin Secker 1929)

REMARQUE, ERICH MARIA, *All Quiet on the Western Front* (1929; trans. 1929; new trans. London: Jonathan Cape 1994)

ROTH, JOSEPH, *Flight Without End* (1927; trans. London: Chatto & Windus 1983)

ROTH, JOSEPH, *Tarabas* (1935; trans. London: Chatto & Windus 1987)

ROUAUD, JEAN, *Fields of Glory* (1990; trans. London: Harvill 1994)

SASSOON, SIEGFRIED, *Memoirs of a Fox-Hunting Man* (London: Faber and Faber 1928)

SASSOON, SIEGFRIED, *Memoirs of an Infantry Officer* (London: Faber and Faber 1930)

SOLZHENITSYN, ALEKSANDR, *August 1914* (1971–83; trans. London: Jonathan Cape 1989)

SOLZHENITSYN, ALEKSANDR, *November 1916* (1993; trans. London: Jonathan Cape 1999)

THOMPSON, EDWARD, *In Araby Orion* (London: Ernest Benn 1930)

THOMPSON, EDWARD, *These Men Thy Friends* (London: Macmillan 1933)

WELLS, H.G., *Mr Britling Sees It Through* (London: Cassell 1916)

WILLIAMSON, HENRY, *How Dear Is Life* (London: MacDonald 1954)

YEAYES, V.M., *Winged Victory* (London: Jonathan Cape 1934)

ZWEIG, ARNOLD, *The Case of Sergeant Grischa* (1927; trans. New York: Viking Penguin 1928)

ZWEIG, ARNOLD, *Education Before Verdun* (1935; trans. London: Martin Secker 1936)

Russian Revolution and Civil War

BABEL, ISAAC, 'Red Cavalry', in: *Collected Stories* (1924–37; trans. 1955; new trans. Harmondsworth: Penguin 1994)

SHOLOKHOV, MIKHAIL, *And Quiet Flows the Don* (1929; trans. London: Putnam 1934)

Spanish Civil War

FURST, ALAN, *Night Soldiers* (London: The Bodley Head 1988)

HEMINGWAY, ERNEST, *For Whom the Bell Tolls* (London: Jonathan Cape 1941)

LEE, LAURIE, *A Moment of War* (London: Viking 1991)

MALRAUX, ANDRÉ, *Days of Hope* (1938; trans. London: Hamish Hamilton 1968)

SIMON, CLAUDE, *The Palace* (1962; trans. London: John Calder 1987)

Second World War

ANATOLI, A. (KUZNETSOV), *Babi Yar* (1966; trans. London: Jonathan Cape 1970)

BALLARD, J.G., *Empire of the Sun* (London: Victor Gollancz 1984)

DE BEAUVOIR, SIMONE, *The Blood of Others* (trans. 1944; London 1948)

BEGLEY, LOUIS, *Wartime Lies* (London: Picador 1991)

DE BERNIÈRES, LOUIS, *Captain Corelli's Mandolin* (London: Secker & Warburg 1994)

BINDING, TIM, *Island Madness* (London: Picador 1998)

BÖLL, HEINRICH, *Group Portrait With Lady* (1971; trans. London: Secker & Warburg 1973)

BÖLL, HEINRICH, *A Soldier's Legacy* (1982; trans. London: Secker & Warburg 1985)

BÖLL, HEINRICH, *The Silent Angel* (1992; trans. London: André Deutsch 1994)

BÖLL, HEINRICH, *The Stories of Heinrich Böll* (trans. London: Secker & Warburg 1986)

BOOTH, MARTIN, *Hiroshima Joe* (London: Hutchinson 1985)

BOWEN, ELIZABETH, *The Heat of the Day* (London: Jonathan Cape 1949)

BUCHHEIM, LOTHAR-GÜNTHER, *The Boat* (1973; trans. London: HarperCollins 1975)

BURNS, JOHN HORNE, *The Gallery* (London: Secker & Warburg 1948)

BUZZATI, DINO, *The Tartar Steppe* (1945; trans. Manchester: Carcanet Press 1996)

CALVINO, ITALO, *The Path to the Spiders' Nests* (1947; trans. 1956; new trans. London: Jonathan Cape 1998)

CUNNINGHAM, PETER, *Consequences of the Heart* (London: Harvill 1998)

CURTIS, JEAN-LOUIS, *The Forests of the Night* (1947; trans. London: John Lehmann 1950)

VAN DIS, ADRIAAN, *My Father's War* (1994; trans. New York: The Free Press 1996)

ENDO, SHUSAKU, *The Sea and the Poison* (1957; trans. London: Peter Owen 1972)

ENDO, SHUSAKU, *Stained Glass Elegies* (1979; trans. London: Peter Owen 1984)

FARRELL, J.G., *The Singapore Grip* (London: HarperCollins 1978)

FAULKNER, WILLIAM, 'Two Soldiers' and 'Shall Not Perish', in *Collected Stories* (London: Chatto & Windus 1951)

FOWLES, JOHN, *The Magus* (1966; revised London: Jonathan Cape 1977)

FULLER, JOHN, *The Burning Boys* (London: Chatto & Windus 1989)

FURST, ALAN, *The Polish Officer* (London: HarperCollins 1995)

FURST, ALAN, *The World at Night* (London: HarperCollins 1997)

GALLICO, PAUL, *The Snow Goose* (London: Michael Joseph 1941)

DEL GIUDICE, DANIELE, *Take-Off* (1994; trans. London: Harvill 1996)

GRASS, GÜNTER, *The Tin Drum* (1959; trans. London: Secker & Warburg 1962)

GRASS, GÜNTER, *Dog Years* (1963; trans. London: Secker & Warburg 1965)

GREEN, HENRY, *Caught* (London: Chatto & Windus 1943)

GREENE, GRAHAM, *The Ministry of Fear* (London: Jonathan Cape 1943)

GROSSMAN, VASILY, *Life and Fate* (1980; trans. London: Harvill 1985)

HARRIS, ROBERT, *Enigma* (London: Hutchinson 1995)

HELLER, JOSEPH, *Catch-22* (London: Jonathan Cape 1962)

HELLER, JOSEPH, *Now and Then: From Coney Island to Here* (London: Simon & Schuster 1998)

HENDERSON, MEG, *The Holy City* (London: Flamingo 1997)

HERSEY, JOHN, *The Call: An American Missionary in China* (London: Weidenfeld & Nicolson 1985)

HUGHES, DAVID, *The Pork Butcher* (London: Constable 1984)

JONES, JAMES, *From Here to Eternity* (London: Hodder & Stoughton 1952)

JONES, JAMES, *The Thin Red Line* (London: Hodder & Stoughton 1963)

KADARÉ, ISMAÏL, *The General of the Dead Army* (1970; trans. London: Quartet 1986)

KOEPPEN, WOLFGANG, *Death in Rome* (1954; trans. London: Hamish Hamilton 1992)

KOESTLER, ARTHUR, *Arrival and Departure* (London: Jonathan Cape 1943)

MACLEAN, ALISTAIR, *HMS Ulysses* (London: Collins 1955)

MAILER, NORMAN, *The Naked and the Dead* (London: Alan Wingate 1949)

MALAMUD, BERNARD, 'Armistice', in *The Complete Stories of Bernard Malamud* (London: Vintage 1998)

MALOUF, DAVID, *The Great World* (London: Chatto & Windus 1990)

MANNING, OLIVIA, *The Balkan Trilogy* (London: William Heinemann 1987; comprising *The Great Fortune*, 1960; *The Spoilt City*, 1962; and *Friends and Heroes*, 1965)

MANNING, OLIVIA, *The Levant Trilogy* (Harmondsworth: Penguin 1982; comprising *The Danger Tree*, 1977; *The Battle Lost and Won*, 1978; and *The Sum of Things*, 1980)

MICHAELS, ANNE, *Fugitive Pieces* (London: Bloomsbury 1996)

MONSARRAT, NICHOLAS, *The Cruel Sea* (London: Cassell 1951)

MORANTE, ELSA, *History: A Novel* (trans. Harmondsworth: Penguin 1974)

MULISCH, HARRY, *The Assault* (trans. New York: Pantheon 1985)

ONDAATJE, MICHAEL, *The English Patient* (London: Bloomsbury 1992)

PALMER, WILLIAM, *The Pardon of Saint Anne* (London: Jonathan Cape 1997)

PRITCHETT, V.S., 'The Voice', in *The Lady from Guatemala: Selected Stories* (London: Vintage 1997)

PYNCHON, THOMAS, *Gravity's Rainbow* (London: Jonathan Cape 1973)

SARTRE, JEAN-PAUL, *Iron in the Soul* (1949; trans. London: Hamish Hamilton 1950)

SHUTE, NEVIL, *A Town Called Alice* (London: William Heinemann 1950)

SIMON, CLAUDE, *The Flanders Road* (1960; trans. London: John Calder 1985)

SIMONOV, KONSTANTIN, *Days and Nights* (London: Hutchinson 1945)

SKVORECKY, JOSEF, *The Engineer of Human Souls* (1977; trans. London: Chatto & Windus 1984)

STEINBECK, JOHN, *The Moon is Down* (London: William Heinemann 1942)

STYRON, WILLIAM, *Sophie's Choice* (London: Jonathan Cape 1979)

SZCZYPIORSKI, ANDRZEJ, *The Beautiful Mrs Seidenman* (1986; trans. London: Weidenfeld & Nicolson 1990)

VIDAL, GORE, *Williwaw* (New York: Dutton 1948)

VONNEGUT, KURT, *Slaughterhouse-Five* (London: Jonathan Cape 1969)

VONNEGUT, KURT, 'A Nazi City Mourned at Some Profit', in: *Palm Sunday; An Auto-biographical Collage* (London: Jonathan Cape 1981)

WAUGH, EVELYN, *The Sword of Honour Trilogy* (Harmondsworth: Penguin 1984; comprising *Men at Arms*, 1952;

Officers and Gentlemen, 1955; and *Unconditional Surrender*, 1961)

WOLF, CHRISTA, *A Model Childhood* (1976; trans. London: Virago 1983)

Korean War

SALTER, JAMES, *The Hunters* (1956; reissue London: Harvill 1998)

Vietnam War

CAPUTO, PHILIP, 'In the Forest of the Laughing Elephant', in: *Exiles* (New York: Alfred A. Knopf 1998)

COETZEE, J.M., 'The Vietnam Project', in *Dusklands* (London: Secker & Warburg 1982)

FRENCH, ALBERT, *Patches of Fire* (London: Secker & Warburg 1997)

GREENE, GRAHAM, *The Quiet American* (London: William Heinemann 1955)

HASFORD, GUSTAV, *The Short-Timers* (New York: Harper & Row 1979)

HEINEMANN, LARRY, *Paco's Story* (London: Faber and Faber 1986)

HEINEMANN, LARRY, *Close Quarters* (London: Faber and Faber 1987)

HOLLAND, WILLIAM E., *Let a Soldier Die* (London: Transworld 1985)

HUONG, DUONG THU, *Novel Without a Name* (trans. London: Picador 1995)

JONES, THOM, *The Pugilist at Rest* (London: Faber and Faber 1994)

KOCH, CHRISTOPHER J., *Highways to a War* (London: William Heinemann 1995)

MASON, BOBBIE ANN, *In Country* (London: Chatto & Windus 1986)

MASON, BOBBIE ANN, 'Big Bertha Stories', in *Love Life* (London: Chatto & Windus 1989)

NINH, BAO, *The Sorrow of War* (1991; trans. London: Secker & Warburg 1994)

O'BRIEN, TIM, *Going After Cacciato* (London: Jonathan Cape 1978)

O'BRIEN, TIM, *The Things They Carried* (London: Collins 1990)

OLEN BUTLER, ROBERT, *A Good Scent from a Strange Mountain* (London: Secker & Warburg 1993)

OLEN BUTLER, ROBERT, *The Deep Green Sea* (London: Secker & Warburg 1997)

DEL VECCHIO, JOHN M., *The 13th Valley* (London: Sphere Books 1983)

WEBB, JAMES, *Fields of Fire* (London: Granada 1980)

WOLFF, TOBIAS, 'Soldier's Joy', in *Back in the World* (London: Jonathan Cape 1986)

Gulf War

BEINHART, LARRY, *American Hero* (London: Century 1994)

BLINN, JAMES, *The Aardvark Is Ready For War* (London: Doubleday 1997)

FARLEY, CHRISTOPHER JOHN, *My Favourite War* (London: Granta 1997)

ACKNOWLEDGEMENTS

Georges Borchardt, Inc.: Excerpt from *The New Confessions* by William Boyd, copyright © 1988 by William Boyd. Reprinted by permission of Georges Borchardt, Inc.   *Counterpoint Press:* Excerpt from *The Hunters* by James Salter, copyright © 1997 by James Salter. Reprinted by permission of Conterpoint Press, a member of Perseus Books, L.L.C.   *Jean-Louis Curtis:* Excerpt from *The Forests of the Night* by Jean-Louis Curtis (John Lehmann, 1950); originally published in France as *Les Fôrets de la Nuit* (René Juillard, 1948).   *Dell Publishing:* 'A Nazi City Mourned at Some Profit' from *Palm Sunday* by Kurt Vonnegut, copyright © 1981 by Kurt Vonnegut. Reprinted by permission of Dell Publishing, a division of Random House, Inc. *Doubleday:* Excerpt from *HMS Ulysses* by Alistair MacLean, copyright © 1955 by Alistair MacLean. Reprinted by permission of Doubleday, a division of Random House, Inc.   *Dutton Signet:* Excerpts from *Regeneration* by Pat Barker, copyright © by Pat Barker. Reprinted by permission of Dutton Signet, a division of Penguin Putnam Inc.   *The Estate of Erich Maria Remarque:* Excerpt from *All Quiet on the Western Front* by Erich Maria Remarque.   *Im Westen Nichts Neues,* copyright © 1928 by Ullstein A. G., copyright renewed 1956 by Erich Maria Remarque. *All Quiet on the Western Front,* copyright © 1929, 1930 by Little, Brown and Company, copyright renewed 1957, 1958 by Erich Maria Remarque. All rights reserved. Reprinted by permission of the Estate of Erich Maria Remarque, administered by Pryor Cashman Sherman & Flynn LLP.   *Farrar, Straus and Giroux, LLC:* Excerpts from 'a thousand points of light'

Louis-Ferdinand Céline, translation copyright © 1983 by Ralph Manheim. Excerpt from *The Sea and Poison* by Shusaku Endo, translated by Michael Gallagher, copyright © 1958 by Bungei Shunju Co. Ltd., Tokyo, copyright © 1972 by Peter Owen. Reprinted by permission of New Directions Publishing Corp. *Pantheon Books:* Excerpt from *The Sorrow of War* by Bao Ninh, copyright © 1995 by Bao Ninh. Excerpt from *Corelli's Mandolin* by Louis de Bernières, copyright © 1994 by Louis de Bernières. Reprinted by permission of Pantheon Books, a division of Random House, Inc. *Penguin Books Ltd.* 'Treason' from *Collected Stories,* by Isaac Babel, translated by David McDuff (Penguin Books, 1994), copyright © 1994 by David McDuff. Reprinted by permission of Penguin Books Ltd., London. *PFD:* Excerpt from *A Moment of War* by Laurie Lee (Viking UK, 1991), copyright © 1991 by Laurie Lee. Reprinted by permission of PFD on behalf of The Estate of Laurie Lee. *Random House, Inc.:* Excerpt from *Enigma* by Robert Harris, copyright © 1996 by Robert Harris. Excerpt from *Man's Hope* by Andre Malraux, translated by Stuart Gilbert and Alastair MacDonald, copyright © 1938 and renewed 1966 by Random House, Inc. Reprinted by permission of Random House, Inc. *George Sassoon:* Excerpt from 'Finished with the War' by Siegfried Sassoon (published in *The Times,* London, July 1917), copyright © 1917 by Siegfried Sassoon, and an excerpt from *Memoirs of An Infantry Officer* by Siegfried Sassoon, copyright © 1930 by Siegfried Sassoon. Reprinted by permission of George Sassoon, administered by the Barbara Levy Literary Agency, London. *Scribner:* Excerpt from *A Farewell to Arms* by Ernest Hemingway, copyright © 1929 by Charles Scribner's Sons, copyright renewed 1957 by Ernest Hemingway. Reprinted by permission of Scribner, an imprint of Simon & Schuster Adult Publishing Group. *St. Martin's Press, LLC:* Excerpt from *The Silent Angel* by Heinrich Boll, copyright © 1994 by Heinrich Boll. Excerpt from *Hiroshima Joe* by Martin Booth, copyright © 1985, 2003 by Martin Booth. Reprinted by permission of St. Martin's Press, LLC. *Suhrkamp Verlag:* Excerpt from *Death in Rome* by Wolfgang Koeppen, translated by Michael Hoffman, copyright © 1986 by Suhrkamp Verlag, Frankfurt am Main (Hamish Hamilton UK). *University Press of New England:* Excerpt from *Life in the Tomb* by Stratis Myrivilis, translated by

P. 44